"IF YOU THINK YOU CAN TREAT ME LIKE YOUR BOUGHT WOMAN, YOU'VE GOT ANOTHER THING COMING!

I won't be manhandled by any man, even my husband! When I take a man it's because I want him, and you've given me damned little reason to want you these last months!"

Wyatt moved like a coiled spring to reach her, and then he had her by her shoulders and was shaking her. "You'll take me when I want you to take me! As you just pointed out so charmingly, you're my wife!" Lifting Roxanne, he threw her back on the bed and threw himself on top of her.

There was no escape for her this time. And suddenly her own blood began to race through her body, as flame spread through her, enveloping every inch of her, consuming her...

Books by
Lydia Lancaster

Desire and Dreams of Glory
Passion and Proud Hearts
Stolen Rapture
The Temptation

Published by
WARNER BOOKS

To Those Who Dare

by
Lydia
Lancaster

WARNER BOOKS

A Warner Communications Company

WARNER BOOKS EDITION

Copyright © 1982 by Lydia Lancaster
All rights reserved

Warner Books, Inc., 75 Rockefeller Plaza, New York, N.Y. 10019

W A Warner Communications Company

Printed in the United States of America

First Printing: January, 1982

10 9 8 7 6 5 4 3 2 1

To Those
Who Dare

1

Mary MacDonald's heart beat faster as she came within sight of the lights. The torches had turned the meeting grounds at Chestnut Grove from darkness to a brightness that rivaled that of the midday sun. She had been walking fast, but it was the excitement of the unknown and of very real danger that brought the flush to her cheeks and a sparkle into her hazel, Scotch-Irish eyes. She had no business here; she'd be fined, and probably even discharged from the textile mill, if she were discovered. In this year of 1835, the rules were strict and not to be broken. All the same, it was worth the risk.

Even from the outskirts, it was easy to see why the more fastidious citizens of Athens, New York, chose to remain at home during this week when folk from miles around converged at the revival grounds. Camp meetings were the high point of their monotonous and work-filled lives. Weddings and funerals helped, and a few holidays such as Christmas and the Fourth of July, but these only lasted for one day, while camp meetings went on for a glorious week!

The approach to the meeting ground itself was bedlam. On every hand, booths had been set up as if this were a carnival or a fair rather than a serious religious gathering. The booths were gaudy, with banners that shouted out the goods their proprietors offered. Kill-divvie, gumption and belly-whip vengeance were among the more potent alcoholic beverages for sale, along with the more conservative whiskey and gin and rum.

The crowd itself was motley. There were gaudily dressed Cyprians from as far away as Albany who had come in by

7

canal packet from Troy. There were Bowkers hawking lewd ballads and outrageous takeoffs from the Bible itself. There were self-styled doctors offering cures for the pox, and grimy-handed women offering sly promises to girls who had been either foolish enough or fortunate enough to find their legs broken above the knee and were in need of means to rid themselves of the unwanted consequences. Charms were thrust under the noses of any would-be patron who looked as though he needed a love potion or a concoction to bring a rival to grief. Turnpike and towpath scum were out in force, along with canallers and Skenekers, railroaders who worked on the Albany to Schenectady line.

To Mary's unsophisticated eyes, the scene was no less than breathtaking. In spite of her excitement, her footsteps slowed, and she felt a moment's panic. Lordy, but this was going to be a hard place to make her way through, alone and unprotected as she was! She'd better catch her breath, so that she could make a run for it and try to gain the safety of the benches on the meeting ground proper. Or should she go back, after all? She had no idea of the riffraff that would be here, even though Mrs. Simms, her nightmarm at the Livingston Textile Mill, had spent the last two weeks warning all of the female mechanics in her dormitory of the danger of as much as setting foot on the streets of Athens for as long as this revival meeting went on.

Her chin came up and her mouth firmed. No! She wasn't going to miss the preaching, miss getting to hear the great evangelist Carlton Booth himself, just because of the no-man's-land that stood between her and her goal. She took a deep breath, gathered up her skirts, and set out running, never realizing that her action only served to draw attention to herself, the very thing that she wanted to avoid.

"Well, well, what have we here! What's yer hurry, lass? Slow down and tell Art all about it! Lost yer sweetheart? Never mind, I'm a better man than he is, you won't be sorry for the trade! Lemmie buy yer a drink, you looks like yer needs one."

Mary jerked her arm in a vain effort to free it from the grasp of the man who'd accosted her. Her eyes were glazed with fright, but not so glazed that she couldn't make out that he was as big as a house, and drunk. A canaller! All of the mechanics had been warned about them, over and over.

Drunken, godless men, Mrs. Simms told them, and don't as much as look at one or you'll end up ruined!

Not that any of the nightmarm's charges had much chance to look at one, unless it happened on a Saturday when the mill closed at sundown, or unless it happened in the wintertime when sundown came early so that the streets were still populated by late shoppers and early revelers, the latter almost certain to be canallers. The Erie Canal had brought prosperity to Athens, and to all the rest of the country it had opened up to cheap transport of goods, but you couldn't have a canal without having canallers.

The only other opportunity the young women fortunate enough to have positions at the mill had to glimpse a canaller was if one happened to be abroad early enough of a Sunday morning. The nightmarms herded their charges to services at the First Methodist Church of Athens, and if Mrs. Simms spotted a canaller on their side of the street she herded her chicks to the other side with admonitions to keep their eyes lowered and not risk as much as a peek.

"Let me go! I'm meeting someone!" Mary cried. She wondered fleetingly, because there wasn't time to speculate on it, if she would be called to account in the hereafter for telling a lie, even if it was such a necessary one. "Let me go this instant!"

"Now, you don't wanta be like that! Tell yer what, I'll buy yer honest-to-goodness whiskey, none of that stuff that'd rot the insides out of a tender little morsel like you. Art'll show yer a good time, wait'n see if he don't! Don't you fret that I ain't got the money to buy whiskey, I've got a wad, and if we gets along like I know we're gonna I'll spend it on yer freer'n that sweetheart of yours would! No cheap gin for you, my pretty, whiskey it'll be!"

"I don't want any whiskey! I want you to let me go! Let me go or I'll scream!"

The man threw back his head and laughed, displaying a mouthful of very large teeth. "Playful, aren't yer? Well, that's the way I like 'em!" He began to drag Mary toward the nearest booth. Mary was frantic. If she screamed, she'd be found out and sacked, but if she didn't scream—Her imagination shuddered at what, much worse, would happen to her. Why hadn't she stayed behind at the dormitory, as she'd been supposed to do?

The man who called himself Art dragged her so fast that she stumbled over a rut, and her bonnet bobbled half off her head. She made a grab for it, almost as frantic about the bonnet as about the danger she was in from the canaller. She couldn't lose her bonnet, it was the only one she owned and Mrs. Simms would demand to know what had happened to it when it was time to go to services next Sunday.

"Atta boy, Art! Hang onto her, she's a looker! If you can't handle her, give me a chance! You're too big for her anyways, she's more my size!"

Half a dozen other men were encircling them now, laughing, hooting, finding her plight as entertaining as a sideshow. Desperate, Mary wondered what would happen if she slapped her captor, or kicked him. Would he let her go, or would he make an outcry that would attract an even larger crowd of spectators and make sure that she'd be pegged as a mill mechanic who was out of bounds?

Drawing a deep breath, her lower lip clenched between her teeth, Mary kicked him. He howled and cursed, taken enough by surprise so that his grip on her arm relaxed just enough for her to wrench herself away. She took off like a frightened hare, dodging this way and that in an attempt to avoid other clutching hands. She felt a sharp searing pain in her ribs as two men collided with each other, lurching into her. They fell, taking her down with them, and one of their feet drove itself into her side as she went down.

"Hands off 'er," the huge canaller bellowed. "She's mine, I saw her first!"

Cringing, holding her side against the pain, Mary's blurred eyes saw him reach down for her. She tried to roll away but it was too late. He grabbed her arm and drew her back to her feet, none too gently, angered because she'd tried to run away from him. Her eyes were so misted with tears of terror and pain that she wasn't aware of a newcomer looming up behind them until his hand fell on her captor's shoulder, bringing him to a halt.

"What's this, Franklyn? It seems to me that I heard this young lady tell you that she didn't care for your company."

"Aw, common, Cap'n. She wants a good time, she does, else why'd she be here?"

"Let her go. You heard me, Art. That's an order!"

Incredibly, Mary's arm was free again. She looked over

her shoulder at the same time that she rubbed the place where there was sure to be a bruise by morning. The man who had come to her rescue was younger than the one named Art Franklyn, but in spite of that he wore an air of authority that was backed up by his uniform and the caster hat that pegged him as a canal boat captain. All of the captains wore caster hats, made of beaver or rabbit skin and painted with some kind of a nautical symbol. In this case the symbol was an anchor with a fanciful if not artistically perfect mermaid sitting on one of the curves. Seaweed clinging to the most vital portions of her anatomy provided a modicum of decency.

Her rescuer doffed the offending hat and smiled at her. "I hope he didn't frighten you, Miss. Franklyn isn't a bad sort, except when he's had a drop too much, else I wouldn't keep him on as a member of my crew. Did I hear you say that you're meeting someone? You'd better let me help you find your friend so there won't be another unpleasant incident. I'm afraid that these outer precincts of the meeting grounds aren't the safest place for an unescorted lady."

"I . . . yes . . . no . . . " Mary was so confused that she didn't know what to say. She was still thoroughly frightened, almost as much by the tall, brawny canaller as she had been by Art Franklyn himself. Even if she dared to take his goodwill at face value, she didn't dare to enter the meeting grounds with him. If Mrs. Simms or any of the other girls saw her not only where she wasn't supposed to be, but in the company of a canaller, her goose would be cooked.

"I've changed my mind. I think I'll leave. Thank you for helping me, sir." Mary reached up to set her bonnet straight, and the resulting twinge in her ribs made her gasp.

"You're hurt!" The canaller's very blue eyes darkened with concern.

"It's nothing." The words were brave enough, but her voice broke with the effort of keeping from crying from pain. Lord have mercy, were her ribs broken? Every breath she took, every movement brought on another onslaught of agony.

"I'll find you a place to sit down. Make way there, let us through!" His hand on her arm was surprisingly gentle in spite of his size. He steered her through the crowd toward an upended keg occupied by a man with a heavily stubbled chin. His eyes bleary, he'd spotted it as a resting place after he'd imbibed so much that he was no longer steady on his feet.

"You, give the seat to the young lady, move off!"

Even in her pain and agitation at the predicament she found herself in, she couldn't help but notice that all of the other men made way for the captain, looking at him with respect. The light of the torches and lanterns was bright enough for her to see that he could be no more than in his twenties, and that the hair under his caster hat was a light brown, almost blond where it was sun-streaked. He was a good head taller than she was, and his blue eyes were kind. His jacket, removed because of the warmth of the night, was slung over his shoulder.

She still trembled, now more from the effect of his sheer masculinity than from fright or pain. As the drunken man scuttled off the keg, Jim Yarnell helped her to take his place. Her face, uplifted to his as she thanked him, was pale, and her mouth quivered.

He studied her as intensely as she was studying him. "Good Lord, you're hardly more than a child! You're far too young to be out alone after dark, let alone in a place like this. Whatever possessed you?"

"I wanted to hear the preaching."

"But alone?" Jim's voice was incredulous.

"The other girls went on without me. I was on cleanup."

He understood then. Although Mary had changed into her Sunday calico, the best of the three dresses that were all she owned, and was properly although cheaply bonneted, she was one of the mechanics at the textile mill. This meant that she had no protection in Athens except that afforded by the mill and by some nightmarm who was supposed to take care of her.

"Wouldn't you have been fined, if you'd been discovered attending the camp meeting alone?"

"Fired," Mary said.

"And you risked it, just to hear the preaching?"

"It's exciting, I wanted to come. I've never been to a revival meeting, we always lived too far to leave the farm just with the boys to look after things."

Jim's heart felt an unaccustomed twinge. Poor girl! He had an idea of how drab the mechanics' lives must be. The girls were little better than slaves, they enjoyed virtually no freedom, and at wages that should have made the mill owners flock to camp meetings themselves to throw themselves on God's mercy.

He studied Mary more closely. He'd only come to her rescue because she'd looked so young. He had three younger sisters and he'd been raised in a decent family; he felt bound to help any girl who appeared to be in difficulties. Now he saw how young she actually was. Fifteen, at the most, maybe no more than fourteen. And pretty, too, for all that she was so frightened. Her hair was a light brown that just escaped being a honey blond. Her lashes were darker, tipped with black, framing extraordinarily lovely hazel eyes.

"How old are you?" Jim demanded, his voice so gruff that Mary started.

"Seventeen. Almost eighteen."

Seventeen! He wouldn't have thought it, but looking even more closely he decided that she might be telling the truth. Those were very real curves under her tight bodice, curves that filled the material to capacity because she'd grown while the dress had shrunk. But she was still far too young to be in a place like this, alone and unprotected. Ed Hanney, the town constable, and his part-time deputies had always found it the better part of discretion not to patrol the meeting grounds too carefully. In case of trouble, which invariably erupted, they were outnumbered, and it would take a more courageous man than Hanney to risk being maimed or killed through an attempt to do his duty and keep order.

"Do you think you can walk now? I'll take you back to your house, to make sure you get there safely."

"I think so." Tentatively, Mary stood up and walked a few steps, but her wince showed him that she was hurt even more badly than he'd thought. This was a pretty kettle of fish! What the devil was he to do with her? If he did as he should, found her nightmarm and turned her over to her, she'd almost certainly be discharged. On the other hand, he couldn't simply carry her back to whichever dormitory house she lived in, and dump her on the doorstep to fend for herself.

At a loss, he scanned the crowds searching for a solution, and then he gave a sigh of heartfelt relief. How lucky could he get, to have Galen Forbes come along at this precise moment? The young doctor had only recently come to Athens to assist Dr. Harding, whose practice had grown beyond his ability to handle it alone. Forbes had patched up or dosed members of

Jim's crew on several occasions when they'd stopped at Athens to discharge and take on passengers and cargo.

In the next instant he frowned: Galen wasn't alone. A young lady walked on either side of him, each of them of unmistakable quality, and it took him only seconds to recognize Adelaide Livingston, the daughter of Athen's textile mill owner, and her friend Geneva Burton. He'd better not ask Dr. Forbes for help, after all.

Too late! Forbes had seen him, and Geneva Burton, her dark gray eyes alight with interest, was urging him forward toward them.

"Hello, Jim.. Is something wrong? Miss Burton thinks that the young lady is in some kind of distress," Galen Forbes said.

Beside Jim, Mary's breath caught and her face went even paler. She'd also recognized Miss Geneva Burton—everyone in Athens knew Miss Burton by sight—and no one could fail to recognize Miss Adelaide Livingston, the seventeen-year-old, fairy-tale lovely daughter of Herndon Livingston himself! It was all up. She might as well resign herself to start walking back to the farm as soon as these dratted ribs of hers would let her set out walking.

"She fell," Jim Yarnell said. "I think she's hurt."

"Then we'd best get her home so that I can examine her, unless her family would prefer to call in Doctor Harding." Galen's eyes, as hazel as Mary's, were keen. "Miss Burton, you won't mind dropping us off? I'll try not to cause more than a few moments delay."

"Of course I won't. But the buggy's going to be overloaded. I think you'd better take the young lady, Doctor. Perhaps this gentleman will be kind enough to escort Adelaide and me on foot."

Jim belatedly remembered to remove his hat, cursing himself for his oversight. "Captain Yarnell, ma'am, at your service. I'd be only too happy to act as your escort, but it's a long walk for ladies."

"Oh, Addie and I wouldn't mind that!" Geneva's eyes were on Mary's face. "We don't know each other, do we?" she asked Mary.

Mary flinched, and then faced up to the fact that there was no way out of her predicament. "No, Miss Burton. I'm from the mill."

"But you aren't supposed to be here alone, or with a gentleman!" Adelaide's sky blue eyes flew wide under her ruffled and beflowered bonnet. "At least, I don't think you are."

"No, Miss Livingston." Mary's voice was miserable. "I just came, since the others couldn't wait for me because I was on cleanup."

Geneva realized that Mary was terrified of the consequences of her rashness in coming to the revival meeting alone. Her heart, always warm toward stray dogs and cats and any human being in difficulties, went out to the little mechanic.

"I know what we can do. If Captain Yarnell will still offer his escort, we'll just go back to the meeting and find the group from the mill to make sure that they don't leave for at least an hour. The nightmarm in charge can't very well walk out if Addie chooses to talk to her for a long time. It would be highly impolite of her to cut short a conversation with Mr. Livingston's daughter."

Galen gave her a startled look, his face registering disbelief. He scarcely knew Miss Burton. As the lowly assistant to Dr. Harding, he was hardly on a social level with families like the Burtons or the Livingstons. He had met Geneva and Adelaide only once or twice at minor social functions.

Galen's escorting the two young ladies this evening was nothing more than a fluke of chance. He'd come to the revival alone, out of curiosity. Geneva had spotted him and immediately called on him to act as escort for herself and Adelaide because her brother Cyril, who'd brought them to the meeting, wanted to get away and prowl the outskirts where the action was. There hadn't been any way Galen could refuse, although he hadn't liked the idea at all. Young ladies like Miss Geneva Burton and Miss Adelaide Livingston were to be avoided above all else, and he had good and valid reasons for his avoidance of them.

Not that there was any danger for him from either Miss Burton or Miss Livingston. Geneva was unofficially engaged to Wyatt Livingston, Adelaide's brother and the heir to the Livingston fortune. Adelaide herself was much too young to become interested in a doctor who would still be years in getting himself established, even if her parents would have allowed it.

He was jerked back to the present by the young mill mechanic's voice, filled with anguished hopefulness.

"You honestly won't snitch on me, Miss Livingston? And you'll keep Mrs. Simms busy while the doctor looks at me? My ribs do hurt a lot." Struggle against it as she might, Mary's eyes filled with tears. The thought of being discharged and blackballed frightened her even more than the possibility that she might actually be injured.

"Of course I won't. None of us will." Addie, even more softhearted than Geneva, felt her own eyes sting with tears of sympathy. "Just tell us what Mrs. Simms looks like, so we can pick her out."

"She's kind of old, about forty, and plump, and her hair is sort of going gray with the brown, and she's wearing a gray bonnet, her Sunday one, and she'll be with the girls from my dormitory, sixteen of them. I expect she's wearing her Sunday dress; it's gray too, with a white lace collar."

"We'll find her." Geneva's voice was confident and encouraging and there was a sparkle of mischief in her eyes. This encounter with the mill girl was giving spice to what had otherwise been a fairly boring evening. It wasn't that Geneva wasn't a religious person. She was, her faith in God was absolute, but this particular brand of religion wasn't to her liking. All the shouting and exhorting was distasteful to her.

Galen cast another thoughtful look at Geneva before he took Mary's arm. "Come along, then. I doubt that you have a broken rib, but I know that it probably feels that way."

"Will you recognize the buggy?" Geneva wanted to know.

Galen's mouth twitched with amusement. "I will if Cato's with it." He doubted that there was a person for miles around, even small children, who didn't recognize Bobo Burton's trotter when he saw it. Like the rest of the population of Athens, which had grown to an incredible eleven thousand since the advent of the Erie Canal, Galen had fallen into the local habit of calling Geneva's brother Cyril Burton nothing but Bobo.

"Cato's with it. I don't think you'll have any trouble with him hitched to the buggy instead of Bobo's gig. Just be firm with him."

16

Although every breath she took pained her, Mary managed to reach the outskirts of the grove escorted by Galen. Her eyes widened when she saw the smart buggy, its wheels painted red, and the horse that stood between its shafts. Cato was a magnificent animal, his roan coat gleaming in the reflected light. She'd never ridden in a buggy in her life, but only in her father's farm cart, pulled by old Brownie, their plough horse.

Galen cocked a wary eye at the trotter. "You behave yourself, Cato," he said. "Don't go giving me any trouble."

"Do you think he will?" Mary's voice sounded nervous. Although as a farm girl she'd lived most of her life around horses, she'd never been up behind an animal like this.

"Probably not, but hang on to your teeth. From all accounts he's a handful. Up you go . . ." He paused, searching for a name for the girl.

"I'm Mary. Mary MacDonald," Mary supplied.

Strong and gentle, Galen helped Mary climb to the high seat. She could feel his concern for her through the flesh of her arm, and she shivered a little, hardly daring to believe that she, Mary MacDonald, was in the company of such a distinguished and handsome young man, riding in a buggy that only the wealthy could afford, and behind a horse that the whole town of Athens envied Bobo Burton for owning. The doctor was a gent, he was, a real gent, like some hero out of one of those novels that Mrs. Simms sometimes read to the mechanics in lieu of more edifying works, during their cultural hour before lights-out every evening. And the thought of what might have happened to her if Captain Yarnell had walked her home made her shiver. This was more exciting than listening to the preaching, a dozen times more exciting. The thought that she'd never dare to brag about it to the other girls she worked with was a sharp and painful disappointment.

Cato stepped out smartly, and in spite of Galen's qualms about handling him, gave no trouble. The horse sensed the authority in the hands on the lines, and his perfect, high-stepping trot brought them to the dormitory house in record time. Mary thought it was like flying. She could almost close her eyes and imagine that she was Miss Geneva Burton or Miss Adelaide Livingston, except for the pain in her ribs.

But once in her upstairs dormitory room, alone with Galen, the unorthodoxy of what they were doing overwhelmed her. Her face burned with embarrassment as Galen told her to remove her dress and get into her nightgown and lie down, even though he was thoughtful enough to step outside into the hallway until she was safely covered. Her whole body burned red at the enormity of letting a man, even a doctor, examine her.

She looked small and vulnerable in her cot at the end of a long row of them lining one wall. There was another row against the opposite wall, and a small chest at the foot of each cot to hold personal possessions. A hook beside each cot was for the girl's dress and shawl and bonnet. The only other amenities in the room were two washstands, a smoky mirror to aid in the neatening of hair, and a small rocking chair for the nightmarm to occupy while she read to her charges from educational or morally uplifting books until lights-out at ten o'clock sharp every night.

When Galen laid back the sheet and slipped his hands under her nightgown to probe at her ribs, the sensation that went through Mary drowned out the discomfort. No man had ever touched her so familiarly before, not even her father. She was surprised that the wave of heat that engulfed her didn't set fire to the cornhusk mattress.

"Just as I thought," Galen told her. "You're well bruised but there is no break. Once I strap you up, you'll be able to move and breathe with a great deal more comfort. Only we seem to have run into a problem. I didn't bring my bag with me to the revival meeting, so what can we use for bandages?"

It was a dilemma. Mary's face puckered, and then she made a supreme sacrifice. Her extra petticoat, her second-best, would have to be proffered. She winced as Galen tore strips from its bottom. She couldn't afford to buy another one, even if she could have done it without Mrs. Simms or the other girls finding out about it. And how was she to manage to dress every morning, in her Sunday petticoat, without anyone noticing?

But that problem faded into insignificance, compared to what came next. She hadn't thought, it hadn't entered her mind, that she'd have to bare herself to the waist for Galen to effect the strapping.

"Close your eyes and pretend I'm not here," Galen instructed her, trying to keep amusement out of his voice. Amusement, and then a moment of shock as he realized that

18

this girl was nowhere near as young as he'd thought she was. No wonder she was so embarrassed! She wasn't a child after all, she was a young woman. "I can't do it without seeing, you know."

Her face flaming, Mary submitted to his ministrations. She'd never be able to look him in the face again, or Mrs. Simms, or any of the girls she lived and worked with! But she had to be strapped up, she had to be able to work, so that she wouldn't be found out and dismissed and blackballed for insubordination. She'd only have to slip her dress on after slipping her nightgown barely off her shoulders, and that wasn't much of a problem because all of the girls did the same thing, modesty being one of the rules of the mill.

"Thank you, Doctor. I won't be able to pay you until next quarter, but I promise I'll pay you."

"There's no charge. It was your petticoat," Galen teased her. "Now go to sleep, and try not to lift your arms high for a few days. Good night, Mary. I hope I'll see you again soon."

She watched him leave, closing the door behind him carefully, before she got out of bed to blow out the lamp. Then she groped her way back beneath the sheet and pulled it up under her chin, staring into the darkness with her eyes wide open. Now that her ribs were strapped, the pain had abated, but her heart was beating so fast that she could feel it thudding against her chest.

Dr. Forbes, Galen Forbes! Galen had to be the most beautiful name in the world. It just matched him, Mary thought. She could remember every plane in his lean face, exactly the way his dark brown hair tried to curl over his forehead although the rest of it was straight. He was her knight in shining armor who'd rescued her from a fate worse than death. She was in love. The thought that she might not have dared to go to the revival meeting alone, that she wouldn't have met Dr. Forbes if she hadn't, made her bury her face in her pillow and tremble. She'd never realized before that being in love made you feel a little bit sick to your stomach.

2

As he drove back to Chestnut Grove, Galen was still amused at Mary MacDonald's agony of embarrassment when he'd strapped up her ribs. She was a sweet little thing, as pretty as a picture, uncomplicated and without a wile to her name. Whatever man had the sense to snap her up would be a lucky cuss, and Galen hoped that he'd realize his good fortune.

He enjoyed the return journey more than he had the trip to Mary's dormitory house, because now he could give his full attention to handling Cato. Envy was an emotion he couldn't afford, but it was a pleasure to be behind the fast-paced trotter, its action a symphony in perfection. Only one other horse in Athens or its environs could match him, and that was Red Boy, Wyatt Livingston's trotter. If he ever had the luck to be a spectator at a race between the two champions, he didn't know which one he'd lay his money on.

The carnival-like atmosphere of the outkirts of the meeting grounds had intensified since he'd left. Nearly every man he saw, canaller, raftsman, towpath hobo, was by now the worse for drink. The hawkers were more raucous in the touting of their wares, the Cyprians more brazen as they solicited customers.

He had to forcibly remove a tawdrily dressed bawd's hand from his arm as he pushed his way through the mob, and his smile turned to a frown of outrage as he saw another girl in trouble. This one was very young, with a shabby shawl drawn close around her body in spite of the warmth of the evening. She was tendering a few coins that she certainly couldn't afford to the eager hand of a crone who was selling Bellyease, an abortifacient that would probably do no more than produce severe cramps and nausea, leaving the young girl in the condition she was so desperate to be rid of. Scoundrels, cheats, liars! If the girl took enough to do the job, it would likely kill her along with the burden she carried under her shawl. It was unprofessional, it was against all ethics, but he strode up to the girl and placed his hand on her arm.

"Don't take that filth," he warned her. "It will do you a deal more harm than good."

"I gotta take it, an' it's none of yer business!" The girl jerked away from him and ran, clutching the brown bottle, and Galen's eyes darkened as he watched her disappear in the milling throng.

There was nothing he could do about it. What was needed were laws to keep charlatans from peddling such concoctions, and he was a doctor, not a politician. He'd do well to keep his mind off outrages he could do nothing about, and apply himself to doing good where he could.

He was still amazed that Geneva Burton and Adelaide Livingston had been so kind as to help rescue Mary MacDonald from the results of her folly in venturing to the revival meeting alone. He quickened his step. Any further delay in escorting the two young ladies home, as he'd assured Bobo Burton that he would, would be inexcusable. Besides, Jim Yarnell would be chafing at the bit, wanting to go about his own business of seeking entertainment without being burdened with two young and socially prominent females. It had been as good of Captain Yarnell to pull Mary out of her predicament with the drunken canaller as it had been of Geneva and Adelaide to manufacture the time for him to treat the little mechanic, but their patience must be wearing thin by now.

He was mistaken about that. Jim Yarnell was thoroughly enjoying himself in the company of the two young ladies whom he ordinarily wouldn't dare to nod to on the street. He supposed that Athens was as democratic as any other small town, but there were still clearly defined social distinctions. Canallers, farmers, mill workers, clerks and artisans who worked with their hands did not socialize with the higher class of citizens, the owners of businesses, the clergy, the mill owner, physicians, and the like. They spoke to each other on the street, nodded to each other in church, but no closer association existed. For a canaller to be found escorting two young ladies of Geneva Burton's and Adelaide Livingston's social prominence, no matter the reason, was unheard of, even if he was a captain, and he was savoring every moment of it.

Geneva was also enjoying herself, because she made a point of enjoying any situation in which she might find herself. She had a lively interest in people, and was enchanted by the rantings and ravings taking place on the improvised platform of bare planks. There was a portable lectern for the speakers and a few straight-backed chairs for the sundry pastors and deacons who were basking in the reflected glory of having Carlton Booth, the evangelist, in their midst.

Sixteen-year-old Addie, her blue eyes shining, was ecstatic. She knew that when she returned home her father would be angry because of the lateness of the hour, but just being here for this extra time was worth any tongue-lashing or penalty he could impose on her.

The subject of Addie's worship was speaking now, his tawny hair spilling over his noble forehead in his passionate eloquence. His eyes, as blue as her own, flashed with ardor as he pleaded, threatened, cajoled and promised eternal hellfire to anyone who did not heed his words.

Matthew Ramsey, twenty-four years of age, was the newly ordained assistant who relieved the Reverend Jebbidiah Tucker of some of his more tedious and time-consuming duties. Matthew had been in Athens only a little longer than Galen, but it had been long enough for Addie to fall headlong and devastatingly in love with him.

Addie was no longer reluctant to face the monotonous sermons every Sunday. Ever since the first Sunday that Matthew Ramsey had appeared on the podium with Reverend Tucker, Addie was the first one of her household to arise on Sunday morning, ready to get started so as not to miss one second of being under the same roof with the young minister who had enslaved her heart.

Matthew's time to speak came when Reverend Tucker, and more importantly, Carlton Booth, ran out of breath. It was true that Matthew's time was curtailed, since the lung power of the evangelist was phenomenal, and that of Jebbidiah Tucker almost on a par with Booth's; but here he was, showing his worth, proving to everyone that he was the best, the most eloquent, the most magnificent minister who had ever walked the earth.

Addie was going to marry Matthew. She'd made up her mind about that the second Sunday he'd been in Athens. The first Sunday she'd been too busy falling in love with him to have time to consider such secondary things as marriage.

They weren't engaged yet, of course. Her father was slow in giving his permission. Herndon Livingston had bigger game in mind for his only daughter, preferably Cyril Burton, but barring him there were three or four others who would do almost as well, all of them young men of impeccable family, background and fortune. A young minister, without two coins in his pocket, and still without a church of his own, was hardly a worthy candidate for the hand of Miss Adelaide Livingston. Wyatt was to marry Geneva Burton, and if Adelaide were to marry Cyril, it would keep the largest part of the money, as well as social supremacy, in the family.

But even a Herndon Livingston's best-laid plans can come up against a snag. Addie had no romantic inclinations toward Bobo Burton at all. Bobo was handsome enough, if a face filled with puckish humor could be thought of as handsome. It was an open face, his brown hair forever rumpled, his mind ever questing for something interesting and amusing to relieve the tedium of applying himself toward his chosen profession, the law, thus following in his father's footsteps. There was no doubt that his career would be brilliant. He was enough of his father's son for that, but he was still only Bobo, almost as much a brother to her as Wyatt was, entirely too familiar to find him romantic.

Matthew was sitting down again, and once more Carlton Booth took up his stance, his voice and his breath restored to full force by his brief rest.

"Christians, let us pray!" Carlton Booth shouted. "Let us pray that tonight, every lost soul in this gathering will be saved from eternal hellfire!"

A catcall came from the back of the crowd. Booth rose to the occasion, his fingers pointing, his voice electric with force.

"There's a sinner! Pray for him, brethren and sistern! Pray with all your might, that he'll see the error of his ways and leave his life of sin to come forward and accept God's everlasting mercy! Come forward, sinner, let the light of the

Lord shine upon you, throw yourself on His mercy before it's too late! Your sins are black, black, but they can be washed as white as snow this very night if only you will repent!''

Galen made his way, apologizing in whispers, until he reached the three people for whom he was searching. Geneva saw him first, and she whispered to Addie.

"Here's Doctor Forbes, come to take us home. Addie, don't look so crestfallen! It's nearly eleven. Matthew won't get another chance to speak tonight and I have to get you home before your father sends a search party for you! Captain, thank you for stepping into the breach. We appreciate it a great deal. I hope we haven't ruined your evening.''

Beside Geneva, Mrs. Simms, the nightmarm, was hissing at her charges to be ready to leave as soon as the evangelist stopped praying. She'd have had them at home and in bed long ago if Miss Adelaide Livingston and Miss Geneva Burton hadn't been kind enough to engage her in conversation, their interest in her great responsibility for so many young mechanics gratifying in the extreme. In all her years as a nightmarm, she'd never dreamed that Miss Livingston herself would ever take any notice of her, and the honor was overwhelming.

"It was a pleasure, Miss Burton. I don't know when I've enjoyed myself so much. You should be up on that platform. You could talk a bird out of a tree if a cat was waiting at the foot of it with its mouth open. The way you kept Mrs. Simms here, so that that pretty little mechanic wouldn't get in trouble, was a pleasure to behold!'' Jim told her truthfully.

Geneva laughed. She'd taken a liking to the canal boat captain. Her father would enjoy hearing about tonight's adventures, and be amused at the way she and Addie had outwitted Mrs. Simms.

People were giving them outraged looks and shushing them for the small commotion they were creating. As they made their way to the end of the row, apologizing and attempting not to trample on any feet, Geneva's own amusement increased as she noted that nearly every face registered shock at seeing her and Addie in company with a canaller, albeit a captain and a respectable-looking one. Word was sure to fly all over Athens. There would be no serious repercussions at her own house. Her mother would be disapproving, but her father would laugh, pointing out that Dr. Forbes wouldn't have left their daughter and Addie in the company of a man who couldn't be trusted, and that he'd lay his money on Geneva any day even if the man had turned out not to be as dependable as Dr. Forbes thought he was.

Herndon Livingston, though, was an entirely different matter. His outrage would be genuine, and strong enough to take steps against Galen Forbes himself, unless Geneva could come up with some story that would mollify him. Otherwise, Addie would be in for it, and Herndon kept her on a mighty short leash as it was. The poor girl never even got to see Matthew Ramsey except at services and prayer meetings and choir practice, from which proper activities he was allowed to walk her home but never to dally along the way. Herndon timed them. He knew how long it took to walk from the First Methodist Church of Athens to his home, and that was exactly as much time as they were allotted before Matthew had to enter his house with her and pay his respects to himself and Mrs. Livingston and continue whatever conversation he might have been having with Addie in full view and earshot of her parents.

But glory be, here was Matthew now, walking so fast that he was almost running, his hair slightly rumpled as he strove to maintain the dignity proper for a minister at the same time that he was trying to catch up with his sweetheart before she left the revival grounds.

Geneva's heart ached with sympathy for Addie as she saw how her friend's face lighted up when Matthew called her name just as they reached the buggy.

"Go ahead. Walk a little ways with him, just over there under those trees," Geneva said. "Doctor Forbes and I won't peek, I promise, we'll just wait for you here. But don't be long, it's already late and I don't want you to get into trouble at home."

The look Addie gave her was so filled with gratitude that even Galen noticed it. Young love, he thought wryly. Another thought followed on the heels of the first one: was there was no end to Geneva Burton's good deeds? First Mary MacDonald, the little mill mechanic, and now this young heiress who was so obviously head over heels in love with Matthew Ramsey that it was pitiful. How could it be possible that any girl of Geneva Burton's status—wealthy, spoiled— could care so much about other people? All of his past experience proved to him that girls like Miss Burton cared for no one but themselves. It had to be an act; she was playing a part for no more noble reason than to bolster her own opinion of herself and other people's opinion of her.

As she walked away from them with Matthew, Addie longed to reach out her hand and take his, but it would never do. Someone might see them, and it would be sure to get back to Papa.

"You were wonderful tonight, Matthew!" Her face flamed as she realized that she was being improper. They weren't even officially engaged, even though the whole of Athens was expecting the announcement daily. Had Matthew noticed that she'd called him by his first name, would he think that it was very forward of her? She stumbled on, tripping over her words. "Your preaching was the best of all, even better than Mr. Booth!"

"It's sweet of you to say that, but I'm afraid it isn't true. It'll be a long time before I can match the evangelist. I was afraid that you wouldn't be able to come, Miss Livingston. You'll never know how happy it made me to see you in the congregation. If I talked well, it was because you inspired me."

Even under the shadow of the trees, Addie's eyes were like stars. To be Matthew's inspiration was the fondest dream of her life. She meant to dedicate herself to him entirely, to work for his success for as long as she lived, asking nothing more than to bask in his reflected glory. To be loved by such a man, head and shoulders above all other men, was the ultimate in happiness, it made her blessed above all other women!

"Miss Livingston—Adelaide—I must speak to your father again soon!" The emotion in Matthew's voice made Addie feel faint. "Do you think he's softened toward me at all, that he'll permit our betrothal?"

"He thinks I'm too young." Addie's voice was filled with despair, but then it brightened. "But Mama is on our side! He'll relent soon, I'm sure he will! I'll get Wyatt to talk to him, Wyatt will always do what I ask, he's the most wonderful brother in the world."

Her words were more confident than her thoughts. It was true that Wyatt was a wonderful brother. He'd always been kind to her, he loved her and he'd never teased or tormented her as other older brothers do their sisters. All the same, she wasn't sure that Wyatt liked Matthew that much. He'd told her not to take this first love too seriously, that she was way too young to decide what man she wanted to marry. Sometimes it seemed that everybody was against her, just as everyone had been against Juliet and Romeo!

"I'll be the happiest man in the world, the most fortunate man who ever lived, as soon as we receive your father's consent," Matthew told her. "Being sent here to Athens was the turning point of my life. When I think that I might have been sent somewhere else, that I might never have met you, it frightens me so that I can't sleep. It was fate, Adelaide. I'm convinced that God ordained it."

Had ever a girl been so loved! Addie's eyes filled with tears. Oh, yes, Matthew was right, it had been ordained in heaven, else it never would have happened!

And then something even more wonderful happened. Unable to restrain himself, Matthew leaned down and kissed her cheek. If Addie had died on the spot, she would have died the happiest girl who had ever lived.

They had to go. Geneva and Dr. Forbes were waiting for her, and if she was any later in getting home, her father would never let her see Matthew again, much less marry him.

Watching the young lovers walk back to the buggy, Geneva knew that Addie had been kissed, even if it had only been on her cheek. The way Addie kept reaching up to touch the spot on her cheek where Matthew's kiss was still glowing spoke volumes that any girl with half an eye would be able to read. She looked at Galen Forbes to see if he too had noticed, but the doctor was busy running his hands over Cato's sleek hide, lost in admiration for him.

"We're ready to leave, Doctor Forbes," she said. She didn't blame Galen for admiring Bobo's horse, but it was something of an insult for him to devote his entire attention to Cato when he was with her!

With Galen once again taking a boyish pleasure in driving Cato, they delivered Addie to her doorstep and escorted her to the door. Just like the first time he'd ever seen the Livingston house, Galen had to surpress a whistle. Mill owners made money, that was for sure. The white clapboard house on the summit of Elm Street was enough to make any ordinary man whistle. A castle for a princess, Galen thought, and Addie Livingston, with her golden curls and porcelain complexion and those sky blue eyes certainly fit the part, as dainty and lovely as any princess in a fairy tale.

The door was opened by a manservant in butler's livery. A liveried butler, right here in Athens! Galen had not yet had the honor of being summoned to the Livingston mansion as a doctor, much less as a guest, and so he was caught by surprise.

"Geneva, thank you for talking Bobo into taking us. Arnold, have my mother and father retired?"

"Yes, Miss Adelaide."

Addie's sigh of relief barely escaped being audible, but she covered it up with a smile. "Then you might as well go to bed too, if Wyatt is in." It was a pity that there'd been a breakdown in the spinning room at the mill, and that Wyatt had had to stay this evening to supervise the repairs, so that he hadn't been able to go to the revival with them. But then, it was probably just as well, because Wyatt wouldn't have been able to overlook the little mechanic's flouting of the rules as she and Geneva had. Not that he wouldn't have wanted to, but as the mill owner's son, and the second-in-command, his conscience would have made him adhere to the letter of the rules.

"He's already in, Miss Adelaide." Arnold bowed his head toward Geneva and Galen. "Good night, Miss Burton. Good night, Doctor Forbes."

"Whew!" Galen burst out when Arnold closed the door behind them. "How do the Livingstons manage to function in all that formality?"

Geneva's tone was dry. "It isn't easy, at least for Addie and Wyatt. Do you know where I live, Doctor Forbes? It's only around the corner, on North Street."

"I know the place. Will a butler be waiting up for you, too?"

Geneva's laugh rang out, silvery and filled with amusement greater than his own. "We don't have such pretensions, Doctor. The nearest thing we have to a butler is Emma Martin, who still insists on calling herself a hired hussy even though she's been our housekeeper since before I was born. And I assure you that she will have been in bed for hours!"

The Burtons' door opened before Galen and Geneva reached it, and a hearty voice greeted them. "So you're back at last! Come in. That isn't Bobo, Geneva! What happened to that young scalawag who was supposed to be looking out for you and Addie? It's Doctor Forbes, isn't it? I expect Bobo turned his charges over to you, so that he could go helling around with the other Corinthians in the Sin for Sale area. Come in, Doctor, and have a nightcap, while Geneva tells me if anything worth seeing happened at the revival."

Galen wasn't sure that he liked this turn of affairs. Helping out in a crisis was one thing, but he had no desire to cultivate people like the Burtons. Having been in Geneva's presence for just this little while was enough to make the bile rise in his throat, even though he was honest enough to admit to himself that if she'd been as poor as Mary MacDonald, he'd have found her confoundedly attractive.

Nevertheless, common courtesy constrained him to follow his host in through a hallway with stained-glass windows, and on into a living room of such warm comfort that it seemed to reach out a welcome to anyone who entered it. The furniture was of the finest quality, but most of it was old and well worn. The rug glowed with color, the curtains at the windows were drawn back and the windows were open to admit the soft night air, so that there was none of that sense of stuffiness so common to most sitting rooms of the affluent.

Nor was Galen unaware of the honor of being invited into the Burton home. As much of a newcomer as he was, having been in Athens only a few months, he was aware that the Burtons surpassed even the Livingstons in social importance, for all that they chose to live more modestly. Marvin Burton's wealth—half inherited and half earned by his own ability as a lawyer—equaled the Livingstons' with their textile mill. The Burtons had been a power in Athens and its environs for generations, and Marvin Burton had added even more prestige to the name.

The lawyer walked over to a small table where decanters and glasses were set out. "What will you have? Brandy, whiskey, rum, wine? I recommend the brandy." Without waiting for an answer, he poured a liberal amount into one of the cut-glass glasses and handed it to Galen, and then supplied his daughter with a glass of sherry.

"Brandy's the drink for conversation." Mr. Burton indicated a comfortable armchair and lowered his long frame into another. Geneva pulled up a tapestry stool and sat close to her father's knees, her eyes sparkling at Galen over the rim of her glass. Seen under the lamplight, with her bonnet laid aside and her cheeks still flushed with the excitement of the evening, she was even more attractive than Galen had realized. Her eyes, of that deep, almost slate gray, were remarkable, and her brown hair was smooth, disdaining the myriads of round sausage curls that were so much in vogue among the ladies. In the lamplight, her eyes took on a silvery sheen, and the simple hairstyle brought out the perfect bone structure of her face.

He tore his eyes from her and studied his host. Marvin Burton wasn't as tall as his thin frame made him appear to be, but there was a lean strength to his body. Galen surmised that he never suffered from ill health. A closer scrutiny told him that his daughter had inherited much of her attractiveness from him, including the same gray eyes and brown hair, although Marvin's was touched with gray, now that he was in his late forties. His face was intelligent and filled with humor, his mouth sensitive and prone to smile. In different circumstances, Galen would have been pleased to have him as a friend.

"I'm waiting to be amused," Marvin prodded Geneva. "What went on at the meeting? You didn't feel called to go forward and get yourself saved, did you now, Geneva?"

Geneva's grin was impish. "No, I didn't. There were enough others to do that without me to add to Carlton Booth's glory. There were the usual fits, people crying and becoming hysterical and falling down and shaking, as well as some booing and catcalls by rowdies who slipped in from the outer fringes. It promises to be a triumph before it's over. After all, this is only the first night. By the time the week is out the evangelist should have every soul in the Athens area safely in the fold. Except for the rowdies and the canallers, of course. Even Carlton Booth wouldn't expect to save them!"

Marvin chuckled, and then turned his attention to Galen. "And what do you think of our fair city, Doctor Forbes? Does Athens come up to your expectations? How do you like working under that pompous ass, Stephen Harding?"

For a moment, Galen was too taken aback by Marvin's choice of words to answer. Then he threw back his head and almost choked with laughter.

"You said it, I didn't!" he gasped, wiping at his eyes. The brandy he'd just begun to swallow when Burton had come out with "pompous ass" had gone down the wrong way.

Geneva was on her feet, thumping his back. "All right now? Father, I'm afraid that Doctor Forbes hadn't been warned about your particular brand of humor."

"Pompous ass I called him, and pompous ass he is. I'd as lief call Les Peterson to treat me as that old fool. Forbes, would you believe that when Geneva was seven, Stephen Harding diagnosed her as having a common cold, and it turned out to be diphtheria? We all but lost her, and it was our nursing that saved her, not any of his pills or potions. How are you at diagnosis, Forbes?"

"I think I could recognize diphtheria." Galen's voice was cautious. "Not that I could do much more about it than Doctor Harding, you understand. You were fortunate that your daughter lived."

"Put that down to her stubborn refusal to die." Marvin chuckled. "She was angry with Bobo because he'd broken one of her dolls, and she couldn't wait to get well so she could smash a wagon he'd built himself, to get even. She kept making us promise not to let him in her room lest he catch her disease too, and foil her by dying."

"But I didn't break his wagon, Father. I only wanted to make him think I would," Geneva responded. "You know what a tease he always was, still is for that matter. He told me he was going to break Amanda, and then he did, but it was only a clumsy accident, he didn't mean to do it." Her eyes were dancing as she turned to explain to Galen. "I tried to snatch the doll from him, you see, and he dropped it and stepped on it. He was more horrified than I was, and then I came down with diphtheria that very evening, and all the time I was sick I could hear him begging Mother and Father not to let me die before he could save up enough to buy me another doll."

Marvin chuckled, his face registering mirth. "He did save up enough, too, only he saw a very special jackknife in the store when he went to buy the doll, and he bought the jackknife instead! He offered to let Geneva go shares with it, though. She wasn't that stupid. She took the knife, all four blades of it, and on Christmas she gave him a doll! It wasn't until New Year's Eve that they finally got together and effected a trade. Doctor, raising children is an experience. It's a shame that some people are cheated of it.''

He got up and replenished both Galen's glass and his own. ''You treat the mill workers, don't you? Isn't there an unusual amount of illness among them?''

''Unusual! It's disgraceful! How could it be otherwise? Working fourteen, fifteen, sometimes sixteen hours a day, the air filled with lint, kept cold in the winter, their diet inadequate—''

Marvin held up his hand. ''I'm aware of the conditions. But Stephen Harding doesn't agree with you. He claims heredity, that the workers come from bad stock and so nothing else can be expected.''

''Balderdash! I beg your pardon, Miss Burton.''

''Double balderdash!'' Geneva said, her voice agreeable.

''I find it hard to believe that any man, even a mill owner, could be so blind to the fundamental human needs of his workers,'' Galen said, his voice tight with anger.

''You'll find out more about Herndon Livingston almost immediately,'' Marvin told him. ''Athen's biggest day falls on the day after tomorrow.''

Galen looked at him, puzzled, wondering what on earth the lawyer was talking about.

''Herndon Livingston's birthday. Certainly you've received your invitation to the celebration at his home? As Harding's assistant, you're sure to have been included in the guest list.''

''Oh, that. Yes, I did receive an invitation. I'd forgotten.''

''You'd best not forget it again, if you want to make yourself useful in Athens. For those who are honored with an invitation, attendance is mandatory. You'll want to go in any case, so that you can evaluate the man for yourself and form your own opinion. All of Athen's elite will be there. You'll get a very good idea of what it means to live in a mill town, of who runs things and of how difficult it will be to institute any changes.''

''We met one of Mr. Livingston's mechanics this evening, Father.'' Geneva leaned forward, her face grave now, the corners of her mouth compressed. ''She'd been on

32

cleanup duty and was left behind while the others went to the camp meeting. She'd gone on alone, against all orders, and somehow got herself slightly hurt in some sort of a contretemps on the outskirts. Doctor Forbes took her back to her dormitory and strapped her ribs while Addie and I made sure that her nightmarm didn't take the other girls back in time to find her out."

Marvin's eyebrows shot up. "And you and Addie stayed on at the revival alone?"

"Indeed not. We were very well protected, by a canal boat captain. Doctor Forbes knows him, a Captain Yarnell."

"Yarnell. I know the man, by sight at least. He seems to be a decent sort, in spite of his calling. Not that I subscribe to the popular opinion that all canal men are scoundrels and drunkards. I don't doubt that you were in good hands, but I hope that that devious feminine brain of yours has come up with some excuse to hand along to Herndon, for Addie's sake."

"I expect you to help me with that." Geneva's voice was demure, but her eyes were dancing. "He was appointed our bodyguard, for instance, while Doctor Forbes was called to attend an emergency?"

"Capitol! I couldn't have done better myself. Doctor, if this girl of mine weren't a female she'd have made a topnotch lawyer. Always use enough of the truth so that the rest will slip by unnoticed."

Galen rose to his feet. "It's been a privilege to talk with you, Mr. Burton, but it's late and I have a full day tomorrow. I'll see you at the Livingston affair."

"And keep your ears open while you're there. We'll get together some time, discreetly, so that you won't be drummed out of town for agreeing with me that changes should be made. We need your sound medical opinion. I'll tell Bobo to cultivate you, no one will think anything of it if he takes a liking to you and invites you here regularly. It's either that, or you'd have to pretend you're courting Geneva, and Wyatt Livingston might take exception to that."

In spite of the fact that her father was obviously making one of his jokes, Geneva felt her cheeks burning. Galen only looked startled, as if he was ready to take to his heels at any such suggestion. A moment later Galen was gone, and Geneva kissed her father good-night, but she didn't think that she'd sleep well in spite of the lateness of the hour. Galen Forbes disturbed her, there was something about him that got under her skin. Not for the first time in recent months, while all of Athens waited for her engagement to Wyatt to be announced, she wondered if she really wanted to marry him. Was she being pushed into it simply because they'd known each other all their lives and people expected it?

But there was no use worrying about Galen's effect on her. Being more than normally intuitive, she had the distinct impression that Galen wanted nothing to do with her. Perhaps he'd left someone back home, wherever it was he'd come from. Or maybe he was one of those men who simply don't care for the opposite sex. Every time she'd caught his eyes on her, she'd felt a wave of wariness, even of dislike. And it wasn't because of anything that had happened between them.

Brushing her hair, she pondered again the question of Wyatt. Up until the first time she'd met Galen Forbes, three weeks ago, it had never entered her mind that she might not love Wyatt. Since then, and especially tonight, the prospect of being Mrs. Wyatt Livingston, of taking her undisputed place as Athen's social leader, and of an endless round of morning calls and afternoon teas, dinner parties, sewing circles, talk of babies and diapers and colic, of servants and fashion, appalled her.

There had to be more to life than that, even though ninety-nine girls out of a hundred would envy her. But society being what it was, what else was there for a girl of her wealth and breeding?

She was helping her father gather material for a history of New York State that he was writing, with particular emphasis on the Erie Canal and its impact on the population every place it touched. The advent of the canal, that miracle of modern engineering, had had such a tremendous effect that it took her breath away. The whole country was in a flux of change, of growth, of prosperity such as had never been known before. People in the remotest communities had been brought in touch with civilization and its advantages, and existing towns were not only growing but more were springing up where none had been before.

It was so exciting, so filled with adventure and challenge, that Geneva yearned to be a part of it all. The struggle that her father predicted, a struggle to improve the lot of the mill workers, filled her with excitement. In the midst of all this prosperity, it was unthinkable that the lot of the mechanics should remain stable, that they should be underpaid and overworked while the rest of the country thrived. Her father was determined to do something about it, in spite of the fact that it would make enemies of a good many men of influence who profited by the cheap labor.

Geneva was fully cognizant of the fact that her father was a remarkable man. Of all the men she had ever known, he was virtually the only one who was convinced that every human being had the right to fight to better his lot, that a person's ability counted more than the station in life to which society had committed him. His convictions were all the more remarkable because he did not confine them to the male sex only, but also to women. Geneva had been taught to think for herself from the time she'd begun to walk and talk, and she was accorded more freedom of movement and choice than any other girl in this age where women were allowed no independent thoughts or opinions.

But things were changing, and the changes were so exciting that they made her blood race. Ever since the Erie Canal had been built, women all over the country enjoyed more freedom from the backbreaking and time-consuming toil that had been their lot. They were turning their energies more and more to uplifting movements. They were banding together to make their wishes known and to accomplish their desires.

The great majority of men didn't like it. Men of means and influence were too used to having their own way, to holding down both women and the lower classes for their own comfort and convenience. The changes underway enraged them. Only a few men, her father foremost among them, applauded the changes and worked to further them.

And now there was Galen Forbes. Geneva didn't know how he felt about women, but she had learned tonight that he was furious about the lot of the mechanics. He would be a part of this long-needed reform. Geneva longed to plunge into the battle herself, but as Herndon Livingston's daughter-in-law it would be impossible. The course of history was being changed, and she wanted her part in it!

Exasperated, she threw down her hairbrush and got into

bed. If Galen Forbes had shown the least bit of interest in her, her problem would be half solved. Having a choice between two men, one adhering to the old conventions, the other open-minded and welcoming change, would give her an option.

But Galen had shown no interest in her. Why didn't he like her? The question nagged at her, making her toss and turn and thump her pillow. And why should she care whether he liked her or not? She had Wyatt, if she wanted him, and a girl could hardly be any luckier than that. And if she decided that she didn't want him, because by marrying him she'd be walking into the prison men had devised for wives and daughters, then she didn't have to accept him. She still had a choice. She didn't have to have any man at all!

There it was again, the old unfairness between men and women. No man was looked down on because he did not choose to marry. Only women were labeled with derogatory terms if they chose to remain single. Spinster, old maid! Maybe part of this new movement forward would include women not choosing to marry unless they could find a man who would concede that they had a right to freedom.

She'd see Galen again at Herndon Livingston's birthday party. If he still evinced no interest in her, she'd accept Wyatt. Ever since she'd been old enough to know the difference between boys and girls, she'd taken it for granted that she would marry him. She'd known him all her life. He was handsome, witty, and fun to be with. She'd always supposed that she loved him. She knew that she liked him at least, and that she was terribly fond of him. There was no doubt that they would be happy together. And she could use a woman's gentle influence to persuade him to make changes in the policy of the mill. Women had done such things before. When one way was closed to them, they found another.

Only would that be enough to satisfy her? Wouldn't she spend the rest of her life chafing against the bonds that kept her from doing more, from plunging into the upcoming struggle with a whoop and a holler?

And not only that, she admitted to herself. Wouldn't she spend the rest of her life wondering if she had missed out on something wonderful, on experiencing a love that flamed and burned until it consumed her, but miraculously left her more whole than she had ever been before? She could laugh all she wanted to about the way female novelists ran on about flaming and consuming romance, but every girl who was ever born longed for it. Without it, she would have been cheated.

Before she finally slept, she thought about Mary MacDonald. She hoped that the little mechanic wouldn't get into any trouble because of her ill-advised adventure. Why had Mary done such a thing?

Half asleep, Geneva laughed. In Mary's place, she'd have done exactly the same, only she wouldn't have let some ruffian terrify her, she'd have terrified him instead! She wasn't a timid little mill girl. The man had yet to be born who could frighten her. But that was because she'd been fortunate enough to be born Geneva Burton rather than Mary MacDonald. Once again she hoped that Mary wouldn't be found out. She determined to check up on it. If Mary got into any trouble, she could at least persuade Wyatt to intervene for her.

Her other problems would have to be worked out as they came up. And worked out by herself. No one else, not even her father, could do it for her.

3

Wyatt Livingston's stride was fast as he approached his home on the evening of his father's birthday celebration. He was all but late, and if he didn't get dressed in record time and present himself in the front hallway to help his parents greet their guests, Herndon would be mightily displeased.

He shouldn't have stayed at the Cayuga so long, fortifying himself against the boredom of the evening that loomed ahead of him. He'd meant to have no more than one drink, but Bob Maxwell had been there, and Paul Towndson, and his envy of their freedom had got the better of him.

Even in his hurry to get into the house undetected and make himself presentable, Wyatt grimaced as he saw that Addie had forgotten to pull the drapes across the windows of her bedroom at the front of the house. Checking his stride, he saw his sister's figure pass in front of the windows, dressed only in her petticoats. Then his eyes went to the house that was situated directly across the street, and his grimace turned into a black frown. Damn! That old lecher, the banker Henry Maynard, was in his own bedroom window. Wyatt saw the lace curtain move as Maynard got himself an eyeful.

It wasn't the first time it had happened, and Wyatt had to check his impulse to force his way into Maynard's house and knock the Peeping Tom down his own stairs. But the three drinks he'd had hadn't clouded his mind enough to let him carry out the impulse. Instead, he entered his own house and took the stairs three at a time to rap sharply on Addie's door before he thrust it open. He crossed the room to yank the drapes across the windows.

"Wyatt, you scared the daylights out of me!" Addie protested, snatching up a dressing gown.

"Then remember to pull the curtains before you dress or undress!" Wyatt's voice was unnaturally gruff. "Anybody walking down the street could see you!"

Addie's hand flew to her mouth, and her face flushed scarlet. "I did forget! Could they really see me, Wyatt?"

"I did." Still curt, Wyatt's voice softened. He was fond of his younger sister; he'd kill the man who would hurt her, and it wasn't in him to go on being angry with her. She was overexcited at being allowed to join the adults for the first time for this party, and she was innocent enough and had been so overprotected all her life that the idea of men looking into her bedroom windows would never have entered her mind. "Just try to remember, Addie. I've got to rush." Pecking her cheek with a kiss that almost missed, he dashed past her on his own way to dress.

He was shedding his own clothes even as he kicked his bedroom door shut. A glance at the clock on his bureau confirmed that he'd have to get dressed faster than he ever had before in his life. Only the thought that Geneva would be here tonight, that he'd have an opportunity to get her alone out in his mother's garden, made the evening that loomed ahead bearable. If Geneva gave him the answer that he wanted, a dozen such evenings as this would be a small price to pay. Whistling, he began to smile, both his sister and Henry Maynard forgotten.

Herndon Livingston himself was a contented man on this evening of his fiftieth birthday. Not many men could boast of having accomplished as much as he had in the half century since his birth. It was true that he had inherited the textile mill from his father, Emmerson Livingston, as well as the old family home on North Street, but Herndon was the one who had expanded the mill, who had brought it to its present state of prosperity, who was the largest single employer in Athens, and who had built this house on Elm Street which dominated the town.

At the head of the table in his thirty-foot dining room, Herndon surveyed his guests through benevolent eyes. The cream of Athenian society had come to pay him homage, which he accepted as no more than his due. Without him and his textile mill, the wheels of Athenian commerce would grind to a halt.

His gaze came to rest on Geneva Burton, approving her gown and her general appearance. If he was the king of Athens and his wife Lillian the queen consort, if his son Wyatt was the crown prince, then Geneva would be an eminently suitable crown princess. When the day came that he would have to abdicate to his heirs, he could rest assured that he would leave his dynasty in capable hands.

His eyes moved on, and a frown appeared between his brows as they rested on the dress that Roxanne Fielding was wearing. The material was a particularly brilliant green, complementary to Roxanne's flame of auburn hair, but in Herndon's opinion it was far too sophisticated for a young lady of nineteen, the same age as Geneva. Earl Fielding ought to keep a tighter rein on his daughter, but then Earl himself was flamboyant, lacking in the finer nuances of social graces. There was no old money behind Earl. He was a self-made man who'd got his start with a single canalboat years ago and bought a second with the profits made by the first, then another and another until he owned a fleet that had made him one of the wealthiest men in the state.

Herndon was well aware of the extent of Earl Fielding's wealth. Henry Maynard, who owned the Mercantile Bank of Athens and who was one of Herndon's closest associates, had given him some idea of the amount of cash that Earl safeguarded in his financial institution until he drew it out to invest in one or another of his other enterprises. Maynard's bank paid no interest on monies kept there, but merely safeguarded them, making its own profits by offering loans at twelve and a half to fifteen percent.

Earl Fielding's financial status had earned him a place at Herndon's table, but his background left a great deal to be desired. If it hadn't been for his growing influence, he wouldn't have been allowed past Herndon's door, and Roxanne would not have been numbered among Adelaide's friends.

Herndon allowed the merest flicker of a smile to play around his mouth as his gaze moved on to his daughter, three years younger than Geneva and Roxanne. This was the first time that he'd permitted her to attend his birthday dinner.

Adelaide (he never, even in his own mind, referred to

her as Addie as her brother and her friends did) was gowned most becomingly and suitably in white, with eyeletted ruffles at her shoulders. Her camelia-fair complexion was tinged with the pink of excitement in spite of the fact that she was unreasonably upset. That young minister who'd come to assist Reverend Tucker had had to send his regrets, as his presence was needed at the revival meeting. Herndon himself was as well satisfied that the revival coincided with his birthday. It was time that he took steps to nip that unsuitable romance in the bud.

His self-satisfaction with his life deepened as he regarded his son and heir. At twenty-one, Wyatt was everything a man could ask for in a son. A little too dashing, perhaps, and Herndon regretted Wyatt's association with that brash young element that termed themselves Corinthians, aping the antics of other wealthy young men, a decade or so ago, in England. Their members sported ruffled shirts and skintight pantaloons; they carried slender walking sticks and dashed around the streets of Athens and the surrounding countryside in their suicide gigs, so-called because they had such high wheels that they were top-heavy and dangerous to life and limb. But then, a young man of Wyatt's position could hardly have avoided belonging to that society. As long as his son ran up no overwhelming gambling debts and avoided getting himself into any other disgraceful scrapes, he could afford to overlook such minor infractions.

Wyatt and Geneva. Herndon could ask for no more perfect birthday gift than to have the matter settled, but Geneva, for some inscrutable reason of her own, had chosen to keep Wyatt dangling.

No matter. Who else could the girl marry? She was intelligent enough to realize that she'd never find another young man as well qualified to be her husband as Wyatt. If Marvin Burton weren't so unconventional as to believe that females should be allowed to have minds of their own and a voice in how their lives were to be disposed of, the matter would have been settled long since.

Herndon had a particular need for a marriage between Wyatt and Geneva. He wasn't overextended, even by the standards of the most conservative businessmen, but the time had come to expand, to enlarge his mill and thereby enlarge his profits. The enlargement was going to involve a great deal of money that Herndon did not have available for the purpose. Marvin Burton, whose fortune rivaled that of Earl Fielding, would make him a loan at much less than Henry Maynard would charge him as soon as the engagement was announced. With Wyatt and Geneva married, the money would all be in the family, after all.

Herndon's mouth, always hard, hardened a trifle more as he thought about Marvin Burton. Any other father would have seen that his daughter accepted such an advantageous proposal without all this shilly-shallying. For a man of such solid intellect and background, the lawyer had notions that passed the bounds of common sense.

There was one other person present tonight who was as concerned about whether the marriage would take place as Herndon, or as Wyatt himself. Roxanne Fielding's thoughts were in violent contrast to the smile on her face as she made all the correct responses to the guests seated on either side of her. If Geneva accepted Wyatt tonight, as Roxanne was desperately afraid she would, Roxanne's last chance of enticing Wyatt away from her would be gone.

And it was all such a waste! Why couldn't Wyatt see that she would make him happier than quiet, serious-minded Geneva who'd rather have her nose in some dusty book or take up the cause of lost mongrels, or spend hours compiling her father's notes?

Wyatt was so alive, so vibrantly, excitingly alive, and so was she! And she was prettier than Geneva, everyone knew that. Heads never failed to turn when she walked down a street or entered a room; she could have any man she wanted by merely snapping her fingers, any man but Wyatt. But Wyatt was the only man she wanted or had ever wanted, and Wyatt had always been Geneva's, who didn't have the sense to appreciate him!

It had always been that way, ever since her father had brought her from Albany. They'd bought the original Livingston house on North Street, only half a dozen doors removed from the Burton's house. Roxanne's mother, a former actress, was a beautiful, auburn-haired woman. Roxanne resembled her so closely that Earl's heart twisted every time he looked at his daughter. She had died when Roxanne was ten. After her death, Earl, unwilling to let Roxanne out of his sight, had taken her everywhere with him, living a good share of the time on his own canalboats. Roxanne's first inconsolable grief for her mother had abated under the excitement of canal life. She'd taken to it as if she'd been born on a barge.

As her sixteenth birthday approached, Earl had realized that a young lady had no business racketing around the country in the company of all the canal scum and riffraff, no matter how well his name and reputation protected her. It was time that she took her place as a young lady of society. No expense was too great, no effort too demanding, to give her everything she should have. His beloved wife hadn't lived to enjoy the full fruits of his success, but Roxanne was to have it all: wealth, social prominence, and a brilliant marriage into one of the best families. He could afford it, and by God, she was going to have it!

The house in Athens was exactly the right setting for this jewel of a daughter. Anyone who lived in the old Livingston house was accepted without question. But Earl, who had struggled his way up from the slums of New York City, had no idea that the furniture he bought was too showy, that the rugs were too bright and gaudy, that the window hangings he ordered were festooned with too many gold tassels. And Earl himself, in his habitual garb of tight checkered trousers, and gaudy waistcoats in the latest fad, sported too many ruffles on his shirts. The ruby stickpin and the diamond ring he wore every day were too flashy to be anything but vulgar.

Roxanne, who'd inherited a sensitivity from her mother which Earl was totally lacking, knew these things but would have bitten her tongue off before she'd crush her father's feelings by telling him that everything about him, including the house he'd bought as a setting for her, was wrong. She'd manage to get where she wanted to in spite of her father's help, not because of it. And so far she'd managed very well. It hadn't taken her any time at all to tone down the language she'd learned on the towpath, to make friends with the socially prominent girls of Athens, to institute gradual and subtle changes in the house, changes that her father never noticed. Roxanne was, as her mother would have said, a quick study.

At nineteen, Roxanne had arrived, as far as social position in Athens was concerned. The fact that there was still, and always would be, a degree of withholding the last, final acceptance that girls like Geneva Burton and Adelaide Livingston had been born to, was something that Roxanne shrugged off, not caring a whit. There was only one thing she wanted now, and that was Wyatt Livingston. Because Roxanne loved Wyatt, she loved him blindly and with excruciating agony. But Geneva had Wyatt now, just as she'd always had him, even though she couldn't seem to make up her mind whether she wanted him or not.

Not want him! Not want Wyatt with his crisp black hair? Wyatt, whose eyes were so blue that looking into them was like drowning in a mountain lake, eyes soot-touched with black brows and lashes. Wyatt, who moved as lithely and powerfully as a jungle animal; whose mouth curved in a smile that made Roxanne want to kiss it until her senses left her!

He was so handsome in his evening clothes that Roxanne's hands clenched until her fingernails bit into her palms. Geneva must be made of solid stone, not to feel that attraction that would make any other woman willing to lay down her life in return for one smile, one kiss. And he only had eyes for Geneva. He hadn't looked at Roxanne once, or barely once, when he'd greeted her when she and her father had arrived. Greeted her as one pal to another, as casually as if she'd been one of those Corinthians he ran with! Wyatt liked her, they were friends. If she'd been a man, she would undoubtedly have been his best friend. But she wasn't a man, she was a girl, and she loved him and Geneva had him. If Geneva accepted him tonight, Roxanne would feel as if her life had come to an end.

If Roxanne had been convinced that Geneva loved Wyatt, everything would have been different. She liked Geneva, she liked her better than she liked any other girl she'd ever known. Geneva had been good to her, Geneva had been the first to welcome her to Athens, to reach out with unfeigned friendship to draw her into her own circle of friends and see that she had a place there. If Roxanne had been blessed with a sister, she would have wanted that sister to be Geneva. In any other matter than Wyatt, she would have been loyal to Geneva to the death.

She was still loyal to Geneva, that was the trouble. If Geneva wanted Wyatt, Roxanne would never, as long as she lived, lift a finger to come between them. She wanted Geneva to be happy. Her own happiness would always come second after that.

But she wanted Wyatt to be happy, too. And how could he be happy, if he and Geneva married and then they found out that it was all a mistake because Geneva didn't love him? Their lives would be ruined, and Roxanne's along with them.

If only things had been different! If only Geneva knew, without question, that she didn't love Wyatt, if only Wyatt loved *her* instead of Geneva!

So here I am, Roxanne thought. And there's Geneva, and there's Wyatt—three people in a mess that can't be resolved. But I'm the only one that knows it and there isn't a thing I can do about it. It isn't fair, and it isn't right, but that's the way it is. So smile, darn you, Herndon Livingston's looking at you, and what's more important, so is your father. She wouldn't give a hoot if Herndon Livingston saw that she was unhappy, but she'd rather cut her heart out than have her father find out that there was something his money couldn't buy for her.

All this tomfoolery about her taking her place in society, about her having to be some kind of a social queen! It was all for her father. She couldn't have cared less. She'd been happy living on her father's canalboats, and she'd be happy living in a shack as long as it was with the man she loved. But Earl Fielding wanted everything for her, and she couldn't let him down. All he'd accomplished, all of his labor and determination to succeed, had been for her. If he knew that she wasn't happy it would kill him. Roxanne had a deep and abiding love for her father, and she'd rather die than hurt him.

Roxanne's smile was brilliant as she met her father's eyes. She had the satisfaction of seeing him beam, filled with pride because she was in this place at this time, a guest at the most important social affair of the year. He'd done this for her, he'd made it happen, and he was happy. Only Roxanne knew that half of the sparkle in her eyes came from the tears that she refused to shed.

At her own place at the table, Geneva's thoughts were almost as disturbed as Roxanne's. Where was Galen Forbes? How dared he be late, or—a thought that appalled her—not show up at all, after he'd been warned that not to put in an appearance would mean incurring Herndon Livingston's wrath, to say nothing of the censure of Dr. Stephen Harding, on whom she depended to gain a foothold in Athens? She could see that opposite her at the table, Harding was becoming more annoyed by the moment at his young assistant's dereliction.

Geneva was shaken at how strongly she cared about what happened to Galen Forbes. There was something about the tall, intense young doctor that seized her imagination, that convinced her that he was someone worth knowing, someone whose company she would never fail to enjoy.

She saw, dismayed, that Herndon Livingston was looking with severe disapproval at the glaringly empty chair where Galen should have been sitting. Even her father looked a little perturbed, and Marvin Burton was seldom ruffled.

There was an interruption as Arnold appeared between the sliding doors that had been rolled back into their slots at either side of the dining room archway, and crossed the carpeted floor to whisper something to Lillian Livingston. Lillian looked both startled and alarmed, and her nervous blue eyes went to her husband as if she didn't know quite what to do about Arnold's whispered message. "Mr. Livingston, Doctor Forbes has arrived," she managed to get out. "He sends his apologies for being late."

Herndon frowned, and Geneva held her breath. It was several seconds before Herndon said, "Show him in, Arnold."

Geneva breathed again. Was not late better than never? At least he was here; it remained to be seen whether his reason for his tardiness would be acceptable.

Galen's suit was neat, his shirt modestly ruffled. Only his hair looked slightly disheveled, as if he'd taken a quick swipe at it while making a dash for the door after having dressed. He went directly to his hostess and made his apologies in person. His delay had been unavoidable, and it was good of her to overlook it.

"Unavoidable?" Herndon's displeasure was patent. Galen started as he was about to take the empty chair, well down the table from the more important guests, and Geneva held her breath again.

"I'm afraid so, sir. There was an unfortunate accident at the mill and I was called in. It isn't a subject for the dinner table, however. I can only beg your indulgence."

"Quite so." Herndon addressed himself once more to his roast beef and Yorkshire pudding, heavy fare for so warm a night. Accidents, especially serious enough accidents to necessitate the calling in of a physician, should never be discussed at a dinner table in the presence of ladies.

Down the full length of the table, Galen's eyes met Geneva's. She tried to look stern. She ended up smiling. Galen returned the smile, his eyes slightly mocking. Geneva's hand trembled almost imperceptibly as she toyed with her water glass, and this outward sign of her agitation made her angry. Why should she care so much if Galen were to discredit himself with the powers that made the wheels of Athens turn?

He'd mentioned an accident. What kind of accident, how badly had the unfortunate worker been injured? She wanted to know, but it was certain that she wouldn't find out until the party was over and she asked her father about it. The other ladies would be told nothing of it, and she suspected that outside of herself none of them would even think to ask their husbands or fathers. If an accident happened to one of their friends or social peers, they'd be concerned, but as this one had happened at the mill it could have no possible significance to them. The shallowness of their existence was brought home forcibly to Geneva. They weren't supposed to think; their only duties, as females, were to be good wives and mothers, and reasonably decorative.

Trapped in the drawing room with the other ladies after the gentlemen had been left to their port and cigars, Geneva felt that she was suffocating. The chatter all around her was so meaningless, so inconsequential, that she wondered that any woman with a modicum of intelligence could indulge in it, much less enjoy it as they were giving every indication of doing. Even Roxanne looked animated as she listened to some tidbit of gossip, and her own mother, Cora Burton, who should have something more in her head after twenty-five years with her father, seemed to be enjoying herself thoroughly.

She couldn't bear it another moment. She made some inane excuse to Mrs. Casper, who was enthusing about the amount of preserves that would fill her cellar shelves before the summer was over, and in a moment she was in the entrance hall and walking out of the front door.

It wasn't fresh air she was seeking, but a place directly outside the dining room windows, where she'd be able to eavesdrop on the gentlemen's conversation. It was reprehensible of her and she knew it. Eavesdropping was as bad as stealing or lack of charity, but she had to know what the gentlemen were talking about, and she felt a compelling need to know how Galen Forbes was conducting himself on this most important occasion that would seal either approval or disapproval of his welcome in Athens.

Thank heavens that it was such a warm evening that the windows had been half opened. Geneva stationed herself directly beside one of them, although well out of sight, just in time to hear ". . . ten-hour day." Who was talking? She wished that she dared risk one peek through the window.

"A ten-hour day! Preposterous! I can't credit my ears, Mr. Burton."

"Nevertheless, it's what they're pressing for in England. A ten-hour day for all the textile mill mechanics, and it looks as if they might get it."

"It'll be the ruination of England, then! The country will become a second- or a third-rate power. They'll ruin their entire commerce! A ten-hour day, indeed! Why, it isn't even godly!"

"Not godly, Mr. Livingston? How did you arrive at that rather peculiar conclusion?" Even without being able to see, Geneva knew that it was Galen Forbes who had challenged the mill owner.

"Doctor Forbes, it's obvious that you know nothing of finance or trade. Can't you picture the chaos that will result if the common workingman puts in only ten hours a day at his place of labor and has all the remainder of his time to spend in carousing, in throwing his money away on strong drink and gambling? God Himself set the working hours for the laboring man, from sunrise to sunset!"

"Except in the winter months, I take it." Galen's voice was sardonic, and Geneva felt her blood begin to race. "In the winter months, they labor far beyond the hours between sunrise and sunset."

"You are being facetious, sir! Why, every factory in England will grind to a standstill if those agitators get their way! There will be anarchy, mark my words. The country will sink into anarchy!"

"I'm afraid that I don't follow your line of reasoning, sir. Twelve hours, fourteen hours, sixteen hours of labor wreaks havoc on any worker's physical well-being. Men, and women as well, grow old before their time, succumb to diseases that they'd be able to throw off if their bodies weren't worn out. To say nothing of children! I've seen children of ten with wizened faces that looked old, and known that few of them would survive to full, healthy adulthood.''

"Balderdash! Working is the salvation of those children. It keeps them out of mischief, it keeps them from running the streets and turning into thieves and pickpockets and worse! It adds to the security of their families by bringing in extra money. Work never hurt anyone. It's unlimited leisure to bring down destruction on themselves that does the harm. Ask any businessman, ask any factory owner, and he'll tell you the same.''

Herndon Livingston was angry. His anger was in his voice and Geneva knew that if she could see him, she'd see the anger in his cold face, in his cold eyes. Galen was digging his grave with his own tongue.

"I can't say that I'm entirely in agreement with you, Herndon,'' Marvin Burton said, and Geneva thought, Go on talking, Father, so that Galen can't!

"And why not? You of all people should recognize the importance of keeping the lower classes gainfully employed, in keeping them busy so that they have no time to cause trouble!''

"That may be so up to a point, but fourteen or sixteen hours a day is too much for a female to work, to say nothing of children. They haven't the strength for it. Like our young physician here, I've seen the results of such hours, and am disturbed by it.''

"Speaking of children, young Dan Nolan is a case in point. He fell asleep on his feet this evening, and I had to stitch his forehead up where he fell into the machinery. I found him to be exhausted, yet he was discharged on the spot for causing a few moments' loss of production. Added to that, I expect that his father will beat him for losing his position, and he's no more than eleven.'' Galen's voice was as angry as Herndon's.

"How parents discipline their children is not our concern, Doctor Forbes.'' Herndon's voice was icy.

Galen refused to be warned. "The point is, Danny shouldn't have been working at all, at such long hours.''

Once again Marvin Burton stepped in. "The proposed

new English legislation will prohibit any child under nine years of age from working, and stipulate that children under eighteen work no more than twelve hours a day, that children under eleven work no more than eight hours, and that schooling must be provided for them during factory hours. Personally, I would like to see similar legislation passed in this country.''

''The United States will never do anything so reprehensibly foolish! And if the fools in power in England bow to the whims of the ignorant, it will mean the end of England as we know it.'' Geneva heard the sound of a chair being moved back. ''Gentlemen, I suggest that we put an end to this unprofitable discussion, and join the ladies.''

Geneva lifted her skirts and ran. By the time the gentlemen appeared in the drawing room, she was sitting beside Addie, her breathing carefully controlled, and hoping that her face wasn't noticeably flushed.

Wyatt's face lighted up as his eyes searched her out, and he went directly to her, holding out his hand. In spite of having expected it, Geneva wished that it could be put off. But there was no help for it. Every pair of eyes in the room was on them, some of the ladies all but simpering and the men looking wise. Her mother, still pretty and almost girlish-looking at forty-five, looked expectant, hopeful. The thought of her daughter walking down the aisle to marry Wyatt Livingston, the most brilliant marriage of decades, was dear to her heart. Geneva wasn't getting any younger, if she didn't accept Wyatt soon she'd end up an old maid. Only Geneva's father's face showed a rather sardonic amusement, as if he were telling her that this was her problem and that she'd have to handle it herself, with no help from him.

''Let's walk in the garden, Geneva.'' A long time ago, when they'd been children, Wyatt had tried to get away with calling her Jenny. She'd refused to answer, so stubbornly that he'd finally capitulated and called her by her correct name. ''I could do with some fresh air, after all that cigar smoke.''

Across the room, still in conversation with Marvin Burton, Galen watched them go. This is it, he thought. In a few more minutes it wouldn't matter whether he was attracted to Miss Geneva Burton or not. She'd be spoken for, officially engaged. It was just as well. He couldn't afford to waste time thinking about a girl he'd never dream of wanting for his wife. Roxanne watched them go, her smile painted on her face, her heart like a stone.

It was a beautiful evening. The air was sweet and fresh with the scent of Lillian Livingston's prize roses. Still Geneva's steps hesitated, reluctant to carry her on to wherever Wyatt was leading her.

"Wyatt, will your mother execute me if I pick this rose?" It was a white rose, luminous under the starlight. Its petals were covered with dew, and its scent was so sweet that it almost made her dizzy. She didn't want the rose, she had no need for the rose. Her mother's garden at home was filled with roses as beautiful as this one, and besides, this particular rose had long and very sharp thorns.

"I'll get it for you." Wyatt released her arm and grasped the blossom by its stem.

"Be careful! You'll be lacerated. I shouldn't have asked for it."

"If you want it, you'll have it." Wyatt's voice was determined as the thorns dug into his flesh, but it was tinged with laughter as well. If Geneva said yes tonight, he'd let his hands be torn to shreds and never notice the pain. Harding wouldn't even have to patch him up. Still, he swore under his breath as one of the thorns pierced deep.

"I told you!" Geneva said. "Here, let me get it out. You're bleeding." Without thinking, she put his finger in her mouth and licked the blood away.

Wyatt lost control. "Don't do that, damn it! Geneva, can't you see that you're driving me crazy?" He caught her in his arms, and the rose was crushed, forgotten, between them. His mouth sought hers, his arms trembled as he held her even closer. The whole hard length of his body pressed against her in a manner that would have made the ladies in the drawing room gasp and reach for their smelling salts if they could have seen it.

He kissed her as she'd never been kissed before, even by him. He was all through playing at courting. He wanted her, he had to have her, she belonged to him and nothing in the world was going to keep her from him from this moment forward.

Geneva's lips parted under his, she felt a streak of electric excitement race through her body. For a moment, she felt light-headed. She strained against him, telling herself that this was good and right, this was what she wanted. She must have been a little addled not to have accepted Wyatt long since. It was time, past time, that she was married. She was ready for it, ripe for it, and she loved Wyatt. She did, didn't she?

"Geneva? Is it yes?" Wyatt's voice was tense.

Geneva shook her head. "No, Wyatt. I'm sorry, but no."

Stung to near madness after his conviction that this was the night when Geneva would say yes at last, Wyatt shook her as though she were a rag doll, shook her until her head bobbled back and forth, until she cried out in outraged protest.

"Damn you, Geneva Burton! Damn you to hell! You can't say no. It isn't possible. You know you belong to me!"

Geneva felt like crying. She'd never wanted to cry as much in her life. She held back the tears with an effort that shook her.

"Wyatt, I'm sorry. I'm sorry! I don't want to hurt you, you mean more to me than almost anyone in the world. But it's still no, and don't ask me why because I can't explain. Not so that you would understand. I only know that I can't say yes, that it wouldn't be fair to either of us."

"How much longer am I supposed to wait?" Wyatt's eyes were blazing with the rage of his hurt. "Another six months? Another year? Two years?"

Geneva's face was as pale as the rose that had fallen to the ground at their feet. "I don't want you to wait at all, Wyatt. That would be even more unfair to you, because I'm afraid that my answer will always have to be no."

She reached out to touch him, to touch the face that was so dear to her and that was contorted with rage and grief and a sick disbelief, and then she dropped her hand. There wasn't anything more to say, and touching him would only add insult to what she had already done to him. She turned and walked away from him, leaving him standing there as though he'd been lightning-struck and rendered incapable of movement.

In the drawing room, Roxanne saw her come back in, and her heart leapt. Geneva had said no. Roxanne could tell by the look on her face, even though Geneva had composed herself as well as she could after such a distressing scene.

It wasn't too late, there was still a chance for her, if only Geneva didn't change her mind! Wyatt would be devastated.

He'd need her now, need the special friendship that only she could offer him. Maybe it wasn't much of a chance, seeing how much Wyatt loved Geneva, but it was better than none at all. He couldn't go on forever loving someone who didn't love him! Wyatt was very much a man; it was against nature. Roxanne was the one he would turn to, simply because she intended to be there at every possible opportunity. It wasn't as if she'd be betraying her friendship with Geneva, now that Geneva had turned him down.

She turned her attention back to Henry Maynard, who'd come to sit next to her when he'd seen that there was no way he could get near Addie. Bobo, bless his heart, was seeing to that. Geneva's brother was monopolizing Addie, fending off all the banker's approaches. If Roxanne wasn't mistaken, Bobo had a soft spot for Addie. It was too bad that Addie had fallen in love with Matthew Ramsey. As Roxie saw it, Bobo would make her a much better husband.

The smile she bestowed on Henry almost undid him. Disgusting old lecher! He'd tried to put his hands on Roxie more than once, at different social affairs, but she was more than a match for any dirty old man who slavered over young girls. He should be at the revival meeting, and go forward and confess his sins and throw himself at the seat of mercy! That's where he needed to be, more than those poor sinners who only lusted after strong drink or things they couldn't afford to buy.

Roxanne had been making a point of watching out for Addie whenever Henry Maynard was around, because Addie was still as innocent as the day she'd been born. If the old fool thought that she crowded in between them and demanded his attention because she wanted it for herself, then let him be happy thinking it. She grinned to herself, as she thought of how many times she'd felt like punching him in his round paunch instead of simpering at him to get his filthy mind off Addie.

Now, as she smiled at him again, his face turned the color of an overripe tomato and he very nearly drooled.

Wyatt, Roxanne thought. Watch out, Wyatt Livingston! I'm coming after you, and this time you aren't going to get away!

4

On the evening after Herndon Livingston's birthday celebration, Roxanne sat on one of the front benches at the revival meeting, which was in full swing halfway through the week blessed with Carlton Booth's presence. On one side of her, Hiram Miller sat correctly straight, his gaunt face showing his approval of every word that was being thundered from the pulpit. On Roxanne's other side, Mrs. Miller's plump body quivered with religious fervor. Roxanne had the uneasy feeling that the sixty-year-old matron might slip from the bench at any moment, the way several of the congregation had already done.

In the row in front of Roxanne and her escorts, whom she'd asked to accompany her because her father was away on one of his business trips, Miss Minnie Atkins, who was in charge of the Athens Reading Rooms, rose to her feet. Moaning and weeping, she scrambled over obstructing feet and knees until she reached the aisle. Her arms outstretched, she half ran toward the evangelist.

Carlton Booth waited for her, his face aglow. "Another soul saved! Hallelujah! Hallelujah!"

Booth stepped down from the platform and Miss Minnie threw herself at his feet. He lifted her, his face raised toward heaven, and placed his hands on her head, which was shaking on her skinny neck as though it were getting ready to fly off.

Sinner! Roxanne snorted under her breath. Miss Minnie Atkins wouldn't recognize sin if she met it face-to-face in a dark alley at midnight. Her life was exemplary, she'd probably never been kissed, she hadn't missed services, prayer meeting or choir practice once in the last twenty-five years. Roxanne knew that, because Miss Minnie had been presented with a New Testament to commemorate her perfect record, only last month.

The congregation, almost to a man, were on their knees or in the process of lowering themselves to their knees, their collective voices raised in hallelujahs along with Evangelist Booth's. Mrs. Miller was shaking harder than ever, so that Roxanne had to help her back up onto the bench when the hallelujahs were finished.

"Mrs. Miller, I see some friends at the back. Would you mind very much if I went to sit with them? I might be able to prevail upon them to see the light."

Mrs. Miller's eyes brightened, her smile was beatific. Roxanne wiggled her way to the end of the bench.

Roxanne's mention of friends in need of saving had been a blatant lie, but she felt not one ounce of compunction. She'd prevailed upon the Millers to let her accompany them for one reason only, and that was to get here without causing tongues to wag by coming alone. Not that she had any personal fears of the throng that milled around the approaches to the meeting grounds, patronizing the booths and raising general hell, but even as lenient with her as Earl Fielding was, he'd have raised the devil if she'd come alone.

Wyatt would be somewhere in the mob of rowdies. Likely he'd be in company with half a dozen or more of the Corinthians he ran with, but after Geneva had refused him last night, she wouldn't have much trouble enticing him away from them in favor of sympathetic feminine companionship. He'd be in a black mood, in need of all the sympathy he could get, and a soft shoulder to lay his head on.

She received a great deal more than her share of attention as she pushed her way through the throng that milled around the booths. Cyprians gave her wary eyes, hostile at unfair competition until they either recognized her or saw for themselves that in spite of her flaming beauty, she was a lady and no threat to them. Masculine eyes lighted up, hands reached out for her. She was tendered drunken and not so drunken invitations, indecent or barely bordering on the decent.

Roxanne wasn't in the least frightened. She'd spent enough time in her impressionable years in close proximity with men like these to be able to give back as well as she took.

"Back off, buster! Not tonight, I've another engagement," she said, pushing hands away from her, dodging others. "Don't bother me, I'm busy."

Her smile took the sting away and even the most intoxicated of the men took no umbrage. Most of them knew her, or of her, and knew her father, so she was in considerably less danger than a strange woman would be. She was a good sort, Miss Roxanne was, even if her father was a nabob. It wouldn't do, and it most definitely wouldn't pay, to insult Miss Roxanne Fielding. If she couldn't take care of herself, and all but the most ignorant of them were convinced that she could, then they'd have Earl Fielding to reckon with later, and it wasn't worth it. Earl Fielding's fists, his prowess in a brawl, were too widely known to be taken lightly, even if he didn't blackball them so they'd never find another day's work on the canal, or anywhere else where Earl's influence reached.

There! Roxanne paused and her eyes brightened. There was a group of Corinthians, resplendent in their narrow pantaloons, their shirt ruffles gleaming white in the light from the lanterns and torches. They all wore tall hats and carried whippety canes. And there, right in the center of them, was Wyatt, more than a little intoxicated and clearly intending to become more so before the evening was over.

Roxanne couldn't make out, from this distance, whether he was drinking whiskey or rum or kill-divvie. It wasn't gin, because he had an aversion to gin, claiming it was a stableboy's drink, not fit for gentlemen. But whatever it was he'd already imbibed a quantity of it and even as she watched he downed another glass, shuddering, nearly choking, and wiping his mouth with a snowy handkerchief. The good stock, the smooth blends, were not offered for sale at these booths, which were patronized by men who didn't care whether liquor was good or bad as long as it was potent, and cheap enough so that they could afford all they wanted of it.

Roxanne stopped where she was, planning her strategy. The best thing would be to approach him directly, explain that she was without an escort and ask him to offer his services in that capacity. Even as lenient as Earl Fielding was with his daughter, Wyatt would realize that he'd be furious if he knew that she'd been at the revival meeting alone.

Before she could set herself in motion again, a canaller lurched past the group of elegantly attired young gentlemen and stumbled against Robert Maxwell, the son of the owner of Maxwell's Emporium, Athen's largest mercantile store. The stumble caused the hand that Bob was in the process of lifting to his mouth to jerk, and the contents of the glass that the hand was holding splashed over his face and his immaculate ruffles.

"You clumsy lout! Why don't you watch where you're going?" Bob spluttered.

"Who's a lout? Whyn't yer go home an' tell yer ma to tuck you in bed with yer passifier? Yer too young to be suckin' on a bottle lessen it's got milk in it!" The canaller threw back his head and guffawed at his own joke. "Har, har, har! Milk, that's what yer'd oughta be drinkin', fancy-lad!"

Enraged at this insult to his honor, Bob struck at the canaller with his cane so as not to soil his hands on such scum. The next instant, the cane was wrenched out of his grasp as the canaller's temper exploded. Cane him, would he, the young whippersnapper? Cane Dan Jenkins, the terror of the towpath!

Contemptuously, Jenkins broke the walking stick in two and flung the pieces away from him, and then struck Robert across the face with an openhanded blow that took the young Corinthian off his feet and sent him crashing back against the booth. Bottles fell from the counter, glasses flew, and as two of the other Corinthians moved in on Jenkins, Wyatt one of them, the delighted shout of "Fight!" went up.

Roxanne said a word under her breath that she hadn't dared to say aloud since she'd been taken from her delightfully adventurous life on her father's canalboats. That idiot, that complete and utter idiot! Wouldn't you know that it would be Bob Maxwell, with his touchy pride, that the canaller had stumbled into? Now the Corinthians would be in for it, because all of the other canallers would come to his aid, only too happy for the opportunity to bloody a few aristocratic noses and knock out a few teeth to ruin the smiles of these fops who looked down on them.

The constable! Where was the constable and his deputies? They were supposed to be here, keeping an eye on things and at least attempting to prevent any out-and-out riots. Not that there was anything that Ed Hanney could do at this stage of the game, except join in the fray himself with his deputies and hope they'd live through it.

Canallers were already converging on the trouble spot.

From the outskirts of the crowd, half a dozen more young dandies, flourishing their whippety sticks as well as fists that were reasonably 'versed in the manly art of fisticuffs, came pelting to the aid of their peers. Roxanne was jostled, nearly knocked off her feet as two canallers parted company to pass on either side of her, without leaving her enough standing room.

"Jackasses!" she screamed at them. One of them had the gall to look back over his shoulder and wink at her and shout back, "Just be patient, you pretty thing, I'll be back as soon as we've taught these town fops a lesson!"

Roxanne was furious. Why had it had to happen before she'd got Wyatt away? There were always fights at the camp meetings. Human males being what they were, especially the lower orders who gravitated to such doings on the outskirts of the meeting area, it was inevitable that there would be fights. As long as the trouble stayed within the bounds of the canallers and other riffraff, Ed Hanney was inclined to look the other way. He saw no reason for having his own head bashed in in an attempt to keep the peace.

Wherever Ed Hanney was now, he wasn't in the immediate vicinity, and neither were his deputies, who were no more than adequate to lead Verne Baldwin, the town drunk, to jail when he'd had too much to drink and needed a place to sleep it off, or shake their fingers at naughty boys who were playing ball too close to vulnerable windows.

The fight had begun in earnest now, with fists flying, walking sticks thrusting and flailing, broken noses and spattering blood. Roxanne was jostled this way and that as onlookers, not interested in joining the fray, crowded around to cheer on their heroes. The press of the mob made it impossible for her to see who was winning, and she seethed because she wasn't tall enough to see over their heads.

She made up her mind. Gritting her teeth, she surged forward, kicking shins, and using her elbows to force her way to the front where she'd have a clear view of what was happening. Some distance away, the preaching went on without pause as the exhorters used the opportunity to decry mindless violence, brought on, without doubt, by the hard spirits that robbed men of their minds and ultimately of their souls.

"Satan is loose amongst us! You can hear his cohorts now, fomenting evil! They have turned deaf ears to our entreaties to come forward and avail themselves of God's mercy.

They have damned themselves by their very actions. But it needn't be too late for you, brethren and sistern! No, it needn't happen to you, not while you have strength in your limbs to come forward and breath in your bodies to beg the Lord for mercy!"

In the thick of the melee, just as Roxanne had thought, Wyatt's nose was already spurting blood and one of his eyes was closed. His left cheek was abraded where iron-hard knuckles, used to the heaviest and roughest sort of work, had connected with it. He himself had laid out two canallers and sent another staggering off to catch his breath. He fought back to back with his fellow Corinthians, all of whom were well-versed in all kinds of fighting, from the Marquis of Queensbury rules to the rough-and-tumble of such frays as this. But although in ordinary circumstances few men would care to stand up against them when their blood was up, this time they were outnumbered and becoming more so by the moment as more canallers and towpath scum threw in against them. And now Wyatt was down, and in no little danger of being trampled. With one last extreme effort, Roxanne reached him.

"Hey, you girl, get outa here! This ain't no place for a lady!"

"Get out of here yourself!" she shouted. "You're crowding us, give him air, you . . . ."

The canaller's mouth gaped open as Roxanne let loose with the choicest Erie language she knew, and there was very little of it that she didn't know.

"Make yourself useful, drat you! Grab him under his shoulders and help me drag him out of here!"

Still stunned, the canaller obeyed. "Miss Roxanne, you shouldn't oughta be here! What's your father going to say?"

"I don't care what my father's going to say. I've got to get Wyatt out of here before he gets himself killed! Can't you drag him any faster?"

It wasn't easy in that mob, but the canaller put his back into it. "It's Wyatt Livingston, isn't it? Sure it is. His old man's going to have a word or two to say about this, even if yours doesn't. Where at do you want me to put him, Miss Roxanne?"

They were out of the immediate vicinity of the fight now, but Roxanne bit her lip, at a loss as to what to do with Wyatt now that he'd been rescued from the danger of being trampled. He was still out cold, and even if she could revive him she doubted that he'd be able to navigate on his own for a while, much less dare to go home where his father would see the condition he was in. Herndon Livingston took a very dim view of public brawling, not to mention public brawling with canallers. Disciplinary measures would be taken, for all that Wyatt was twenty-one. Of all times, now wasn't the time that Roxanne wanted his activities curtailed. If she couldn't have access to him, how was she going to convince him that she was the one he'd wanted to marry all along, rather than Geneva Burton?

"I expect his horse and gig are here somewhere," Roxanne said. "Do you think you could carry him until we locate it?"

Without a word, the canaller hoisted Wyatt over his shoulder and set off, Roxanne lengthening her stride to keep up with him.

She could take him to her own house once she had him in his gig. But he'd have to be carried inside, and someone would be sure to see them, and with her father away there'd be a scandal that would rock the town to its foundations. Mrs. Carey, the cook, and Freda and Norah, weren't at home. They, along with a good share of Athens's population, were at the revival meeting and they wouldn't be home until it was over for the evening.

In the hitching grounds, children slept in and under farm wagons, bedded down when they'd no longer been able to stay awake. Buggies, gigs, carts, saddle horses, every means of transportation were cheek by jowl. But Wyatt's suicide gig, and his trotter Red Boy were easy to pick out. The canaller whistled through his teeth as he slung Wyatt up onto the seat.

"You sure you can handle that animal, Miss Roxanne? He looks mighty powerful to me."

"I can handle him." Roxanne's voice was firm. "And thank you for helping me. If you'll tell me your name, I'll pass it along to my father. He might be able to return the favor some day."

The canaller beamed. A good word from Earl Fielding might stand him in good stead if Cap'n Yarnell got tired enough of his drinking and brawling at every opportunity to throw him off his crew. "Art Franklyn, Miss Fielding. Glad to have been of help." Then he began loping back to the scene of the melee, intent on not missing any more of the action than he had to. Revival meetings only happened one week out of the year, and every red-blooded canaller who was lucky enough to be where they were had to make the most of the opportunity. It was only by chance that the Undine was still in Athens, laid up for repairs after it had been rammed by another boat whose captain was determined to get ahead of it at one of the locks. That had been a good fight, too, even if the Cap'n had kept him from killing the other captain.

Roxanne reached up to make sure that her bonnet, resplendent with cabbage roses, was straight, glanced at Wyatt to make sure that he wouldn't fall out of the gig, and gathered up the reins. She'd simply drive along the country roads outside of Athens until Wyatt regained consciousness and, hopefully, a measure of common sense. She could take him to the Burton house where he'd be administered first aid, but as things stood between him and Geneva she suspected that he wouldn't appreciate that.

It was a beautiful evening. The moon was nearly full, and the stars hung low. A night for romance, Roxanne thought wryly, not without humor. Only how could she find romance with a man who was battered and unconscious, and suffering the pangs of unrequited love at that? Still, this was better than nothing. He should at least be grateful to her for rescuing him from being trampled.

She made another wry face at the thought. For a man to feel beholden to a woman was scarcely conducive to romance. Men resented being beholden, especially to a woman. But she couldn't have left Wyatt there on the dusty, churned-up ground, at the mercy of the riffraff's boots. A dead or crippled man was even less prone to romantic feelings than a beholden one.

She drove for half an hour, Red Boy's easy trot sending the ribbon of country road spinning away behind them. The air was balmy, redolent of clover. The scent was enough to make her feel light-headed.

"What the devil?"

Beside her, Wyatt stirred, and his undamaged eye opened. The effort made him wince, and his hand went to his other eye, intensifying the grimace. "Is that you, Roxie?"

"It isn't my Aunt Matilda." Roxanne's voice was cheerful.

"Turn around! I wanna go back. Got unfin . . . . unfinished business."

"Your business at the revival meeting is finished for tonight, I think. You've taken all the punishment you can stand, till you've had time to recuperate."

"I'm alright! Turn around, blast it! Here, give me those lines!"

Roxanne fended him off. It wasn't difficult, considering the amount of liquor he'd imbibed and the state of both his body and his head. "You aren't going back. At least, not tonight. Not unless you want to get out and walk."

Wyatt glowered at her out of his good eye. "It's my horse and gig!"

"And I'm a lady. You don't expect me to get out and walk, do you? On second thought, you can hardly leave me alone and unprotected on a country road even if you walk and leave me the gig. And I'm not going back, so you can't either." She slapped the lines against Red Boy's back to make him smarten his pace.

"What kind of female are you? What makes you think that you can dictate to me?"

"I'm a smarter female than you are a male, at the moment. What you need is a lot of fresh air and time to sober up."

"I'm not drunk! You've never seen me drunk!" Wyatt leaned back and folded his arms across his chest, glaring straight ahead, his mouth set in a grim line. But his dignity lasted for only a few seconds.

"Ohmigod! Stop the gig, I'm going to be sick!"

It wasn't a ruse. He was already gagging. Roxanne pulled Red Boy to a halt and turned to support him, but he was already clambering down to cling to the side of the gig and retch. Roxanne watched him with what amounted to awe. She'd seen her father with king-sized hangovers, for Earl was a lusty man who enjoyed his pleasures, but she'd never seen him sick like this. Earl had a cast-iron stomach and the constitution to go with it.

"What on earth did you drink?"

His stomach empty, Wyatt walked a short distance off the road and collapsed on the ground under a maple tree.

Roxanne climbed down from the gig, put out the weight to keep Red Boy from wandering off, and went to sit beside him and take his head into her lap.

"A little of everything. I felt adventurous." Wyatt shuddered, his face pasty from the dregs of the nausea that was still with him. "I feel like death!" he moaned.

"It serves you right." Roxanne was disgustingly cheerful. "Maybe the next time you'll know better. Darn it, I thought you had better sense!"

"Geneva turned me down."

"If this is the way you're going to act every time you don't get your own way, I don't blame her. Maybe she knows you better than you know yourself."

"She didn't have a reason. She couldn't give me one solitary reason! It's been understood ever since she put her hair up. She always just asked for more time, but this time she said she isn't going to marry me at all!"

"Geneva has a right to turn down any man she wants to, even you. You've known her for too long, anyway. It would be almost like marrying your sister. How do you feel now?"

"Awful."

"You're a sissy. You can't take it. Well, I'm bored. If you don't feel up to coming with me, I'm going to take Red Boy and see just how fast he can step out. I've always wanted to drive him and see what he can do, and this is my chance."

Wyatt sat up, his face filled with alarm. "The hell you are! You think I want one of his legs broken, or to have you bring him back windblown?"

"Then come with me and see that nothing like that happens. But I'm going, whether you come with me or not."

Groaning, Wyatt got to his feet. He was a little unsteady but he managed to get to the gig. Behaving in a most ungentlemanly manner, he climbed in and left Roxanne to get in by herself. She didn't hold it against him. In his state, it was all he could do to climb up himself without helping her.

"Here we go!" Her voice was filled with excitement as she gathered up the lines. "Giddap, Red Boy! Let's see what you can do!"

"Ohmigod!" Wyatt said, and he covered his face with his hands.

For half an hour, Roxanne exulted in the exhilaration of bowling along the country road as Wyatt's magnificent trotter made mincemeat of the miles. She had no trouble with him; like Cato when Galen Forbes had driven him, the animal recognized the authority of her hands on the lines. There was enough light so that the dirt road stood out clearly, and there was no danger of missing a bend or running into a deep rut. Roxanne's blood raced through her veins, and once, in the wildness of her elation, she even burst out singing, a bawdy towpath ditty that made Wyatt wince even in his present condition.

Oh, but it was glorious, there was nothing like it! Darn her father anyway. He was so set on her being a proper lady that he refused to allow her to have a trotter of her own, an animal equal to or even better than Red Boy and Cato. As indulgent as Earl was concerning all of her other wishes, he was as much afraid of the impression she'd make as he was that she'd be hurt.

A horse and buggy was at her disposal, but Pansy was fat and docile, the buggy stodgy for all its bright paint, nothing like a real trotter and a gig. After tonight, she'd never be satisfied with Pansy and the buggy again. If she had a trotter and a gig of her own, she might even beat Wyatt and Bobo in a race, and wouldn't that stand Athens on its ear!

She broke off her singing suddenly and looked at Wyatt. He'd stopped complaining about her speed and skill a good ten minutes ago. What if he'd relapsed into unconsciousness again? A fine nurse she was, forgetting her patient just because she was having the time of her life! As soon as her glance fell on him she drew Red Boy up. "Whoa, whoa!"

Obediently, having had enough of this uncalled-for after-dark exercise, Red Boy slowed to a stop. Roxanne dropped the lines and caught Wyatt just as he was in the process of falling off the high seat. He was a deadweight in her arms. Panic-stricken, her fingers explored his head, and the egg-sized lump she found told her why he was unconscious. He'd taken a harder blow in the melee than she'd realized.

It was no easy task to prop him up while she climbed over him, got her own feet on the ground, and it took every bit of her strength to ease him down. Even so, his weight on top of her put her off balance and sent them both into a heap in the road, and she had to fight and struggle to crawl out from under him before she could grasp him under his armpits and drag him onto the grassy ditch bank.

She wasn't very good at telling time by the stars, but she knew that it was getting late. She sat there, with Wyatt's head in her lap, and wondered what on earth she should do. He probably needed a doctor, but there was no way she could lift him back into the gig and hold him there while she drove all the way back into town. Should she leave him here and rouse up some farmer to hitch up his wagon and drive them back?

It took her only seconds to reject that possibility. Wyatt would be humiliated. He'd never forgive her if he was carted back to Athens in a farm wagon, like a sack of potatoes. The story would be all over town, he'd never live it down. Not only that, but the repercussions from Herndon Livingston would be awesome. Wyatt's breathing was steady, and his pulse, when she managed to find it, was strong. He was only knocked out. She'd just have to wait it out.

Whether she could tell time by the stars or not, she knew that it was very late when Wyatt moaned and stirred. She tried slapping his face, gently at first, and then harder. "Wyatt, wake up! Can you stand on your feet, do you think you can climb into the gig?"

Wyatt's right hand darted out and caught hers. "You don't have to hit me. I'm all right! Roxie, you're a pal. You're a real friend. If you hadn't got me out of that mess back at the revival grounds, my goose would have been cooked! The way I felt, I'd have gone on drinking till I had to be carried home, and the roof would have caved in!"

"Sure I'm a pal. Haven't I always been your pal?"

In the moonlight, Wyatt's face was very serious. "You're more than that. I don't know what I'd do without you. I need you, Roxie, do you know that? We get along together, you always stick by me, you'd never treat me the way Geneva does! You know something, Roxie? I love you."

Roxanne's lips twitched, half in amusement and half in pain. "Does this constitute a proposal?" she asked, having to fight hard to keep her voice light.

Wyatt sat up. His face was pale but his eyes burned with intensity. "Sure it does. Why not? Geneva doesn't want me. I'll just show her, that's what I'll do! I'll show her that if she doesn't want me, somebody else does! We'd get along, Roxie, we'd make a great pair! We could make a go of it. Your father would be tickled. You'd be the queen of Athens, and he'd like that."

Roxanne turned her face away so that he wouldn't see her wince. She had her proposal at last—she could have Wyatt if she wanted him, all she had to do was hold him to it. He wasn't so drunk now that he wouldn't have some recollection that he'd asked her.

"I'll think about it," she managed. He'd asked her to marry him, but only to show Geneva that somebody else wanted him! For one wild moment, she was tempted to accept him. Wasn't this what she'd wanted for years?

But a half-drunk, despairing Wyatt tonight, and a sober Wyatt tomorrow, were two different things. If he asked her again tomorrow, she'd have him at the altar so fast that Athens would count on its fingers until nine months had passed. And if he didn't, she'd call herself a hundred kinds of a fool for the rest of her life for not having accepted him tonight. But that was something she'd have to risk. There was a chance, a good chance, that after he had time to think it over, he'd still realize that he and she would make a good pair, that they were right for each other and they could make a go of it. And in that case, he wouldn't be marrying her only to show Geneva that he could get someone else.

"Let's get on home. Try to get in the gig," she urged him.

It took him three tries, but he finally made it.

Dawn was brightening the sky when a disgruntled Red Boy entered the outskirts of Athens. Wyatt, almost completely recovered, took over the lines before they turned into North Street.

"What if you're locked out?" he asked, his voice sounding nervous. Marvin Burton might have overlooked it if it had been Geneva coming in with him at this hour, but Earl Fielding was another matter entirely.

"I won't be, I have my own key. What about you? Can you get into your house without rousing everybody?"

"I'll sleep in the stable." Wyatt's grin was crooked. "They'll assume that I spent the night with Bob or one of the others. Thank the Lord that nobody's up and about yet, or you'd be well compromised and then you'd have to marry me!"

Was he already having second thoughts? "Don't worry about it. Nobody's going to see us."

The words were no more than out of her mouth when a

head poked out of an upstairs window in the house across the street. Wyatt groaned.

"Just our luck! It's Mrs. Miller, and she'll have it spread all over town before nine o'clock this morning!"

Roxanne couldn't control her laughter, although she did her best to suppress it, with the result that she nearly strangled. "And I told her that I was going to see if I could lead my friends to the light! Now she'll be convinced that you've led me down the path to Hades!"

"I fail to see anything funny about it!" Wyatt snapped at her. "If you had to lie, why did it have to be to her?"

"Because she was the one I happened to be with. I had to get to the revival somehow, didn't I?"

"No. Or if you did, then you should have stayed with her!"

"You ungrateful wretch! If I'd stayed with her, what would have happened to you? You realized that not so very many minutes ago! Or have you already forgotten that you had the grace to thank me?"

"I'm sorry." Darn him, why did his voice have to be so stiff? "I am grateful, Roxie. I just wish I hadn't got you into so much trouble. It would have been better if you'd stayed with Mrs. Miller."

"What? And missed all that fun? You'll have to escort me to the door, Mrs. Miller is still watching."

Grimly, Wyatt climbed down, and his hand under her elbow was anything but gentle. Roxanne's amusement, he felt, was out of place. Maybe she thought that all this was funny, but he had sense enough to know that their coming back to town alone at the crack of dawn was nothing to be laughed about.

"If Mrs. Miller wasn't watching, I'd wring your neck!"

"No you wouldn't. If you did, you wouldn't have my nice soft shoulder to cry on."

Wyatt didn't dignify that with an answer. His head throbbing and his stomach turning cartwheels again, he stalked back to the gig. This would turn into a scandal that would all but ruin both of them. Not only that, but Earl Fielding would probably kill him.

After the wedding had taken place, of course.

5

Wyatt's morose prediction came true on schedule. Fired by Mrs. Miller's scandalized stories of the hour and the condition in which Roxanne Fielding had been escorted home by Wyatt Livingston, the flame of the scandal spread throughout Athens by midmorning of that same day.

Herndon's first reaction, when the story reached his ears, was one of furious indignation. How dared his son bring disgrace on the family name. He ought to be horsewhipped, punished so severely that he'd never again have the temerity to cause his father embarrassment!

His second reaction came hard on the heels of his first. Perhaps something could be salvaged, after all, something a good deal more important than Roxanne Fielding's reputation. Earl Fielding was by far the most affluent man in Athens, indeed in all the surrounding territory. The canaller had used a combination of recklessness and solid business acumen not only to build up a fleet of canalboats that was the envy of nearly every other canal man on the Erie, but he'd doubled and redoubled his profits by buying up property both in Rochester and Buffalo, canal ports that were booming at a rate that was astounding to all but the most farsighted. Waterfront property, for the most part, and hotels, restaurants, saloons; everything that would skyrocket in value as trade on the Erie Canal grew with every year that passed.

The growth of this trade was little short of phenomenal. Herdon Livingston himself had not foreseen the impact that the canal would have on the prosperity of the country. But Eric Fielding had. Fielding had believed in it from its earliest days, and he'd put his strength of purpose and his enormous vitality where his beliefs lay. He had enough ready cash to advance Herndon all he needed to effect the expansion of the mill. And an alliance between the two families, through Wyatt's marriage to Roxanne, would insure that the loan would be forthcoming.

Except for her father's wealth, Herndon was none too pleased at the prospect of having Roxanne Fielding for a daughter-in-law. The girl was not only too flamboyant to conform to his ascetic tastes, but she was also strong-willed. It was a pity that Geneva Burton had refused the honor of becoming Wyatt's wife. But what was done was done. For some fathomless reason, Geneva had decided against Wyatt, and therefore second-best would have to do. And no doubt Roxanne would conform to Livingston standards after a period of having her rough edges polished by constant association with Herndon and Lillian, once the marriage had taken place and Roxanne had come to live at the Livingston house.

With that thought in mind, Herndon paid a visit to Earl Fielding, in his office on Canal Street, early the next week as soon as he learned that Earl was back in town. There was no doubt in his mind that Earl would be delighted to see his daughter married to Wyatt. It was common knowledge that Earl wanted the best for Roxanne, and in Athens and its environs Wyatt Livingston was the best.

Herndon put on a jovial manner as Earl rose from a battered desk. The canalman's office was small and shabby, giving no indication of the stature of the man who conducted his business there. The lavishness with which he lived at home found no echo here. Business was business, Earl maintained, and needed no fancy trappings. It was money that talked, money and ability, not window-dressing.

"Well, Earl." There was no hint of Herndon's inner wince as he felt it expedient to address Fielding by his given name. "I expect you've heard of our offsprings' little peccadillo the other night. It's caused quite a ripple in Athens."

Earl regarded the uncrowned king of Athens calmly, his strong, highly colored face giving away nothing. "I've heard a rumor or two."

"And what do you think should be done? I can't tell you how sorry I am that my son should have placed your daughter's good name in jeopardy. However, I'm sure that Wyatt will be eager to make it right." Herndon said that with full confidence; if he told Wyatt that he was to marry Roxanne, Wyatt would marry Roxanne. His own decency would assure his compliance, even if he might have had any inclination to defy his father.

Earl's thick, sandy eyebrows, a shade darker than his hair, shot up. "Just what do you have in mind, Herndon?" He clipped the end off a cigar and held a match to it, waiting while he pulled to get the cigar going. He didn't offer one to Herndon, who never indulged in tobacco in any form, either eating or smoking.

"I should think it would be obvious. The young people must be married, of course. Anything else would be unthinkable."

Herndon, accustomed to being in command of any situation, had an uncomfortable feeling that there was a glint of amusement in Earl's eyes.

"You think it's as bad as all that?"

"I'm afraid that it is. It was after four o'clock in the morning when Wyatt brought your daughter home from the revival meeting, and they were alone, completely unchaperoned! Certainly they must be married. Wyatt will call at your home this evening to ask Roxanne to do him the honor of becoming his wife."

"Then I'd better warn her. She'll want to make sure there's no dust on the piano." Earl's voice was dry, but once again Herndon had the feeling that the man was laughing at him. What was wrong with him, that he couldn't see how serious the situation was?

"Shall we say seven-thirty?"

"Sounds all right. We eat at six. I reckon those overpaid hired hussies can have the table cleared by then, and Roxanne'll have time to make sure that her nose isn't shiny. Glad you stopped around, Herndon. Girls don't like to be caught unawares."

Earl stood up, the interview clearly at an end. He didn't escort Herndon to the door, he simply looked at him, deadpan, until Herndon let himself out.

Once he was alone, Earl smashed one fist into the open palm of his other hand. His jaw clenched so that his teeth ground together. Damn that arrogant young puppy of a Wyatt Livingston! Earl was fully aware of Roxanne's love for the boy, and up until this had happened, nothing would have made him happier than for her to snare him right out from under Geneva Burton's nose. Not that he had anything against Geneva. She was a nice girl—intelligent, well bred, and damned pretty in her own right even if she couldn't hold a candle to Roxie.

But a forced marriage, a marriage tainted by scandal, was something else entirely. If Wyatt walked through the door right now, Earl would be inclined to choke the life out of him. Wyatt was lithe and agile and there was nothing wrong with his muscles, but Earl—despite his age—could still break him in two without trying.

It rankled that this marriage was exactly what Herndon Livingston wanted, now that Geneva had turned Wyatt down. Damn, but he'd almost rather not have Roxanne marry Wyatt at all, than to give Herndon the satisfaction of being in a position to ask for the loan that Earl wouldn't be able to refuse him once Roxie was Mrs. Wyatt Livingston. Not unless he was willing to have Roxie suffer the consequences of Herndon's displeasure. Roxie could take care of herself, but it would be nicer if her father-in-law didn't take an instant hate for her. He'd let the old bastard have the money, all right, but it would go against the grain.

He shook his head and sat back down at his desk, pulling a ledger toward him and taking up his pen. The only thing that really mattered was whether Roxanne would be happy. And if she wasn't happy, if Wyatt Livingston didn't make her happy . . . In that case, Wyatt Livingston would have plenty of cause to wish that he'd never been born.

Walking back to the mill, Herndon was seething. The effrontery of the man! He was actually treating this whole matter as a joke! Still, he must keep his temper in check. No matter how distasteful it would be to have the Livingston name affiliated with the Fieldings, the marriage must take place. Visions of expanding his plans, of making the mill even larger than he'd hoped, helped to restore his equanimity.

In his own office, with its rich walnut furnishings and an oriental rug on the floor, his desk twice the size of Earl's and innocent of the least scratch, the first thing Herndon did was send for Wyatt.

Wyatt had had ample time to recover from his drinking

bout and the free-for-all that had followed, but his face still paled when his father made his ultimatum.

"Marry her? That's ridiculous! Nothing happened between us, damn it! To be perfectly truthful, I was in no condition for romance even if I'd been inclined. I was out like a light a good deal of the time, and the rest of it was spent in retching while Roxie held my head."

Something flickered in the depth of Wyatt's memory. He had an uncomfortable but certain feeling that there had been more than that. Hadn't he made a damned fool of himself, crying all over Roxie and asking her to marry him so he could show Geneva a thing or two? But he didn't have any recollection of her accepting him. She hadn't, had she? Roxie had more sense than that! They were friends, good friends, but she didn't love him any more than he loved her. He wished that that fight had started before he'd had so much to drink, and then none of this would be happening.

He gathered up his courage, no simple task in the face of the way his father was glaring at him. "There was nothing that calls for marriage, and Roxie will be the first to tell you the same thing."

"Nevertheless, her name is ruined. And as you're the one who ruined it, you are to marry her. I've made arrangements for you to see her this evening at seven-thirty. You will do me the favor of being prompt."

"Jehosephat! You can't be serious!"

Herndon regarded his son with cold eyes. "I've never been more serious in my life. You are to ask the young lady for her hand tonight. There's no need to consult her father first, as I've already taken care of that." He dismissed Wyatt by picking up a sheet of paper, and began to study it.

In his own smaller office, scarcely larger than a cubbyhole, Wyatt put his head into his hands and groaned. He wished that he kept a bottle in his desk as so many businessmen did, but his father allowed no spirits on the premises.

Marry Roxanne! But he didn't love her. He loved Geneva, he'd never love anybody but Geneva. He felt like a rat in a trap.

Damn it anyway, why had Roxie had to haul him away from the meeting grounds, why hadn't she let him lie where she'd found him? Even if he'd been trampled, it would have been better than this. He hadn't been in that much danger;

Bob Maxwell and Paul Towndson and Emery Ledbetter and the other Corinthians would have dragged him out from under the booted feet before he'd suffered much damage. This was what came from women minding men's business!

A sudden suspicion made his eyes narrow and glint with anger. Was it possible that Roxie had had something like this in mind when she'd virtually kidnapped him? Everybody knew that she wanted to be on the top rung of the social ladder—how better to get there than by marrying him? Top rung! She'd be the Queen of Athens, that's what she'd be; that was exactly what she wanted; and now it looked as if she was going to get it.

For a few minutes, Wyatt considered running away, making a bolt for it, putting as much distance between Athens, and Roxanne, as possible, and staying away until she gave up on him and settled for somebody else. But even as the thought went through his mind he knew that it wasn't possible. He was a gentleman, and if Roxanne's name was being dragged in the mud, then he had to make things right.

Besides, he'd never be able to come back home if he bolted. His father would never forgive him. Even worse, the chances were that Earl Fielding would hunt him down no matter where he tried to hide, and kill him. Wyatt was no coward. Wyatt would match his strength and courage with almost any man he knew, but Earl Fielding was something else again. He couldn't lick Earl in a fight, and even if he could, it would be shameful to fight a man so much older, and for such a reason.

His life was ruined no matter what course he took. The only choice was between degrees of ruination, and marrying Roxie was the lesser of two evils. Maybe it wouldn't be so bad. Roxie was a good sort. He'd always got along with her. She was more like a good friend than a girl. If they weren't in love with each other, maybe they could be good enough friends so that it wouldn't matter that much. It wasn't as if he had any chance with Geneva anyway. Geneva had made that clear to him. And if he couldn't have Geneva, then he might as well marry someone else. He supposed that Roxanne would be better than almost anyone else he might settle for.

It was seven-thirty to the second when Wyatt lifted the knocker at the Fielding house on North Street. Two houses away, the Burton house sat serene in the late evening sunlight, adding to his misery. What would Geneva think, when she heard that he and Roxanne were to be married? Groaning, he surmised that she'd think that she was well rid of him, and thank God for her lucky escape.

It was Freda, the older of the Fieldings' two hired maids, who answered the door. The expression on her face told Wyatt that she was fully aware of the purpose of his visit.

The whole of Athens was probably aware of his visit to the Fielding house tonight, Wyatt thought savagely. He wished with all his heart that he was entering the Burton house instead, with Nellie telling him that she'd saved him a piece of berry pie, and to remind Geneva that he wanted it before he went home.

There was one saving grace as he entered the living room. Earl Fielding himself was not in evidence. Only Roxanne was there, blowing dust off a bunch of cattails that sat in an ornate vase on the mantel.

"Dirty things. Can't keep the dust off them for anything," Roxanne greeted him. "I see you're right on time. Did your father have to give you a push, or did you make it out of your front door on your own?"

"Roxie, cut it out. I take it you know why I'm here."

Roxanne blew one last time at the cattails and turned to face him. "My, that's the most romantic proposal I've had all day! Aren't you supposed to get down on your knees? Or didn't your father coach you in the finer points of asking a girl to marry you?"

"Be serious."

"I am being serious. Run on home to your daddy, Wyatt, and tell him that I turned you down."

Wyatt would never—nor anyone else—know what it cost her to say those words. Turn him down—turn down what might be her only chance to get him!

But she didn't want him like this. If he had come to her yesterday, or the day before, she'd have been the happiest girl in the world. If he'd come to her on his own, and told her that now that he was sober and in his right mind he still thought that they could make a go of it, she'd have accepted him.

But he hadn't. He'd waited until he was forced into it. And no matter how much she loved him and wanted him, she would never take him under those circumstances.

"What did you say?"

"I said to run along home. You're off the hook, Wyatt. I don't want to marry you. I will not marry you. Now wipe that misery off your face and give me your old happy smile, and scat."

"Roxie, you don't know what people are saying!"

"Of course I know. And I couldn't care less. Great jumping bullfrogs, you look like you're going to fall on your face! Here, have a drink. It's rum. It's the only thing Papa will drink, and it's potent, so take it easy."

"How do you know it's potent?" Wyatt managed to get out, before he accepted the glass she handed him and felt its fire burn all the way down to the pit of his stomach.

"I've tried it. Thanks, but no thank you! I'll stick to wine, or better still, a mug of beer, any day."

Beer! Even knowing Roxanne as well as he did, Wyatt was taken aback. Most of the ladies he knew took a little wine, but no lady of his acquaintance ever drank beer, which was strictly a workingman's beverage. His mother would probably swoon at the very notion that any well-bred young lady in their stratum of society would lift a mug of beer to her lips. Earl Fielding must have been out of his mind to let Roxanne travel with him on his canalboats all those years, rubbing shoulders with the worst kind of riffraff.

But that was beside the point right now. "What will your father say, when you tell him you turned me down?"

"He'll say 'good for you!'" Roxanne said, and her laugh was near enough to normal so that Wyatt didn't notice the difference. "Don't worry, he won't come looking for you with either a pistol or a horsewhip. I've already told him that I was going to say no."

Wyatt downed the rest of the rum and felt considerably better. "You're a good sport, Roxie. They don't come any better."

"That's what I keep telling everybody, only half of them don't believe it. Go on home, Wyatt, and put an end to your father's suspense. I hope he doesn't take a notion to horsewhip you because you couldn't talk me into it!"

Fool! Roxanne raged at herself after Wyatt had left. In spite of her assertion that she couldn't bear rum, she helped herself to a liberal tot before she went upstairs and closed her bedroom door behind her, not to give vent to tears, as most other girls would have done, but to glare at her own face in the mirror and call herself every name she'd picked up along the towpath.

"But I'll get him yet!" she vowed. "You just wait and see! I'll get him, and I'll keep him, and it'll be on my own terms. He's going to love me, or my name isn't Roxanne Fielding!"

Faced with the ruination of his plan, Herndon Livingston was forced to seek other means to accomplish his goal. Earl Fielding, when he went to call on him in his office on the morning after Wyatt had apprised him that Roxanne wouldn't have him, had proved adamant. Who Roxanne married, or whether she married at all, was strictly up to Roxanne, Eric had informed the mill owner. He'd thanked Herndon for his concern, but the matter was closed.

Herndon was convinced that the world was going mad. First Marvin Burton, and now Eric Fielding, both insisting that their daughters had the right to choose their own husbands, that they themselves had no right to force them into obedience even when it was for their own good! It was beyond belief, it was even beyond common sense.

But the fact remained that there would be no money from Earl Fielding. Faced with this truth, Herndon had no choice but to take himself yet again to Henry Maynard's Mercantile Bank, to try once more to negotiate terms for a loan, terms that wouldn't cripple him.

The banker was in no hurry to talk business. He insisted on inquiring after Herndon's family first, and most particularly about Adelaide.

"Your daughter is a beautiful young lady, Herndon. An extraordinarily beautiful young lady! It's amazing how she's grown. It seems only yesterday that she was a child, and here she is of an age to marry and have children of her own."

"Hardly that, Henry. Adelaide is only sixteen, a bit young for matrimony."

Henry pursed his lips, his small eyes shrewd. "A good many girls marry at sixteen, sometimes even younger. I hear that young Matthew Ramsey has his eye on her. Hardly the choice I'd make for a husband for her, Herndon. An impecunious young minister with his reputation still to build and not even a church of his own. No, hardly the right choice for Adelaide. I should think that you'd want a man of solid background for her, a man whose financial and social background leave nothing to be desired.''

''I have no intention of allowing my daughter to marry anyone for some time yet,'' Herndon said stiffly, finding it difficult to suppress his annoyance.

''Still, if someone eligible were to offer for her, someone whom you knew you could trust with her welfare and happiness, you might reconsider.''

What was the man getting at? This was going beyond the bounds of polite social exchange. Herndon chafed under the delay.

''An older man, Herndon. A man who has already proven himself. Then your worries about arranging a suitable marriage for Adelaide would be over.'' As Henry folded his hands over his round stomach, mute proof that he himself had prospered, and made a belated effort to hold it in, Herndon began to catch the drift of where this extraordinary conversation was leading.

For a moment, shock held him immobile. Henry Maynard, and his Adelaide, his sweet, innocent sixteen-year-old daughter? It was unthinkable!

''Henry, about that loan . . .''

''Sixteen percent,'' Henry said.

''Sixteen! It's out of the question, you've never asked more than fifteen, and for an investment of this magnitude, I'd counted on your lowering it to twelve, at the very most.''

''It's because of the magnitude of the loan, Herndon. You understand that it's not personal. But I have to protect my investment, I have to have some extra compensation for the risk of loaning out such a large sum. I'm glad that you aren't considering allowing your daughter to marry Matthew Ramsey anywhere in the near future. It would be to her worst disadvantage. What if he never becomes a success in his chosen profession? Very few ministers achieve any sort of financial security. You should consider her future as a whole. As mature, sensible men, we both know that romantic love doesn't last much beyond the honeymoon. It's other considerations that are important in the long run. It's up to fathers to make sure that their daughters will never have to suffer poverty or insecurity or lack of social status, even if it means that you must refuse to let them have their own way while they're still too young to know what's best for them.''

"Henry, what are you getting at? Surely you aren't hinting that you would like to offer for Adelaide?"

"And why not? Where could she do better? Where could you find any man who could offer her what I have to offer?"

"She's scarcely more than a child!"

"A fully developed, healthy young lady," Henry corrected him. "And that's all to the good. I'm a lonesome man, Herndon. I need companionship, and I need a child or two to carry on my name. Once she had the children, Adelaide would be content, as other women are. After all, the Almighty Himself designed women for motherhood, made it the most important thing in their lives."

"Adelaide would never consent."

Henry regarded him without blinking. "She's your daughter. She'd be obliged to accede to your wishes. Or are you one of those men like Marvin Burton and Eric Fielding, who let their daughters dictate to them, holding the ungodly opinion that females should be allowed to direct their own lives?"

Herndon came near to wincing. Henry's remark had struck home. Marvin Burton and Eric Fielding, indeed! Idiots, unfit to be fathers! If it weren't for men like them, Herndon wouldn't have found himself in this awkward financial position now.

"There's no great hurry. Take time to think about it." Henry rose to his feet. "Let me add just one thing, Herndon. If things should come about as I so fondly wish, I might find it possible to extend you a loan for, say, eight and a half percent." He extended his hand, and stunned by the figure that had just been mentioned, Herndon took it.

Eight and a half percent! An unbelievably low figure. But with strings attached.

Walking from Henry's office to his own, Herndon shook his head, his face set. It was unthinkable. Adelaide was only a child, far too young to marry, let alone marry a man who was old enough to be her grandfather. If not her grandfather, certainly her father. Henry Maynard was older than Herndon himself. Lillian wouldn't hear of it. She and Adelaide would both raise such a fuss that the obstacles would be insurmountable. To say nothing of Wyatt. In disgrace over this Roxanne Fielding scandal or not, Wyatt was extraordinarily fond of his sister, and he'd raise the very devil.

Angry, filled with fury at the banker's outrageous suggestion, Herndon resolved to put it out of his mind. But resolving wasn't the same as doing. All the rest of that morning, all during his dinner hour at home, and all during the afternoon back at his office, all during the supper hour, and long after he had gone to bed that night, Herndon thought about it.

Eight and a half percent, and the loan would be as large as he needed. And wasn't it true that everything Henry had said was sensible? A mature man, an established man, a man who had the means to cherish Adelaide and give her everything she needed for her lifelong contentment. Henry's position in Athens left nothing to be desired. He was a pillar of the church, his position on the social scale was as high as it could become unless he supplanted Herndon himself, or Marvin Burton. Adelaide would lack for nothing, and Henry would take the kindest care of her.

Granted that she was young, but that in itself could end up being an advantage. She was bound to outlive Henry, and then she'd be a wealthy widow, able to pick and choose a man to her own liking. She was almost certain to be widowed while she was still young enough to bear more children. If Henry's wish came true and she presented him with a son or a daughter or both, then the years in between would be filled with motherhood and the rearing of her children. That would more than make up for any lack of romantic feeling for her husband.

Such marriages were commonplace. It was a sad but established fact that many men outlived two or three wives, and married progressively younger women to be their helpmates and raise the children of their previous marriages along with their own.

He slept poorly that night, but by morning his mind was made up. Unlike Marvin Burton and Eric Fielding, he was the master in his own household, and he would choose Adelaide's husband, as was only right and proper. The marriage would be to her advantage as marriage to Matthew Ramsey could never be. The only thing now was to find the means to accomplish it with the least amount of dissention.

With that in mind, Herndon sent for Matthew Ramsey to call on him at his office, at his earliest convenience.

Matthew lost no time in complying. As soon as he'd read

the hand-delivered message, he set out, feeling not a little trepidation. He was well aware that Mr. Livingston didn't look kindly on the romance that had sprung up between himself and Adelaide. All the same, he'd had high hopes, because there was no doubt that Adelaide truly loved him and would refuse to accept anyone else.

Outside of his love for Adelaide, which was real enough, the advantages of marriage to her stood out strongly in Matthew's mind. Having a Livingston for a wife would be a strong factor in obtaining a good church of his own, already well established. Adelaide would attract the more affluent people to his church, and hold them there, as his superiors would know very well.

It was with more nervousness than he cared to admit that Matthew stood in Mr. Livingston's office and faced the man whom he hoped would become his father-in-law. If he'd been called here to be told that his attentions to Adelaide were no longer welcome, the blow would be a hard one. All the way to Herndon's office, he'd tried to formulate arguments in his own behalf, but knowing the mill owner, he wasn't at all convinced that Herndon would consider his worth, a fact that rasped against his pride and made him rail at a world that considered wealth, especially inherited wealth, to be of more account than uprightness and moral character. Matthew himself had no doubt of his own worth, and that he would make a worthy husband for any girl lucky enough to have won his devotion.

To his relief, Herndon shook hands with him with every appearance of affability, and Matthew's hopes soared once more.

"I understand that you and my daughter are serious about each other. So serious that you are considering marriage," Herndon began.

"Yes, sir, that's true." Matthew took a deep breath, and plunged ahead, determined to get it settled today if it were at all possible. "And as you have not voiced any objections, I've allowed myself to hope—"

Herndon cut him off, but he was still smiling, and Matthew's hopes climbed another notch.

"Just as I thought. But you understand, of course, that Adelaide is very young. Far too young, as a matter of fact, to be sure of her own mind in a matter of such importance. For her sake, and for your own, I have a proposition to make."

"Yes, sir?"

"It isn't an unreasonable proposition, as I'm sure a man of your intelligence will agree. It is simply that I believe that Adelaide should go away for a while, for several weeks at least, to see if her feeling for you remains constant during a long separation. Her Aunt Vanessa Rutherford, who resides in Syracuse, will be delighted to have her for as long as necessary. My sister is a widow, with no children of her own, so Adelaide's visit will be a blessing to her. I have no objection to correspondence between you, you may exchange as many letters as you like, providing, of course, that my sister shall read all such missives."

Matthew's first reaction was one of blazing anger entirely unbecoming to a man of his calling. But as Mr. Livingston's words sank in, he realized that as disagreeable as a separation would be, it was a good deal better than having Adelaide's father forbid him from courting her at all. This was no more than a delay, and entirely within Mr. Livingston's rights in order to protect his daughter's future happiness. He had no doubts at all that Adelaide would continue to regard him with the same sweet love that she'd already professed to him. And he knew that he himself wouldn't change. Their marriage couldn't have taken place in less than a year in any case, anything else would have been scandalous.

"May I make one stipulation, sir?" Matthew asked, seeing an advantage and determined to press it home.

Herndon inclined his head.

"It's just this—that the necessary year of courtship might begin today. I'm sure that that would be within the bounds of propriety, as everyone already knows of our intentions."

Herndon pretended to give this request some thought before he answered. "Yes, I think that that would be all right. And as we are agreed, do I have your word that you will make no attempt to see my daughter, that you won't go traipsing off to Syracuse, once I've sent her to her aunt?"

"Of course you have my word." As the two men shook hands again, Matthew felt elation surge through his body. The engagement was all but official. A few weeks from now, a few months, and his path to lifelong happiness and success in his chosen field would be assured. To all intents and purposes, it was already assured.

"You may call on Adelaide this evening, at eight o'clock." Herndon's face was wreathed with as much benevolence as it was capable of expressing, largely because he was convinced in his own mind that he was doing the right thing even though he had been forced to take this devious means of accomplishing it. "I was so sure that you'd see things my way that I have already made arrangements for Adelaide's journey to Syracuse. We will leave in the morning. I, of course, will accompany her, to see her safely settled with my sister until we can be certain that your marriage would not be a mistake."

At eight-thirty that evening, Adelaide, her face almost as pale as the white, rose-sprigged muslin she was wearing, threw herself into Matthew's arms, her cheeks drenched with tears.

"Matthew, how am I going to be able to bear it?" In her anguish, she didn't care if she was addressing him too familiarly, that to throw herself at him like this would shock the whole of Athens if anyone had known about it. Nothing mattered but that they were to be separated, for an unspecified length of time. It wasn't fair, her father was an ogre, she'd die if she couldn't see Matthew every day!

Matthew held her gently, and talked to her as he would have talked to a disconsolate child. She was a child, or hardly more; a child waiting for him to direct and guide her as a husband must always direct and guide his wife.

"I know, my dear. But the time will pass, and more quickly than you think. Syracuse isn't the end of the world. You'll be back home before we know it. Then we'll announce our engagement and you'll have our wedding to look forward to."

"It won't pass quickly! I don't want to go, I don't want to leave you!" Her heart was breaking, she wished that morning would never come. But all of her begging and pleading, to her mother, and even to Wyatt, had been useless. Even Wyatt was against her! He thought, just as her father thought, that she needed time away to make sure of her feelings.

As if she needed such time! She'd known since the first moment she'd seen him, just as she knew now, that she couldn't live without him. I won't be alive until I come back, until we're together again, she thought desolately as she lifted her face to him, his image still blurred by tears.

Matthew kissed her. It was the first time he'd ever kissed her, except for a fond, brief caress on her cheek, and even that had been hard to accomplish, chaperoned as they'd been every time they'd been together. Her head began to spin, her bones turned to water, things were happening to her that she'd never dreamed of. Many nights, as she'd lain awake after the rest of the household was asleep, she'd tried to imagine what being kissed by Matthew would be like. Even her wildest imaginings had been nothing like this. If she'd been heartbroken before at the thought of being separated from Matthew, now she was sure that she would die.

Matthew held her away from him at last, his beloved face filled with emotion almost as strong as her own. "Addie, Addie, don't cry. Let me see you smile, darling, I want to remember you smiling."

Her mouth trembled as it turned up at the corners, but it was only a caricature of a smile. And then her father rapped on the door of his study where he'd allowed them a few moments of privacy to say their good-byes, and she opened the door and ran past him, blindly.

She crashed into Wyatt on the stairs, and turned on him, her voice lashing out. "Even you!" she cried, her voice wild with her grief. "Even you've turned against me! I hate you!"

Wyatt winced as she continued her flight to find sanctuary in her room. Blast it! He hated to see her like this, but for once he was forced to agree with his father. Addie was too good for that sanctimonious young minister. If being away from him for a while put a stop to her adolescent crush on him, all her tears would be worth it.

Lillian Livingston was waiting for her daughter in Addie's bedroom, and she opened her arms to take her into them and comfort her. "My poor little girl, my poor baby!" Lillian murmured. "But your father knows best, darling. You must believe that. He's doing this for your own good."

Addie wept on her mother's breast, shaking uncontrollably. She didn't lash out at Lillian as she had at Wyatt, because even in her pain and anger she knew that her mother had no influence on, or control over her father. Lillian Livingston compressed her lips and thought, rebelliously, that it wasn't fair even if Herndon did know best. Because being Herndon, he'd have it his way, whether it was right or not.

Frightened by her disloyal thoughts, she held Addie closer, and went on trying to comfort her. Of course Herndon knew best, hadn't he always? All the same, it was a man's world, and sometimes it became very irksome.

6

Mary MacDonald's stomach was growling with outraged protest when the breakfast carts were rolled in. Another
minute, and she thought she'd have fainted from lack of
nourishment, as healthy as she was. But now the two-hour
stint before breakfast was over, and they had a full twenty-
five minutes to eat and rest before they went back to their
looms to work until dinnertime, when the carts would be
rolled in again. Supper was brought to them in their rooms.

The meals for the mill workers were catered, by whoever
put in the lowest bid. Nancy Steele, and Dorothy Monroe,
who'd been at the mill longer than Mary had, told her that
they used to get better food, but shortly before Mary had been
recruited, Herndon Livingston had found another caterer
who had contracted to feed them for a lower price. Mary
wished that she could have got in on some of those better
meals.

Breakfast, for instance, was the same, every day, winter
and summer: oatmeal or cornmeal porridge, with molasses to
sweeten it but no milk; imitation coffee, and a piece of bread.
It was hearty and filling but the monotony, and the imitation
coffee, were enough to make her want to scream. Back home
on her parents' farm, she'd at least had an egg when she'd
wanted it, when the hens obliged, and milk to drink if the cow
hadn't run dry.

The day that the recruiter for the Livingston mill had
come to her father's farm was still vivid in her mind. She'd
been fifteen, her birthday had been only a few weeks before.
Her mother had baked her an applesauce cake but there

hadn't been a present. The MacDonalds had no money for such things as birthday presents. They were lucky to get home-knit stockings and mufflers and caps for Christmas, or anything that could be contrived from materials found on the farm. Mary had had a wooden doll that her father had hand carved from a tree limb when she was six. It was dressed in scraps that her mother had labored over with her work-worn hands by the light of the oil lamp after the day's work had been done.

The recruiter, Carl Jakes, had arrived by shunpike, driving an enclosed black wagon. He'd paid a penny for a meal, and given her father a cheap, reeking cigar as he extolled the merits of working at the mill.

"It's a virtual heaven on earth for any young miss. She gets food, shelter, and nine shillings a week—imagine that, nine shillings! And she's able to save almost all of it if she isn't frivolous. She can help her family, and save toward the future, and wear silk dresses while she's doing it!"

Carl had leaned back in his cane-bottomed chair, hooked his thumbs in his braces, and expanded on his theme. "And besides all that, it's a cultural opportunity that few girls are ever privileged to have. She not only learns a valuable trade so that she never need go without work for as long as she lives, but the young ladies read from books during their leisure hours, from uplifting books! If they can't read, other young ladies or their nightmarm reads to them. They're guarded and cherished, you can depend on that, guarded and cherished! Every dormitory has a nightmarm to protect them, a genteel lady who teaches them genteel manners. No young lady in her charge ever comes to harm. Yes indeedy, any girl fortunate enough to work at the Livingston Textile Mill is a fortunate young lady indeed!"

Mary had listened, entranced, filled with wonder that such things could be. Light, easy work, Mr. Jakes said, and good food—three meals a day and no stinting—and nine shillings a week, as well as books to read, and the adventure and excitement of living in a town, of becoming a cultured city girl, a real lady.

When Carl Jakes had left, Mary had gone with him, her extra dress and her shoes and her comb and brush wrapped in her shawl. Her father had been relieved to have one less mouth to feed; her mother had been sad to lose her but elated that at least one of her daughters was to escape the life of unremitting slavery that had been her own lot. Her younger sisters had been awe-stricken at her good fortune; her brothers openly envious because the mill only wanted young females.

The MacDonald farm had been the first stop on Jake's route. For each of the young ladies Jakes delivered to the mill he received a bounty of one dollar. He did his recruiting far from Athens for the very sensible reason that if any young lady decided that she didn't care for her new good fortune, it would be extremely difficult for her to leave and make her way back home.

Mary had started as a bobbin-doffer, but she'd worked her way up to having a loom of her own before long. Sometimes two looms, for which she received not one penny more than she received for tending only one. That was one of the matters of contention among the mechanics, that they should be forced to attend two looms, at considerably more expenditure of energy, for the wages of tending one.

Not that there was much extra energy to expend, because their working hours precluded any excess of energy. The factory bell began its ear-shattering clangor at four-twenty every morning, and kept on ringing until the sluice gates set the mill wheels turning. All mechanics were required to be at their looms ten minutes before the power started. To be tardy meant being shut out for the day, and a fine on top of the loss of wages. Being tardy more than once meant the loss of your job, and an excuse was seldom accepted. If a mechanic was only seconds late, the fine was still sixpence.

Once the day's work began, the mechanics worked for two hours before breakfast was rolled in on carts, and by that time they were ravenous enough to eat what was offered even though it left a good deal to be desired. Nearly all of the mechanics gulped their portions down as fast as they could so they could lie down on the floor to snatch a few minutes rest before they had to be back at their looms. Some of them were tired enough so that they actually fell asleep for a few minutes, but for one of them to be even a second late back at her loom almost never happened because of the fines.

They were subject to fines for almost everything. They were fined for being late, they were fined for talking, they were fined for unsuitable dress and for contumacy toward their employer. They were fined for eating candy, or stopping a loom, for any damage to a length of cloth even if it wasn't their fault.

There was no increase in their wages for additional hours worked over and above the normal fourteen-hour day. On Saturdays, the mill closed at sundown. As sundown came late in midsummer, the mechanics were not happy with the rule during the summer months. To balance things, their employer deplored the necessity of shutting down early on Saturdays during the winter months when sundown came in the late afternoon.

No fires could be started in the chunk-burning stoves that heated their dormitories unless the temperature dropped below forty degrees. They woke and dressed in bone-chilling cold during the winter months, and washed in icy water. Washing every morning was mandatory, whether they were chilled to the bone or not. They were all ladies here, and ladies do not go dirty no matter the weather.

It was virtually mandatory, also, that any shopping they did be done at the company store. They were not allowed to see the prices of goods they purchased; the total was extracted from their quarterly wages, and so they had no way of proving if they were being cheated. Mary was convinced that they were cheated, and so were most of the girls she worked with, but any complaints were regarded as contumacy and sure to bring on a fine, or, the worst that could happen, dismissal and being blackballed.

The promised books, the reading aloud, was a reality. Some of the girls couldn't read, but when those who could begged off because they were busy washing their clothes or mending or tending to other personal needs, Mrs. Simms, their nightmarm, read to them.

Mary loved to hear the reading. She knew her letters and she could make out a good many of the words, for her mother had taught her the alphabet and how to read from the dog-eared Bible that held the place of honor in their almost unused sitting room at home. But she had trouble with the longer, more elegant words. Listening to Mrs. Simms, who was an educated woman having gone all through grammar school, was a joy, even if most of what was read was from books of sermons, or essays, or other cultural or educational material. Still, Mrs. Simms was a good-hearted soul, and occasionally she could be prevailed upon to bring back a real, exciting romantic novel from Minnie Atkins's Reading Rooms. The young ladies' heads were filled quite full of impossible dreams of villas in France, or passionate love in English manor houses, after one of these rare treats. Mrs. Simms had to caution them that such things are very unlikely to happen to mill mechanics in real life.

This was Mary's life, the heaven on earth that Carl Jakes had promised her. She was fed, she was housed, she was provided with honest employment and she was able to send most of her wages home to her mother, as all of the girls were encouraged to do. Girls who did not make a practice of sending most of their wages home were discriminated against, until their fines ate up so much of their wages that they might as well have conformed in the first place. It was a very practical form of insurance against the mechanics being able to save up enough to return home if they took the notion to quit.

Mary herself incurred very few fines, but as she conformed to the unwritten rule about sending the larger portion of her wages to her family, there was no way she could get back home either, outside of walking. But although town life and working in the mill was a far cry from the paradise that Carl Jakes had promised, she had no intention of either quitting her job or losing it, if she could help it. Her mother needed every shilling she sent. The rack rents were high and her father barely managed to scrape out a living for his family. It would have been nice, though, to be able to afford a silk dress of the elegance that Mr. Jakes had said all of the mechanics could afford.

Mary spooned her porridge into her mouth, taking care not to grimace, because that might be construed as a criticism of the fare that was furnished, and bring down a fine. Beside Mary, Agnes Barlowe made no attempt to control her own distaste for their breakfast.

"Ugh! This prog isn't fit for pigs!" Agnes said.

Mary didn't like Agnes, who was the oldest of all the girls in her dormitory, a full twenty-two although she tried to deny her age. Agnes was overbearing, belligerent, forever appropriating the other girls' personal belongings whether they wanted to lend them or not, and in general acting superior to the others because of her seniority. Worst of all, Agnes was a tattler. She'd turn any fellow mechanic in in order to gain approval for herself, whether it was for talking during working hours, or eating candy during working hours, or any other infraction of the rules.

Why is she like that, Mary often wondered. Agnes was prettier than almost any of the other girls, in spite of a slight coarseness of feature. Her hair was nearly black, and curly, her full mouth was an enticing, deep pink, and her eyes were big and brown and fully lashed. Even her work dress wasn't able to conceal the generous endowment of curves that nature had given her.

In spite of her dislike, Mary flinched. "Be careful. Somebody'll hear you and you'll be fined for contumacy."

"Let 'em dare! If things don't get better around here, there'll be a turnout, mark my words, and then old Livingston will see that it doesn't pay to set his mechanics against him! We could bring his looms to a standstill and he'd lose money every minute they weren't running. Other mills have had turnouts; it happens when the organizers come in and tell us mechanics our rights."

Mary was agonized. "Stop it! Somebody'll hear you for sure, and turn you in!"

"Pah! Nobody'd dare!" Agnes retorted. She tossed her head, making her dark curls dance, and her face was filled with scorn. "They know what'll happen to them if they do!"

The trouble was, Agnes was right. None of the other girls dared to turn Agnes in because of the retaliation she meted out. One mechanic had been discharged only last month because she'd refused to lend Agnes her merino shawl to wear to church on a rainy Sunday morning, having needed it herself. Agnes had wanted it because it was prettier than her own, and she'd been outraged when the girl had refused to swap for the morning.

"I'll tell you something." Agnes leaned forward and lowered her voice so that it would reach only Mary's ear. "There's an organizer coming to town, and pretty soon, too! And if these ninnies that work here and take all the dirt that's dished out to them listen to him the way they oughta, things'll change around here. There'll be a turnout that'll make old Livingston's hair turn white! And he'll meet our demands, too, unless he wants to be left with idle looms till he's bankrupt!"

Mary's eyes went round. "Agnes, you're just saying that!"

"No, I ain't. He's coming, you can bet your next quarter's pay on it! And I'm going to be right there when he talks, and cheer him on!"

"But how do you know that he's coming?"

"I got ways. I don't just work and eat and sleep the way the rest of you ninnies do. I get out, an' go places an' hear things. My gentleman friend told me, an' others too."

Just thinking of the risks that Agnes Barlowe took at least two or three nights a week, when she skinned out of the upstairs window and let herself down to the ground with her tied-together bedsheets, in order to spend time with her gentlemen friends, made Mary's heart quail. Agnes wasn't the only one who did it, girls being what they are, driven by nature itself to come in contact with the opposite sex, but she did it a lot more often than any other girl. Most of them were so frightened at their own temerity that they never tried it the second time. Mary guessed that Agnes was driven harder by nature than the rest of them, because she skinned out so often.

"Shhh! Mrs. Jackson's looking this way, she's looking right at us. Besides, it's time to get back to work."

The mechanics were hurrying back to their looms and Mary followed suit. Agnes took her time and was at her post with only a second to spare. The other girls whispered that Agnes got away with so much because of Carl Jakes. It was Mr. Jakes she met when she skinned out, and as recruiter Mr. Jakes had influence with the foreladies to keep her out of trouble. Mr. Jakes could be mean, and even the foreladies were wary of him.

Mary was so excited and nervous about what Agnes had told her that she had a hard time keeping her mind on her work. Only her fear of letting the threads tangle or break kept her from being reprimanded and fined.

Was it possible, could it be true, that an organizer was coming to Athens? And if it was true, would the mechanics listen to him, and stage a turnout? Just thinking about it made Mary tremble. She knew that reforms were needed. The girls whispered about it after lights out, when they'd been locked in their dormitories for the night. She knew that there had been trouble at other mills. Turnouts, and even riots. In spite of the laws against it, men still tried to organize the laborers. They were fined, jailed, and starved while they were in jail, because if their fines amounted to all they had in their pockets and they couldn't afford to buy their own provender, they had to go without. No one in a mill town dared to take them either food or money. Not only would any mill worker be discharged and blackballed for such an action, but his or her entire family would be prohibited from working for one full year. The laws were hard, and they were enforced. The government knew where profits came from—the employers, not the common mechanics.

What would she do, if an organizer did come? Would she dare to follow the lead of any mechanics who listened to him, and join in a turnout? Merely listening to such a man was cause for being discharged and blackballed.

All the same, it was exciting. The very idea that the mechanics might gain higher wages and shorter hours was enough to make her blood run fast. She'd do it! She was a human being. She had rights too, as well as the Livingstons and their like. Maybe Miss Adelaide Livingston was nice, she'd certainly been nice to Mary when she'd helped her get away with attending the revival meeting without being caught, and maybe Mr. Wyatt was nice. At least three-quarters of the girls at the mill were in love with Mr. Wyatt, even if he didn't know that they were alive.

Only she guessed that Mr. Wyatt really did know that they were alive, even if he could never as much as think of falling in love with one of them, being in love with Geneva Burton as he was. He was always nice to all of them. He spoke to them as if they were real people, and didn't even discharge them if they slipped up and sounded like they were complaining.

Mary had heard, and she believed, that Wyatt had had quarrels with his father about the way the mill was run. Wyatt thought that the mechanics should be paid more and their hours should be shortened. As Wyatt was inclined to shout when he had differences of opinion with his father, word of their quarrels got back to the mechanics in short order. Wyatt didn't think that his father should be planning to expand the mill until something was done to better the working conditions of the employees. Nothing would come of his being on the mechanics' side, of course. Wyatt didn't have that much influence with his father, who never let anything but his own desires influence him.

Just the same, Wyatt listened to the girls when they had a legitimate complaint. Not that many of them ever had a chance to talk to him. Herndon Livingston kept his son's nose at columns of figures most of the time. But when Wyatt had occasion to walk through the mill to check up on something or just to see how things were going, he was nice. If Mary hadn't already been in love with Dr. Galen Forbes she might have been in love with Mr. Wyatt herself.

A motion caught the corner of her eye and she risked a glance just in time to see Agnes dip surreptitiously into her pocket and slip a licorice drop into Becky Pratt's hand. The sweep-up girl, whose only duty was to keep scraps of cloth and ravelings and lint cleaned up, grasped it in her eager, grubby hand and popped it into her mouth. It was a mouth that was habitually slack, just as her eyes had a vacant look, because Becky was a natural. She wasn't quite right in her head, she'd been born lacking. Nearly fourteen years old, she'd never be able to handle a loom, or find any employment better than she had, and she only had that because her family were Athenians and kept her at home so that her wages were less than half of Mary's.

Mary's indignation flared. It was bad enough giving Becky candy during working hours, but a licorice drop! She'd get black around her mouth, and she'd be caught, and this time she'd be sacked because she'd been caught before. Being not quite all there in the head wouldn't excuse her. Agnes had a mean streak in her. She enjoyed causing trouble, and picking on Becky was one of her chief sources of enjoyment.

Just as Mary thought, it wasn't two minutes before Mrs. Jackson noticed the black around Becky's mouth. Mary seethed as the forelady marched over to the hapless child and pried her mouth open. Becky might be dim in her wits but she knew that the way to make a piece of candy last was to suck on it, not chew it up and swallow it down. Most of the licorice drop was still in her mouth, damning evidence that couldn't be ignored.

"Becky, don't come back tomorrow. I'll let you finish out the day, but after this don't come back again. I have to put you on report."

Despite Becky's dim-wittedness, she knew what being sacked meant. Her mouth wide, she began to howl, blubbering and digging her fists into her eyes. Her father would beat her for losing her job. He'd not only beat her, he'd see that she didn't get her fair share of food, and there wasn't that much at home to begin with. Them as don't work, her father said, don't eat. That was the way of the world, and that was the way it was in Luther Pratt's house.

Gritting her teeth till her jaws ached, Mary managed to hold her temper until she and the other girls clattered up the stairs of their dormitory and spilled out into their room. It wouldn't have done any good to tell on Agnes. There wasn't any rule against giving someone candy during working hours, there was only a rule against eating it. If she'd told, all she'd have accomplished would have been to make Agnes her deadly enemy for squealing, and Becky would have been sacked anyway.

The moment the door was closed behind them, she turned on Agnes. "You did that on purpose! You got Becky fired. You knew she'd be caught! Licorice, to a natural!"

"Shut yer trap. What's it to you? I was only being nice to the dimwit. You know how she loves candy and Gawd knows her old man doesn't leave her a ha'penny to buy any."

"You knew she'd get it around her mouth, Mrs. Jackson sees everything, and you knew she'd be fired this time!"

"I'm sick of seeing that silly face of hers, that's what! And half the time drooling or slobbering, especially when she eats!"

"You'd probably drool and slobber too if you were a natural! Becky can't help it, and she tries not to."

"But I ain't a natural! I've got all my buttons, and it's just too bad for them that don't! People like that shouldn't oughta be inflicted on normal people. They make me sick to my stomach!"

"I'll make you sick to your stomach!" While their roommates watched, their eyes wide and holding their breaths, Mary doubled up her fist and drove it into Agnes's stomach with all her strength.

"Oooww! Why, you sneaky little hick! I'll teach you a thing or two!" As soon as she'd managed to straighten up, Agnes dove in for the attack. She grabbed Mary's hair and yanked. Mary, screeching, retaliated in kind. Like two terriers, the antagonists went round and round, pulling each other by the hair. The only difference was that now Mary was silent, her teeth clenched, while Agnes kept up a steady stream of shrieks.

"Little Jenny-come-lately thinks she can teach me manners, does she? I'll show you, you filthy little rat!" Agnes spat at Mary between her cries of pain and fury.

A particularly hard yank that made her feel as if part of her scalp had been yanked out drove Mary to retaliating with a swift kick to Agnes's shin. Agnes howled. Mary kicked her again, and followed it up with a poke at Agnes's eye. Agnes followed suit, and Mary saw stars.

"Young ladies, young ladies, stop that this minute!" The door had burst open and Mrs. Simms came bustling in, her face flushed with horrified indignation. "We do not fight in this house. We are all well-bred young ladies!"

Mary let go of Agnes's hair, and after one more second, Agnes too obeyed the nightmarm's orders. Even Agnes dared not to go on brawling in front of Mrs. Simms, who would be forced to put them on report if the brawl didn't stop immediately. Fighting among the young ladies was strictly forbidden. Even arguing was forbidden. The Livingston mill promised culture for its young ladies, and arguing and fighting was not a part of its image. If this contretemps went on report, both Mary and Agnes would be discharged and blackballed as potential troublemakers.

There was no reading from an uplifting book that evening, much less from a romantic novel. In its stead, Mrs. Simms served up a lecture about the evils of causing trouble, and the sinfulness of young ladies engaging in physical combat and verbal abuse.

Mary's eye was black the next morning, but Agnes's eye was blacker. It being Sunday, every young lady in Herndon Livingston's employ was obliged to go to church—the First Methodist Church, of course, where Herndon's practiced eye could see at a glance whether the count was short, and also note that each and every one of them dropped at least twenty cents into the collection plate. Mary's eye would pass, if she kept her bonnet pulled well forward, but Agnes's was far too black to escape notice.

"Agnes, you will have to stay behind," Mrs. Simms told her, her voice filled with regret. "In order to protect both you and Mary from being discharged, that eye of yours must not be seen. You are to read from the Bible until we get back."

Each dormitory room was provided with a Bible in case any of the mechanics might not have one of her own. "I'll mark out the chapters you are to read."

"Yes'm," Agnes said. Mrs. Simms looked at her sharply, but Agnes didn't smirk until she turned away. Like fun Agnes would read the Bible! She'd spend the time to better advantage, taking down the neckline in her Sunday dress with no spying eyes to watch. She could wear a scarf tucked in when she went to church, so that Mrs. Simms or even worse, Herndon Livingston, wouldn't notice, but she wouldn't look so raggle-taggle, so downright frumpy, the next time she went out the window. If there was any time left over, she'd experiment with her hair. Would she dare cut herself some bangs? But how would she curl them? Curling irons or curling papers were forbidden, as implements of vanity, which were in turn implements of the devil.

Mary too was not in exactly a religious frame of mind as she left with the other mechanics to be escorted to church by the nightmarm. Agnes was the one at fault, Agnes was the one who'd been cruel enough to get Becky discharged, but Agnes was the one who got to stay home from church, and Mary knew perfectly well that Agnes would spend the time in primping. She herself had to attend services as usual, even though there was nothing she'd like better than to spend the two and a half hours doing a little primping of her own. Something exciting with her hair, and perhaps she could try to refurbish her bonnet if she had anything to refurbish it with, just in case Galen Forbes might look at her during services next week. She wished that she owned a decent dress, not just her Sunday calico that had begun to fade, so that Dr. Forbes would notice that she was a grown-up, attractive young lady, and not just a young mechanic whom he'd taken pity on in a time of need.

Sometimes he looked at her, and he always smiled. *Dr. Galen Forbes, Galen Forbes, Galen.* She savored the name on her tongue, almost tasting it. Her only consolation was that if she'd been the one with the blacker eye, and the one to be left behind, she wouldn't get to see Galen Forbes today.

Jim Yarnell felt more than a little sheepish as he entered the First Methodist Church that Sunday morning. He was one of the last, and had to find a place well at the back. It had been a long time since he'd attended church services, although he'd been brought up in a church-going family. As a young tad, he'd never missed Sunday School, or services either, along with his parents and his two younger sisters. But when he'd struck out on his own and ended up on a canalboat, he'd got out of the habit, unless his conscience troubled him thinking how upset his mother would be if she knew that he didn't attend church in whatever town he found himself on a Sunday.

His conscience was bothering him a little this morning, not because of thinking of his mother being upset, but because he was in church for an entirely different reason, having nothing to do with worship. He was a good Christian, or at least he held himself to be. He didn't drink, and he didn't smoke or chew tobacco or indulge in snuff, and he seldom visited any of the taverns or houses of ill repute that other canallers frequented whenever they had the chance. His family were Calvinists, who took a strict view of such matters, and it was hard to shake the habits of a lifetime.

This Sunday morning in July, however, Jim sat in church because he wanted to get another look at the girl whom he'd helped to rescue from her dilemma at the revival grounds—Mary MacDonald. He hadn't been able to get her out of his mind since that night, even though his lineboat had pulled out the next day, with his crew the worse for their carousals at that same meeting.

Jim was proud of the *Undine*, and of the crew that he had handpicked. His steward was one of the best on the canal, providing catered meals and liquid refreshments paid for by charging one cent a mile for each passenger that the boat carried. Besides the steward, there was a cook, a helmsman, two bowmen, a cabin boy, and two drivers, both of whom were boys in their early teens. Nearly all of the drivers on the Erie were boys, with the exception of the fast packets, which hired burly men who could hold their own in the sometimes vicious maneuvering for place at the locks. Fights at the locks were commonplace, and sometimes men were severely injured in the competition to maintain the fastest schedules.

It took Jim only a moment to pick out the sizable group of female mechanics from the mill, along with the plump figure of Mrs. Simms, their nightmarm. Mary was with them, her bonneted head bent over her hymnal as the congregation rose to lift their voices in "Bringing in the Sheaves." Even among all the other voices, Jim could pick out Mary's clear contralto, and as he joined in the singing with his own deep baritone, he felt a thrill like warm water travel up his spine. She sang like an angel, and she knew all the words without referring to the hymnal. His glance went to the choir, looking for Miss Livingston, whom he knew was a member, but she wasn't among them this morning. The young Livingston girl was sweet, and he hoped that she wasn't sick, but he forgot her in another second as he strained his ears to hear nothing but Mary's voice.

The sermon was a long one. Jebbidiah Tucker was in good voice and in no hurry to release his captive audience, but Jim found himself enjoying the discourse. It took him back to his younger days, when, like most of the other tads whose posteriors squirmed on the hard benches of the Calvinist church he'd attended with his family in Albany, he'd longed only for his freedom.

There was the usual crush at the door after the services ended. Jim himself was the object of a great deal of attention. Several of the ladies of the higher social planes looked undecided as to whether to speak to him or not. As Christian women, it was their duty to invite him to come back and see to the salvation of his soul, but to speak to a canaller was so far removed from their everyday experiences that they couldn't quite bring themselves to it.

And then a lady worked her way toward him and offered him her hand. It took Jim only a moment to recognize her. It was Miss Minnie Atkins, of the Athens Reading Rooms.

As the keeper of that cultural establishment, Minnie was definitely a lady. On the other hand, the spinster was as poor as the proverbial church mouse. Her family had never been prominent, and she was not a member of the circle in which the Livingstons and the Burtons moved, or any of the other monied families who drew a subtle but impenetrable social line which could not be crossed without the most ironclad references. Minnie herself, with a sense of humor which sometimes startled and even frightened her, thought that she existed in a sort of never-never land, neither one thing nor the other.

Nevertheless, she was a lady, and if a canaller came to her church, he should be welcomed so that he would feel free to come again. The Good Lord knew that the canallers needed saving, and someone had to hold out the first hand.

"It's good to see you here, Captain. I wish that more of

the canal people would avail themselves of spiritual guidance. Will you come again, when you're in town?''

''I will indeed, ma'am, and thank you kindly.''

''Perhaps you could prevail on your crew to accompany you. I'm sure they'd be welcome.'' Minnie wasn't as sure of that as she sounded, but she summoned up her courage and said it anyway. She'd welcome them, at least, even if no one else did!

Working with the motley assortment of people that he did, Jim had become an expert at reading emotions, and he had a very good idea of what this was costing the librarian. By and large, the canallers were considered a godless lot whom the devil had marked for his own. Efforts had been made by people like this matron and those of even higher classes, to save their souls from perdition, but had met with indifferent success. The canallers insisted that they were as Christian as the next man in spite of their calling, and they resented organizations that banded together to force their missionary work on them.

By the time he made his way out into the sunshine, Mrs. Simms and her group were some distance ahead of him, walking sedately, for all the world like a Mother Goose with a gaggle of young goslings, but Jim's long stride caught up with them in short order.

The girls stopped, some of them with their mouths agape and their eyes all but popping out of their heads at the phenomenon of a canaller actually accosting them on the streets of Athens on a Sunday morning.

He removed his captain's hat, his tone deferential. ''Ma'am, I'd appreciate being allowed to have a word with Miss MacDonald. I had occasion to see her family recently, and her mother asked me particularly to pass along their love and news of all of them.'' Lying, bald-faced lying, and on a Sunday, directly from church! Still, Jim could think of no other excuse to offer that might gain him a few words with Mary.

Mrs. Simms studied him as if she were memorizing every detail of his appearance so that she could describe him to the constable in case he was a wanted felon. But Jim's eyes, clear and candid, prompted her to nod, albeit reluctantly.

''In that case, it might be permissible. Mary, you may walk ahead of us with Captain . . . Captain . . .''

"Captain Yarnell, ma'am, and thank you kindly."

"Mind you don't get too far ahead. Ladies, we will walk a trifle more slowly, if you please. You are to take Miss Mac-Donald directly to the dormitory house, Captain."

"Yes, ma'am."

Mary's face was flaming. Of all the people in the world she never wanted to see again, it was Captain Yarnell. Not only was she mortified because he knew of her indiscretion, but to be seen with a canaller, to have to walk right on down Seneca Street with him in broad daylight, would ruin her reputation. What would Dr. Forbes think if he should see them together? He'd think that she was a loose woman—how could he possibly think anything else? She felt like crying, except that would only make matters worse than they already were, and so she reacted by attacking.

"You lied to Mrs. Simms, didn't you? You couldn't possibly have seen my family, they don't live anywhere near the canal."

"I'm sorry, Miss MacDonald, but I wanted to see you again, and make sure that you were all right. You weren't badly hurt then, the other night?"

Jim's eyes widened with shock when he got his first full look at Mary's face as she lifted it to him accusingly. If that wasn't a black eye, then he'd never seen one! Her bonnet had hidden the discoloration before, but now it stared back at him, unmistakable. "Mary, what happened to you?"

Mary's hand flew to her face, and her face grew even redder than it had been before. "I was in a fight. But Agnes deserved what I gave her. She couldn't even come to church because her eye is so much blacker." In spite of her humiliation, there was a note of pride in her voice. "I gave her a good one, I did, it's what she deserved for getting poor Becky Pratt sacked."

"Good for you!" If it hadn't been Sunday and if Mrs. Simms and her brood hadn't been so close behind them, Jim would have thrown back his head and laughed. Mary Mac-Donald had spirit and he liked that in a girl. He'd been right to want to see her again. Of all the girls he'd ever known, Mary intrigued him the most. He wanted to get to know her better, a great deal better.

The thought sobered him. Getting to know a mill mechanic better—they were guarded as carefully as novice nuns in a convent—posed problems that he'd never before had to face.

"We turn here," Mary said. She kept her eyes on the ground, afraid to look at him. "Thank you for wanting to know how I was. I'm all right. Nobody found out that I went to the revival meeting. I'd have been sacked for sure if they had. I'd have been sacked last night, if Mrs. Simms had reported me for smacking Agnes, but at least I had a good reason for doing that."

Suddenly her face went pale as she risked a quick glance at the canaller, mostly to satisfy her curiosity by seeing for herself if he looked as wicked as all canallers were reputed to be. Lord preserve her, there was Dr. Forbes, and there was no way to sink through the ground as she'd like to do so that he wouldn't see her with Captain Yarnell!

"Jim! It's good to see you. Checking up on my patient, I see. She looks none the worse for her adventure—" Galen broke off, as startled as Jim had been a moment ago. "Jumping Jehosephat, what happened to your eye?"

"She smacked another girl for getting poor Becky Pratt sacked," Jim answered for her when Mary's voice failed her. "But you ought to see Agnes! She couldn't even come to church."

"Agnes Barlowe, I'll be bound," Galen said. And like Jim, he added, his face filled with admiration, "Good for you!"

"Well, she deserved it," Mary said.

"I'm sure she did. Jim, how long are you going to be in town?"

"We pull out in the morning. Doctor Forbes, I'd like to talk to you, after I've seen Miss MacDonald home." Maybe Galen Forbes would have some ideas on how a canaller could go about getting to know a young mechanic better. "How about walking back to the *Undine* with me? I can offer you the best cup of coffee on the Erie, as well as some victuals that do our steward proud."

"Undine? What does that mean?" Mary's forehead creased, and her curiosity made her forget her embarrassment at being caught by Dr. Forbes, not only in the company of a canaller, but with this disgraceful black eye.

"Water nymph," Jim explained. "It's a little fanciful

for a lineboat, but I like it. Mr. Fielding let me name the boat, and that's what I picked."

"I think it's a pretty name. Undine," Mary repeated, so that she'd remember it. She liked to store things away in her mind. It helped make up for not being able to read as well as she wished she could.

The dormitory had come in sight, and Mrs. Simms and the other girls were bearing down on them. "Thank you for asking how I was, but you can see I'm all right." The words were hurried as she directed her voice at Jim while she kept her eyes on Galen's face, drinking in every feature as if she were afraid that she'd never see him again. It was a pity that she was so healthy. She'd never get sick and get to see him that way. Remembering just how much of her he'd seen when he'd bound up her sore ribs made her face flame, and she dropped back to melt in with the other girls as Mrs. Simms clucked and prodded them into the house.

"Mary has a beau!" Dorothy Monroe twitted her. "Now what do you think about that? Mary has a canaller for a beau!"

"Two beaus, it looks like. Doctor Forbes, as well as the canaller!" Nancy Steele jumped in. "But a lot of good it'll do her, the way we never get to go out at night!"

"I do not have a beau! You stop saying that!" Mary's hands clenched into fists, although she had no inclination to smack either Dorothy or Nancy. They were her friends, nothing like Agnes Barlowe, and their teasing was friendly, not jealous or mean.

"Young ladies, young ladies! We will have no talk of beaux." Mrs. Simms frowned at them. But her face was both kind and concerned as she added, "And it would be a good idea not to mention Mary's escorts in Agnes's hearing. She might use the information to do Mary a hurt."

"All the same, Mary's dozened with the doctor. I saw the way she looked at him!" another girl put in. "Fancy that. She's dozened with the doctor, and he isn't anywhere near as handsome as the captain! Me, I'd take the captain, any day!"

"All right, then, take him and welcome!" Mary shot back. "I don't want him, that's for sure!"

Dorothy put her arm around her as they started up the stairs. "The more fool you," she said, her tone friendly. "All right, the rest of you, let's stow it. Agnes has ears like a fox.

Mrs. Simms, can we go for a walk this afternoon, instead of just hanging around here reading stupid books? Please, can we?''

"*May* we, Dorothy, *may* we!" But Mrs. Simms capitulated. "Very well, I think that we all might benefit from a nice walk during such salubrious weather. We'll go directly after we've had our dinner.''

Having Mrs. Simms accompany them wasn't exactly what Dorothy had had in mind, but it was better than nothing. "Maybe we can walk along the canal. Maybe we'll see the captain's boat.''

"The *Undine*," Mary said. "That means water nymph.'' Her breath quickened. She hoped that the girls would eat fast, and that Mrs. Simms would be ready to start as soon as they'd finished. What if they walked past the *Undine*, and Dr. Forbes was still there? She'd get to see him again even if she didn't get to speak to him. Seeing Galen Forbes again, even for a few seconds while they were passing by, would be better than Christmas.

7

Jim was on deck as Mrs. Simms and the group passed. He bowed to them, his face flushing with pleasure when he saw Mary.

"Laws, ain't he handsome! I wish I had something nice on, instead of this frumpy old calico!" Nancy Steele mourned.

"Come along, young ladies. We must not linger in these environs. I should never have allowed you to persuade me to come this way in the first place, and the sooner we get out of the vicinity the better."

Jim stood looking after the group of chattering girls, until they turned a corner and were out of sight. Lord, but Mary was prettier every time he saw her! It was too bad that Galen Forbes hadn't been able to come up with anything that would help him to see her again, but at least he'd promised to put his mind to the problem. Jim would see him again as soon as he got back from his next haul.

Mary's thoughts were in a different channel. He wasn't there, she thought, almost sick with disappointment. I wonder where he is?

At that precise moment, along with not only Marvin Burton but also both Bobo and Geneva, Galen was walking along the canal bank some distance from the *Undine*. He'd enjoyed his noon dinner on the lineboat, good, hearty fare that Jim Yarnell had reason to be proud of serving to his passengers. Having traveled via canal on many occasions, Galen had not been surprised at the quality and quantity of the food set in front of him. Fried chicken, boiled potatoes, gravy, bread and butter, jam and jelly, pickles, peas and chopped carrots and greens, pork chops and berry pie and spice cake, coffee with thick country cream, and cheese. Any canalboat worthy of its name would be ashamed to offer less than two kinds of meat and two different desserts at one meal, including breakfast.

He'd turned down the offer of brandy or rum or cider after he'd eaten, not knowing how his hostess, Cora Burton, would take to his appearing at her home on a Sunday afternoon with spirits on his breath.

As it happened, he hadn't seen Mrs. Burton when he'd arrived. Cora had decided that she could use an afternoon nap to help her recover from her own hearty dinner and the warmth of the day, having arrived at that decision after Marvin Burton had put the idea in her head. Cora was apt to become upset at talk of politics or reform, and to object when Geneva insisted on entering discussions that were considered the province of the masculine gender.

Marvin Burton's reaction to his dinner and the warmth of the day was a desire for exercise to stir up his circulation, and both Geneva and Bobo had fallen in with the suggestion with enthusiasm.

"Yes, let's do!" Geneva said. "Just let me change out of this ridiculous harness Mother insists I strap myself into for church, and get into something I can move in without turning purple." Her eyes sparkling, she ran up the stairs as if she hadn't been laced into a corset at all, to appear in an amazingly short time, divested both of corset and the fashionable dress she'd worn to church. She was garbed now in a simple dimity, its pink a trifle faded and, Galen suspected, wearing only two petticoats under it.

Not only had she changed in that short time, but she'd taken the pins from her hair and bundled it in a loose knot on top of her head, with a few tendrils escaping to curl around nape and forehead.

"That feels better!" Geneva said. "You men don't know how lucky you are, with your short hair, and not having to wear half a dozen petticoats and strangle yourselves in laces! Glory, I can breathe again! Let's go, the afternoon is too beautiful to waste. We'll walk along the canal bank, shall we?"

"Geneva, you're shocking our young friend. Medical man or not, I doubt he's used to hearing ladies discuss their undergarments in mixed company."

"Then it's time he learned the facts of life. Petticoats and corsets are an abomination." To Galen's further consternation, she linked one arm in her brother's and her other in his. "He ought to be glad that I shed the pesky things, else I'd never have been able to keep up with you!"

Bobo grinned. "Galen, don't be surprised if she takes off her shoes and stockings when we get far enough out of town, to dangle her toes in the canal. And you'll be lucky if that's all she does. If it was just the two of us, she'd probably shed more than that behind the most convenient bush, and go all the way in."

Galen looked alarmed, not at the thought of Geneva's shedding most of her clothing to cool off in the canal, but because of the danger involved in such an unorthodox procedure.

"Great Scott, aren't you afraid she'd drown?"

The grin on Bobo's good-natured face deepened. "Geneva drown? She swims like a fish! Once I came near to drowning in a pond, and she dived in and pulled me out, and she was no more than thirteen at the time. Hit my head on the bottom, like a fool! The next thing I knew she had me on the bank pumping water out of me and calling me every name she could turn her tongue to for daring to scare her like that!"

"I'm afraid that my daughter doesn't conform to the general pattern of a well-brought-up young lady," Marvin told Galen, not without sympathy. "I believe in giving young people all the freedom they can handle. Give them room to grow and develop, as it were. Minds as well as bodies can atrophy from lack of room to spread out, don't you agree?"

What Galen thought was that Geneva Burton was spoiled rotten, like every other wealthy woman he had ever known. Not that he'd come into contact with many, but the one he had had intimate contact with set the pattern for all the rest. He'd learned by bitter experience that wealthy women didn't care whom they hurt.

"And in the case of my offspring, I can't see that it's done any harm," Marvin finished complacently.

"Well, it's done me harm! I've had to punch more than one nose in her defence, when some fellow or other had the temerity to hint that my sister wasn't exactly ladylike. Not that I minded." Bobo's tone was mild, filled with admiring amusement rather than ire. "Boys always welcome a reason to punch someone."

Galen found himself liking Bobo. The young man who was going to follow in his father's footsteps in law had a mind almost as keen as Mr. Burton's, even if he did cover it up, for the most part, with an attitude of lazy good nature. Galen appreciated Cyril Burton's sense of humor and the way he let life roll off him, rather than taking things too seriously.

"Go on. Mostly you were too lazy to chase the name-caller to punch him in defense of my honor!" Geneva scoffed. "Isn't it a beautiful day! It isn't even too hot, now that I'm out of those churchgoing trappings." She gave a little skip, her face flushed from the pleasure of this outing. She'd started out with a hat, but as soon as they'd left the town's streets behind she'd removed it, and the sun glinting on her hair turned it to polished chestnut.

"We should have brought our fishing poles. I haven't been fishing in a donkey's age," Geneva added.

"And who'd fry them up for supper, with Mrs. Brady off Sunday afternoon and evening?" Bobo asked her, his eyebrows shooting up.

"I would, ninny. You'd clean them, of course. I can't see Mother doing it. Can't you just imagine her face if we put a string of fish in her hands and told her we wanted her to cook them? But darn it, we didn't think to come prepared, so Doctor Forbes will just have to settle for cold meat and salad and cake, after all."

Geneva Burton was altogether too attractive. Galen had a vivid picture in his mind of what a girl like her could do to the career of a young doctor who had dedicated himself to the care of the poor. Remembering David Harshey brought a knot to the pit of his stomach.

Even thinking about David Harshey made Galen wince. As an adolescent boy, the younger son of a blacksmith whose wife had blessed her husband with five girls between his brother's birth and his own, Galen had helped in the blacksmith shop. He'd loved the horses, and as his father had also been the most knowledgeable man in their section of upstate New York when it came to animals' ailments, he'd seen a good many injured and ailing creatures. He'd learned at a young age how to apply poultices to swollen joints and sprains, how to treat sores and colic. He'd had a feeling for it, and a good many of the farmers and carters in their neighborhood had predicted that he'd grow up to be an even better horse doctor than his father.

It was because of this that he'd come into contact with young Dr. Harshey. David had brought his horse in with a lamed foreleg, and he'd been impressed at the way Galen had treated the animal, Galen's father having gone to a farm to look at a cow that was having trouble calving, and his brother being busy shoeing a cart horse.

"You're almost as good a doctor as I am, Galen," David had said. "Maybe you'll be a doctor, when you grow up."

The sixteen-year-old boy had taken the joke seriously, and his face had tightened. "I'm afraid not, sir. There wouldn't be any way for me to learn."

Sensing the boy's feelings, David had felt a quick sympathy for the bright lad. "But you have a knack, Galen. You could learn if you put your mind to it. Would you really like to learn?"

The transformation in Galen's face had been startling. His eyes had seemed to take fire and his voice was intense as he said, "More than anything else in the world! I reckon I'd die happy, if I was to get me a chance to learn."

That had been the beginning of a friendship that had lasted for years. David Harshey was a dedicated doctor, a young man bent on alleviating the sufferings of the lower classes in particular. His zeal had found a ready ally in Galen, whose natural sympathy for any suffering creature made him determined to work for humanity. David Harshey took the boy under his wing and began to teach him all that he could absorb.

Galen was a ready pupil, seeming to absorb everything David taught him with little effort. Of all the people in the world, Galen had looked up to David, had worshiped him.

What plans they made, the two of them! Galen would walk home from David's dispensary with his head in the clouds, not caring that he'd be so tired in the morning that his father would shout at him and call him a fool for trying to be something he could never be.

Whenever he could, as often as his father would give grudging permission, Galen went with David on calls. He experienced the agony and the glory of seeing new life come into the world, and he went through the despair of watching the fatally ill and the aged die while David used every means within his power to ease their passing. He helped to stitch up and bind up limbs mangled in farm accidents, he learned the value of joking and sympathizing with a child with severe respiratory attacks until the medicated steam and the chest rubs took effect.

And perhaps the hardest lesson of all, he learned how to go without sleep for long periods of time, how to keep on his feet and go on functioning no matter how tired he was after a night call that lasted until dawn, only to have to go directly to the smithy and put in a full day's work under his father's and his brother's jaundiced eyes. It was a full three years before they began to give their grudging approval, when it became apparent that Galen was going to make it. His mother had always approved, prayed for his success, and his sisters had been awe-stricken at his new importance, but the opinions of females didn't matter.

"Do you know something, Galen?" David asked him, four long and bone-weary years after the day Galen had tended David's horse. "You're a doctor. I've taught you everything I know, and the rest you'll learn by experience. It's time you and I became full-time partners."

As tired as he'd been, so tired that even staying on his feet was an agony, especially after fifteen full hours of helping David battle to save a man who'd stepped on a rake and developed blood poisoning, Galen's elation was overwhelming. He knew that anything else that might come to him in his life would pale by comparison. Their patient was going to live, and he was a doctor!

The partnership had been satisfying even beyond his expectant dreams. He looked on David as a brother, as a father image, as a hero more noble than any hero of mythology. They worked well together, bending all of their efforts toward treating the poor and hopeless. The hours were long and there were the inevitable failures that plunged them into despair, but there were also the successes that made it far more than worthwhile. Given his choice of any occupation in the world, Galen would still have chosen to be a doctor and David's partner.

And then, two years after their partnership had begun, David fell under the spell of Miss Arabel Crandall. They'd met at a charitable affair, where Arabel had taken a starring role as a dispenser of largess to the poor and unfortunate, a role that the young society lady had played with relish.

Almost outrageously beautiful, the only daughter of the wealthiest and most socially prominent family in the county, Arabel had captivated David with her porcelainlike beauty and lustrous dark hair and violet eyes. And although Arabel had traveled extensively, and had turned down dozens of more eligible men, David had caught her interest, probably because he was so different from any other man she had ever known.

Galen himself had fallen headlong in love with Arabel, and with more excuse, because he was ten years younger than David and a great deal less experienced with women, never having had the time or the money to indulge himself with feminine companionship. He'd known from the first that he didn't have a chance against David's handsomeness and charm, but somehow he'd come to terms with his jealousy and wished his mentor and partner only the best of luck, although there were times when he'd been hard put to keep his jealousy under control.

But little by little, Galen had seen a change taking place, until his jealousy turned into uneasiness. Having decided that David was the perfect complement for her, Arabel took him under her wing and persuaded him, an inch at a time, to expand his practice, to tend friends of her family and her friends, for suitable compensation. At thirty-three, David had an air of confidence and capability that assured his success in this more lucrative field, and he merged into high society with little trouble.

Galen fought down his qualms. He told himself that it was still no more than crass jealousy of his friend's good fortune that made him have his doubts about the advisability of this union. David had worked like a slave for years. It was time that he began to achieve recognition and compensation for his abilities. With himself to continue caring for the poorer element among their patients, there was no reason why he should not. All the same, in unguarded moments, he fretted over the change in David as the older man pushed more and more of their less lucrative cases onto his shoulders.

David and Arabel were to have a traditional June wedding. Galen was to be the best man, and even though his first blind infatuation for Arabel had given place to a more cynical view of her character, he still wondered how he'd manage to get through it without letting his still seething jealousy make him crack up. Flawed jewel or not, Arabel still had the power to make any man overlook her shortcomings and go on worshiping her in spite of them.

The biggest event of the year was the New Years party that the Crandalls always held in their home. It had been an exceptionally bitter winter, and Galen's own special patients had suffered greatly from it. Early on December the twenty-eighth he'd been called in to treat a young boy, and as was not unusual, he found that he'd been called too late. The boy, one of Galen's favorites whose name was Tim, had already developed pneumonia.

There was little evidence that Christmas had just passed in this house, a dilapidated clapboard that was little better than a shack. Tim's father was a carpenter, and there was little work for a man in his trade in the winter. Tim's mother was stooped from years of hard labor, and Tim, along with his brothers and sisters, was too thin, and had that particular pale look associated with the children of poverty.

Still, by checking in on Tim three times a day, by seeing to it that the five-year-old boy was kept warm, that the steam kettle was never allowed to run dry, Galen was sure that he'd be able to pull him through.

On December the thirty-first, he knew that the crisis was near. He intended to stay with Tim all night, pitting every ounce of his strength and knowledge against the spectre of death that threatened to cut the young life short.

"I ain't askeered," Tim whispered, as his fever-hot hand clung to Galen's. "Long's you're here, I ain't askeered at all." The words had ended in a fit of coughing, and Galen had supported the frail body until it passed, cursing both heaven and earth because he didn't know more.

An hour before he was going to go back to Tim's house to spend the night, a panic-stricken farmer had pounded on his door. Galen had attended the man's wife in childbirth before, and he'd warned the farmer that another pregnancy might very well kill her. Now the woman had gone into labor two months prematurely. There was no help for it, he had to go, or he'd have her death on his conscience.

Grim-faced, he set out for the Crandall mansion, where

preparations for the gala that would end with a midnight supper to celebrate the New Year were well under way. David was already there, being ordered about by Arabel as the last touches were put on the decorations.

"Look, David. This is important. Party or no party, you have to be with Tim tonight. If one of us isn't there, he's likely to die." He held David's eyes with his own, his face demanding. "The crisis is building fast. I wouldn't ask you unless it was absolutely essential."

"Go along and take care of Mrs. Lindquist. And mind you remember everything I taught you about premature births!" David clapped his hand on Galen's shoulder, his voice hearty. "I'll see to Tim. You needn't have a moment's worry."

Galen spent all of that night and more than half the next day battling to save two lives, those of the suffering farmwife and her unborn child. He despaired of saving either of them even as he refused to give up. But in the end he'd won. The mother was weak from her excruciating ordeal and loss of blood, but she'd live, this time, and the infant, a boy, had been persuaded to breathe and to go on breathing.

Leaving the mother and infant in the care of a capable neighbor farmwoman, himself so exhausted that he was grateful that his hired horse knew its own way back to the livery stable, Galen still turned the animal's head toward Tim's house before he returned it to its owner and sought his bed. In spite of his exhaustion, he felt a sense of accomplishment, of the meaning of his life through his work. Once he'd seen Tim and knew that all was well with him, he'd be able to sleep without one of his recurring bouts of jealousy of David's good fortune in capturing Arabel.

One of the children answered his knock. The little girl was wide-eyed, her eyes rimmed with black shadows and filled with grief and bewilderment at things she was too young to understand.

"Tim?" Galen asked, but already his heart was sinking. He'd seen that look too often not to know what it meant.

The little girl jerked her head. Galen walked on through to the kitchen, the warmest room in the house and therefore the one where Tim's cot had been brought to nurse him during his illness.

Mrs. Adler sat in a straight chair beside Tim's bed, her

hands folded in her lap, staring at nothing. Tim's eyes were closed, his hands folded on his breast.

"When?" Galen's voice was a croak. He couldn't take it in. Tim had been supposed to live.

"About midnight."

"What did Doctor Harshey say?"

"He weren't here. He come once, 'bout seven o'clock, but he went away again and he didn't come back. My Tim, he stopped breathing about midnight."

Half an hour later, not having found David at the house and office they shared, Galen pounded on the Crandalls' door and pushed aside the servant who answered it. He strode into the drawing room, drawn by David's voice and Arabel's silvery laughter. Another second, and he was across the room and his hands were around David's throat.

"You didn't go back! You didn't go back, and Tim's dead!"

Arabel screamed. David clawed at Galen's hands, his eyes popping as he failed to be able to combat the insane strength with which Galen was throttling him.

"You killed him! Damn you to hell! You let him die, because you thought a party was more important than a little boy's life!"

Arabel's shrieks went on, and Arabel's father, and two or three servants rushed in. It took all of them to pry Galen's hands from David's throat and subdue him.

David took a few staggering steps and collapsed into a chair, gasping for breath. His face was purple. "Galen, I thought he was doing fine. I meant to go back but . . ."

"You murderer!" Arabel screamed. Not at David, but at Galen, who was shaking hs head, his eyes losing their mad glaze as he returned to sanity. "You tried to kill him, you tried to kill David! Father, call the constable, have this maniac locked up!"

"No," David croaked. "Don't do that, Arabel."

"David is right. We don't want any of this to get out, it would be a scandal," Arabel's father said. Behind him, Mrs. Crandall, an older version of her daughter, agreed with him, wringing her hands. "But as for you, Doctor Forbes, I'd advise you to leave town as soon as it can be arranged. You're through in Bingingham. This town does not want nor need a doctor who verges on insanity."

And Galen was through. A few words from the Crandalls had their immediate effect. The Crandalls were powerful, and even though David tried to intervene in Galen's behalf, they were adamant.

For as long as he lived, Galen would never forget the shame in David's eyes as they had said good-bye. And just as bad, even now, Galen was filled with self-distrust, not sure that under similar circumstances he might not again revert to some form of violence.

The wealthy! He had no sympathy for himself, but it was because of the whim of a wealthy, shallow girl that Tim was dead, and that his friendship with David was shattered. David had betrayed his own ideals for the love of a girl who wasn't worth it. A rich and pampered girl like Geneva Burton.

He was jolted out of his black thoughts as Geneva tugged at his arm to gain his attention. "Doctor Forbes, come back! You were miles away. Did you notice how glum Matthew Ramsey was this morning? Actually, I don't blame him, with Addie away for the rest of the summer. But even so, I can't help hoping that Addie'll get over him before she comes home. I'd hate to see her tied to him for all the rest of her life, no matter how noble that handsome brow of his is!"

Bobo looked at her, his eyes twinkling. "If you were tied to him, I can guarantee that you wouldn't be walking bareheaded, with your hair looking like a magpie's nest, and only two petticoats, on a canal bank on a Sunday afternoon."

Geneva laughed. "If I were foolish enough to get myself tied to him, I'd deserve to be miserable all the rest of my life! Not that Addie's stupid. She isn't, she's just young and this is her first crush. As I said, I hope she gets over it!"

"I'm afraid there's nothing you can do about it, if she doesn't," her father told her. "Doctor Forbes, do I look like a writer to you? No, don't answer that! But that's what I'm doing now that Bobo's back to take over a good share of my legal business. I'm writing a history of this section of the state, with special emphasis on the impact of the Erie Canal on industry and on society in general."

"It sounds interesting." Galen wasn't just being polite, he was interested.

"It is, it's a fantastic subject. The canal has not only doubled and tripled commerce, it has brought a freedom to the common people that was undreamed of before it came into existence. Do you realize that farm women in particular have been freed from hours of drudgery every week, now that they can buy, at reasonable prices, things that they used to have to make at home? Cloth, clothing, soap—the list is endless. It's given rise to so many movements that it's hard to keep track of them."

"Movements?"

"Yes, movements. The women are turning their energies to every cause you could think of. Antislavery, Christian centers to board and house and look after the boys who drive the canalboats to save them from perdition, temperance, clothing the heathen. Name it and they're into it up to their necks. It's somewhat of a mixed blessing. A good many of the objects of their zeal would as soon not have their personal lives tampered with."

"At least it gives them something to do. And it's time that they didn't have to work themselves into early graves." Galen's mind went, inevitably, to Mrs. Adler, Tim's mother, whose life had been nothing but unremitting drudgery. He wished that the canal had been able to save her from some of it. "And to occupy their minds."

"So you concede that women have minds!" Geneva teased him. Her father gave her a warning look, not willing to have frivolous comments intrude on the seriousness of his subject.

"Expand their horizons, yes. It's done that, all right. And I'm glad it has. This country is riding on a wave of prosperity that's unprecedented, Doctor, and the canal has done it. Geneva's helping me with my research, and she'll make the final copy of everything I write, in handwriting that won't send any editor I send it to blind. It will be a full-time job, and I'm grateful that she's interested enough to help me."

Galen glanced at Geneva, who didn't look the least bookish or even serious, at the moment. He had an uncomfortable impression that she was laughing at him for being so surprised.

"Perhaps your daughter will develop into an author on her own account." He hoped his comment didn't sound as wry as he felt.

"God forbid, if you're thinking of those sticky-sweet, asinine novels that they seem to be restricted to! No daughter of mine is going to waste her God-given brain power on trash like that! She might delve into history, or social trends, but that's up to her. All I ask is that she never let her brain atrophy."

Bobo interrupted them. "Look there. We're about to have company." A large group of young women was bearing down on them, and it took Galen only a few seconds to identify them as mechanics from the mill, out for a Sunday afternoon airing with their nightmarm herding them along.

"Exercise period," he commented, only half humorously. "They remind me of a bunch of prisoners or orphans who're walked around for an hour or two a week under the name of health and recreation."

"Unfortunate creatures," Marvin agreed. "And they'll be even more unfortunate if that organizer comes and talks them into a turnout. If they don't win, and at this time I don't see how they could prevail against Herndon Livingston, the lot of them will be blackballed, and their families right along with them. It'll take more courage for them to stand their ground than you and I can dream of."

"There's Mary MacDonald! I expect she'll never dare to step out of bounds from the mill rules again, after the fright she had at the revival grounds," Geneva said.

"I expect she won't either." Galen's face was grave. Mr. Burton's wonderful Erie Canal hadn't done much for Mary and the other mechanics like her, not even giving them time to expand their minds by joining various movements.

Marvin bowed to the young ladies as the group approached them, and Bobo and Galen followed his example.

"Good afternoon, Mrs. Simms. May I present Miss Burton and her father, Mr. Burton, and Cyril Burton?" Galen was as formal as if the nightmarm and her charges rated the same courtesy as Geneva herself, or any of her friends.

There was a chorus of awed oh's and ah's at this unexpected bonus to their stroll. Mrs. Simms flushed with pleasure.

"How do you do. I'm very glad to make your acquaintance, I'm sure. I see that you too are taking advantage of this lovely afternoon."

In the center of the group, Mary's eyes were begging Geneva not to let on that she knew her. Geneva smiled at her to let her know that neither she nor Galen would dream of giving her away. Mary's relief was apparent on her face as she returned the smile somewhat tentatively.

"It is indeed a lovely afternoon. It's hard to realize that in a few short weeks, autumn will be here, and after that winter will descend upon us," Marvin Burton remarked, quite as if he found nothing unusual about exchanging pleasant amenities with a group of mill mechanics and their nightmarm. His manner held nothing to indicate that he found them his social inferiors, and Galen's already high opinion of him climbed several more notches. It took a real gentleman to treat others who were not as fortunate as equals.

"Young ladies, we must be getting along," Mrs. Simms said. "Good afternoon, Mr. Burton. Good afternoon, Miss Burton and Doctor Forbes." Still beaming, her face reflecting her gratification, the nightmarm herded her group together and urged them into motion.

Geneva's face was thoughtful as she watched them walk away. "They have so little to make them happy, almost nothing to look forward to. I wish there were something we could do for them." She thought for a moment, a cloud coloring her eyes, and then her face brightened.

"Father, couldn't we put on a picnic for them? We could have it at Chestnut Grove, and invite all the mechanics, everyone who works at the mill. Don't you think they'd really enjoy that?"

"I'm sure that they would, but have you thought of how much work would be involved?"

"Oh, Geneva won't mind frying up a few dozen chickens and baking a couple of dozen cakes, and making a few gallons of lemonade," Bobo put in, his face merry.

Geneva picked up a stick and threw it at him. "You can take that look off your face, because I won't mind! Besides, I'll get Roxanne and some of the other girls to help me. It's too bad that Addie isn't here. She'd enjoy doing something for her father's workers, but we'll manage without her."

The wealthy young society lady out to do good works, Galen thought sourly. It struck a chord that brought back bitter memories. Arabel Crandall had played at being a benefactress, too, not from real goodness of heart, but to make people admire her. She'd snagged David that way, and David was still caught, only half the man he used to be.

"You ought to hit Herndon up to foot the cost, seeing that it's for his employees' benefit." Bobo's face showed still more merriment. "Can't you imagine his reaction at the idea of being asked to pay for a picnic for his mechanics?"

"We'll leave Herndon Livingston out of this!" Geneva said, her voice firm. "We'll just notify him that the picnic is an accomplished fact, or else he might find some reason why we couldn't have it. That's your job, Father. You can tell him tomorrow morning, and don't take any back talk! Galen, you'll come, won't you? You wouldn't want to miss it. And Bobo must round up his Corinthians, to set up the tables and fetch and carry and help things run smoothly. Maybe doing a good deed will help erase some of the black marks against their souls. Goodness knows Bobo could use some help in that direction."

"My soul is without blemish," Bobo told her. "But you'd better look to your mechanics' souls if you intend to turn the Corinthians loose among them. Or the Corinthians' souls, for that matter! Some of those girls must be mighty man-hungry, after being locked away in Herndon Livingston's nunnery for so long!"

Behind his good-natured banter, Bobo was delighted with the opportunity to be in the thick of Geneva's plans. It would give him something to do to take his mind off Addie Livingston. Ever since the night he'd taken his sister and Addie to the revival, he'd realized that Addie had grown up, that she was a deucedly attractive girl. If he'd had his wits about him a year ago, he'd have seen that she was going to grow up almost overnight, and got his licks in before Matthew Ramsey had come to town and captured her heart.

But a year ago Addie had been only fifteen, a child, and although Bobo had been inordinately fond of her, a romance between them had never entered his head. Blind ass, he told himself now. And the worst of it was, now that he knew that Addie was the girl he wanted, that she was the only girl he'd ever want, she was so much in love with the minister that she couldn't see straight.

It wouldn't do any good to talk to her, to point out to her that Matthew was all wrong for her, that a life as his wife would stifle her. Concerning Matthew, Addie was blind and deaf. Bobo's only chance was that she'd realize it herself before her father got around to letting her marry him. And if she didn't, there wasn't a thing in the world he could do about it. You can't go around punching a minister in the nose!

At least Geneva would be on his side, if the chance ever came. His sister wasn't all that enthralled with Matthew Ramsey herself. So he'd better stay on Geneva's good side, so that she'd throw her influence his way when and if the time came. And it had to come, or it would be one of the greatest miscarriages of human happiness since the world began! Addie was too good for Matthew, she'd been held down under her father's thumb every year of her life. It would be disastrous for her if she simply passed from Herndon Livingston's domination to Matthew Ramsey's, when Bobo could and would devote his entire life to making her happy, to letting her spread her wings and fly.

Geneva's voice, teasingly sweet, jerked him back to the present.

"The Corinthians are your responsibility, brother mine. I'll hold you responsible for their behavior. It's all settled, then."

"It may be, or it may not." Marvin Burton's voice was suddenly serious. "Some of Athens's more upstanding citizens might not approve of the idea of holding a picnic for the mill girls. You're apt to run into opposition. Do you think you can handle it?"

"They can like it or not." Geneva shrugged. "We're going to do it." There was a look in her eyes that boded ill for anyone who dared to cross her.

Galen made up his mind. He'd attend the picnic, if only to strike a blow for the common people. Geneva Burton herself had nothing to do with his decision.

8

Marvin Burton's surmise had been correct. The town of Athens split right down the middle at the idea of having a picnic for the mill mechanics. Most of the more affluent were against it. They felt it was pampering the workers and giving them an inflated notion of their importance. The less affluent, for the most part, were for it.

Bobo spent the better part of a morning persuading Jebbidiah Tucker that giving the mill workers a treat was an act of Christian charity. It would also be beneficial to the souls of his sister and the other young ladies who had volunteered to help her.

"Good works, Reverend Tucker! We must remember the importance of good works! You could come up with a powerful sermon on the subject. And of course, we will expect you to attend, and to lead us in prayer." The idea was to go to the top, because with Tucker's sanction it would be hard for anyone to come flat out against it. Even Herndon Livingston wouldn't care to come out publicly against anything that the Methodist minister approved.

As it happened, Herndon approved the project for reasons purely self-seeking. With the rumor of an organizer coming to Athens, it might prove to his advantage to have his mechanics in a good frame of mind, just in case the man managed, despite his precautions, to speak to the girls. After having made merry, and stuffed themselves with good food, they'd be in a mood to look on him as their benefactor, someone to whom they owed undivided loyalty.

Jim Yarnell heard about the picnic even before the

Undine pulled into Athens on the Saturday before it was to take place. News traveled fast on the canal.

Albany, Troy, Schenectady, Little Falls, Utica, Rome, Syracuse, Lyons, Rochester, Lockport, Buffalo was the route from east to west, and now Jim was halfway back again, to stop at Athens to unload and reload, and thank God that Earl Fielding was among the shippers who did not run his boats on Sundays and holidays.

The controversy over Sunday operation was a violent one, with both sides putting forward arguments that were sensible and to be considered by any thinking man. The Seventh Day Adventists and other Sabbatarians were for Sunday operation, while others argued that the canallers would only use Sundays to get drunk and gamble their money away; that canal traffic would back up for miles and cause three-day jams at the locks if the Erie were to be shut down on Sundays. Some lines actually advertised for customers who were against the sin of traveling on a Sunday.

Earl Fielding's reasons for not operating his line on Sunday had nothing to do with morals or religion, but sprang from having come up from the ranks himself. He knew how much a day off meant to the canallers. If they chose to gamble away their wages or spend them on strong drink or women during their day off, that was their affair. He wasn't their conscience, he was only their employer, and he had a strong conviction that every man had the right to decide things for himself.

Chestnut Grove gave the appearance of a bustling beehive as Jim approached it that Fourth of July afternoon. He had only one of his crew in tow, having received word by the grapevine that he would be welcome, although the other canallers would not. Both he and Ezekiel Oldham, who answered only to Ike, were scrubbed until their faces were raw, their clothes pressed and immaculate. They were filled with anticipation that made them feel as if their skins might burst. Jim was old enough to know better, but Ike had a good deal of excuse, being only fifteen.

One of the ship's two drivers, Ike had started a year ago. A refugee from his stepfather's farm, Ike was hungry, dirty, exhausted, and filled with a determination to die rather than go back. The only thing Ike had carried with him except the clothes on his back was a notice he'd torn from a newspaper, to the effect that his stepfather offered one penny and a bucket of ashes for his return, the usual value set on runaways whose return was not wanted.

Falling in with Jim had been the turning point of Ike's life, even though the life of young drivers on the canal was hard. Six hours of walking, driving the teams, and six hours of riding, in all sorts of weather. The canalboats had to keep moving, which meant the drivers had to keep walking to keep the horses moving.

But the night that Jim had stumbled over Ike, huddled in a miserable heap against the side of a saloon where Jim had gone to drag one of his crew back to the *Undine,* had been like admission through the Pearly Gates. Hardly more than a sack of bones, Ike had been slung over Jim's shoulder and carried to his boat; there, Jim had filled him with more and better food than the boy had ever known, had stripped his filthy rags from him, scrubbed him down, dressed him in whole clothing, and given him a job.

If Ike was sick, which almost never happened, he didn't have to work, he could lay in his bunk until he felt better. If the other crew members, or the older boy who was the alternate driver, thought to hassle or torment him, they answered to Jim. In return, Ike looked on the *Undine*'s captain as next only to God, and gave him his worshipful and undivided loyalty. Still skinny, because no amount of food would fill out that young frame until he was older, his freckled face topped by hair the color of a carrot, Ike would have laid down his life for Jim Yarnell without thinking twice.

"Ain't this something!" Ike crowed. "A picnic, an honest-to-goodness picnic! I never got to go to a picnic. I never even got to go to a camp meeting, I always had to stay home to look after the stock. You think they'll mind that you brought me?"

"I can't see why. You aren't old enough to cause any problems with the young ladies." Jim slapped his back, chuckling. "All you have to do is stuff your face and join in the fun and games."

As they entered the fringes of the crowd, Jim caught sight of a head of bright auburn that he'd recognize on a moonless night in the rain. Miss Roxanne Fielding, setting plates and cutlery on one of the long plank tables. Jim shook his head as he took in the tables. Tableclothes, would you believe it? Miss Geneva and Miss Roxanne must have stripped their linen closets bare to furnish all those tablecloths! And flowers, too. The rosebushes in their gardens must look mighty bare about now. When these young ladies put on a picnic, they did it right. Real silverware, and real chinaware, and tablecloths and roses—no wonder the mechanics' eyes were all but popping right out of their heads!

"The lady with the red hair is Miss Roxanne Fielding," Jim told Ike. "Come along and I'll introduce you." He felt easy about presenting his driver to Roxanne, because there wasn't a trace of snobbery in her, and from all he'd heard, she'd insisted on trying her hand at driving her father's canalboat horses when she was knee-high to a grasshopper.

"Gosh! She's beautiful!" Ike's voice held a trace of awe. "I don't reckon I ever saw any lady as beautiful as she is, before." And then Ike saw a girl come up beside Roxanne and stand there talking to her, and his breath caught in his throat and gurgled there. Maybe she wasn't as downright beautiful as Miss Fielding—she was a sight less colorful, for sure—but if Ike hadn't known it was impossible, he'd have thought that an angel had come down from heaven to lend her blessing to this gathering.

"Who's that one?" he managed to get out, after he'd stopped gurgling.

"That's Miss Burton, Miss Geneva Burton. She's the one whose idea this all was." Jim put his hand under Ike's elbow and strode along until they came to the table where the two young ladies were laughing at something even as they dealt out plates and glasses and knives and forks and believe it or not, linen table napkins!

"Captain Yarnell!" Geneva was the first to see them. She held out her hand, her smile of welcome so genuine that Ike's heart melted into a puddle of pure adoration. "I'm so glad you could make it. I've been keeping my eye out for you."

Her astonishingly beautiful eyes, like molten silver, rested on Ike, and her smile deepened. Ike had the feeling that he was suffocating, but if this was what it was like to die of suffocation then he was ready to give up his soul to his Maker.

"Miss Burton, this is Ezekiel Oldham, my driver."

Geneva's hand felt as soft as a little white dove in Ike's

rough and callused paw. "I'm glad that you could come, too, Ezekiel."

Ezekiel, Ezekiel, who in thunder was Ezekiel? Covered with confusion, Ike finally remembered that that was his own name. "Pleased to meet-cha, ma'am." His hand felt naked and forlorn when Geneva released it, and he thrust it into his pocket to try to retain some of the warmth and softness of hers.

"Bobo and Doctor Galen and my father are around somewhere, they'll be glad to see that you're here," Geneva said. Now Ike was convinced that she was an angel, because only an angel could have a voice like that, as soft and sweet as a brook murmuring in the forest.

"Hello, young Ike." The auburn-haired beauty's voice was nowhere near as musical as Geneva Burton's, but its deep warmth made Ike feel warm and good. It was a friendly voice, a voice that said that its owner liked people. Roxanne too took his hand. "I'm glad the captain brought you. Jim, have you any idea where that old reprobate, my father, is? I expected him home last night but he never showed up."

Jim had a hard time keeping his face expressionless. He knew perfectly well where Earl Fielding was, but it wasn't something he could pass on to a young lady, especially Earl's daughter. Miss Fielding wouldn't even know about the establishment in Buffalo, an establishment that her father had financed, that housed Miss Jewel Southern and her bevy of young ladies.

If Earl was where Jim had seen him last, he was in Jewel's company and in no hurry to leave it. Soft in the head over Miss Southern, Earl was. He'd marry her in a minute, not giving a puff of wind about her reputation, if it wasn't for his daughter on whom he could hardly inflict Jewel Southern as a stepmother.

Roxanne laughed. "All right, Jim, I'll let you off the hook. Give my regards to Jewel when you see her."

Jim almost choked. How in thunder had Miss Roxanne found out about Jewel? But he couldn't very well ask her, not with Geneva Burton standing right beside her. And darned if Roxanne wasn't laughing at him, enjoying his discomfiture!

"Geneva, there's Mary MacDonald, as pretty as a picture," Roxanne continued.

Jim's breath stilled in his throat. He'd come to this picnic just to see her, and he'd have sworn that he'd remembered exactly what she looked like, but she was even prettier than he'd remembered. Her face was all pink with excitement and her eyes were shining, and her soft brown hair looked like silk. Just seeing her made him want to touch her, and if he touched her he'd set himself on fire. If he didn't get a chance to touch her, he'd burn anyway.

"Mary, over here!" Geneva called. "Would you like to help Roxanne finish setting the tables? I have half a dozen other things to check on."

Mary's face had lit up when she'd seen Geneva, but now her eyes fell on Jim and her color faded. If it wouldn't have been downright rude, she'd have refused to join the little group. As it was, she had no choice but to go over and say that she'd be pleased to help. Every time she saw the canaller, she was filled with more confusion than she'd been the last time. The way he looked at her disturbed her. It was as if he thought she was pretty, and he'd like to get to know her better.

Now it was even worse, because the captain decided to help her with the table setting when that beautiful Miss Roxanne Fielding went dashing off to speak to somebody. She jumped as if she'd been burned when his hand brushed against hers.

"Sorry," Jim said, his hand jerking back. "I didn't jab you, did I? Here, let me see." Before Mary had a chance to snatch her hand away he had it in his, examining it.

"I'm all right. You didn't jab me." Mary pulled her hand away, and Jim released it with reluctance. This was getting worse and worse. Desperately, she sought for a means of escape.

To her dismay, Jim sensed her discomfiture. "Miss MacDonald, you aren't afraid of me, are you? I don't eat little girls, especially when they're as pretty as you are. You remind me of my sister, and I'd be mighty displeasured if anyone were to frighten her."

Mary's face flushed scarlet. "Of course you don't scare me! Why should you? You've been nice to me. It's just that Mrs. Simms won't like it if she catches us talking to each other. We aren't supposed to have anything to do with canallers."

Appalled at what she'd said, she flushed even redder, and felt like either bursting into tears or taking to her heels and running, or both. She felt dizzy with relief when Galen Forbes spotted them and came over to speak to them. Now she wasn't alone with the captain any more. Besides, she'd wanted to see Galen more than she wanted anything else in the world.

"Miss MacDonald. Jim. What do you think of Miss Burton's brainstorm? From the looks of it, she and her friends are really going to feed us! I never saw so much fried chicken in my life. Ike, how are you doing?"

"Fine, sir. Miss Burton is a fine lady, isn't she?"

"A fine lady indeed." Galen hoped that none of them detected the dryness of his voice. Lady Bountiful! "Miss MacDonald, if you've finished with the tables, why don't the four of us walk down to the brook, where it's cooler?"

Galen had no desire to walk to the brook, but he intended to find some excuse to take Ike in tow and leave Mary and Jim together, to give Jim the chance he was dying for. It would be his good deed for the day.

Mary's ecstatic pleasure at the chance to spend a few minutes with Dr. Forbes was diluted by her displeasure that the captain would be with them. Oh well, half a loaf, as her mother was fond of saying. Besides, she had the extreme gratification of seeing Agnes's eyes widen and her face take on an expression of sour jealousy as the four of them walked past her, Mary with a handsome man on either side of her and Ike bringing up the rear.

Her gratification vanished after a few minutes, because they'd hardly reached the brook when Galen snapped his fingers and exclaimed, "I almost forgot! I promised Bobo Burton that I'd find him. Ike, why don't you come along? Bobo and his sister wanted to consult me about something, and I might as well get it over with before we eat."

It had been on the tip of Ike's tongue to refuse to leave the captain until the doctor had mentioned Miss Burton. At this, he fell in step with Galen without a backward glance.

Galen winked at him as soon as they'd left the others. "I'm afraid I told a lie," he confided in the boy. "I didn't think that the captain appreciated our company, now that he has a chance to be alone with Mary. You don't mind, do you?"

"We aren't going to see Miss Burton?"

Galen looked at Ike's crestfallen face with instant comprehension. "I wouldn't be surprised if we could find her. And I have a very good idea that she'd appreciate an offer of help. She probably needs a strong young man like you to fetch and carry."

If Geneva was surprised when Galen appeared by her side with the young driver in tow, offering the lad's services, she was tactful enough not to let it show. "I certainly can use some help! Some of these dishes are heavy, and that brother of mine and his fine friends have made themselves scarce so that I can't draft them. Roxanne, we have two volunteers!"

One volunteer, she revised, as Galen murmured an apology that she couldn't quite make out, and left them. Drat the man, what ailed him? Anybody would think that she was contagious, the way he avoided her! Sometimes she was certain that he was interested in her, but then he'd go shying away like a skittish horse that's seen a scarecrow standing in the middle of the road.

And just wait till she got her hands on Bobo! He and those friends of his were probably trying to break as many hearts as they could manage, all in the mistaken belief that they were giving the poor little mechanics a treat by being attentive to them. It had probably been a mistake to let Bobo and those Corinthian friends of his anywhere near this picnic. Next time, she'd know better!

For the next hour Ike was in a daze of happiness as he carried heavy platters and hampers piled high from the buggies that had brought them, to the picnic tables. He didn't consider it work. Just to be near his newfound idol was enough. When Geneva smiled and thanked him, his face turned so red that his freckles disappeared. It was hard to tell where his face left off and his flaming hair began.

He flushed even hotter when an older woman approached Geneva, her plain but kind face expressing interest when Geneva introduced them. "Mother, this is Ezekiel Oldham. He's been kind enough to do most of the heavy work for us, seeing that that worthless son of yours has disappeared. Ike, this is my mother, Mrs. Burton."

Ike bobbed his head. He'd have given five years of his life if his own mother, and his stepfather, could see him, be-

-ing introduced to Mrs. Marvin Burton herself, just as if he was an equal!

"That was nice of you, Ezekiel. We'll be sure to see that you have plenty to eat, in compensation. Are you here with someone?"

"Captain Yarnell, ma'am. He's my captain. Of the *Undine*."

Ike held his breath, wondering if the kindly interest in Mrs. Burton's face would change to distaste, but Geneva's mother smiled again, and nodded.

"A canalboat. The canal, and the canalboats, are an important part of the welfare of this country. Or at least Cyril and Geneva and my husband tell me so." Mrs. Burton looked a trifle confused, but willing to accept their word for it. "It must be an interesting life, I'm sure. Geneva, I'll be sitting at the head table with Mr. and Mrs. Livingston and the Reverend Tucker. The mechanics do seem to be enjoying themselves! I believe that it was a very good idea after all for you to plan this picnic for them."

She turned away a little vaguely, and Ike felt an instant liking for her. Why, she wasn't uppity at all, for all she was Lawyer Burton's wife, and, next to Mrs. Livingston, the Queen of Athens's society! Even above Mrs. Livingston, if all the gossip he picked up along the towpath was true. If he knew how to write, he'd of written to his mother just to tell her about how wonderful his life was with the captain, and about today, and how he'd got to rub elbows with the society people!

Dismissed from his duties, he looked around for the doctor, but Galen was nowhere to be seen. He decided that he'd better get back to the brook and find the captain.

Still in a daze, he nearly missed noticing the groups of mill workers. They were drifting back and forth seemingly aimlessly, but Ike was an observant boy. He had to be to survive on the towpath, where he had to keep his eyes open for anything unusual that might cause trouble. Something snapped alert in him when he noticed that as one or two drifted off, one or two more converged on the same spot. They were off to one side, but what caught Ike's interest was that one man, a small, nondescript fellow who might have been a laborer himself, never moved. More than that, he was the one who was doing all the talking. The others were listening to him as if what he had to say was almighty important.

His curiosity whetted, Ike drifted nearer, but found that he had to worm his way right onto the edge of the ever-shifting group before he could hear what the man was saying. He moved so quietly and kept himself so small that nobody noticed him.

"You can do it, all it takes is sticking together. You aren't slaves. No man in the world has a right to work you like slaves and pay you starvation wages, hardly enough to keep your souls in your bodies. And how many don't manage to keep their souls in their bodies, just think about that! If you get sick because you're overworked, you get fired, and where's the money to come from to pay a doctor to cure you? Do you have savings, anything put aside, on your salaries?"

The man hardly paused to take breath, as if he had to say what he had to say quickly. "They've done it in other places, I tell you! They've had turnouts, and they've refused to go back till their demands were met! All it takes is courage, and sticking together. You're human beings, just like the owners, curse their black souls. You're just as human as they are and you have just as much right to a decent living for the work you do, and a few hours to call your own; instead of working fourteen or sixteen hours a day and falling into your beds at night just to get up next morning and do it all over again!"

A piece of paper changed hands, passed from one mechanic to the other. Ike's sharp eyes saw a young mechanic stuff another piece of paper just like it down the inside of her dress.

"Pass them around, see that everybody gets a chance to read them! And if you can't read, God bless you, why no more could I till I was older than you. Somebody'll have the kindness of heart to read them to you. You'll see that I'm right. You'll see that it can be done, as sure as my name's Philo O'Brian!"

Ike backed away, moving as carefully as he had when he'd moved into place so that he could find out what was going on. Jumping Jehosephat, it was the organizer! If he was caught here, all hell would break loose! He'd be thrown in jail, and every mill mechanic who'd listened to him would lose her job. At the same time, Ike couldn't help having the most profound admiration for the nerve of the man, daring to infiltrate the picnic grounds right under Herndon Livingston's nose!

As soon as he was far enough away not to attract attention, Ike broke into a trot. The captain had better be where he'd left him, because he had to tell him about this. He breathed a sigh of relief when he saw Jim, with Mary Mac-Donald still with him, by the brook, sitting under the shade of a tree. Mary's hands were filled with wild daisies, and someone else had joined them. He wasn't sure until he got closer, and then he came to a stop. It was Miss Burton's brother, one of the ones who'd throw the organizer in jail as fast as sneeze.

Jim had seen Ike approaching on the double, and he was puzzled when the boy came to such an abrupt halt. Knowing Ike as he did, he knew that something was bothering the boy.

"What is it, Ike?"

"Nothing." Ike rubbed the toe of his shoe in the grass. His eyes went from Jim to Bobo, and Jim got the message.

"Excuse me. I have to find out what's on Ike's mind." He walked over and took Ike's arm and pulled him a little ways away. "All right, what is it? You're fair to bursting, so spill it out."

"The organizer's here. I saw him and I heard him, talking to the mechanics."

"Good Lord!" Jim was so startled that he spoke more loudly than he'd intended, and Bobo came loping over.

"Trouble, Jim?"

"There might be. Ike saw the organizer who's been expected, right here talking to the mechanics."

Bobo's usually carefree expression changed, and he looked dead serious. "That isn't good. How the devil did he dare, with Herndon Livingston here? We'd better get back there and see what's going on, and see if there's anything we can do about it." Remembering Mary, he went back and took her arm. "Come on, we have to return you to your friends, the captain and I have some business to attend to."

Mary felt nothing but relief at the chance of escape, but it was an uncomfortable relief because she had to half run to keep up with the two men as Ike led them back to where he'd seen the organizer.

"There!" Ike said, and he pointed.

"And there!" Jim's voice was grim. "Isn't that Carl Jakes, sidling away?"

"It certainly is! And he'll be heading right for Herndon, and our organizer'll find himself in jail before he knows what hit him." Bobo's face lighted up. This promised excitement where there'd been nothing but boredom. His eyes searched the crowd until they came to rest on Bob Maxwell and Emery Ledbetter, his Corinthian friends whom he'd drafted to help set up the tables and to keep a general eye out for any attempted invasion of the picnic grounds by undesirable elements.

"I'm going to create a diversion. You grab our foolhardy man there and take my gig and get him out of here!" A light of pure joy in his eyes, Bobo sprinted full-steam ahead to collide head-on with Bob Maxwell, sending him reeling. Bob's mouth, opened to protest, snapped shut again at Bobo's terse orders. "Diversion! We're going to keep Herndon Livingston and Carl Jakes from getting past us."

Diversion! The word was a call to battle stations to all of the Corinthians, who had used these tactics on more than one occasion to get themselves out of scrapes or to direct unwelcome attention elsewhere. Bob immediately shoved Emery, who took off running directly into the path taken by Herndon Livingston and a grim-faced Carl Jakes, with Marvin Burton, looking worried, following close on their heels.

"Oops, sorry!" Emery lost his balance, or so it seemed, and made a grab for Herndon to regain it, while Bob, only a stride behind him, pretended to lunge for him in some game they were playing and careened into Jakes. A pantomime of duck-and-weave followed, with the Corinthians ostensibly attempting to get out of the way of the two determined men while managing to block them instead. "Sorry, Mr. Livingston, there you go. . . ."

There he went, as Bobo's foot somehow got in the way of Herndon's leg while he pretended to come to the mill owner's rescue. Herndon went down. Carl Jakes stooped to help him up, both of their faces flaming with rage, but somehow when Bob and Emery made to assist them, they all ended up in a tangle, their arms and legs inexplicably entwined so that it took valuable time to get themselves disentangled. Marvin Burton, with no idea of what his son was up to, nevertheless knew Bobo well enough to decide to help matters along by grasping Herndon's hand, hauling him free, and then releasing it again an instant before Herndon had his balance, so that he went down again. This was more fun than he'd had in years.

Paying no attention to the contretemps behind them that was drawing a clapping and cheering crowd of spectators, Jim grabbed one of the organizer's arms while Ike grabbed the other. They hustled him away, overriding his protests.

"Don't ask questions, just move!" Jim pulled the man faster, only holding back from a run because it would have attracted attention even with the madhouse Bobo and his friends were creating.

They reached the hitching grounds, and Jim literally boosted the rescued man off his feet and hurled him into Bobo's gig, scrambling up beside him while Ike untied the reins from the hitching rail. Once Cato got his feet moving, nothing in Athens could catch up with him, seeing that Wyatt hadn't come to the picnic because of Geneva.

The campgrounds well behind them, Jim turned his head toward his passenger. "You were about to be taken into custody. I'll drop you off wherever you say, but you'd better given Athens a wide berth for a while. Mr. Livingston's man Carl Jakes got a good look at you and he'll recognize you if he sees you again. You'd better believe that they'll be watching for you."

"Thanks." The man thrust out his hand, a hard, callused hand that told its own story of a lifetime of hard manual work. "Philo O'Brian, and I appreciate your help. Was all that fuss back there just to get me away?"

"It was, and you can thank Bobo Burton for that." Jim's eyes were twinkling. "And his young Corinthian friends."

Philo whistled. "Corinthians! I'd have thought they'd be the first to try to lay hands on me!"

"Not Bobo Burton. He's all right, and so is his father, the lawyer. Do you think you got through to any of the mechanics? Will they make an attempt to stand together to get better working conditions and wages?"

"They have to, unless they want to go on the way they are for as long as they live."

"It's a pretty dangerous thing you're doing. The cottonocracy is all out against men like you. You must spend most of your time either running or hiding, or behind jailhouse bars."

Philo O'Brian grinned, and the face that had seemed so nondescript leapt into life, sparked by the light of battle in his eyes. Jim got the distinct impression that the hardships, the jail sentences, meant nothing to the man, compared to the joy of pitting himself against the all-powerful cotton-ocracy.

"It's worth it. One of these days we'll show those black-hearted bastards that we aren't their slaves! This ain't Ireland, by Gawd, where a man has to knuckle under or starve, and starve even if he does knuckle under! We've stood together in other mills, and got our way, and we'll do it here too, in spite of Herndon Livingston! The mechanics listened to me today, they listened good. It won't take much more to set the spark that'll light a fire under Herndon Livingston that he won't forget in a hurry!"

Thinking of Mary, Jim wished O'Brian luck. God knew that she, and all the others like her, were in desperate need of better wages and shorter hours. But he was afraid that there'd be trouble, bad trouble, before what O'Brian was working for came to pass. He wished that there were some way that he could keep Mary safely out of it.

He took the organizer to the *Undine* and fed him. The way that Philo O'Brian wolfed the cold meat and bread and cheese told him that it was the first decent meal he'd had for a long time. Then he bedded him down among the cargo. "Stay put. I don't know if Mr. Livingston will institute a search of the whole town, but I wouldn't put it past him."

"I'll stay put, never fear. I can use the rest. I walked all last night to get here." Philo grinned at him, the corners of his mouth expressing his glee at this stroke of unlooked-for luck.

Jim drove back to Chestnut Grove and hitched Cato in the same place he'd taken him, but he was disappointed in his hope of seeing Mary alone again. She'd insinuated herself among the girls from her dormitory, and she steadfastly refused to notice him. Face it, Jim told himself desolately, she doesn't like you. She's had it pounded into her too hard and too long that canallers are poison. It would be a long time, if ever, before he'd be able to beat his way through her defenses. If he wasn't an upright man who remembered what his mother had taught him, he'd be tempted to curse.

Then fate, in the person of Geneva Burton, came to his rescue. He felt a touch on his arm and looked around to see Geneva motioning him toward one of the tables.

"The excitement seems to be over, and we're going to

eat. Bobo and Roxanne are saving us places. Go and sit down and I'll see if I can persuade Mary to join us.''

There was no way that Mary knew of to refuse Miss Burton's invitation. The other mechanics looked on with astonishment as she walked with Miss Burton herself to a table where important people were sitting. Agnes Barlowe's face showed a good deal of malice, intensified because Mary's friends, Nancy Steele and Dorothy Monroe, were so happy at Mary's being singled out for such an honor.

To her intense discomfiture, Mary found herself seated between the captain and Galen Forbes. Then her eyes sparked into laughter as the thought struck her that she was, as it were, halfway between heaven and hell. As there was no immediate way to move nearer to heaven or further from hell, she might as well settle down and enjoy herself. It was probably the only time in her life that she'd find herself in such exalted company. It was almost as if every word that Carl Jakes had told her, when he'd recruited her, was true, that life as a mill mechanic in Athens was the next thing to Paradise.

What a crazy world this is, Geneva thought. Her observing eyes noted the unmistakable fact that Mary MacDonald was in love with Galen Forbes, and the equally unmistakable fact that Jim Yarnell was in love with Mary. As for herself, she was still intrigued by Galen. It must be a wonderful thing to be so dedicated to a profession, to a cause. The fact that there was almost no monetary advantage in it for the doctor only made it the more intriguing. Maybe that was why she was so taken with Galen, and why she'd turned Wyatt Livingston down even when she knew that she had been a fool to do it.

What a tangled web this was, Geneva thought. But tangled or not, one thing was certain, it wasn't boring. Meeting Galen's cold glance, her own was amused as she turned her attention to Bob Maxwell, who had scrambled to obtain the place beside her. She could hardly wait to see how it would all come out.

9

It was a glorious September day. The sky, with only a few tufts of white clouds for contrast, was that wonderful blue that only happens in the autumn. The air was cool but not chilly, the kind of weather that makes most people glad that they're alive. Even Aunt Vanessa's rather stuffy parlor benefited from the season.

But the beauty of the day was lost on Addie, who sat with her hands lying limply in her lap, staring at nothing. Aunt Vanessa's suggestion that a walk in the sunshine would benefit her had fallen on deaf ears. The dresser runner the girl was embroidering lay in its workbasket. Vanessa Rutherford, her pale, thin face filled with concern, was at a loss to know what to do with the girl.

It was really too bad of Herndon to ship Adelaide to Syracuse and demand that his sister withhold her mail from her. Vanessa wasn't cut out for intrigue; she wanted only to be left in the peace and quiet of her widowhood, without having to cope with a girl who'd barely passed her seventeenth birthday. That event, falling on the second day of September, had been commemorated by the arrival of lavish gifts from Lillian and Wyatt, a discreet locket from her father, and a letter from Geneva expressing the hope that she'd return home soon. Another letter from Roxanne suggested she stay in Syracuse because Athens was boring. Aunt Vanessa had given her a hand-knitted muffler, in case the weather turned cold before she went home. Seventeen, old enough to marry, no matter what her father thought!

Vanessa jumped, her nerves ragged, as Addie's voice

startled her after a full half hour of silence. "Aunt Vanessa? Are you sure there was no letter for me?"

"I'm sorry, Adelaide. I am sure. You know that there was no mail for you at all, except the letter from your mother three days ago."

Lillian Livingston never failed to write to her daughter at least twice a week, but her letters were unsatisfactory. They consisted of general gossip, household matters, and complaints of headaches. She never mentioned Matthew at all, probably because she thought it would only make Addie feel worse. Geneva hadn't mentioned him either, or Roxanne. Something was wrong, she knew it.

Six weeks! It had been six weeks now, with no letter from Matthew. She'd written to him every week. She'd have written to him every day except that Aunt Vanessa insisted that it would be highly improper, especially as Matthew's letters had dwindled down to none at all. There had been two letters, a week apart, after she had arrived at Aunt Vanessa's, and then a week with no letter, and one after that, and then none at all.

Addie had no way of knowing, and in her innocence would never have dreamed, that her aunt's hired girl, who picked up the mail, withheld all letters addressed to her and gave them to her mistress, in the kitchen, when Addie wasn't around. Any letters from Lillian Livingston or Geneva or Roxanne were given back to the woman to be handed over in Addie's sight the next time the mail was picked up. The hired woman saw nothing amiss with the arrangement. Young ladies of such a tender age had to be protected from undesirable missives from gentlemen, and it was done on this particular young lady's father's orders. By the same token, Addie's letters to Matthew had dwindled at the same rate, the hired girl not posting them as Addie thought she did, but giving them over to her mistress instead.

Now Addie jumped to her feet, her hands twisted in front of her. "Something's happened to him. He's sick, and nobody's told me because they don't want to worry me. It has to be that. Aunt Vanessa, I have to go home. I'm going to pack right now."

Vanessa was dismayed. "Adelaide, I appreciate your concern, but I assure you that if your fiancé were ill, your father would have apprised me of the fact even if he wanted to spare you. And it is out of the question for you to return home. I cannot possibly leave, with so little warning, and you cannot travel without a chaperone.''

"Tomorrow, then, or the next day at the latest!" Addie began to pace the floor, her distress almost canceling out Vanessa's wince for the damage that such pacing might do to the carpet. "Please, Aunt Vanessa, you must see that I have to go home!"

"The best I can do is to write to your father and ask his permission. I'm afraid that you will have to be patient until we receive his reply. If there is need for you to return, he will no doubt come to escort you himself, or send Wyatt to do so.''

At that moment, Vanessa hated her brother. The lies she'd had to tell, during these weeks, were enough to prohibit her from passing through the gates of heaven. If it weren't for her absolute financial dependence on Herndon, who made up the difference between what her husband had left her and what it took to subsist, she'd take the child back herself, and tell Herndon that she'd have no more to do with the matter.

Think of the devil! The coincidence was enough to make Vanessa's blood run cold as a hired hack pulled up in front of her house and Herndon himself disembarked, carrying a valise. Herndon here, entirely without advance notice!

"Father!" The cry was torn from Addie as she tripped over her skirts in her rush to open the door. "Father, why didn't you let us know you were coming? Something's wrong, I know it, tell me!''

Herndon's face was grave as he kissed his daughter's cheek. Then he turned to his sister, who was staring at him in that annoying, almost popeyed way she had when she was upset and unable to cope. "Vanessa, would you leave Adelaide alone with me? I'm afraid that I do have grave news for her.''

Vanessa was only too glad to escape to the sanctuary of her bedroom. She only hoped that if Herndon had come to take Adelaide away, he'd relieve her of those letters that reproached her even from their hiding place in her bureau so that she could hardly sleep at night for knowing they were there. And poor dear Adelaide! Oughtn't she pray that the news that Herndon was bearing wasn't too dreadful?

In Vanessa's parlor, Addie stood facing her father, so still that she might have been a statue.

"Father, what is it? Matthew's ill, he's had an accident, he's dead!"

"No, no. Matthew is all right. But it distresses me to have to tell you that his affection for you has cooled. You are overly young to be a minister's wife, he needs someone more mature, more able to be a real helpmate to him in his duties. It isn't surprising that he's had second thoughts on the matter. I myself knew from the beginning that marriage between you and Matthew would be unsuitable."

"I don't believe you! Matthew never would have changed! Has he told you he has? Has he told you that he doesn't want me anymore?"

"Not in so many words." Being an intelligent man, Herndon knew that adhering as closely to the truth as possible was always the safest course to take. So he told the truth, not adding that he himself had all but put the words in Matthew's mouth. "He mentioned your extreme youth and expressed doubts about the wisdom of your union, when I saw him only two days ago." He gave no hint that he himself had directed the conversation, leading Matthew to concede that the engagement should be a long one, even though it had been obvious that nothing would please him more than to have the wedding as soon as the shortest decent period of courtship was over.

Addie stared at him, her shock making her go rigid. "No, no, it isn't true! He'd have told me himself—"

"Adelaide, I'm afraid that all this is beside the point. The real reason I came is to tell you that your mother isn't well."

For a moment Addie couldn't take it in. One shock on top of another was too much. "What's wrong with Mother?"

"She's ill, as I'm trying to tell you." Herndon pressed his hand against his forehead and then let it fall to his side, a gesture calculated to convey his despair. "Doctor Harding has told me, privately, that she will never be well again, that she will need the best and gentlest of care all the rest of her life, however long that might be. It depends a great deal on shielding her from any shock, on making sure that she lacks no comfort and ease of mind."

"But that can't be true! Mother has written to me, she would have told me if she was that ill!"

"She doesn't know the gravity of her condition,

Adelaide. Doctor Harding believes, and I agree with him, that to tell her would have a most deleterious effect. She must be protected, kept from knowing how ill she is. These things happen, and we must bear them with what fortitude we can.''

Herndon sat down, his face very grave. ''I'm going to need your help, all the help you can give me. Especially as I myself am facing the gravest of situations at the mill.''

Addie tried to swallow. She felt as though she were suffocating. ''I don't understand.'' The words came from between lips that were suddenly cracked and dry.

''I'm afraid that I'm faced with considerable financial difficulties,'' Herndon told her. ''In fact, with ruin. I've overextended, the mill needs to be expanded, and there's no way to finance it or even to meet my outstanding debts. There's a very good chance that we will lose everything, and then your mother. . . .'' This was safe ground. Adelaide knew less than nothing about financial affairs or matters pertaining to the mill. Like most females of her day, she had always been protected against the crassness of business life.

''No!'' It was as though Addie were trying to push her father's statements away from her with words. ''It can't be, you're a wealthy man, you're richer than anyone in Athens, except for Mr. Fielding and Mr. Burton. And they're your friends, they'll help you!''

''I'm afraid they won't. I've already tried them.''

''But there's Mr. Maynard! He's always let you have whatever you need, Father!'' Addie knew that much, from overhearing conversations between her father and Wyatt. ''Surely you can get a loan from him!''

This couldn't be happening. Outside Aunt Vanessa's parlor windows, the sun was still shining, a soft breeze was romping with fluffy white clouds. Matthew lost to her, Mother desperately ill, Father on the brink of ruin!

''Mr. Maynard considers it too poor a risk,'' Herndon told her. ''I wouldn't be able to pay him the interest he'd ask, and continue to operate. But he might, under certain conditions, let me have what I need at a lower rate of interest; under certain, extraordinary circumstances. But only under those circumstances.''

Addie found herself groping for the back of a chair to support herself. ''I don't understand.''

"Adelaide, you are aware that Mr. Maynard is a widower?"

"Of course I am! Everyone knows that!"

"And are you aware that he is desirous of marrying again? So desirous of it that he would let me have what I need, if it could be accomplished?"

"What has that to do with us?" Addie cried. "Father, you're confusing me, I don't understand what you're talking about!"

"I'm trying to tell you. I had hoped to put it to you more gently, but I can see that there is no other way. Mr. Maynard holds you in the deepest affection, Adelaide. In other words, if you would consent to become his wife, he would give me the loan that I must have to keep from going under, and your mother would be assured of the care and protection that it is essential for her to have."

Addie's knees seemed to have turned to jelly. Her legs wouldn't bear her weight. She wondered, almost dispassionately, if she were dying. Henry Maynard! But he was old, he was as old as her father, even older! It was impossible, it was ludicrous, she'd rather die! Oh, Matthew, Matthew!

Die. The word pounded against her forehead from the inside. It wasn't she who was going to die, it was Mother.

"You don't have to give me an answer now, Adelaide. I know that that would be expecting entirely too much of you. Why don't you go to your room and lie down? I'll have Vanessa bring a cold cloth for your head, some tea . . ."

Addie lay on her bed, the cold cloth pushed away onto the floor without her being aware of it. Her aunt's worried face hovered over her.

"Adelaide, dear, are you feeling better?"

"Yes, thank you, Aunt Vanessa." The words were listless, lifeless.

"Do you think that you could see your father for a few moments? He's very worried about you."

Returning to her parlor, where Herndon was waiting, Vanessa wondered how it would feel to kill someone. But she'd never know, because she lacked the courage to find out. She had always been a coward and she always would be. She still didn't know what this was all about, Herndon disdained to take her into his confidence; but he'd done something to that poor child upstairs and it had something to do with those letters. If she had any courage at all, she'd turn around and go up to her room and get them and give them to Adelaide.

Halfway down the stairs, Vanessa paused, and then she went the rest of the way down. Herndon would stop his financial aid to her, she would lose this house, she'd be impoverished, she might very well end up at the Poor Farm. Adelaide was Herndon's daughter, what transpired between them was none of her affair.

All the same, she didn't think that she'd be able to say her prayers that night, because if she hated herself so much how could she expect God to love her? If He ever had. Sometimes Vanessa thought, wickedly, that God had no love for any woman, else He wouldn't have created them weak and helpless in the hands of men.

Eyes closed against the hurting sunlight that filled her room, Addie lay and listened to her father's voice, only dimly aware of what he said to her.

"Mr. Maynard is willing, even eager, to come to Syracuse so that you may have the opportunity to become better acquainted with him. He'd stay at an inn, of course, but call on you every day and escort you wherever you might wish to go. If you decide to accept him, I can assure you that he will cherish you as you deserve to be cherished."

By now, Herndon believed every word he was saying. Compared to Matthew Ramsey, Henry Maynard was far more desirable a husband for his daughter. Solid, established, a match that Adelaide would thank him for in years to come. "A great many young ladies would be happy to have the opportunity of becoming Mrs. Henry Maynard, with all of the advantages that such a title entails. The very fact that he is considerably your elder will assure that he will treat you with the utmost care and consideration. I know that he holds you in the highest esteem."

Her father's voice droned on and on, and Addie closed her ears to it, floating in a sort of unreal never-never land. She wished that Wyatt were here, he'd tell her what to do. All of her life, she'd depended on Wyatt, who had never failed her. She wanted him now, she needed him desperately.

She opened her eyes and struggled to sit up. "I want to see Wyatt."

"I'm afraid that that isn't possible. Wyatt isn't available right now, or I'd have brought him with me to help lessen the shock of what I've had to tell you. He's traveling, visiting other mills throughout the New England states, with a view of learning more efficient management, something that will be essential for our own mill's continued operation.''

Of course Wyatt was away. Herndon had sent him, immediately before he'd set out for Syracuse, to keep him well out of the way. Lillian would believe anything he told her. But Wyatt was another matter entirely. His son was nobody's fool. He'd realize that something was going on when Herndon packed up and went off to Syracuse for several days, knowing his father detested Vanessa and avoided her company whenever possible.

Addie lay back against the pillows, her face waxen. Herndon felt a moment's qualm at her pallor, but then he told himself that she was only behaving like any foolish young woman with the vapors. She'd recover rapidly, once she'd made up her mind to face what must be faced. Relentlessly, he pressed on.

''May I tell Mr. Maynard that you will receive him, when he calls?''

There was no immediate response, so that for a little while he was afraid that she hadn't heard his question. He was just about to repeat it when Addie nodded. Herndon's mouth pressed together with satisfaction. Although Addie had no way of knowing it, Henry was already in Syracuse, too eager to commence his courtship to wait until Herndon should summon him. Tomorrow, after Addie had had a night to recover from her shock, he would call on her.

Herndon had laid his plans well, leaving nothing to chance. Lillian was forever ailing, subject to headaches and a nervous stomach, and ever since the onslaught of that certain time of life that all females must suffer through, she'd had periods of faintness and weakness. As these occurred every few days, he'd had only to wait until one of her spells before he'd told her that he had urgent business in Syracuse and would of course take the opportunity to visit Adelaide while he was there.

''You must take care of yourself, my dear. Feeling as you do, you can on no account accompany me. Later, when you're feeling better, we'll make a special trip so that you can see Adelaide.''

Henry Maynard presented himself in Vanessa's parlor

promptly at four o'clock the following afternoon, in time for tea. He was so solicitious of Addie's health, so eager to please her, that she couldn't help but feel contrition because her response to him was so listless. It didn't seem possible that he'd been in love with her ever since she'd grown up, but his adoration of her showed in every word.

She mustn't think about Matthew. Matthew was lost to her, she must try never to think of him or else she was sure she'd go mad. Even if he hadn't decided that he didn't want to marry her, she would have had to marry Mr. Maynard anyway, in order to save her father's mill, for her mother's sake.

Herndon stayed on, making sure that his sister let Henry's courtship progress without too much chaperonage. The four of them hired a carriage and made excursions to the countryside, to visit all of the local points of interest. At these times Herndon would take Vanessa aside, out of earshot and eyesight, so that Henry could use his privacy with Adelaide to his best advantage.

"My dear Miss Livingston, you cannot imagine how happy it makes me to be in your company! How I've longed for the day when I could be alone with you and tell you how I feel about you! There's nothing I wouldn't do for you, my dear. My only concern in life is to make you happy, to bring a smile to your sweet lips."

Addie's smile was pathetic, but she tried. If Mr. Maynard was to be the instrument that would save her mother, he deserved at least that much.

There were dinners out, where Henry ordered the most special delicacies to tempt her appetite. If they strolled in the evening, he carried her shawl and draped it lovingly around her shoulders at the least hint of a breeze. His kindness was overwhelming. Even in her shock and heartbreak Addie felt a twinge of guilt because she couldn't respond.

"That is only to be expected," her father told her when she expressed her feelings to him. "A good majority of marriages start out without love on either side. A woman learns to love her husband after marriage, Adelaide, or at least develops a fondness for him that makes her life agreeable and happy. It's the natural order of things. Henry will be so good to you that you won't be able to help loving him."

Maybe it was true. Her father was so much smarter than

she was! She prayed that it was true, that this ache that was consuming her would fade as time went by, so that she wouldn't wake up each morning wishing that she were dead. She couldn't die, she wasn't allowed to. She had to marry Mr. Maynard.

But to marry him so soon! Her father told her that the marriage must take place immediately or it would be too late. And Henry was anxious, wanting her to be his wife as soon as possible.

"But Father, how can we be married so soon? What of the engagement? The year of courtship?" Even in her benumbed state, being told that the marriage was to take place within a few days appalled her. She couldn't, there was no way she could do it!

"In this case, my dear, the sooner your marriage to Mr. Maynard is an accomplished fact, the better. It will save everyone concerned a good deal of embarrassment, as well as insuring that I'll receive Henry's loan in time for it to do me any good. Would you want Matthew to have to tell you that he's changed his mind? An immediate marriage will spare him that, and spare you the embarrassment of explaining to your friends that your brief affair of the heart was a mistake."

For Matthew to tell her! Heartbroken, devastated, Addie still had pride. She didn't care what her friends would think, but for Matthew to have to tell her, in so many words, that he didn't love her and didn't want to marry her was too much to bear.

"But how will we explain to Mother?"

"That depends largely on you, I'm afraid. You must realize how important it is that she thinks that marrying Mr. Maynard is your own idea, that you were the one who changed your mind about Matthew when you saw how much better a husband Henry would be. Tell her that you couldn't face life as a minister's wife, that the duties would have been onerous to you, that Henry is so charming and kind that you realize that he will make you much happier. She must never guess that you're doing it for her. The shock alone might carry her off."

Sick at heart, so heartsick that she couldn't think straight, Addie asked again for Wyatt.

"Wyatt will be here, won't he? I want him so much! I don't know how I can face it without him."

"I'm truly sorry, Adelaide. But I'm afraid that there is no way we can wait for Wyatt. I don't know where he is. I left his itinerary entirely up to him."

That much was true. "It's time you showed some real responsibility," he had said. "I'm trusting you with this mission, and I hope you are aware of how important it is. Choose which mills you want to visit first and stay as long as you like, all I ask is a comprehensive report when you return."

Wyatt had been delighted with the task his father had put on his shoulders. Improving the efficiency of the mill had long been a bone of contention between himself and his father. If he could bring back cold figures to prove that with better management, they could afford to cut hours and raise wages, it would be a major victory. And getting away from Athens for a period of several weeks was a godsend, now that he dreaded running into Geneva. It would be impossible to go on never seeing her at all for much longer, especially in a town so small. He needed time to absorb his hurt and learn to live with it. More than that, getting away from his father's displeasure and the whispers engendered by his peccadillo with Roxie made this trip all the more desirable. Give things time to cool off and settle down, he thought, as he set off in a happier frame of mind than he'd known since the night of his father's birthday party.

The days passed in a daze for Addie, each waking hour an agony, her nights restless and filled with nightmares when she finally fell asleep. Her father left to return to Athens to bring her mother to Syracuse for the wedding, but Henry stayed on, determined not to let his prize slip through his fingers. He was still unfailingly kind, unfailingly solicitous of her welfare. He presented her with a sapphire ring, to match her eyes, her betrothal ring. It was beautiful and costly, and the weight of it on her finger was a constant reminder of all she had lost. She thanked him for it, a smile on her lips, but her eyes were bleak and filled with pain.

Lillian Livingston was both amazed and filled with delight when her husband arrived at home only to tell her that now that she was feeling better, he'd take her to Syracuse immediately. She hadn't been feeling better, she missed Addie and Wyatt and she'd had another dizzy spell, but the prospect

145

of spending several days with Addie brought on a remarkable recovery.

Herndon told her nothing about the upcoming wedding. Although Lillian, as a proper wife, never questioned him as to his decisions, she was still a woman, and in this case he did not want her to have time to think about Addie's decision to marry Henry Maynard when she'd been so much in love with Matthew only a short time ago. If she had time to think about it, she'd poke and pry. He had confidence that he could fend off her objections to such a rushed marriage, but she'd be sure to question Addie much too closely if the whole affair wasn't carried off quickly.

Addie threw herself into her mother's arms the moment Lillian alighted from the carriage that brought them to Aunt Vanessa's house. She was trembling, although she was trying to control herself. It took all of her strength not to cry out her anguish, but Mama looked pale and tired and she remembered how ill she was.

"Mama, how are you feeling? Are you all right?"

"Why, I'm fine, dear. I did have a bad spell a few days ago, but I'm quite recovered. These dizzy spells are such an annoyance, but I'm fine now."

Her words, spoken with such innocence, sounded a death knell in Addie's heart. Dizzy spells, faintness—what Father had told her was true, her mother was very ill. Protected as she had been, told barely what she'd needed to know at the onset of her own passing from childhood into that mysterious and frightening change in her bodily functions when she'd been thirteen, Addie wasn't even aware that women go through another period of change in their middle age. Such things were never discussed before young ladies, any more than the more intimate details of the marriage relationship were discussed.

Lillian was startled half out of her wits when Mr. Henry Maynard appeared beside Vanessa, his round face unnaturally pink and beaming. "Why, Mr. Maynard, what are you doing here?" she blurted out.

"Let me do the explaining." Herndon's hand was relentless under Lillian's elbow as he propelled her into the house and up the stairs to the room that Vanessa had prepared for them. "Adelaide, you can talk with your mother later, after she has rested. The journey was fatiguing to her."

"But it was a delightful journey! I enjoyed every moment of the voyage on the canal!" Lillian tried to protest. But it was already too late. Her husband had closed the bedroom door behind them and was pushing her, gently but very firmly, into a chair.

"Married! Getting married tomorrow!" Lillian's mouth hung open a moment later, as her disbelieving eyes searched Herndon's face, searching desperately for some hint that this was some kind of a joke even though Herndon had never made a joke in all the years they had been married. "It's impossible, I cannot believe it! Adelaide is in love with Matthew Ramsey, and Mr. Maynard is an old man. She scarcely knows him! It's unheard of, and to rush into it like this! Herndon, you must be out of your mind!"

She eluded his restraining grasp and rushed to the door, calling for Addie, her voice shrill as it had never been before.

Her face pale but her eyes resolute, her hands clasped tightly in her lap to keep them from betraying their trembling, Addie answered her mother's questions. She reconfirmed her father's statements about how she had reconsidered marrying Matthew, that having had time away from him to think it over she'd realized that she could never be happy as a minister's wife. She got through the story, often rehearsed, of how Mr. Maynard had called on her as a neighborly duty when he'd come to Syracuse on business. She added how much she had liked him, as soon as she'd got to know him better.

"I fell quite in love with him, Mama," Addie said. "He's so kind, so thoughtful! And just think, I'll be living right across the street from you, I won't have to pick up and follow him to some other town, as I would have had to do with Matthew when he was assigned a church of his own! I couldn't have borne that. I love Henry and I'm going to marry him tomorrow."

Lillian's horrified arguments were smothered by Herndon's reasonableness in explaining how this quick marriage, amounting to an elopement, was better for everyone concerned, how having Addie and Henry return to Athens as man and wife, an accomplished fact, would save embarrassment all around.

Addie came through the ordeal of talking to her mother even better than he'd hoped for. Now, with Lillian white and trembling from the shock, was the time to dose her with the calming powders that Stephen Harding supplied her with.

He gave her a double dose of the powders. It wouldn't hurt her, she'd have to have much more than that for it to do her any real harm, but it would assure that she would experience a fuzziness in her mind and would sleep the night through.

"I mustn't!" Lillian tried to protest. "I have to talk to Adelaide, I have to explain things to her, she doesn't know—"

"Vanessa will perform that duty for you," Herndon told her, urging the potion on her. "You must rest now, my dear. Everything will be all right."

But it wasn't right. Nothing about this was right. And it was a mother's duty, not an aunt's, to tell her daughter what would be expected of her on her wedding night. Only Addie had already left the room, and Herndon was assisting her to remove her dress, and then the bed awaited her, and she was very tired, after all.

In the morning, her head ached, the pain was intolerable. Herndon dosed her again, more lightly this time because she had to get through the ceremony, but enough to keep her quiet. When it was all over with, he could tell her, truthfully, that she had made no further objections. "This is the happiest day of our daughter's life," he told her sternly. "You mustn't spoil it for her. Take your medicine, dear." And her head hurt her so that she took it, although she had an uncomfortable, nagging feeling that she shouldn't.

Addie was dressed in white. It was not a wedding dress, for this was not a formal wedding, but a marriage performed in Vanessa's front parlor, with only the family present. Aunt Vanessa had pinned late white summer roses in her hair, and she held a tiny bouquet of white roses and baby's breath. She looked at her mother. Lillian had a smile on her face but it was like a smile painted on a wax doll, without life, her eyes were vague. Not knowing that her father had dosed her mother, Addie's heart contracted, as she thought how very ill her mother looked. There could be no turning back. Her mother had to have the care and comforts that this marriage to Henry Maynard would provide her with.

The minister was looking at her, and so was Mr. Maynard. Had she done something wrong? She was supposed to say something. She remembered then. She had been to weddings, and an instant before her father had to prompt her, her lips parted and she whispered "I do."

There was a ring on her finger, a wide gold band. She looked at it as if she didn't know what it was. Henry kissed her cheek, his mouth hot and dry, an old man's mouth. Aunt Vanessa's lips were cold as she followed suit, and Addie felt her aunt trembling as she folded her in her arms. Poor Aunt Vanessa, all this had been too much for her. But at least Aunt Vanessa wasn't ill, as Mother was, and she'd recover once they were all gone and she had peace and quiet again.

Her mother kissed her last, her mouth hot and feverish, her hands clutching as though she didn't want to let her go. "Be happy, Adelaide," Lillian whispered, her eyes flooding with sudden tears.

"Mama . . ."

"Mothers always cry at their daughters' weddings," her father told her. "She'll be all right, Adelaide. Leave her to me, I'll take care of her."

And then she and Henry were in a carriage, and Henry was talking about all the things he was going to show her.

"We'll spend three days in Auburn. The Exchange Hotel there is a marvel. It has three hundred beds, can you imagine that? And it boasts a stationary bathtub, the only one in the country! Naturally you won't use it, my dear, it wouldn't be suitable, but I am certainly going to try it out."

Addie nodded, trying to look interested because he was so kind. Henry beamed, and rumbled on.

"We'll take the tour through the State Prison as well, and see the Theological Seminary, it's one of the most beautiful places you can imagine. And Owasco Lake is lovely, one of the loveliest of the Finger Lakes. It will be a pleasure to show it all to you, my dear, a real pleasure."

And then it was evening, the sky already streaked in sunset, and they had arrived at the Exchange Hotel. With dinner in the dining room, Henry urged her to drink the wine in the glass at her place, but she didn't want it.

"You're tired, my dear. And little wonder, you've had a long day. I think we will retire to our room, if you're sure you don't want your dessert or the wine." Henry himself had already finished his dessert, and three glasses of wine. Eating was the third greatest pleasure in his life, next only to making money, and what was in store for him tonight.

They went up a flight of carpeted stairs, and stopped in front of one of the many doors that led off the hallway. Henry opened the door and stood aside to let her enter. He entered after her, closed the door and locked it, his face flushed and beaming as he looked at his bride.

He put his arms around her, crushing her to him. His mouth was loose and wet as he crushed it against hers, and Addie shuddered with revulsion as he forced her lips open and thrust his tongue into her mouth.

She struggled, fighting against nausea. "Please—" She'd never imagined a kiss like that, that such a thing could be possible! It was horrible!

Henry's hands were rough as he ran them over her body, pressing and pinching at her breasts, probing at a place even more intimate. "Get your clothes off!" he told her. He was panting, his eyes were glittering like some excited animal's.

"But you must leave the room . . ."

"My dear Adelaide, you're my wife." His words made her turn cold. But then he laughed. "Very well, then. We must preserve your maidenly modesty, I suppose, according to custom. I'll give you five minutes."

Addie hurried, her fingers numb and trembling as she struggled with buttons and snaps. In her haste to get herself under the covers, she left her dress and underthings draped over a chair instead of hanging them away. Her nightgown was high-necked and modest, but she still pulled the sheet up under her chin as she lay there trembling, her stomach churning, dreading Henry's return and another of his revolting kisses.

The lamp was still lighted, and Henry didn't turn it out when he returned and began to shed his own clothing. Horrified, Addie closed her eyes. "Henry, the lamp," she whispered.

"I want it on, I want to see you." Naked, the skin of his arm and legs sagging, his stomach round and protruding and hairy, Henry yanked the sheet off and threw it onto the floor. Addie's eyes flew open at the unexpected gesture, and she gasped.

Aunt Vanessa had told her nothing. She'd thought that Lillian had instructed her daughter. Addie thought, as most girls of her age and social class thought, that marriage consisted of gentle kisses and fond caresses, of sleeping in the same bed hand in hand. She'd never seen a naked man in her life, not even a naked male baby. What she saw now made her eyes go wild with shock.

And then Henry was on her. He yanked her nightgown up around her neck as his hands glided all over her. Probing, hurting.

"Spread your legs," he commanded. He forced them apart, and Addie screamed as his searching fingers entered her. The scream was smothered as his slobbering mouth covered hers, cutting off the sound.

His hand captured one of hers, forced it downward. He removed his mouth from hers only long enough to command, "Take it! Don't let it go soft!"

Addie fought against it, sobbing. Her fingers cringed and flinched away. Infuriated, Henry shifted his position.

"All right then, we'll try another way!"

Helpless, every inch of her body and soul screaming with horror and agony, Addie was initiated into perversions that even her mother had never heard of nor dreamed existed. She knew that she had entered the gates of hell and that they were locked behind her.

10

Roxanne was out of breath from walking so fast when she mounted the steps to the Burtons' front porch and rapped sharply with the knocker. She could hardly contain her impatience while she waited for Nelly to answer the door. When the self-styled hired girl appeared she didn't wait to be invited inside, but brushed past her. "Where's Geneva?" she demanded.

"Up in her room. Is something the matter, Miss Roxy?" A privileged character by virtue of having worked for the Burtons for twenty years, Nelly assumed the right to call all of Geneva's friends by their first names or nicknames.

"We'll tell you later." Roxanne took the stairs as fast as she could, holding her skirts up out of the way so that she wouldn't trip. She burst into Geneva's room without ceremony.

"Geneva, you'd better sit down."

Geneva paused in her task of folding her freshly laundered lingerie, as surprised as Nelly had been at Roxanne's unceremonious entrance. "Roxanne, whatever is the matter?"

"Addie's married. She's married to Henry Maynard."

The chemise that Geneva had been folding dropped to the floor. She stared at Roxanne as if she didn't credit her ears. "You're out of your mind."

"Drat it, Geneva, this isn't a joke! They're married. My father got in just a few minutes ago, and he told me that Henry Maynard himself told him when he stopped in to put some money in the bank. They were married in Syracuse.

You know that Addie was staying with her aunt there because Herndon Livingston wanted to separate her from Matthew Ramsey for a while. And old Henry left town a few days ago, or hadn't you heard? And he and Addie were married right there in Syracuse and they just got back from their hymenal tour and if you can tell me why she married him, I'll be mightily grateful! She was so much in love with Matt Ramsey she was about to perish of it, and now she's married old Henry, and if there wasn't some hanky-panky about the whole thing my name isn't Roxanne Fielding!"

"Oh, my lord!" Geneva picked up the chemise she'd dropped and sat down on the bed, dumbfounded. "Addie and Henry Maynard? Roxie, that's awful!"

"Isn't it just!" Roxanne sat down beside her, her voice filled with indignation. "I tell you, it isn't natural! There's been funny business, and I could just cry, only it wouldn't do any good. Geneva, can you imagine having to go to bed with Henry Maynard? Everybody in Athens knows what he is. Well, maybe you don't. He wouldn't ever have tried to put his sweaty hands on you because you're too much of a lady, but he's tried to put his hands on me. And besides, I keep my ears open and I keep my eyes open too, especially whenever that old coot's with reaching distance of me!"

"Why, Addie's just a baby! She's barely seventeen! And she's as innocent as the day she was born. I'd swear she doesn't even know the facts of life!"

Roxanne's voice was flat. "We aren't supposed to know them either. But I'll lay you any bet you care to make that if Addie didn't know them before, she knows them now! And I'll bet everything I ever hope to have that Herndon Livingston is behind this whole thing! He's strapped for money to expand his mill. He came to my father wanting a loan, and was turned down. Father has no interest in investing in a mill when he can make so much more by speculating in property in Rochester and Buffalo. You know how they're booming. And I'll lay you odds that he went to your father, too, and was turned down. So he had to sell poor Addie to Henry to get the money he needed."

"Roxanne, even Herndon Livingston wouldn't do a thing like that! I don't believe it, not his own daughter!"

"You mean you don't want to believe it. Even I don't want to believe it, and I'm not as charitable toward people as

153

you are. But we all know that Herndon Livingston was dead set against Addie marrying Matt, because Matt hasn't any money and doesn't even have his own church. It all ties in, and he did it, I know he did. The whole thing stinks to high heaven. Why Lillian Livingston allowed it, I'll never know, I always thought better of her even if she is under Herndon's thumb and hardly dares call her soul her own. But I'll tell you one thing, Geneva. When Wyatt gets back and finds out about it, there's going to be the devil to pay!''

"Yes, I rather think there will," Geneva agreed. "Roxie, we'll have to do everything we can to help Addie. I have a feeling that she's going to need all the friends she has."

"I'd like to get Herndon Livingston on one of Father's boats, I'd push him overboard and jump in after him and hold him under till he drowned!" Roxanne raged. "And Henry with him, if I could manage it! Geneva, what are we going to do?"

Geneva shook her head, her face still pale with shock. "There's nothing we can do. If they're married, they're married. Oh, poor Addie!" She broke off, to add a few seconds later, "I wonder how Matthew Ramsey is going to take it? The last I heard, he was upset because Addie hadn't answered his last several letters. As much as I was against Addie marrying him, at least until she knew him better, I can't help feeling sorry for him."

"Save your pity for Addie," Roxanne advise her bluntly. "Matt isn't married to that old goat, Addie is. Matt can find someboy else but Addie's stuck with that horrible old lecher for all the rest of her life. Or his life," she added as an afterthought. "After all, he's old. I think I'll be attending church faithfully from now on, to pray that he won't live to be much older!"

"Roxanne!"

"Well, don't you feel the same way?"

"Yes, I suppose I do, but we can't pray for someone to die, for all that. Besides, if God were going to do something about Mr. Maynard he'd have done it before they were married, so they wouldn't ever have been married at all."

"Logic, logic!" Roxanne's fury showed no signs of abating. "If it would do any good to cry, I'll bawl my eyes out!"

"And so would I. But all we can do now is try to help Addie in any way we can."

"Do you think we should go over to see her?"

Geneva shook her head. "Not the first day she's back. We'll probably see her on Sunday, in church, and have a chance to speak to her and ask her when we can come."

"And I don't doubt that Jebbidiah Tucker will have the largest congregation he's ever enjoyed," Roxanne said. "Everybody in Athens will try to crowd in to get a look at the bride and groom."

Roxanne's prediction turned out to be true. On Sunday morning, the First Methodist Church of Athens was packed to its doors, people squeezed so tightly in the pews that they hardly had room to pick up their hymnals.

Roxanne had come with the Burtons, and she was pressed close against Geneva on one side and Bobo on the other. Beside Geneva, Cora Burton looked bewildered, and Marvin Burton's face was grim, but not as grim as Bobo's.

Bobo had known Addie Livingston all her life, and up until this summer, when he'd returned to Athens to take over his father's law practice, he'd regarded her as no more than his sister's beautiful little friend, almost as a younger sister. This summer, though, he'd been surprised at how much her loveliness disturbed him, and the depth of his disgust at her wasting herself on that dull stick, Matthew Ramsey, had shaken him. If only she hadn't had the lack of sense to fall in love with the young assistant minister, Bobo would have revised his feeling for her into waiting another year or two until she was old enough to marry, and then he'd have seen to it that no amount of competition would beat him out.

Actually, he hadn't thought that there was any great hurry. Addie was so young that it was inconceivable that her parents would allow her to marry anyone for at least two years, and that would have given him plenty of time to undermine Matthew Ramsey and claim her for himself, which he had had every intention of doing.

The news that Addie was married to Henry Maynard had hit him like a fist in the pit of his stomach, knocking the breath out of him and leaving him dazed. Not Matt Ramsey, which would have been bad enough, but Henry Maynard! The man wasn't only a lecher, he was old enough to be Addie's grandfather! Bobo's knuckles were white as he grasped his hymnal to have something to do with his hands which seemed to be possessed of a life of their own, wanting nothing more than to wrap themselves around Henry's throat and squeeze the life out of him.

How could Addie have done it, whatever had possessed her? But Bobo, like Roxanne, was sure he knew the answer to that. There'd been treachery and Herndon Livingston was behind it. His grip on the hymnal tightened as his hands seemed to feel Herndon's throat between them as well as Henry's.

In front of the congregation, Matthew Ramsey was already in his place, ready to take his small part in conducting the services. His face was pale and stony, and he gazed over the congregations' heads, but Bobo could see that he was having to exert an iron control to keep his face impassive. He must be suffering the torments of the damned, Bobo realized. Then his mouth curled at the corners as he thought, there goes his chance for rapid advancement in the church.

It was an uncharitable thought, especially in connection with a man of the cloth, but Bobo felt no contrition for thinking it. Still, if Addie had had to marry one or the other of them, Matthew would have been the better choice. Anybody would be better than Henry Maynard. In spite of the doors that still stood open because neither the Maynards nor the Livingstons had yet arrived, he felt as though he were suffocating.

Roxanne nudged him. "Bobo, you're mutilating the hymnal! Relax, there's nothing you can do about it."

"Relax yourself!" Bobo hissed back. "Your face is as red as a beet!"

Roxanne subsided. But darn it all, it wasn't right! She wished she could be as calm as Geneva, but she suspected that Geneva wasn't all that calm inside in spite of the habitual serenity of her face. Why didn't Addie get here, so she could see how she was bearing up under being married to Henry? And the Livingstons. It was unheard of for them to be late to services, to say nothing of Henry himself, who should have been at his place at the door to greet the parishioners as they entered. She supposed that he'd been excused from his duty because of his recent return from his wedding trip.

Roxanne wriggled, as much as she had room to wriggle, as a small commotion in the back of the church heralded the Livingstons' arrival. It was a pity that the Burtons' pew was in the front, she couldn't very well turn around and crane her neck to see Herndon and Lillian Livingston, although from the rustlings and whisperings she was sure that a great many of the other parishioners were doing just that.

Then they came into view, the Livingston pew being directly opposite the Burtons'. Roxanne moved her eyes as far to the side as she could to obtain a good view of them as Herndon stood aside for his wife to enter the pew first.

Lillian looked like death. Roxanne could think of no other word to describe it, and Geneva's sudden gasp told her that her friend thought so too. Lillian's face was pale, and the lines around her eyes, that had up until now been nearly indiscernible, showed in high relief. She moved slowly, as though her bones ached, and she sank down onto the bench and bowed her head as though in prayer.

Beside her, Herndon's mouth compressed. He'd had more trouble with Lillian, since they'd returned home, than he would have believed possible. Lillian had always bowed to his will, to his better judgment, without question.

Lillian had been in bed when Matthew Ramsey had called on them on the evening of their return, eager to find out at firsthand why he had not been receiving any letters from Addie, anxious because he was afraid that she might be ill. When Herndon had told him that Addie was married to Henry Maynard, Matthew's voice, already trained to carry, had echoed loudly enough to rouse Lillian from her bed and send her downstairs to see what on earth was the matter.

Lillian was still groggy from the aftereffects of the doses that Herndon had urged on her in Syracuse, but she wasn't so groggy that she wasn't able to grasp the fact that Matthew was furious. Matthew accused Herndon of having used undue influence on his daughter, of having persuaded her to marry Henry Maynard because of Maynard's money and social position. Despite Herndon's telling the young minister that Addie had assured her that marrying the banker was her own idea, Matthew's wild accusations nevertheless raised questions in Lillian's mind. After Matthew had finally left, white and still filled with fury, she had faced her husband.

"Herndon, just how much influence did you use on Addie? This whole affair was rushed through so quickly, I wasn't given time to think or to ask enough questions! If you persuaded Adelaide to marry Mr. Maynard against her will, I'll never forgive you!''

Herndon had managed to stem her doubts that evening, but his respite was short. When Addie returned from her honeymoon, Lillian had seen with her own eyes how unhappy her daughter was, how heartbroken she was. And although Addie, mindful of her father's admonitions that nothing must be allowed to upset her mother, didn't tell Lillian of the abuses that Henry inflicted on her, Lillian was convinced beyond the remotest doubt that her husband had engineered the whole thing. And Lillian had given Herndon no peace since that day. Her natural timidity and her respect for her husband had been pushed into the background as her anger over what had been done to her only daughter strengthened with every day that passed.

Now, on this Sunday morning, Lillian gave an outward appearance of being calm. If she was pale and if her hands trembled, everyone knew that her health wasn't good. Herndon's mouth remained motionless as he said, so low that only his wife could hear, ''Smile! People are looking at us.''

Lillian's head came up, and she smiled. In the pew opposite them, Roxanne's and Geneva's hearts went out to her, and Bobo cursed under his breath.

The congregation was growing restless. It was already five minutes after the time for the services to begin, and still the Reverend Jebbidiah Tucker delayed. It was understandable, as Henry Maynard was one of the four largest contributors to the church, and he'd be displeased if the service started without him. Where were the bride and groom?

People looked at each other, unspoken questions in their eyes. Grimly, Bobo hoped that Addie had brained Henry, as unlikely as it was that such a fragile and gentle girl would do such a thing. But if she had, he'd defend her, and she'd be acquitted to the cheers of the entire town of Athens!

There was no such luck, of course. They were here now, as necks craned again and restless rustlings subsided into absolute silence.

They came down the aisle, Henry's hand solicitously under Addie's elbow. Addie was wearing a periwinkle blue dress and a bonnet made of the same material, with pink satin roses framing the underside of the brim. The pink did its best to reflect on her pale cheeks, but it was a losing battle.

Adelaide's mouth looked swollen and it trembled, although it was obvious that she was exerting the greatest effort to appear composed. Shaded by the bonnet's brim, her eyes looked huge and unnaturally dark.

They took their place in the pew directly behind the Livingston pew, where a space had been saved for them by dint of a great deal of pushing and shoving and sharp whispering. In the next to last pew at the rear of the church, Agnes Barlowe let out her breath and whispered sibilantly, "Look't her dress! And that bonnet, ain't it nice? Ain't she the lucky one, though? Imagine having all that money and then marryin' old Henry Maynard to boot! Some people have all the luck!''

"Agnes, be quiet!" Mary whispered back, her face flaming with embarrassment at Agnes's coarse remarks. As if money mattered all that much, especially if you had to marry an old lecher like Mr. Maynard to get it! Mary didn't understand, any more than the rest of the curiosity-filled congregation, why Adelaide Livingston had married the banker in what amounted to a disgraceful elopement; but she felt in her bones that Adelaide wasn't happy, and Agnes ought to have better sense than to say a thing like that right in church where everybody could hear. People would think that mechanics had no breeding at all. "Do be quiet, or I just might black your other eye when we get home!"

Matthew Ramsey got to his feet and announced the first hymn, nodding to Minnie Atkins at the piano. His face seemed carved from stone, and he didn't look at Addie. In her pew, her eyes fastened on Matthew's face, Addie also seemed to have been transformed into a marble statue. Please, God, don't let her faint, Roxanne breathed. And like Bobo, she cursed under her breath, whether she was in church or not. If God didn't know that something terrible had been done, then it was time that someone else let Him know it!

Addie didn't faint. She joined in the hymn, her voice as true and sweet as it had always been, though it faltered once or twice. The hymn ended, prayers followed, and then Matthew read a text from the Bible. Another hymn, more prayers, the sermon started. The minutes ticked away. But even Jebbidiah Tucker's sermon had to end sometime: the final hymn, the final prayers. There was a general rush to leave the church, a most unseemly rush, as people tried to get outside to take their places so that they could see the principals of this drama walk down the aisle and leave.

Roxanne didn't hesitate to use her elbows to force a way through the throng, dragging Geneva with her, until they came to stand one on each side of Addie, forming a protective guard to shield her from the of the worst stares. Bobo stationed himself as a sort of rearguard. And so they made their way out of the church into the bright sunlight of a perfect September day.

Addie found herself face-to-face with Matthew. Matthew's eyes were as cold as ice as he held out his hand. "Mrs. Maynard," he said. Geneva's arm supported Addie, and Roxanne supported her from her other side.

"Good hymns, Mr. Ramsey. And good Bible readings! Did you select them for this morning?" Bobo reached around Addie to grasp Matthew's hand and pump it, his face a picture of innocence. "You have a way of delivering a Bible text that brings it home to us!"

He dropped Matthew's hand as though it had suddenly turned red hot as he saw that Geneva and Roxanne had moved ahead, with Addie between them, safely away from proximity of the jilted young minister.

"When may we come to see you?" Geneva asked Addie. "We wanted to come as soon as you were home, but we weren't sure that you'd be rested enough after your—" Her hesitation was barely discernible.

Roxie jumped in to rescue her. "How about tomorrow? We've missed you, Addie."

"Thank you. Tomorrow? I don't think . . . . I'm still a little tired, and there's so much to . . ."

"I'm the best organizer you ever saw. Whatever you have to do, I'll help you," Roxanne said, but Geneva's elbow in her ribs made her break off. "Well, of course, if you're really busy we'll wait a few days. But don't make us wait too long."

Then Henry was there, frowning, and propelling Addie away. His own frown turned to a beam as he nodded right and left, accepting congratulations as his due. Roxanne managed to step on his foot as hard as she could, as she and Geneva passed him, and his grunt of outraged pain gave her a small amount of satisfaction. "Only I wish it'd been his neck!" she burst out to Geneva. "Darn it all!"

"Tut, tut," Bobo admonished her. "And we aren't even off the church grounds!"

Even though the thick door to Herndon's study was closed, the sound of Wyatt's voice, filled with fury, reverberated through the house so that the servants held their breaths and looked at each other with something akin to awe. Upstairs, Bessie, Lillian's maid, hovered in the hallway near Lillian's bedroom door in case her mistress might need her to bring her her smelling salts or a cold cloth for her forehead, or her soothing syrup. She knew that her mistress was lying down, probably with her pillow over her ears to shut out that angry voice that threatened to bring the roof down around their heads. Wyatt and his father had had quarrels before, but nothing like this. It was almost the most exciting thing that had happened for years, even if it was frightening.

Wyatt's anger, far from abating, grew as he continued to lash out at his father.

"I wouldn't have believed it even of you! How could you have done such a thing? You sold Addie to Henry Maynard! Don't shake your head at me, don't you dare pretend that you didn't! And you know what Henry Maynard is. If he were a normal man he'd have remarried years ago, someone suitable for him. But Henry wants young flesh, innocent young flesh, he wants a girl hardly more than a child, and you've delivered Addie into his hands, as though she were a bolt of cloth!"

"Wyatt, lower your voice. I am not hard of hearing, there is no need to shout. Adelaide is decently and properly married, and the match is a good one. Mr. Maynard is extremely fond of her, he'll cherish her as she deserves to be cherished. She'll want for nothing."

"Hypocrite! You knew I'd fight you on this, you knew I'd never let you get away with it. That's why you sent me on that tour of the other mills! You had to get me out of the way, because I'd have guessed you were up to something!

"Addie cherished? You make me sick! I've seen her, and she looks like a ghost, like a wraith. There's enough horror in her eyes to make the devil himself cringe! She'd hardly talk to me, she just looked at me as if I were someone she didn't know!

"But she told me the lies you fed her, I got that much out of her! Mother ill—my God, how did you dare tell such a blatant lie, and make her believe it? Bankrupt! You wouldn't go bankrupt even if you were never able to expand the mill. It was nothing but greed that made you do such a despicable thing! Behind my back, behind Mother's back! I feel like killing you. I feel so much like it that I'm getting the hell out of this house before I do it, and I'm not coming back. You can run your stinking mill without me, you can run your stinking life without me. I have no father, and if you ever dare to call me your son, I'll deny it!''

"You're overwrought. What will you do, how do you propose to earn a living? You're trained for nothing except the mill. The positions that would support you as you're used to living are few and hard to come by.''

"I'll find something, you needn't concern yourself about that. I don't have any desire to be as rich as you are, now that I've seen the result of the greed for more and more wealth. I have only one more thing to say to you, sir. I hope you drop dead before you can enjoy the benefits of your mill expansion!''

Upstairs, Lillian lifted her head from her pillow when she heard the door to the study slam with such force that it was a miracle that it didn't come off its hinges. Then she heard Wyatt's footsteps pound up the stairs and the door to his own room slam.

She got off her bed. Her knees felt weak. In all of her sheltered life, she had never heard a quarrel as violent as the one that had just taken place between her husband and her son. She knew that the quarrel was because of Addie's marriage to Henry Maynard. She didn't blame Wyatt. She herself had seen Addie, and she wasn't such a fool. In spite of Herndon's opinion of her mental powers, she knew that Addie was miserable. Now, Wyatt's shouted words had told her everything that she hadn't known. Addie had married Henry Maynard to protect her, because she'd thought that her mother was ill, dying! Addie's life ruined, because her daughter still loved Matthew Ramsey! What other lies had Herndon told their daughter to make her marry Mr. Maynard so suddenly, without even having time to think about it or to talk it over with her mother?

All of her married life, Lillian had refrained from asserting herself. Her father had been the absolute monarch of her childhood and her mother had accepted it as a matter of course. It was a fact of life that women must allow their husbands to rule. Didn't the Bible itself tell women that they must obey their husbands?

But these weren't biblical times. If men still sold their daughters to advantage, and the practice was more common than Lillian could bear thinking about, it still wasn't right! Her Addie, her sweet, beautiful, darling little girl, married to that old man across the street. The old man that Lillian had overheard younger people sniggering about behind their hands!

"Who is it?" Wyatt's voice was sharp as he paused in his yanking out of dresser drawers and piling clothing on the bed, ready to be transferred to traveling bags.

"It's me, Wyatt," Lillian called. "May I come in?"

Wyatt didn't want to see his mother. How much had she heard? He'd been shouting, but he wasn't sure if she had been able to make out what he'd said. But there was no way that he could avoid seeing her before he left, and he might as well get it over with. The shock on her face when she saw that he was already packing made him feel worse than ever.

"You're really leaving, then! Oh, Wyatt, what are you going to do?"

"I'll be all right. I have a little money, not as much as I should have, I admit. I wish now that I hadn't been so extravagant with the salary Father paid me, but I can get along for a little while. I suppose I can sell Red Boy, if it becomes absolutely necessary. He and the gig will fetch a pretty penny; Bob Maxwell's father will lay out any price I ask, and he'll have to bid against competition at that." The thought of selling Red Boy was like a stab in his heart, but he'd do it rather than knuckle under to his father and come back home.

Seeing his mother's stricken face, his own softened. "It probably won't come to that, Mother. I'll find a job. There are plenty I can apply for. In the meantime I'll put up at the Cayuga, and write a few letters to prospective employers recommending myself highly. They'll remember me since I've just finished visiting their mills. They'll know I'm qualified." No use letting his mother know that it probably wouldn't be as easy as all that. All of the mills he'd visited had their own long-established executive personnel, mostly in the family just like the Livingston mills were run. But something would turn up. He was young and intelligent and able-bodied and if he couldn't earn his own living, then it was no more than he deserved.

"You'll let me know where you are, when you find a position?"

"Of course I will." Wyatt kissed her cheek, and she clung to him for a moment, fighting tears. "And before I leave Athens, I'll drop in to see you when Father isn't here, all right?"

He turned away then and began piling things into a bag. Lillian took them all out again, thankful for something useful to do. "Why can't men ever seem to learn to pack properly! Let me do it, or everything will be so wrinkled it'll be unwearable!"

The packing was finished in all too short a time. Wyatt kissed her again and snapped the bags shut; then he picked them up and nearly tripped over the servant as he left the room. He glared at her, his expression so fierce that she shrank back, in spite of the fact that he'd always been so easygoing with all of the servants.

"Bessie, keep your mouth shut, do you understand? And pass the word along to the others. If I hear one whisper of what you've heard today, I'll be back and take it out of your hides!"

"Yes, sir," Bessie gasped. And she dared add, "As if we'd go telling family affairs around! I should think we're better trained than that, sir! And loyal to your mother and Miss Adelaide, too."

Wyatt's smile was humorless as he noted that Bessie hadn't included his father in the servants' loyalty. And then he was down the stairs, the front door closed behind him.

11

In the common room at the Cayuga, Wyatt leaned forward, his fingers still around his glass, and put his question to Bobo.

"What are the chances of me taking Addie away from Henry Maynard? Once I find a job and get myself settled so I can give her a home?"

Bobo set his own drink back on the table and regarded his friend with somber eyes. "There's no chance at all. Addie's Henry's wife. It's virtually impossible for a wife to leave her husband, much less divorce him. A man can get rid of his wife a great deal more easily, although even that is harder than you might think. Henry would have every right to take her back again by force, and keep her by force, if you were foolish enough to try."

"Damn it, why don't the laws protect people, the way they're supposed to?"

"I didn't write 'em, Wyatt, I only studied them. I expect they don't protect people because they're written by human beings with faulty human intellects. Besides, in this case, even the Bible is against you, and you know what the Bible means to most people. You try anything like stealing your sister away from her lawfully wedded husband, and you'll likely end up in a jail that even my father wouldn't be able to get you out of, much less me."

"Then it's hopeless."

"Unless you want to murder Henry. And you'd end up in jail, and hanged, if you tried that. Not that I haven't given it some thought myself. Wyatt, it's over and done with and all we can do is accept it. Geneva and Roxie are going to do everything they can to help her, but outside of that our hands are tied. Why do you think I'm sitting here getting drunk as fast as I can get this stuff down?''

If Bobo was drunk, his appearance gave no indication of it. His face looked as sanguine as ever, his smile was as boyishly innocent, his blue eyes were guileless. But Wyatt knew Bobo, and he knew that his friend was as broken up over this miscarriage of all human justice as he himself was. He'd known Bobo too long and too well to be deceived by appearances.

"Drink up. It can't hurt, and it might help," Bobo said, lifting his glass. "Except for the way your head'll feel tomorrow.''

"I could drink the Cayuga dry, and it wouldn't help.''

"Then let's change the subject. How's Red Boy? You know, we never did have that race. Before you find a job and leave town, I'd like to prove that Cato can beat him.''

"You know Cato can't beat him. There isn't a horse in this county that can beat him, probably not in the state.''

"It still hasn't been proved. What's the matter, are you afraid to put it to the test?'' At this moment, Bobo couldn't have cared less whether Cato could beat Red Boy or not, but he had to do something to take both their minds off their problems.

Bob Maxwell entered the room just in time to hear the last of their conversation. His fair, handsome face brightened as he ran his hand through his blond hair, checking automatically to see if it lay in its perfect waves. Bob wasn't conceited, he was simply aware that outside of Wyatt Livingston, he was the handsomest young man in Athens, and he liked to keep his image intact. He turned to Paul Towndson and Emery Ledbetter, who were with him as they nearly always were when they were out to look for some excitement to liven up their lives.

"A race! That's the ticket, let's have a race! I'll lay ten on Red Boy right now, cash on the barrelhead!''

"Cato can lick Red Boy without even trying," Emery sputtered. "Ten on Cato!''

They'd made no effort to keep their voices down, filled with excitement at the prospect of finding out, at last, which of Athens's champion trotters was the faster. The other men patronizing the tavern that evening pricked up their ears and began crowding around. A race! And not only a race, but a race between Cato and Red Boy! Hands went into pockets, money was taken out and shaken into other faces as the wagering burst into full life even before it was determined that the contest would actually take place.

"Who'll keep tabs?"

"Moody will, of course. Joe!"

Joseph Moody, the Cayuga's proprietor, left off polishing a pewter mug and picked up the piece of chalk with which he marked down his patrons' tally on the slate behind the bar. "I'll lay my money on Red Boy," he said. "One at a time, now, don't confuse me."

At their table, Bobo's eyes challenged Wyatt. Wyatt shrugged. Why not? It was time the issue was decided, and if he had to sell Red Boy, he'd at least still like to be his owner when he beat Cato. And if he didn't have something to occupy his mind, even a race, he was afraid that his head was going to burst from the fury that was still churning inside of him.

"When'll it be? Tomorrow morning?" Emery was so excited that he began to stutter, a habit of his that brought him a good deal of ribbing from his friends. "I'll raise my bet to fifteen, on Cato, who'll m-m-m-match it?"

Bobo's own head was churning from his overindulgence, a thing he'd rarely done even at Harvard when the students had decided to have a real celebration. "Why wait until morning? If my eyes don't deceive me, there's a full moon out tonight and it's almost as bright as day. Unless Wyatt isn't game, that is."

Even through the alcohol fumes, Bobo knew that it wasn't the smartest thing in the world to suggest a horserace at night. As far as he knew, it had never been done. But Wyatt was in a dangerous mood. He'd better get Wyatt's mind on something else in a hurry unless he wanted his friend to come apart at the seams and go hunting for either his father or Maynard. Probably Maynard, because hadn't Bobo himself been idiot enough to make that remark about Addie's only chance of getting free of Henry was to murder him?

As for racing at night, why not? The fact that it had never been done would only add to the excitement. The other men had been struck dumb by the suggestion until it had a chance to sink in, but now their voices were already shrill as they all tried to talk at once.

"At night? Impossible. It's absurd!"

"W-w-why is it absurd? Twenty on Cato!" Emery sputtered, his face flaming red. "There's g-g-g-got to be a first time for everything, and w-w-we can say the Corinthians were the first to do it!"

"It's dangerous, that's why!"

"W-w-why is it dangerous? Didn't Bobo just s-s-s-say it's as light as day out th-th-there?"

"How about it, Wyatt?" Bobo grinned, making small circles on the tabletop with his glass. "Shall we find everlasting fame by being the first?"

Wyatt downed the last of his whiskey. "Miller's Road?" he asked. Not being the county seat, where the fairs took place, Athens had no race track, and such races as took place between gentlemen were ordinarily held on Miller's Road, a long, open stretch so-named because it had originally been the road that led to Fredrick Heinrich's gristmill back when the country had been more sparsely populated.

"Naturally." Bobo stopped playing with his glass and downed the last of his own whiskey. "I'll go and hitch up. And I don't want any company, because I don't want my family to know what's going on. I'll have to be quiet so they won't hear me. My father might not be amenable to the idea of a race at night. I'll meet you back here."

There was a jam-up at the door after Bobo had left. All the others at the inn scrambled to get outside to find whatever transportation they could to the point on Miller's Road where they could have the best view of the race. Most of them opted to station themselves at the curve that led into the gristmill yard. As the men surged down the street and scattered, word of the race spread like wildfire. Every canaller, every piece of towpath riffraff who was abroad got wind of it, and those who could find no transportation set out on foot so as to be in on the end of the race even if they wouldn't be able to get there in time to see the beginning of it. More wagers were laid, without the benefit of being tallied by Joseph Moody, who was the last one out as he shouted to his barmaid to keep things under control until he got back. Custom be damned. With the race in the offing it wasn't likely that anyone would come into the tavern anyway.

Bobo's head felt light as he walked to North Street. He wondered if he'd been foolish to allow the race to be held tonight. He'd drunk a great deal more than usual because he'd still been brooding over Addie's marriage to Henry Maynard. If he'd been sober, he'd have had more discretion. But it was too late now. With the mood that the wagerers were in, they'd tear him apart if he called it off. He'd have to go through with it, and hope for the best. Thankfully, Cato needed virtually no guiding, he'd know what was expected of him and he could be trusted to compensate for his master's lack of equilibrium and good sense. All the same, he wished that his stomach didn't feel so squeamish.

The key to the stable was hanging on its hook just inside the kitchen door, and the kitchen was empty, both Nelly and Mrs. Barnes, the cook, having finished their work and gone to their rooms long since. He managed to get the key and get into the stable without alerting the house, and for once he was glad that his mother sneezed her head off everytime she got within fifteen feet of a dog, so that they had neither house dog nor yard dog to set up a fuss.

His fingers seemed to turn into two full sets of thumbs as he harnessed Cato to the gig, and his head felt strange again as he climbed up onto the high seat after having led the horse down the driveway and into the street at a snail's pace so that the sound of wheels and hoofbeats wouldn't drift to his father's or Geneva's ears. But he was all right. What he needed, he told himself, was a good run in the fresh air and the exhilaration of handling the lines so expertly that there would be no question of which horse would win. That would clear his head. Cato was the better animal, and tonight he was going to prove it. Not that he wished Wyatt bad luck, but losing might give Wyatt something to think about besides his fury over finding Addie married to Henry Maynard.

By the time he got back to the Cayuga, only Wyatt was there, Red Boy already hitched and waiting. There was enough moonlight so that Bobo could see that Wyatt had a worried expression on his face.

"Are you sure you want to go through with this, Bobo? It seems to me that you've had an awful lot to drink."

"Don't be ridiculous," Bobo said, his voice indignant. "Have you ever seen me the worse for drink?"

Wyatt had to admit that he hadn't, but he was still

uneasy. Bobo looked all right, and he talked with no hint of a slur, but by his own admission he'd imbibed a great deal more than he should have, and there was a peculiar expression around his eyes.

"Well, what are we waiting for? Let's get going!" Bobo's impatient voice cut through Wyatt's qualms. "The sooner Cato beats Red Boy, the sooner we can get back to serious drinking. We have to celebrate your independence from your father, don't we? It isn't every day a man wins his freedom!"

With Wyatt letting Bobo lead so that he could keep an eye on him to see if he was handling Cato properly, the two gigs set off for the starting point on Miller's Road, going at a sedate trot to keep the horses fresh. It only took a few moments for them to leave the outskirts of Athens behind them, and a few more to reach Miller's Road and the starting point. The men were already waiting.

Verne Baldwin, the town drunk, was among the cluster, as excited as though he'd been sober, which he was not. He darted away from the others and reached for Cato's bit, making Cato shy and bringing a sharp reprimand from Bobo.

"Mr. Burton, lend me somethin' to bet on the race! Whatever you have, a few shillings even, I'll pay it back when you win and I collect!"

Bobo had to laugh at the man's gall. There was no harm in Verne, except that he couldn't manage to stay sober enough to hold a steady job. Without counting it, Bobo tossed what change he had in his pocket to the excited drunk. "See how much profit you can make with that. And get out from under Cato's feet!"

Another man stepped forward and volunteered to act as starter. The rules were simple. When the man dropped his uplifted arm, the race would start.

"Bobo, are you sure?" Wyatt felt compelled to ask.

Bobo's answer was to maneuver his gig alongside of Wyatt's, the grin on his face mocking. Wyatt shrugged, giving up. They might as well get it over with. Drunk or sober, Bobo was the best driver and owned the best horse of any man he knew outside of himself and Red Boy.

Breaths were held as the starter lifted his arm. Men counted under their breaths, one, two, three, four, and then a shout went up as they roared in unison, "They're off!"

170

The road was dry, and not too badly rutted because it hadn't rained for several days. It stretched like a pale ribbon in the moonlight. In spite of everything else that weighed on his mind, Wyatt felt a wave of elation surge through him as the two trotters stepped out, manes and tails flying, neck and neck. It had been a long time since he'd tested Red Boy against any other horse worthy of giving him a run for his money.

In the other gig, Bobo kept on grinning, his hands expert on the lines in spite of a slight numbness of feeling. "Come on, boy, step along there! You can do it, you know you can, make him eat your dust!"

The horses had their wind, now, and they stepped out eagerly, the excitement of a race coursing through their blood. Ears laid back, hooves flying, they bowled ahead, their action as perfect as flesh and blood could achieve. The spectators felt something like awe as they started to run after the racing horses even if there was no chance that they'd be able to see the finish of the contest. They were so carried away with excitement that they forgot that they'd have to walk all that extra distance back to the Cayuga.

This was a good idea after all, Wyatt thought, his hands holding Red Boy steady, transmitting the message along the lines that he wanted even more speed. He had no fear that Red Boy would break from his trot into a canter or a gallop, which would have disqualified him instantly. Red Boy, like Cato, was a trotter, so well trained that Wyatt doubted that even a whip would make him break his pace.

Eight hooves pounded faster and faster. Wyatt forgot everything except the thrill of the race, the sudden, overwhelming determination to win and prove once and for all that Red Boy was the better horse. All of his fury of the afternoon, all of his frustration at his helplessness to change things, flooded through him as he urged Red Boy faster and faster, until he edged ahead, an inch, a foot, a yard, and they were coming up on the curve in the road that marked the end of the race.

Behind him, Bobo used every ounce of his skill to cut the distance between them. Cato lengthened his pace without losing a fraction of a beat, his hooves moving like pistons. Now they were abreast again, now Cato was a few inches ahead, and the finish line lay just around the bend.

"Go it, boy, go it!" Bobo shouted. His eyes were blurring, but that didn't matter, it was all over but the celebrating anyway. This called for a real celebration, a celebration to end all celebrations! It was too bad that he couldn't let Wyatt win, but that would be cheating and he'd never be able to look himself in the face again, let alone any of the men who had bet on Cato. A gentleman doesn't cheat, even for a friend. Cato was simply the better horse.

And then the high right wheel of the gig struck a rut that Bobo's blurred eyes hadn't seen, and the gig lurched and went over as it tried to take the curve, and Cato, in blind panic, broke into a gallop until the dragging gig slowed him to a stop and he stood with his sides heaving, trembling violently.

"My God, he's dead!"

"No, he isn't, he's breathing. But it looks like he's well broken up. Look at that leg, it's broken, for sure."

His face whiter than the moon that still hung in the sky, Wyatt lifted his head and snapped out orders. "Somebody take my gig. Get to the nearest farmhouse—that'll be the Emerson place—and fetch a wagon, and a shutter or a door to put Bobo on so we can lift him without hurting him any worse than he is. Hurry, man, hurry!"

It took every ounce of his willpower not to retch. He'd known that Bobo had had too much to drink, but he'd still allowed the race to go on. A horserace, at night! No matter how bright the moon was, it still made deceptive shadows. Bobo had never seen the rut that had brought him to grief. If Bobo died, it would be his fault. Looking down at Bobo's bloodless face, Wyatt cursed himself, mindlessly, with a blind fury that knew no bounds.

Bobo was still unconscious, looking as though he were more dead than alive, when Joseph Moody came back with Emerson and the wagon. None of the spectators had come in a cart. Moody had come in his buggy, as had most of the others who'd been fortunate enough not to cover the distance on shank's mare, except for the Corinthians, who'd all come in their suicide gigs, worthless as a means of transporting an injured man.

Wyatt helped to move Bobo onto the door that had been

taken off a shed for the purpose, as more than a dozen hands helped keep the injured man rigid so as not to complicate the injuries he already had. Emerson was a godsend. He'd brought a plank of wood and strips of cloth to rest the broken leg on and tie it into place, and his calmness helped to calm even Wyatt.

"Careful, now. Keep that door level, and don't go bouncing him when you set it into the wagon bed," Samuel Emerson directed. "Mr. Livingston, you and one of the others climb in there with him, and keep the door steady while I drive you on in. Why in thunder you decided to have a horserace at night is more than I can understand. Well, this is what's come of it, but it likely isn't as bad as it looks. Mr. Moody, you skedaddle into town as fast as you can go and rouse the doctor and let the Burtons know, so they can be ready for him when we get there."

In spite of Wyatt's screaming desire for haste, he knew that Sam Emerson was right about taking it slow and easy. All the same, it seemed to take forever to get back to Athens, a sorry procession compared to the jubilation with which they had set out such a short time before.

It was Geneva, always a light sleeper, who awoke when someone pounded on their front door. She came fully awake instantly, every sense alert and her mind leaping to some catastrophe, because no one would pound the knocker like that at this hour of the night, for any lesser reason. Leaping out of her bed, she snatched up her dressing gown and without even bothering to put on her slippers, she ran down the stairs, surefooted from a lifetime of traversing these stairs even in the pitch darkness inside the house.

Her father was awake now, his voice calling groggily, "What in thunder's going on?" Not knowing the answer, Geneva threw back the bolts on the door and opened it without answering him.

Galen Forbes, his black bag in his hand, pushed past her into the entrance hall. "Miss Burton, I'm afraid there's been an accident. Your brother's been injured and Wyatt and his friends are bringing him home. Doctor Harding will be here shortly. While we're waiting, let's get all the light we can. We'll use your dining room table for the examination. Bring all the lamps you can find."

At the head of the staircase, Cora Burton, her hair covered with a frilly nightcap, caught her breath in a gasp that cut through Geneva's heart.

"Cyril! What happened, Doctor Forbes? How badly is he hurt?"

"I understand that there was a horserace, and his gig turned over. You'd better get dressed, ma'am, they should be here shortly. Mr. Burton, would you help your daughter gather up lamps? And we'll want a clean sheet to cover the table, and Mrs. Burton, you can see that Cyril's bed is turned down, ready to receive him when we need it."

Keep them busy, Galen told himself, so that they won't have time to panic. He needn't have worried on that score. None of the Burtons, even Cora, who as a delicate woman of great sensitivity might have been expected to go to pieces, was in the habit of panicking.

Stephen Harding pulled up in front of the house before the preparations were finished, and came puffing in, his eyes snapping. "The dining room table, Doctor Forbes?" he asked huffily. "What kind of medical practice is that? The patient should be placed in his own bed the moment he arrives."

"Don't you think we should ascertain the extent of his injuries before we have him carried up a steep flight of stairs?" Galen kept his voice even, hiding his annoyance with the older doctor. "If any bones are broken, we can splint them more easily on the hard surface of a table."

"Harumph! As long as you've already prepared the table, I expect we can use it." Harding pulled out his pocketwatch and snapped it open, frowning. "They should be here soon. A racing accident, and at night! I don't know what young people are coming to . It wasn't like this when I was a lad, we knew how to behave ourselves, our parents saw to it that we were raised knowing right from wrong!"

Was he ever a lad, Geneva thought? Looking at the portly man, she found it hard to picture him as anything except what he was now. She'd bet he'd been a pompous little boy, just as he was a pompous man.

Nelly hurried into the room with more sheets in her arms. "I'll tear some bandages," she said. "These are the oldest ones I could find, but they're still strong." Her practical self, Geneva noted, in spite of having been disturbed from a sound sleep in the middle of the night.

Why, it was nearly eleven! And that Bobo, wouldn't you know that he'd be the one to get himself into a scrape like this! She'd be willing to wager that that harebrained race had been his idea, and not Wyatt's!

They heard the wagon, its wheels crunching on the road, almost as soon as it turned into North Street. "Mother, go and get dressed, as Doctor Forbes suggested," Geneva urged.

Her face pale but composed, Cora Burton did as Geneva asked. Whether Cyril were injured or not, there were still proprieties to be observed. She was in full enough possession of her wits to call back over her shoulder, "Nelly, you'd better poke up the fire in the kitchen and start a pot of coffee, the gentlemen may need it."

"Emma's already taken care of that." The cook was flustered but she could be counted on to make herself useful. Cora Burton was an easy mistress to work for, but she demanded competence.

Geneva's heart lurched as she saw how white and still her brother lay on the door that Wyatt and some other men had to tilt a little to bring in. For a few seconds, her heart stuck in her throat because she was afraid that he was dead. Then her eyes moved to Wyatt's face, and her heart lurched again as she saw how white he was, almost as pale as Bobo, and the tight, stricken look in his eyes. Wyatt shook his head at her. "He's still breathing."

"This way." Stephen Harding took charge in his usual domineering way. "Into the dining room. Lift him carefully, gentlemen, if you please."

Galen was already there, waiting. "Lift him right on the door. We don't want the bones in that leg grating. Help me ease a sheet under it."

Geneva's hands, small and white but strongly capable, were beside his own. "That's the way. That's fine."

He'd hardly finished speaking when Geneva, without being instructed, began cutting away the trouser leg with a pair of scissors. Galen marveled at how steady her hands were even as he laid his head on Bobo's chest to listen to his heartbeat.

"It's strong," he said. He began probing, his fingers seeming to have a mind of their own, as he searched for other injuries. Outside of a lump the size of a pullet egg on Bobo's forehead, and scrapes and bruises, he could find nothing. "I suggest that we get the leg set before he comes around, it will be easier on him that way, we won't have to get him drunk to ease the pain. It's going to be tricky; the bone is broken in two places."

Incredibly, a glint of amusement flushed into Geneva's eyes. Both she and Galen had had the full benefit of Bobo's breath, which was redolent of all the whiskey he'd already drunk that night.

"Stand aside, everyone stand aside." Harding conducted his own examination. "Doctor Forbes, prepare the splints, and stand ready to assist me."

Geneva straightened, her face and her eyes steady. "Doctor Forbes is to do the setting, please."

Harding jerked as if he'd been shot. "Doctor Forbes? Unthinkable! My dear Miss Burton, he's only my assistant! Do you realize that I have had forty years of experience, while my young associate is barely qualified?"

"I appreciate that, Doctor Harding, but Doctor Forbes is to do the setting." Geneva's voice was firm. "Father, tell him."

"I cannot permit it. It's against all ethics. If Doctor Forbes accedes to your request, I'll have no recourse but to dismiss him as my assistant, and apprise the medical profession as a whole of his unethical conduct." Harding was shaking with indignation, his face a dangerous red.

Geneva's eyes met Galen's, and she saw that he was at a loss. As Harding's junior, his assistant, it would be virtually impossible for him to go against the older doctor's orders without suffering severe repercussions. And if Harding dismissed him, he'd have to leave Athens, where he was so determined to help the poorer people, especially the mill workers whom Harding felt were not worthy of his attention except in the direst emergency.

Everyone's eyes were so riveted on the contest between Geneva and Harding that they were electrified with shock when Bobo opened his eyes and spoke. His voice was shaky, but he'd regained consciousness in time to hear the last exchange of angry words, and in spite of the annoying buzzing in his head he understood what was going on.

"Let Doctor Harding do it," he said. "We don't want to start a feud between our doctors, do we? Well, Doctor Harding? Let's get on with it, it's damned uncomfortable on this door!"

"But Bobo—" Geneva protested.

Bobo tried to grin at her. "Geneva, be an angel and bring me a drink. Make it whiskey. And then get the heck out of here so these medical men can do their work. Wyatt, who won? I can't seem to remember."

"Nobody won. We were nose to nose." Wyatt's voice was tight.

Marvin Burton's face was grave. "It's Bobo's decision," he said. "Do as he asked, Geneva. Bring the decanter while you're at it. And then keep your mother out of here."

Defeated, Geneva turned away. Why did Bobo have to be so darned noble? But there was nothing she could do about it, even though she was convinced that Galen was more capable than Harding. She tried to convince herself that she was worrying about nothing. Granted that there were two breaks, and setting them properly would be tricky, but Dr. Harding had been in practice for twice her own lifetime, just as he'd said.

It seemed that she and her mother waited for hours before Galen and Wyatt and Bob Maxwell, who looked more shaken even than Bobo, finally carried Bobo up the stairs, although the clock on her mother's dresser only registered a quarter after twelve.

"He's going to be all right. He's going to be fine," Galen told them. "He's unconscious again, but that's nothing to worry about, just a little too much whiskey."

"Geneva, may I talk to you?" Wyatt asked.

Cora looked from one to the other of them, and her heart ached. Such beautiful young people, both of them, and so perfectly suited to each other! She couldn't for the life of her understand why Geneva had turned Wyatt down. Maybe this accident would serve some good purpose after all, by bringing them back together again.

"Go along, Geneva. I'll sit with your brother."

Geneva was glad that she'd taken the time to dress, although her hair still hung down her back in a single thick braid, just as she'd worn it to bed.

"In the garden," she said.

There were bentwood benches and chairs under the rose arbor where Cora liked to sit on warm afternoons with her sewing, but Wyatt made no move to sit down. This was the first time he'd seen Geneva face-to-face since she'd told him that she would never marry him, and he couldn't imagine it happening under worse circumstances. If he'd ever had a chance of getting her back, it was gone now, and he admitted to himself that he had still had some last faint traces of hope. He'd hoped that if she didn't see him at all for a long time, she might miss him and change her mind. His face was white and strained as he looked at her.

"It was my fault. I knew he'd had too much to drink. But I was half crazy from finding out about Addie's being married to Henry Maynard. I went along with the idea just to get my mind off it."

Geneva's heart was torn. She felt so sorry for Wyatt in his guilty agony that she wanted to put her arms around him and hold him close, to give him any comfort she could. Only a few weeks ago, she would have done just that. It would have been the most natural thing in the world. He was still dear to her, after all, and it would be so easy to tell him now, when he so desperately needed it, that she loved him. It would solve a myriad of problems and make everybody happy. But something inside of her, something she couldn't control, held her back.

"There's no sense in blaming yourself," she said. "I know Bobo. If he wanted to race, even at night, he'd have found someone else to race with if you hadn't agreed. And he always did want to know which horse was better."

"Geneva—" Wyatt broke off, his hands clenched at his sides, fighting his need to catch her in his arms and hold her close. "Tell Bobo that I'll be over to see him tomorrow. I'm going to go and check on Cato now, we left him with Lester Peterson so he could check for any injuries, there's nobody better with horses. But I don't think Cato's hurt, thank God. Bobo would take it hard."

"I'll tell him. And Wyatt, please don't blame yourself."

For a moment, they stood there looking at each other, and once again Geneva had to fight against telling Wyatt what he wanted to hear. All of Athens already knew that he'd broken with his father, the news had spread through town like wildfire. If ever a man needed a woman's comfort, Wyatt needed hers now. She made a small movement, on the verge of committing herself, but the moment had already passed. Wyatt was walking away, and with her hand pressed against her mouth, Geneva reentered the house to help her mother watch over Bobo.

12

Mary MacDonald's heart beat against her ribs. The pounding almost made them sore as she crept through the shadows toward the jailhouse. What she was doing was dangerous, far more dangerous than when she'd so foolishly decided to go to the revival meeting alone.

It was a crisp autumn evening. Mary could feel the chill through the shawl she wore around her shoulders. It didn't seem possible that so much time had passed since that fateful revival meeting that had changed her life, that it had already progressed from hot summer to autumn, but so many things had happened, so many things had changed, that she had to believe it. She was in love with Dr. Forbes, Miss Geneva Burton had broken up with Mr. Wyatt, Mr. Bobo Burton had been hurt in a gig racing accident, Miss Adelaide Livingston was married to the banker, Mr. Henry Maynard.

Anyway, it was a good thing that it was cold enough for a shawl, because the shawl hid the small bundle she clutched under it. She was still trembling from the exertion of climbing down the knotted sheets from the dormitory window, while her roommates either urged her on, or begged her to let them pull her back up, according to their state of nerves. Agnes Barlowe had told her that she was a fool. She'd be sure to be caught, and then she'd be in jail too, as well as losing her position and being blackballed so that she'd never be hired by a mill again, and probably not by anyone else.

Only Agnes had refused to save a part of her supper to wrap in a scrap of cloth. All of the other girls had sacrificed something, anything that could be carried. Half slices of bread, pieces of boiled potato, a soggy mess of boiled corn. It was hardly a feast, but it would be appreciated.

Philo O'Brian was in jail. He'd been in jail for four days, and the little money he'd had on him when he'd been apprehended had run out two days ago. The organizer had had nothing to eat since then. He'd be famished by now. Starving. He wouldn't care how cold and unpalatable the food was, just so it was something to put in his stomach.

Agnes! Mary thought, her mouth curling with scorn. The brazenly pretty girl had been the most excited of any of them when Philo O'Brian had sneaked back into town and recommenced his agitation for the mill workers to turn out. Agnes had declared, over and over, that she'd be the first one to turn out if only some of the others would have the courage to follow her. But when it came to taking the organizer a few scraps of food, she'd balked. Nancy Steele had been so provoked that she'd slapped her. Only Dorothy Monroe's hand over her mouth, while three of the other girls had held her down, had kept Agnes from making an outcry that would have brought Mrs. Simms to investigate.

Mary knew that she was being as foolish as Agnes said she was, but she couldn't stand by and see a dog or a cat starve, much less a man. Not while she had food to share and two feet to get her to the jail. The thought of the jail's bars was enough to make cold shivers run up and down her spine, having nothing to do with the crispness of the weather.

She knew that Mr. Burton, the lawyer, had tried to get Philo out, but that he'd failed. The older Mr. Burton that was. Bobo, who was a lawyer too, wasn't in any condition to try to get anyone out of jail. He was still laid up with his broken leg, and from what the mechanics had heard, he wasn't ever going to walk without a limp after Dr. Harding had set it.

Mary and most of the other mechanics were sorry about that. They didn't know Cyril Burton personally, of course, except what they'd seen of him at the Fourth of July picnic. He and his Corinthians had been so nice to them, treating them as if they were ladies, just like their mothers and sisters. And poor Mr. Wyatt! He'd left town and nobody knew where he was. They only knew that he'd had a terrible fight with his father about Miss Adelaide marrying the banker, and then he'd had that horse race with Bobo Burton, and

Bobo had been hurt. A few days later Mr. Wyatt was gone.

Mr. Marvin Burton's offer to pay Philo O'Brian's fine had been turned down. The man was to serve his jail term, and that was that. Maybe serving a long enough term, with nothing to eat, would convince him that it didn't pay to come into Athens and try to stir up the mechanics at the Livingston mill. If O'Brian died of starvation, it was on his own head, and there would be one less agitator to be a thorn in the mill owners' sides. It would serve as a lesson to other men who thought to follow in his footsteps. Not that it would come to that. After Philo O'Brian had felt his stomach rubbing against his backbone for a long enough period to keep him from ever wanting to set foot in Athens again, the fine would be accepted, along with Philo's bond that he'd never come back on pain of being arrested again on sight whether he did any more agitating or not.

It was after two o'clock in the morning. Mary had never been up this late before in her life, much less been abroad on the streets. Alone, and frightened half out of her wits, she still kept going, hugging the shadows against the walls, pressing herself into doorways to make sure that no one was around.

Only a little farther now. She was almost there. In a few minutes it would be over, and she could run all the way back to the dormitory house. The girls would pull her back up through the window and she'd be able to sleep with a clear conscience, knowing that Philo O'Brian wasn't lying awake with gnawing hunger pangs.

That thought gave her pause. What if he was asleep now, what if she couldn't wake him to come to the barred window? She wouldn't dare call his name very loudly. As mean as it sounded, she hoped that his hunger was keeping him awake.

She crept around to the side of the jail building, hugging the wall, her nerves screaming. But it was all right, she was here and no one had seen her. Who would be out on the streets this late at night? All she had to do now was call Mr. O'Brian to the window and then she'd give him the package.

"Mr. O'Brian! Please, Mr. O'Brian, wake up!" As low as she kept her voice, it seemed to her that everyone in Athens must hear her. She waited, her heart pounding harder than ever, and then she called again. "Mr. O'Brian, you just have to wake up!"

If the whole town of Athens had been asleep before, the shriek that tore from her throat when a pair of strong hands pinned her arms to her side, imprisoning her, must surely have brought them all awake.

"So! Trying to give aid and comfort to a prisoner, are you? A little bit of a girl like you! You ought to be ashamed of yourself, you ought, going around breakin' the law! Stop that screaming, it ain't goin' to do you a bit of good. I'll just get you inside in a cell right alongside that agitator, and come morning, we'll see what Mr. Livingston and the judge have to say!"

"Damn your mangy hide, Ed Hanney, let the little girl go!" Brian called from his cell window. "Can't you see she's only a child? She hasn't done anything you can arrest her for, you blithering scum of Satan!"

One arm went all the way around Mary, holding her helpless, while the other hand groped under her shawl and grasped the packet that held the bits and pieces from the mechanics' supper. "But she's got it right here! That proves she was goin' to give it to you!"

In spite of her terror, Mary's fighting spirit flared. "Give it to him then, seeing as you've already caught me! If I have to be jailed for bringing him something to eat, he might as well have it, hadn't he?" Oh, Lord, she was caught, she was caught good and proper and there was no getting out of it! And who'd bring her anything to eat, while they held her in jail? She didn't have a penny on her, and nothing left in her chest in the dormitory, and even if the other girls put together the few coins they could scrape up to try to get her out, Mr. Livingston wouldn't allow it. He'd make an example of her, just as he had with Mr. O'Brian. Besides, the other mechanics couldn't afford to pay her fine in the first place. None of them ever had anything to spare what with the wages they were paid.

Shaking in every bone and struggling every foot of the way, Mary was dragged around to the front of the building. Ed Hanney gloated as he dragged her.

"I expected somethin' like this! I'm no dummy. I expected somebody'd try to slip the Irishman something, and then I'd be in trouble, so I kept a good watch. Slept daytimes, I did, when nobody'd dare, and watched all last night and tonight and now I've got you. Mr. Livingston'll be mighty grateful." He licked his lips, thinking of the reward that Herndon Livingston would be sure to give him.

The interior of the jail was pitch dark, because Hanney had kept up his watch without a lamp or candle to give him away. Mary sank her teeth into his forearm as he opened the door to the cell next to O'Brian's. Athens's jail boasted only four cells.

Hanney yelped as Mary's teeth sunk home, and she nearly slipped away, but then he had a tight grip on her hair and dragged her into the cell, giving her a shove that sent her crashing into the far wall before he clanged the door shut and locked it. Nursing his bitten arm, the constable cursed. "Come to think of it, I'll just slip O'Brian the victuals you brought, that'll be proof you brought 'em to him!"

Philo himself was cussing up a storm. He'd never wanted anything like this to happen, even as hungry as he was, and he was so hungry by now that he could have gnawed on one of his own shoes, except that he'd need them to walk out of town whenever he got out of here. From the little he'd been able to see of the girl, she really was hardly more than a child! It was a crime. It was one more count against the mill owners. A little girl had been thrown into jail because she'd had the human charity to bring a hungry man a few scraps of food. He only hoped that she had a family or friends who could take care of her, once she got out. He knew that as things stood now, she'd never be able to find any other work.

Hanney opened his cell door just enough to shove the cloth-wrapped bundle through. "That does it! Now I'll just get a little sleep till it comes time I can go and tell Mr. Livingston I caught a miscreant bringing you these victuals!"

O'Brian lifted his foot with the intention of kicking the packet, and then, so ashamed that tears ran down his face, he picked it up and wolfed down the contents. There wasn't any way he could save it for the little girl. There weren't bars between the cells, but solid walls. If he didn't eat it, it would go to waste, and he still had work to do in this world that treated mill mechanics like animals. Starving wouldn't help his cause, only make a martyr of him.

One hope was uppermost in his mind as his stomach acknowledged the food he swallowed too fast by cramping up on him. Maybe with this little girl thrown into jail along with him, the other mechanics would find the gumption to stage a turnout, in protest.

"Don't cry, little girl. They can't keep you in here forever. Only I wish you hadn't done it."

"I don't. I only wish I hadn't been caught. And I'm not crying! It wouldn't do a mite of good. Did you eat the food?"

"I did, may Sweet Mary forgive me. And I thank you kindly."

"It wasn't much. I was going to bring you more tomorrow night, if I got away with it this time."

"It was plenty, it was a feast," Philo lied. "Try to go to sleep. There's nothing else to do in this place anyway."

Curled into a ball on the hard bunk that was the only piece of furniture in the cell except for a bucket for sanitary purposes, Mary's eyes were wide open in the darkness. It was going to be awful when she had to go home and tell her mother and father that she'd been blackballed because she'd tried to help an agitator. They'd miss the money she sent them. They needed every penny of it. Worse, now her sisters would never be able to work at the mill, either, or any mill. Even though she'd have to walk every step of the way and she'd probably be near to dropping by the time she got there, she'd dread the moment when she had to face her ma and pa and tell them.

And I'll never see Dr. Forbes again, once I go home, she thought. Galen Forbes. Galen. That was when she finally cried.

Roxanne faced Ed Hanney in his tiny office, the expression on her face foreboding. She was wearing green again, her favorite color, and the reflection from her dress made her eyes flash as bright as green fire. There was a basket over her left arm, and her right hand held a parasol, more because it matched what she was wearing than because the sun was bright enough to necessitate it. The basket, covered with a white linen napkin, held fried chicken, fresh-baked bread and butter, jam, apples, and an entire apple pie.

"Do you mean to tell me that you aren't going to let me give this food to Mary MacDonald?"

Ed Hanney wasn't a small man, although his belly had gone to flab. He towered over Roxanne but he took a step backward.

"Now Miss Fielding, you know as well as I do that it's against the law to bring aid or comfort to anyone who's in jail for bringing aid and comfort to an agitator against the mills. I can't let you see Mary or give her the food, it would be worth my job."

"Drat your job!" Roxanne lifted her furled parasol and jabbed Ed in the stomach. It wasn't a gentle jab, it was hard enough to make him grunt with pain and cause his eyes to widen with apprehension. "You just try to stop me, you big bag of blubber! Give me the key to her cell this instant, or your stomach's going to leak like a sieve the next time you take a drink!"

"Miss Fielding, you stop that! You can't go around intimidating an officer of the law! You'll end up in jail right next to Mary MacDonald, if you don't leave off!"

Roxanne jabbed him again, harder this time. "After I have you well punctured, I'm going to break this parasol over your head and wrap what's left of it around your neck! Give me the key!"

"That's telling him, colleen! Go to it, give him what for!" Philo O'Brian called. The Irishman's hands clutched the bars of his cell, and his face was filled with glee.

"You'd better well believe I'll give him what for! And if he dares lay a hand on me, or bring a charge against me, my father will take care of what's left of him after I'm through!"

Ed Hanney paled. Earl Fielding was rapidly becoming a legend in his own time. It was not only for his ability to make money hand over fist, but because there wasn't a man on the Erie or anywhere else within reaching distance who'd dare to tangle with him in a fight. Earl Fielding was something to contend with. Any man foolish enough to lay a hand on his daughter, or even cause her any inconvenience, would be taking his life in his hands. Even Herndon Livingston's anger, which was sure to descend on the constable if he allowed Roxanne to see Mary and to give her food, paled in comparison with what he knew Earl Fielding would do to him the moment he arrived back in Athens.

To prove that she wasn't bluffing, Roxanne raised the parasol and brought it down over Hanney's head. The parasol was a flimsy concoction of silk and lace, and its ribs bent on contact, but it hurt. Hanney had no doubt, looking at

Roxanne's face, that her next step would be to wrap it around his neck just as she'd threatened.

"All right, all right! I'll let you see her for five minutes! But I'll have to report it, you understand that."

"Report it then, and see what it gets you!" Triumphant, Roxanne followed on Hanney's heels, almost treading on them, as he unlocked the door to Mary's cell and stood aside so that she could enter.

Mary's face was still streaked with the tears she'd shed the night before, and now it was pale with apprehension.

"Oh, Miss Fielding, you shouldn't have! You'll get in trouble for sure!"

"Not me I won't! It's other people who're going to be in trouble. As soon as my father gets back we'll have you out of here so fast that Herndon Livingston and Ed Hanney won't know what hit them! Here, have something to eat." Roxanne whisked the napkin from the basket and began taking out food: a drumstick, a piece of breast, an apple, and bread already spread with butter. "Mr. Hanney, give this to that man in the other cell. Wait till I cut him a piece of pie, too. I brought milk, because I didn't think that tea or coffee would keep hot."

"Miss Fielding, you're going too far!" Hanney spluttered, his face so red that it made Mary gasp with nervousness. "I dasn't pass any food to O'Brian, he's the agitator!"

"And you dasn't not to, if you know what's good for you! Consarn your hide, give it to him, or I'll sic my father on you even if you did let me in to see Mary!"

Shaking with indignation, but not daring to disobey the auburn-haired termagant whose threats weren't idle ones, Hanney did as he was told. Philo pounced on the food, chortling with glee.

"Good girl! You're a lass after me own heart. You wouldn't be Irish, by any chance?"

"Wouldn't I now, on me mither's side," Roxanne told him, her voice filled with amusement. "Half Irish she was, and that makes me a quarter, if that'll do."

"A quarter Irish is enough to lick a dozen the likes of Ed Hanney." Philo's voice was muffled and the words hard to understand because his mouth was already full. What Mary had brought last night, bless her heart, had been a lifesaver, but not nearly enough to fill the void in his stomach. But what Miss Fielding had brought was of a sufficiency; it would hold him for two or three more days if it had to. He was used to going hungry. And maybe Miss Fielding would bring more tomorrow, and wasn't it a blessing that there was Irish in her so that she dared to spit in Herndon Livingston's eye, as well as that of Livingston's minion, Ed Hanney.

"Go ahead and eat, honey." Roxanne patted Mary's hand, and then returned to examine the single, thin blanket on the bunk. "Is this all you had to cover you last night? What are they trying to do, freeze you to death as well as starve you? It's time things were changed in this town. One blanket, and so thin it wouldn't keep a shaggy dog warm! And it's probably full of lice, at that."

"That it is, mavourneen, but they have mighty poor pickings, as hungry as they keep us." Philo's voice was cheerful. "A few days in here and we don't have enough meat left on us to fill them up, and that's a fact." He paused to swallow, and then went on. "I suppose you didn't bake this pie with your own lily-white hands, a fine lady like you?"

"No, I didn't, but if I couldn't bake a better one with my eyes closed, I'd be ashamed of myself. Eat it up, there's more where that came from."

"And you're just the girl who'll see that we get it!" Philo swallowed the last of the pie, and breathed a great sigh of satisfaction, followed by a belch. Mary looked embarrassed, but Roxanne laughed. The early years she'd spent on her father's canalboats had inured her to such things. There was nothing about an honest belch by a satisfied man to offend her.

Her laugh put Mary at ease, and she began eating hungrily. She was hungrier than she'd ever been in her life. It was already well past noon and she'd had nothing since supper the night before, and she'd saved half of that to donate to Mr. O'Brian. How good the chicken was, and there was real butter on the bread, and a jar of jam! Still, she controlled herself and ate slowly, using her best manners. Maybe she was only a mill mechanic, or at least she had been until this had happened, but she was still a lady. All of Mrs. Simms's charges were ladies, as the nightmarm never tired of reminding them.

Watching her, Roxanne's heart melted. "Don't you worry, Mary. I'm going straight from here to see Mr. Burton, and he'll find a way to get you out of here. I'd have been here sooner, but I didn't know you were here until my cook came back from marketing. She was good and late because she stopped to gossip about both Mr. O'Brian and you being in jail. Do you know something? You're famous! Everybody in Athens knows you're in jail, an honest-to-goodness martyr because you tried to help Mr. O'Brian!''

"I think I'd rather not be famous, and be out of here." Mary's voiced tried to quaver, but she refused to let it. "And thank you for wanting to get me out, but I don't see what Mr. Burton can do. The law's the law, and I did try to bring Mr. O'Brian something to eat. At least he got it. Mr. Hanney gave it to him to make the evidence against me stronger."

"Marvin Burton's the best lawyer around, and Geneva will see to it that he does something for you." Roxanne's voice was confident. She already knew that the attorney's sentiments were entirely on the side of the mill mechanics, and she was certain that he'd leave no stone unturned to gain Mary's freedom. After that, between him and her own father they'd see that she didn't suffer from lack of employment. As far as that went, Roxanne would give her a job herself, she could always pretend that she needed another maid.

Impulsively, she kissed Mary's cheek and hugged her. "I'm going to see Mr. Burton right now. And if he can't get you out tonight, I'll be back with some good thick blankets, and clean sheets and a pillow, too. Is there anything else you need? A comb and brush, of course. And some clean clothing. Mine would be too large for you but Geneva will lend you something, she'd not too much taller than you are."

In spite of the control she was trying to exert, Mary couldn't help her tears from spilling over. Imagine, Miss Roxanne Fielding herself coming to her rescue, doing so much for her! And Miss Geneva was nice, too, as nice as Miss Roxanne. If she'd had to go and get herself caught, she was the luckiest mechanic who'd ever lived to have friends like Miss Roxanne and Miss Geneva. She wasn't anywhere near as frightened now as she'd been before Miss Roxanne had come.

Leaving the jail, Roxanne set out on foot for the Burton house. She wished that Mrs. Casey had gone marketing earlier, so that she'd have found out about Mary before it was so late in the day. As it was, she'd spent the entire morning going through her wardrobe. She despised sewing and mending, but she was so worried because Wyatt had left town and she'd heard nothing from him for over three weeks that she'd had to keep herself busy or go crazy. When every article of clothing that she possessed was in perfect condition, she'd torn into her bedroom, rearranging all the furniture and then putting most of it back where it had been in the first place.

No one had heard from Wyatt. There'd been only one letter sent to his mother and another to Bobo, both posted from Albany on the same day. It was as if the earth had opened up and swallowed him. Even her father hadn't managed to get a line on him yet, and that was unusual enough to be worrisome. When Earl wanted to find someone, he had the ways and means of doing it.

Roxanne had haunted the Livingston house, calling on Lillian every day. Only yesterday, she'd realized that her constant demand for news only served to make his mother more worried. She'd determined not to call again for at least three days. If Lillian heard anything in the meantime, she'd let her know.

She was so lost in her thoughts that she saw the broad-shouldered figure bearing down on her only at the last possible instant, barely able to get out of his way. She recognized him at the same instant as his startled exclamation told her that he too had been deep in thought and not watching where he was going.

"Miss Fielding? I'm sorry, I should have kept my eyes open."

"And so should I. How are you, Jim? Are you in Athens for the weekend?"

"The *Undine* pulled in less than two hours ago. And the first thing I heard was that Mary MacDonald is in jail. Ed Hanney wouldn't let me see her, so I made tracks to see Mr. Burton to see what can be done about it."

Roxanne saw that his face was set and grim. "That's where I'm going, to see what Mr. Burton can do about it! What did he tell you?"

Jim's hands clenched, and his mouth became more grim than ever. "He says that it's going to take a little time. He's already had it out with Livingston, but he got nowhere. The man's determined to make an example of Mary. According to Mr. Burton, Livingston's afraid that there's going to be a rebellion among his mechanics. He's all out to make certain that none of them will dare listen to another organizer, for fear that they'll find themselves where O'Brian and Mary are now.''

"But he has to be able to do something, he's a lawyer!''

"He's going to do his best. He's already packing up to go to Auburn to talk with Judge Granger. He's pretty sure that he can get a court order for Mary's release, seeing that she's so young and she's never been involved in agitating, or even accused of contumacy against the mills. But in the meantime, Mary's locked up, and she's hungry—''

"She isn't hungry. I just came from there, and I took her a basket of food, enough for Philo O'Brian, too. And if Mr. Burton can't get her out tonight, I'm going to take her blankets and other things. She won't suffer, except from not being able to walk out of there.''

Jim's eyes were filled with gratitude. "How did you get the food past Ed Hanney? He threatened to arrest me and lock me up if I didn't leave, and he meant it. I couldn't do anything for Mary if I was behind bars too.''

"I didn't get it past him, exactly, it was more like through him!'' Roxanne began to laugh, remembering the constable's face when she'd attacked him with her parasol and threatened worse if he didn't let her in. "I have an advantage over you, you see. I'm female, and my father is Earl Fielding, and he didn't dare lay a hand on me or refuse to let me see Mary and give her the food. Brawn isn't everything, women have their weapons, too.''

"I'm downright relieved that Mary isn't hungry! It was good of you, Miss Fielding. Now I reckon all we can do is wait for Mr. Burton to get back from Auburn, and hope that he'll be able to talk the judge into that court order.''

"As long as there's no need now for me to see Mr. Burton, why don't you come back to the house with me? I can give you a meal and we can put our heads together to see what we can come up with in case Mr. Burton doesn't get the court order.''

"I'd like to, but I have to get back to the *Undine*. There's unloading and loading still to be seen to, if we're to pull out Monday morning. Except that if Mary isn't out of jail by then, the *Undine* will either go without me, or it won't go at all!''

All of Jim's fury at Mary's imprisonment was reflected in his voice. His first impulse, when he'd heard that Mary had been jailed, had been to rush over there and overpower Hanney. To tear the jail apart if need be to get her out. But his common sense had told him that that would be the most foolish thing he could do. Even if he succeeded in freeing Mary, she'd be a fugitive. There'd be warrants out for her apprehension, Herndon Livingston would probably offer a substantial reward for her recapture.

He could probably have hidden her until he could get her away to safety, but there was always the danger that she'd be discovered. It would be impossible to take her back to her parents' farm because that would be the first place Herndon Livingston would send men to look for her. And leaving her in some other town or city alone was out of the question. She was only a child, someone had to take care of her. If he spirited her away and she was recaptured or if anything else happened to her, he wouldn't be able to face going on living.

Roxanne looked after him thoughtfully as he strode on to return to the *Undine*. The poor man had it bad. It was a shame that Mary, along with nearly everyone else who lived along the canal, held such a poor opinion of the canallers. Jim Yarnell was a good man. Her father held a high opinion of him. When she went back to see Mary tonight, she'd put in a word for him, letting Mary know that she thought that the captain was a man any girl should be proud to marry.

When he was out of sight, Roxanne went on to the Burtons'. Geneva was only too happy to lend Mary some of her things, and while she put together what they thought Mary would need, Roxanne rapped on Bobo's door.

"If you aren't decent, put something on so I can come in."

Bobo's face lighted up when she suited her actions to her words, and he stood up, leaning on his crutches.

"How's the leg? I hear it isn't doing so well." There was no point in beating around the bush. They'd known and respected each other for too long for there to be anything but complete honesty between them.

"It'll get me around. I won't be winning any prizes for the fast sprint, but I can make it serve."

"What does Galen Forbes say about it?"

"What can he say? One doctor can't go around saying

that another doctor flubbed up, it isn't done. What about you? You have that old battle light in your eyes, what have you been up to?''

Roxanne's account of her encounter with Ed Hanney made Bobo feel better than he had since he'd been injured. Like Philo O'Brian, he said, "Go to it, girl! Give 'em what for! If you don't think one of your parasols is strong enough to do the job when you go back there tonight, I'll lend you one of my crutches!''

It being a Saturday night, there was a greater number of canallers in Athens than there would have been on a week-day. The captains tried to arrive in good time, so that the loading and unloading could be taken care of, and the crews could disperse through the town to seek the amusement they had to do without all the rest of the week. Some barges traveled on Sundays, but those that laid over on that day spilled off their crews, who were intent on making the most of their time off, secure in the knowledge that they'd have all day Sunday to recuperate.

But no thoughts of such revelry were in Ike Oldham's mind as he sat with half a dozen brawny canallers, none of them from the *Undine*, in the Canaller's Roost. He was so indignant at the captain's girl being in jail that he could think of nothing else. Cap'n Yarnell had come back to the *Undine* and told him to go and have a good time. In answer to Ike's query about when Mary would get out, his answer had been short. Not tonight, probably not tomorrow, run along, there's nothing we can do about it until Mr. Burton gets back from Auburn.

But there ought to be something they could do about it! It wasn't right. Mary hadn't done anything wrong. Ike was so riled up that he'd already had two mugs of ale, where ordinarily he never indulged at all; the captain took a dim view of lads as young as he was drinking anything stronger than coffee.

"The cap'n's been teaching me about history," he suddenly blurted. "I'll bet you that something like this couldn't of happened back in 1775! Folks didn't stand for things like this back then. Else they wouldn't have gone an' dumped all that tea in Boston Harbor, would they? Just because they didn't want to pay a piddlin' little tax on it.''

There was nothing that Ike wouldn't do for his captain. His captain had taken him in when he'd been starving and scared half to death that his stepfather would find him and drag him back to a life of slavery on the farm. The captain had clothed him and fed him and given him an important job driving the teams. He had self-respect now. He was self-supporting and no man could look down on him or make him do anything he didn't want to do. If the captain asked him to cut off his hand, he'd sharpen up his pocket knife and do it.

"The tadpole's got something there," Art Franklyn said. Already more than three sheets to the wind, Franklyn was well primed. He'd just come into the Canaller's Roost, but although Ike had started when he'd seen him, the look on Art's face and the tone of his voice gave Ike to believe that Art wouldn't go running to the cap'n carrying tales. "That's the little girl I scared outa her wits, back at the revival meetin', that's in jail. Seems I owe her somethin' for scarin' her like that. How was I to know she was a decent girl, all alone like she was, at a revival meetin'? I say we oughta get her outa there!"

Which was exactly what Ike had in mind, and maybe it was lucky that Art had wandered in here to say it first because the other canallers were more likely to listen to Art than they were to him.

"And the lot of us 'ud land in jail in her place, if we did!" a more prudent voice advanced. "I'd be glad to do it for Cap'n Yarnell, but blamed if I want to go to jail for it!"

"Shucks, don't you know nothin' 'bout history?" Ike demanded. He was so fired up that he ordered another mug of ale. "There wouldn't anybody know who did it! Those Liberty Boys blacked their faces up with burnt cork, or wore pillowcases over them, so's nobody could prove it was them!"

There was a moment of silence as this information was digested. "Could be it would work. And I'd like to do Ed Hanney a piece of dirt, as well as get the little lady out of jail. Herndon Livingston, too, the bastard. Doesn't as much as nod at the likes of us to pass the time of day, chance he sees us on the street. Acts like we're beneath his high 'n' mighty notice! What do you say, mates? We all of us like Jim Yarnell, are we going to let his girl sit there in jail when we can break her out?"

"Of course we ain't!" Ike yelled. He swallowed the rest

of his new mug of ale so fast that he choked until tears ran down his face, but as soon as his back had been pounded sufficiently so that he could catch his breath, he used it to urge his newfound allies on, before they had time to change their minds. "Let's get on with it, I say! Us canallers has got to stick together, don't we?"

Even the one prudent canaller among them nodded at that. Of all things, canallers had to stick together. It didn't matter how much they brawled among themselves, one canalboat crew against another, even to the point of mayhem. When it came to one of their own against the townspeople, they had to stick together.

13

Mary could hardly believe her good fortune when not only Miss Roxanne Fielding, but Miss Geneva Burton as well, came to visit her that evening. And they both brought so many things to make her comfortable! More food, another big basket that was shared with Philo O'Brian the moment they arrived. And blankets, an extra one for Philo too, and a clean shirt for Philo. There was a lovely dress of Geneva's for Mary, made of finely woven wool with lace at the neckline and cuffs, and another, sprigged muslin dress. Also a lawn nightgown with blue ribbons, and a warm dressing gown and bedslippers! There was everything she could possibly need, and the two young ladies acted as if it was nothing at all. If she ever got out of this jail, she'd have something to talk about for the rest of her life.

And she was going to get out. Miss Geneva told her so. "Don't worry, Mary. My father will see to it. He has a lot of influence, Judge Granger will listen to him."

"And you don't have to worry about finding work, either. You can work for me," Roxanne put in. "You can be my personal maid and companion. Then I'll have somebody to go with me when I want to go out, so my father will know I'm properly chaperoned. We'll have wonderful times together, just wait and see." Roxanne made no mention of the fact that she'd balked like a stubborn mule whenever her father had tried to talk her into having a personal maid-companion to accompany her when she went abroad. She wasn't made of sugar. She could take care of herself. Besides, she would rather laugh at smug propriety than observe it.

Personal maid and companion to Miss Roxanne Fielding! Mary couldn't take it in. Not to have to crawl out of bed on freezing mornings in the winter anymore, hours before dawn, and feel like she was starving to death before the breakfast bell rang! She'd get to live in that beautiful house on North Street, and she wouldn't care if it was only a cubbyhole in the attic. If she was companion to Miss Roxanne Fielding, she'd be almost a lady! Companions were genteel, everyone knew that. And she'd work hard at learning how to be a proper companion, she was quick to learn.

But more important than that, more important than anything else, she'd still get to see Dr. Forbes. She wouldn't ever have got to see him again if she'd had to go back to the farm. She might have gone on breathing and eating, you had to eat when you worked hard, but it wouldn't have been living. Why, if she was companion to Miss Roxanne Fielding, she'd be almost on the same social plane as Dr. Forbes! She'd even be able to dress a little better, because it would be expected of her as a companion to a society lady. She'd practice fixing her hair, and maybe Dr. Forbes would notice her. Really notice her, not just look at her as a poor little mill mechanic he was sorry for.

"Don't cry, Mary," Geneva said, when Mary's tears began to flow. "There's nothing to cry about. My father will find a way to get you out of here. And maybe your being arrested and put in jail will do a lot of good. It will bring it home to the other mechanics just how unfair and unjust things are, and that if they don't stand up for their rights and demand better treatment, things will never get better. That's what Bobo says."

"You tell her, Miss Burton!" From the adjoining cell, Philo O'Brian could hear every word that was said, and join in the conversation, which he was in no wise loath to do. He liked to talk even better than he liked to eat. "That's just the way it is. If this doesn't make them stand together and force Herndon Livingston to give them fair treatment, my name isn't Philo O'Brian!"

Ed Hanney was taking in every word that was spoken, and storing it all up in his mind to report to Mr. Livingston. Sunday or not, tomorrow he'd go to Mr. Livingston's house directly after church, and tell him how Miss Fielding and Miss Burton had all but walked over him, bringing more aid and comfort to agitators and organizers than any sane man could conceive of. Mr. Livingston would be livid, but he'd realize that there was nothing that Hanney could have done to stop the young ladies, short of laying hands on them, and that was patently impossible, seeing who they were.

He'd already sent a message to Mr. Livingston, directly after Roxanne's initial visit, but the mill owner had been in conference with Mr. Maynard at the bank. As long as the damage had already been done the messenger hadn't had the temerity to disturb two such important men. And this evening Mr. Livingston was attending a dinner party, and Hanney didn't think it would be wise to disturb him there, either. But tomorrow there'd be a stop put to all this aiding and comforting. Mr. Livingston would know what to do about it. He wouldn't put up with such flagrant breaking of the law, even by Miss Roxanne Fielding and Miss Geneva Burton.

Hanney's back was toward the door, facing the short row of cells the better to keep track of what was going on, and so he didn't know what made Mary gasp. Her hand went up to her mouth just as she let out a terrified scream.

Whirling around, Hanney's hair stood on end and it was all he could do not to do a little screaming himself. A dozen men had walked in, and their appearance was enough to make a braver man than Ed Hanney cringe.

With their faces blacked, with bandanas over the lower parts of their faces, with blankets wrapped around them to hide what clothes they were wearing, they were like something out of the nightmares Hanney sometimes experienced after he'd overpartaken of his wife's New England dinners. But this wasn't a nightmare. The men were real, and advancing on him at this very moment.

"Gimmie the keys," the shortest of the apparitions demanded. "Hand 'em over, and be quick about it, if you know what's good for you."

"Now you see here, you can't do this, I'm the constable and this here's my jail!"

"You want us to prove we can do it?" This speaker was head and shoulders bigger than the others, his very size a menace as he towered over the constable. "Do like you're told!"

Ed considered trying to resist, but he didn't consider it for long. He couldn't reach his firearm because it was in the cabinet across the room, he'd never had any inkling that a thing like this could happen in Athens. Besides, they'd rend him limb from limb before he could get more than one of them. Truth to tell, the thought of shooting anyone horrified him just as much.

In Mary's cell, Roxanne was laughing. She couldn't help it. If that wasn't young Ike Oldham, leading a bunch of rescuers, she'd eat her best Sunday bonnet. A jailbreak, that's what it was! Her father would be tickled when she told him about it. It was just the sort of thing that appealed to his sense of humor.

But Geneva was not amused. "What do you men think you're doing?" she demanded. "Whatever it is, you'd better forget it, and get out of here."

"Not without Mary MacDonald!" the smallest of the invaders shrilled. "She's the one we come for, and we're takin' her out with us, begging your pardon, Miss Burton."

"How about me?" Philo yelped. "Aren't you going to break me out too?"

"Sure we are," the shortest of the ridiculously made-up men affirmed. He already had the key to the cells in his hand. Mary's cell was opened and he made haste to unlock Philo's as well. "Get going!" he advised the organizer. "We'll see that Mr. Hanney doesn't get to go chasing after you till you've had plenty of time for a good head start! Come on, Miss MacDonald, what're you waitin' for?"

Geneva put her hand on Mary's arm. "Don't do it, Mary. I appreciate what these gentlemen"—Roxanne dissolved into another paroxysm of laughter at the term—"are trying to do, but it would bring nothing but a great deal of trouble to you. If you go, you'll be charged with being a fugitive, and even my father won't be able to do anything for you."

Roxanne managed to stop laughing long enough to agree with Geneva. "You stay right where you are, Mary. We'll have you out of here soon enough without the help of these gentlemen."

The would-be rescuers looked as crestfallen as possible under their disguises. This wasn't going at all the way they'd planned. What had been meant as an act of bravado, and a lark that would last them until another one came along, was falling flat.

Geneva's mind was working fast. Philo O'Brian might as well get away, because there was little chance that even her father would be able to defend him ably enough to keep him from receiving a long jail sentence for his agitating. And if his escape was to be effective, Mr. Hanney would have to be prevented from setting up an alarm until at least tomorrow morning. She beckoned to the shortest of the rescuers, and spoke to him in tones so low that Ed Hanney couldn't hear what she said.

"You'll have to gag Mr. Hanney, and lock him in Mr. O'Brian's cell. And you'll have to lock Miss Fielding and me in here with Mary, as well, because we wouldn't have any excuse in the world not to set up an alarm once you've left."

"It's going to be pretty crowded, three of us on that one bunk," Roxanne said, pulling a wry mouth even as she fought against dissolving into laughter again, "but we can stand it."

"And to be sure you can! Isn't there the Irish in you that can stand anything for the sake of justice?" Philo exulted. "I'm off! And may the lot of you be safe in heaven before the divil knows you're dead!" With that, he was out of the door like a streak, pausing only long enough to snatch up his share of the food that Geneva and Roxanne had brought.

"We don't have to gag you ladies, too?" Ike asked anxiously.

"Of course not. We're far too terrified to set up an outcry. In fact, all three of us have swooned." Roxanne reached out to ruffle Ike's hair, but she decided that it wouldn't be wide to push aside the knitted cap he was wearing so that Ed Hanney could get a look at its color. There weren't so many boys of Ike's size with hair the color of a carrot in the vicinity, so that Hanney wouldn't be able to make the connection once he'd gathered his wits. "And besides, we promised before we swooned that we wouldn't make a sound, and a lady never breaks a promise. It would be sinful. Well, girls, it's going to be a long night. We might as well make ourselves as comfortable as possible once our visitors have left us. And young gentleman there, would you be kind enough to get a message to both of our houses not to expect us home tonight? You can tell the Burtons that Geneva is spending the night with me, and my housekeeper that I'm spending the night with her. In the morning, we'll set up a din that'll bring somebody to let us out, all right?"

"If you say so, Miss Fielding. But I still think that Mary'd oughta come with us, now that we've got her cell unlocked."

"No, it wouldn't do at all. Do as Miss Fielding told you, sir." Geneva's mouth twitched. "I promise you that it will be all right. And thank you for trying to help Mary. And tell the others to be sure to wash off every trace of that burnt cork, and dispose of the bandanas and blankets, because we'd rather that none of you were caught with any damning evidence. Now scat!"

With an efficiency that Geneva and Roxanne couldn't help but admire, Ed Hanney was gagged, hands tied behind his back, and bundled into the cell that Philo O'Brian had so recently vacated. He was wrapped up in a blanket which tied around him, more to keep him from reaching the window even if he couldn't yell, than to keep him warm. Reluctantly, Ike turned the key to the cell that the three girls occupied, and dropped the key in plain sight on Mr. Hanney's desk. Then all of the thwarted rescuers were gone. With Mary still protesting against Roxanne and Geneva having to spend the night in jail, the three young ladies settled down to make the best of things.

"We'd better get all the rest we can, because I have an idea that tomorrow's going to be more fun than a barrel of monkeys. We don't want to be too tired to enjoy every minute of it," Roxanne said. And with that, she wrapped herself in a blanket and sat down on the floor, her back against the wall. "We'll take turn about. I'll wake Geneva up in two or three hours, and then she'll wake you up, Mary. That way all of us will get enough sleep to tide us over. Two can fit on that bunk, seeing as it was made to hold a man." And she promptly closed her eyes and dozed off.

Galen's face reflected his bewilderment as he faced Geneva and Marvin Burton and Bobo in Bobo's bedroom. The message from Mr. Burton had told him to come to the Burton house with all speed, and he'd expected to find that someone was ill, or there'd been an accident. But both of the male Burtons, and Geneva Burton, were apparently in the best of health, he hadn't been led to Mrs. Burton's room, and none of the servants were ill.

The jailbreak, and the subsequent uproar the next morning when Roxanne had raised her voice in screams that had made the early churchgoers' hair stand on end, had been a three-day wonder. Nothing else was being talked about, and the subject was still far from wearing itself out.

Nothing would shake the young ladies' stories. They'd been so frightened they'd swooned, and besides, they'd been forced to promise not to raise an outcry until morning. They had not recognized any of the men who'd effected Philo O'Brian's escape. They were law-abiding young women who had managed to prevail upon the men not to rescue Mary MacDonald by force, and Mary was a law-abiding young lady who had declined to be rescued. They were indignant that such a thing could happen in Athens, more protection for decent citizens should be provided.

Ed Hanney was equally vehement that he'd recognized at least two of the black-faced and masked invaders as Ike Oldham and Art Franklyn, but he had no proof because they'd been so well disguised that he had nothing but their sizes to go by. Miss Burton and Miss Fielding were equally vehement in insisting that the smallest of the rescuers had not been Ike Oldham nor the largest one Art Franklyn. And Miss Fielding ought to know, because she knew all of the canallers by sight, if not personally.

Confronted with the fact that the smallest one, who was suspected of being Ike Oldham, had delivered the messages about the young ladies spending the night with each other, Geneva and Roxanne only maintained that whoever he was, he'd only used good sense, in order that no one would come looking for them when they failed to return to their respective homes. As Roxanne had told Herndon Livingston herself, her voice tart, even a moron would know that much.

As Mary corroborated everything that she and Geneva said, there was nothing Herndon Livingston or Ed Hanney could do about it except froth at the mouth, a situation that was even more painful for them because they knew that half the town was snickering at them behind their backs. The general consensus of opinion, except among those businessmen who depended for a large part on the mills for their prosperity, was that the whole affair was hilarious.

Galen wasn't the only one in Athens who suspected that neither Roxanne nor Geneva was as innocent in the matter as they avowed. Knowing them both, he had no doubt that their overnight stay in jail had been voluntary, so that the hue and cry for the escaped organizer couldn't be raised until the next morning.

"How's Mary?" Geneva demanded before Galen had a chance to ask why he'd been summoned if no one in the house needed his professional services. "Have you given her a good going-over to make sure that she didn't suffer any ill effects from her stay behind bars?"

"Mary's fine. Miss Fielding is taking the greatest care of her. The only thing I could find wrong was a good crop of headlice, and that's already been taken care of. Miss Fielding had them, too." Galen couldn't help grinning.

Geneva made a face. "It isn't funny. So did I. You should have heard Mother rave! She's had this whole house turned inside out. I swear that if she'd had her way, I'd have had to cut my hair off to the scalp. Every sheet and pillowcase we own has been boiled, not once but twice, and she burned the clothes I wore that night, right down to the last stitch. Burned them!"

"It's the most effective way I know of getting rid of lice." Galen's eyes were twinkling, his amusement making his mouth twitch at the thought of the very wealthy and very socially prominent Miss Geneva Burton having lice.

Marvin Burton's voice was dry, although not without his own trace of amusement. "A trifle expensive, though. However, as long as she and I between us managed to save Geneva's hair, I expect that I shouldn't complain. Bobo was all for having her cut it off. He thought the whole thing was very funny."

"You could have turned Catholic and entered a convent and become a nun." Bobo grinned from his chair that was placed beside a window so that he could see out. "The discipline would have done you good. At least in a convent you wouldn't be able to consort with canallers and organizers and other riffraff."

"All right, Bobo. It's time we became serious." Marvin's face was suddenly grave. "Galen, we had a message, early this morning, that Philo O'Brian is at the Emerson farm, quite seriously hurt. It seems that he went into their

203

barn, up into the hayloft, to be sure of a good and comfortable hiding place to sleep. He fell on a sickle when he missed his step while descending the ladder just before daylight. Young Luke Emerson, Sam Emerson's younger boy, was the one who came into Athens to tell us. Philo asked him to notify Bobo, because after Bobo helped him escape at the Fourth of July picnic, he knows he can trust him. They didn't dare send word to Stephen Harding's house, because Harding would have notified Herndon and Ed Hanney before he went out to patch Philo up. Luke said that Philo's leg is cut to the bone, he's going to need some stitching, and he lost a lot of blood.''

"I'll go, of course.'' A frown creased Galen's forehead. "But I'll have to borrow a horse and buggy, I don't have one of my own and I can't take Doctor Harding's without telling him where I'm going.''

"We've already thought of that. And in case you're seen driving out of town, which you will be, you'll have to have a good excuse. How would you feel about courting Geneva, for the time being?''

"What?'' Galen's exclamation was both startled and perturbed, and Bobo laughed.

"What better reason could a young doctor have to be driving Cato around the countryside? You'll have to take her, so that nobody will wonder what you're up to. And you'd better get started, it's already after three and it gets dark early these days. It wouldn't do for you to keep Geneva out too long after dark, without a chaperone.''

"I'll have to tell Harding, get his approval.'' Galen's response was reluctant. But outside of Roxanne Fielding, there wasn't any other young lady he could ask to go with him on an errand such as this, and he could hardly insult Marvin Burton's daughter by suggesting that he'd rather take Roxanne.

"Go along then. Cato will be hitched to the buggy by the time you get back. Harding can't very well refuse to let you go, seeing that it's Geneva you want to take driving.''

It was four o'clock by the time they got started, and there was already a chill in the air. Cato was feeling his oats, eager to step out.

"I hope Mr. O'Brian is hanging on,'' Geneva said, worried. "We should have gone much earlier, but you could hardly ask Doctor Harding to let you go courting in the middle of the day. It would be terrible if Philo died before you get there.''

"I doubt that he'll die. Sam Emerson is a capable man, he proved that the night your brother was hurt. Your father said that young Luke told him that they'd managed to stop the bleeding by applying pressure. All the same, it's probably serious, not only the loss of blood but the danger of infection.''

There were still a good number of people on the streets, as they traversed the town to leave by Mill Road. Geneva bowed to those she knew, which was nearly all of them, and secretly hugged herself at their surprised expressions when they saw her out riding with Galen Forbes. Why, this practically compromised Galen! Would she hold him to it, or would she take pity on him and let him go gracefully when Philo no longer needed his attention? Anyway, it amused her to know that before morning, everyone in Athens would have heard that the new young doctor was courting Geneva Burton.

Sitting beside Geneva handling the lines, Galen was thankful that she didn't seem to notice how his ears were burning. This would be almost as much of a bombshell to Athens as the jail escape. He remembered how the town had buzzed when Geneva had broken up with Wyatt Livingston. It seemed that the personal affairs of prominent Athenean citizens were as of much interest to the populace as the doings of politicians. To all intents and purposes, Geneva, or Roxanne, or any of the other wealthy people in Athens were as much in the public eye as actors on a stage. Everything they did was discussed as if it were of the utmost importance. He could understand the reason. There was little enough diversion for the ordinary class of people, so that gossip constituted their chief source of amusement. For himself he couldn't have cared less what the Livingstons' cook served them for supper, or if Cora Burton had worn a new gown to church.

He'd never been good at small talk, especially with young ladies. The only girls he'd ever known well were his own sisters, and they didn't count. What was he supposed to say to Geneva, during the six miles or so they had to travel? He searched his mind frantically, and pounced on something that seemed safe.

"Have you heard anything about Matthew Ramsey

205

since he left town?'' Good Lord, he was gossiping! A few more months in Athens, and he'd be in danger of being as bad as the rest of them.

"Poor Matthew! I felt sorry for him when Addie came back from Syracuse married to Henry Maynard. I felt sorrier for her, of course, but Matthew took it hard. Yes, Father told me, only last week, that he managed to find a place as assistant to the pastor of a church in Lyonsville. The pastor there is ancient and in poor health, and if Matthew pleases the church authorities, he'll inherit the pastorship when the present one either has to give it up because of his health, or dies. It isn't a large church. Nowhere near as large or prosperous as First Methodist here, but at the moment I imagine that he doesn't care about that, just as long as he's away from Athens.''

Geneva paused, sighing, and then she went on. ''Addie looks dreadful. Would it be violating professional ethics to ask if either you or Doctor Harding have been called in to examine her?''

"We haven't. But I should imagine that being married to Maynard would make any girl look dreadful. For what it's worth, Maynard himself consulted with Harding about his own health a few days ago. It seems that now that he has a young and beautiful wife, he wants to live forever! But he'd better keep a tight rein on his temper, and avoid letting anything upset him. He's overweight and his color is too high.''

Galen was violating professional confidence, but he had no fear that Geneva would pass on what he'd said, except perhaps to her father, and it wouldn't go any further than that. All the same, being with Geneva seemed to drain him of his common sense. He'd have to watch himself.

Geneva suppressed a sigh. She was terribly worried about Addie. In all the time Addie had been home after her inexplicable marriage to the banker, her friend had avoided not only her but Roxie as well, and any of her other friends who had tried to see her. Addie attended such social functions as she could not get out of without causing talk, but there were not many of those, and Henry Maynard seemed intent on keeping her entirely to himself.

It wasn't natural. She and Addie and Roxie had been so close. If everything was all right with Addie she'd surely see more of them than she did. Even when they met at some social affair or another, Addie kept close to Henry, evading any attempt on their part to get her alone so that they could talk to her. Geneva knew that Addie never saw her father, that she turned her face away from him and wouldn't look at him when they came into contact.

Geneva was forced to believe Roxie, when she said that Henry must be giving Addie a hard time. If only she could do something about it! If only Addie would talk to her, or to Roxie! But if Addie chose not to, if she chose to keep to herself, they were stalemated. Even Marvin Burton couldn't ferret out the truth behind Addie's strange behavior, and find some legal means to set things right. A man's wife was his property, to do with as he wished as long as he didn't inflict grievous bodily harm on her to the peril of her life. And like Roxie, Geneva believed that Herndon Livingston would have to answer for his sins, if not in this life, then in the next.

They were approaching a crossroad now, and Galen slowed Cato. "I'm not sure which fork to take."

"To the right. We've lived in Athens for so long, for generations, that we know where everybody lives for miles around. Mr. Emerson is a widower, his wife died several years ago. He has two sons helping him run the farm, his daughters are married. You can let Cato out a little more. It's more important that we get there than it is that we get home that fast, he can take it easy on the way back."

As Cato lengthened his stride at Galen's signal on the lines, the young doctor once again had to fight down envy, a commodity that he could ill afford. It would be a long time before he could own a horse like this one. Maybe years. The unbidden thought, one that disturbed him to his core, was that it would be even longer before he could afford a girl like Geneva Burton. And once again, he had to remind himself with bitter force that he wanted nothing to do with Geneva Burton or with any other wealthy girl.

The farmhouse, when they reached it, was at the end of a long lane, isolated from any neighbors. Geneva took the lines while Galen jumped out to rap at the kitchen door. Knowing that farmers did most of their living in the kitchen, it was unlikely that anybody would be in the front part of the house.

The door opened immediately, and a tall, stoop-shouldered man stepped out. He spoke to Galen briefly before he led Cato and the buggy to the barn.

"I'll rub him down," the middle-aged farmer told Geneva, "and give him some water as soon as he's cooled off. Go on in, Miss Burton, get out of the cold. It was good of you to bring the doctor."

The kitchen felt overheated as Geneva stepped inside. A black cast-iron range against one of the outside walls radiated heat to every corner. A younger man who resembled his father pulled a rocking chair with a bright homemade patchwork cushion closer to the stove and smiled at her, his face shy. "You'd best sit down. The doctor may be a while. We've put Mr. O'Brian in the room directly above, where it's kept warm from the stovepipe."

Geneva removed her gloves and held her hands out to the heat, noting at the same time that the kitchen was immaculately clean although it was cluttered. There were curtain rods at the windows, but the curtains themselves had been removed, leaving only a window shade that had seen better days. The room gave mute evidence that the Emerson men were doing the best they could without a woman in the house, and her sympathy, always quickly aroused, went out to them. They were good people, or else they wouldn't have taken in the organizer, and cared for him and sent for Galen, with no thought of collecting the reward that Herndon Livingston had posted on him. A hundred dollars would be a real windfall for people like this, cash money to buy things that they couldn't trade for with produce from their farm. Her father would have called them the backbone of the country: hardworking, with no trace of greed in their makeup.

Still shy, the young farmer poured her a mug of coffee from the battered coffeepot that stood at the back of the range. "I'm afraid it's a mite strong after sitting so long, but it's hot."

She clasped her hands around the mug and smiled at him, and his face turned scarlet. "I'd drink it if it was as thick as mud," she assured him. "Thank you."

Mr. Emerson himself came back from tending Cato, and poured himself some coffee, shaking the pot and handing it to his son. "Better fill it up again, Donald. We'll likely need it."

The second son, Luke, came into the kitchen. He was older than his brother, and already giving evidence that in another few years he'd be a stoop-shouldered image of his father. He spoke to Geneva from the doorway. "The doctor says will you come upstairs, he needs you."

The stairway led up from the dining room. The young farmer carried a lamp that he held above his shoulder to light her way. He nodded toward an open door. "In there. I'm to fetch a basin of hot water and something for clean bandages."

Philo O'Brian lay on a bedstead, his face almost as white as the faintly yellowed pillowcase his head rested on, but he managed a feeble grin. "Looks like you're pegged to play nurse, Miss Burton. I hope you don't faint at the sight of a little blood."

Geneva smiled back at him. "I don't know if I do or not. All the blood I've ever seen has been from nosebleeds and skinned knees." She looked down at his leg then, exposed to Galen's examination, and she winced at the sight of the deep gash that was still seeping blood.

Galen spoke without looking up. "If you're squeamish, I'll have the young man help me, but I'm hoping that you'll be able to do it. It's no time for big, clumsy hands, no matter how willing these people are to help."

"We'll soon find out, won't we?" Geneva spoke lightly. Her stomach felt queasy, and her knees had begun to tremble, but if it had to be done she'd do it and she'd be darned if she'd faint. She'd never hear the last of it from Bobo if she did, as well as letting Philo O'Brian and Galen down.

"I want you to hold the edges of the wound together as I stitch it," Galen told her. "In a way it's good that it bled as much as it did. Wounds that bleed profusely are less likely to become infected. I'll have to leave a small place unstitched for drainage, and it's going to be essential to keep it clean."

"I'd rather she held my hand," O'Brian said, trying to joke. His face twisted into lines of agony as Geneva, under Galen's direction, swabbed the area of the gash with the hot water and soap that Luke brought up. Then Galen began making neat sutures. O'Brian's teeth sank into his lower lip, and he didn't make a sound until it was done. Then he let loose with a string of expletives that would have sent the Wednesday Afternoon Sewing Circle into trauma.

"Beg your pardon, Miss Burton. Dammit, Doc, that hurt!"

Geneva grinned at him. "Go on. Cuss all you want to.

I'll say a special prayer for you tonight and ask God to forgive you."

Luke handed Galen a bottle of rum and Galen said, "Hang on, Philo. I'm going to hurt you some more." He didn't give the organizer time to worry about it, but poured a liberal amount of it over the gash.

The cussing Philo had done before faded into Sunday-school pleasantries in comparison. "Gawdalmighty! You shoulda poured that in me mouth, not on me leg! Come on, man, let me have it before you waste any more!"

Galen tilted the bottle to Philo's mouth. "Go ahead, you've earned it. I want you to be able to sleep. But not too much, mind you, because I don't want you to have a hangover so that you can't eat! You have a lot of blood to build up again."

Philo snorted. "Don't you go worryin' your head about mine! I've got an Irishman's head, and no Irishman ever lived who can't hold more liquor than this bottle holds! Miss Burton, you're an angel straight from heaven, and if iver I get to mass again, I'll be saying prayers for you. I hope I see you again sometime, because the sight of your pretty face brings joy to me heart."

"You'll be seeing her again. I'll have to come back here every night to check on you, and she has to bring me, else you'd have Ed Hanney and all the deputy constables Herndon Livingston can afford swarming all over this farm. Well, Miss Burton? How about a cup of coffee, and then we'll head back."

This time, the coffee was fresher, and they drank it gratefully. They'd been at the farmhouse something less than an hour, but it seemed much longer to Geneva. Her knees still felt shaky as Galen helped her into the buggy.

"You were splendid back there," Galen told her. "Anybody would think you'd helped stitch up gashes all your life."

"I'm glad to have been of service." Geneva tried to keep a light touch to the conversation. Galen's hair was disheveled, and just as she had on the night of Herndon Livingston's birthday celebration, her fingers itched to smooth it back. "Would you like me to drive? You've been under quite a strain, patching Mr. O'Brian up."

"I can manage. I hope you don't mind having to come

back with me every night until I'm sure that Philo will be all right.''

"I'll enjoy every minute of it. Philo O'Brian has become one of my favorite people. And this will raise me several notches in Bobo's estimation. Doctor Forbes, what do you think about Bobo's leg?''

Galen hesitated only for a second. This was no place for a soothing bedside manner. Geneva was entitled to the truth. He was sure that she'd take it without going to pieces, as much as she loved her brother.

"He'll have a limp. Rather a pronounced limp. He'll have to learn to live with it. I'm sorry, Miss Burton."

Geneva's voice was steady, but he detected the pain in it. "And he will learn to live with it. Bobo isn't a quitter. How much will it handicap him?''

"No more than he lets it. He'll still be able to win races with Cato, if he puts his mind to it. Walking, he'll tire more easily than most men, and I don't expect that he'll ever be called on to make a cross-country hike or win a footrace.''

"Then it's all right." Geneva bit at her lower lip, and then burst out, "But darn it, Galen, I wish you'd set that leg!''

"So do I. But no one can say for sure if I'd have done any better a job than Harding did. And wishing doesn't get you anywhere. We can't always have what we want in this world.''

There was a bitterness in his voice that made Geneva start, and she tried to make out his face in the darkness that had settled in while they'd been at the Emersons' farm.

Galen was an enigma to her; always outwardly civil and pleasant, he seemed to hold off any real intimacy. What had happened before he'd come to Athens to make him distrust people?

"Maybe we can't," she said. "But we'd be foolish not to try to get what we want.''

"Or more foolish to try to get it." Galen's voice was rough. "It's probably different in your case. You're one of the fortunate few born to get what they want. We'd better be getting back, we don't want the whole town buzzing. We can't afford to let people think we're serious about each other. It will just have to break off as soon as Philo can do without us.''

His implication was so clear that Geneva felt chilled. He couldn't have made it more plain that he didn't want anything to do with her socially, that he wanted no personal relationship with her. Her anger seethed just under the surface. No man had ever rejected her before. What was the matter with him, anyway? Why was she poison to him? He actually disliked her, and there was no reason for it.

Her furious eyes belying the calmness of her face, she settled back, determined not to attempt any more conversation with him.

Galen addressed all of his attention to driving, but now the pleasure of handling Cato was gone. God, how he wished that this was over with! He'd have to walk a tightrope for the next week or two. He had to have Geneva to accompany him to the Emersons' farm, and he had no wish to alienate himself from Marvin Burton or Bobo, whose good opinion he was anxious to keep. But being thrown into close proximity with Miss Geneva Burton every evening was going to be rough.

All the same, he was damned if he was going to be a rich woman's plaything, or let her coerce him as David Harshey had been coerced. Let Geneva take Wyatt Livingston back, they were suited to each other. The Burton money and backing would come in handy to Wyatt about now.

In grim silence, their antagonism a palpable thing hanging between them, they accomplished the trip back to town in silence.

"I expect you'll need me again tomorrow evening?" Geneva asked coolly as he handed her out of the buggy.

"I expect I will. I regret if it's an inconvenience to you."

"Think nothing of it. As I said before, I thoroughly enjoy *Mr. O'Brian's* company!" With that, Geneva walked into the house with as much dignity as she could muster, but for one of the very few times in her life, she slammed the door hard behind her.

14

Roxanne was alone in her room when the messenger from her father arrived. Mary had gone downtown, eager to listen to the gossip that she might pick up about the unrest at the mill. From what she and Roxanne had heard, the mechanics were on the point of staging a turnout, and Athens seethed with suspense as everyone tried to learn the latest developments.

Earl Fielding was in New York, and Roxanne didn't expect him home for another two days, so her heart leaped into her throat when Freda, the older of the two housemaids, told her that the messenger was waiting in the hall. She brushed past Freda before the woman had finished speaking, and nearly tripped on the stairs before she remembered to gather up her skirts.

The man stood close to the front door, examining the entrance hall with curiosity. "You've come from my father?" Roxanne demanded. The pulse at the base of her throat was beating painfully, but she wasn't the sort to put her hand to it like a frail and delicate female.

"Yes, ma'am, Miss Fielding." His cap in his hand, the man's face registered astonishment at Roxanne's bright beauty. "Mr. Fielding said I was to give you this." He fumbled in his jacket pocket for a letter, the single page folded, written on one side only, leaving the other for the name and address.

Roxanne snatched the letter from him and broke the seal, thankful that her father's handwriting was strong and easily legible.

He'd found Wyatt! His network of informants had located him in Rochester. Roxanne's heart leapt, and then plummeted again as she read on:

It isn't all good news. From what I heard, Wyatt's under the weather, holed up in some room on Second Street just off the waterfront. I'll go directly there as soon as I finish up in New York. Just sit easy, and take care of yourself.

Earl had not yet heard of Roxanne's part in Philo O'Brian's jailbreak, or his letter wouldn't have been so unconcerned. He'd have come tearing home to make sure that she was all right, that Ed Hanney hadn't mistreated her.

The thought was so fleeting that Roxanne scarcely registered it. The only thing that mattered was that she knew where Wyatt was, and that he was sick.

"There won't be any answer," she told the messenger. And then she was back up the stairs again, and ordering Freda to bring a satchel immediately.

"You going somewhere, Miss Fielding?" Freda demanded. "Where are you going, and when will you be back?"

"I'm going to Rochester, and I don't know when I'll be back. Now move!"

Earl would be furious when he found out, but she didn't care. Wyatt was sick, and alone, and she was going to get to him as fast as she could. There was no way she was going to wait for her father to get to him, two or three days from now.

"But Mary hasn't come back yet. Shall I send Norah to find her? She shouldn't have gone out alone, she'll be lucky if that Carl Jakes doesn't waylay her again and try to make up to her."

Freda's mouth was tight with disapproval. Several times since Mary had come to live with Roxanne, Carl Jakes had accosted her on the streets, and tried to persuade her to go out with him in the evening. Mary was not only furious, because she detested him in spite of his coarse good looks, but she was a little afraid of him because of the lustful way he looked at her. No girl was so innocent that she wouldn't recognize that look.

"Yes, yes, tell her to hurry! Tell her to run all the way back. And pack a few things for Mary, too. I'll take care of my own packing."

Knowing the schedules of nearly every canalboat that came through Athens, Roxanne knew that one of the Six Day Packets between New York and Buffalo would be pulling out in less than an hour, and she had every intention of being on it. No waiting for one of her father's boats, which would be so much slower! She threw things into the satchel without regard for neatness. An extra dress, underthings and a nightgown, toilet articles. Snapping the satchel shut, she ran downstairs and into Earl's study, where he always left a good supply of cash. He traveled so much that he didn't want Roxanne to be short on household money or anything she took a fancy to buy for herself. She could have charged anything necessary, but Earl didn't believe in keeping women short of cash and monitoring everything they spent, just because men were the lords and masters.

Roxanne often laughed about the safe that was concealed behind some books on a shelf. The key was kept under the mantel clock. Earl shared her amusement. Actually, the safe was just a place to keep cash out of sight, as Earl didn't believe in tempting servants, either. He had little fear of sneak thieves. It would take a bold thief to dare to steal from him.

Ruthlessly, Roxanne scooped every last bill from the safe. If she was away very long, Freda or Mrs. Casey could charge anything they needed at Maxwell's Emporium or any other shop in town. She didn't even stop to count the money, most of it in gold pieces because her father liked the look and the feel of gold. You knew what a gold coin was worth, and you couldn't always say the same about paper notes. If there wasn't enough, she could get more on the strength of her father's name, in any town along the canal.

Her preparations completed, she paced the hallway floor. Where on earth was Norah with Mary? In a town the size of Athens, with only two blocks of downtown street and a few lesser shops on side streets, it shouldn't have been hard to find her!

Half an hour later, Norah was back, out of breath and red-faced with apology. "I couldn't find her anywhere, Miss Roxanne. I even went to her old dormitory, in case she was visiting Mrs. Simms, but the nightmarm hasn't seen her."

Drat! Well, she'd just have to go alone. She couldn't wait. She'd barely have time to make the packet. The schedule the Six Day Line kept was a horse-killer, but the packets nearly always pulled into either New York or Buffalo on time. It was a mercy that the canal hadn't been closed for the winter yet, else she didn't know what she would have done. Another week or two, and it would have been too late. Snatching up her satchel, she was out through the door before Freda had a chance to protest.

"Well!" Freda said to her retreating back. "What I'm to tell your father, you taking off on a trip without an escort or even a female companion, I don't know!"

Running down the street, holding her bonnet with one hand and the satchel banging against her legs, Roxanne didn't even hear her.

She was the first one off the packet in Rochester, leaving the captain of the packet well roiled up because she refused to wait for him to procure a reliable guide for her. Earl Fielding would have his skin if anything happened to her, even if Earl wasn't connected with the Six Day Line. Staring after her, the captain thanked the Lord that his own daughters were tractable. It would never have entered their conventional heads to behave as this auburn-haired beauty was acting.

Roxanne knew exactly where she was going. She'd elicited the location of the street where Wyatt had a room from the captain almost as soon as she'd boarded his packet. Ignoring the gaping stares of jostling men and slatternly women, she knocked on the door of the first house with a "Rooms-to-Let" sign in the window.

"Wyatt Livingston. He's tall, dark, twenty-one years old, and he'll be well dressed."

She pulled a blank at the first three houses. At the fourth, a hawk-faced woman in a clean overall apron looked at her with suspicion. "You related to him?"

If the district wasn't respectable, the woman obviously was. Roxanne knew that she'd never get past her unless she lied.

"He's my husband," she said. Thank heaven she'd remembered to pull on her gloves before she'd left the packet, the woman couldn't see that she wasn't wearing a wedding ring. "He told me to meet him here."

The suspicion increased. The young woman, obviously agitated, who stood on her doorstep wasn't the kind of young woman who'd travel alone, even to meet her husband. The whole thing was suspicious, because the young man she'd asked for wasn't the sort to take a room in her boardinghouse, either. Well dressed, the young woman had said. Mr. Livingston was so well dressed that Mrs. Campbell had been wary of letting him have a room. He had to be a gambler or an actor to dress that well and seek lodgings in this part of town. She didn't cater to either category. Still, Mr. Livingston had looked tired, and not too well. He'd offered cash in advance for an entire week, so she'd let him in with the mental reservation that if he turned out to be an actor or a gambler, she'd have him right out again.

She still hadn't found out if Mr. Livingston was an actor or a gambler. He was sick, and he was getting sicker, and his room rent had run out. If this young woman had money, then she wouldn't have to put him out when he couldn't even stand on his feet.

"Upstairs, third floor, second door on the left." Mrs. Campbell paused, but only briefly. "If you're going to stay with him, it'll be extra."

"I'll let you know." Roxanne was already climbing the stairs. They were uncarpeted, the boards sagging because the house was jerry-built, but they were clean. At the second door on the left on the third floor, she rapped sharply.

"It's not locked." Wyatt's voice was a croak. He lay on a wooden bedstead, uncomfortable on the sagging mattress. He was burning up, and racked with thirst. In his delirium, he couldn't understand why his mother and the servants didn't bring him a drink of water, why they didn't change the hot and rumpled sheets for cool, lavender-smelling ones, why they'd left him alone for so long when they must know that he wasn't feeling well.

"Drink," he said, when the door opened. "Drink of water, please."

"Wyatt!" Roxanne dropped her satchel, and in another instant her hand was on his forehead. "What on earth have you done to yourself?"

His eyes opened halfway, and they were glazed and dull with fever. Dimly, he thought that he recognized Roxanne Fielding, but he ignored that because Roxanne wouldn't be in his bedroom, it wouldn't be proper. "Water?"

There was a glass and a pitcher on the bureau, but they

were both empty. Roxanne picked up the pitcher and ran pell-mell down both flights of stairs again. At their foot, she raised her voice into a bellow. "We need water! Immediately, if you please!"

Mrs. Campbell came back into the hall, still disapproving. Roxanne thrust the pitcher at her. "Fill it, please. Don't you know that he's ill? What have you been doing for him? Has he had a doctor?"

"He didn't ask for a doctor. It's not my place to call in a doctor that a boarder might not be able to pay for."

"Then send for one! The water first, and then get a doctor here as fast as you can! The best doctor in town!"

"Can you pay?"

"Yes, I can pay!" Exasperated and frantic because Wyatt was so sick, Roxanne gave her a shove, and flew back up the stairs as soon as the resentful woman fetched the pitcher back from the kitchen.

Wyatt was half off the bed, struggling to get to his feet. Roxie was here, he had to find his dressing robe, where had he put it? Couldn't let Roxie see him in his nightshirt, it wasn't decent. Only of course it wasn't Roxie, his mother must have engaged a new maid.

Roxanne's hands pushed him back onto the bed and yanked the sheet up under his chin. "Stay in bed, are you crazy or something? Don't you know you're sick?"

"Sick." Wyatt closed his eyes again. "Water."

There was a four-day stubble of beard on his face and his cheeks were sunken. Roxanne wanted to gather him into her arms and hold him and protect him. Instead, she poured a glass of water and supported his head while he drank a little. Her spirits sank when he turned his head away after only a swallow or two. As is the case with so many fevers, it was difficult for him to drink, he couldn't seem to get it down.

Mrs. Campbell was of two minds about sending for a doctor, let alone the best one in town. She hadn't seen any money yet. What if the young woman was an actress, and Mr. Livingston an actor? Her front parlor window bore a sign that could be found in the windows of nearly every respectable rooming house: "No actors or printers."

The landlady was still trying to decide whether to risk getting a doctor in when Roxanne appeared again, her face white with fury. "Damn you, I told you to send for a doctor! Why are you still standing here?"

"Doctors cost money."

"Wait right where you are." Exasperated, feeling like hitting the woman, Roxanne ran up both flights of stairs again. She'd left her reticule on the bureau. Snatching it up, she dug out a handful of gold coins and went to the landing where she could look down to the ground floor where the landlady was still waiting.

"Here!" Roxanne said. She dropped the gold pieces, five and ten dollar ones. "Now get a move on!"

Mrs. Campbell gasped with what almost amounted to agony. Gold pieces, rolling and bouncing all over the floor, what if she couldn't find all of them? The young woman must be insane! She got down on her hands and knees and scrambled after the coins, finally convinced that she'd found them all. Then, and then only, she stepped out of her house and called to an urchin who was kicking a stone along the street. She told him to go and fetch Dr. Filmore at once. She didn't know if Dr. Filmore was the best in town, but he was the one people in this section of the waterfront sent for if they thought they were going to die unless they called a doctor.

Dr. Filmore looked grave once he'd caught his breath after laboring up the two flights of stairs and examined Wyatt.

"He has a fever," he said. "And congestion."

The idiot! Why didn't he tell Roxanne something she didn't already know?

"I should have been called in sooner."

"But you weren't, so what are you going to do for him now that you have been called in?"

"Keep him warm. Pile on blankets. Pack him with hot bricks. Keep the windows tightly closed and most important of all, withhold water, withhold all fluids. I may have to bleed him, if he hasn't improved by morning. We'll have to wait and see."

"How sick is he? Is he in danger of dying?"

"That, my dear young lady, is in the hands of the Almighty. If I'd been called in earlier, the outlook would be brighter." A fine, snide way of wriggling out of blame if the patient dies, Roxanne thought savagely. It wouldn't be the fault of an incompetent doctor, but the fault of the patient's family! She'd have given everything she owned if Galen were here. How soon could he get here, if she sent him a message? She grasped Mrs. Campbell's arm, her fingers digging in in order to stress her words.

"I want a message given to the captain of the next Six Day Line packet heading east. The captain is to get a message to Doctor Galen Forbes, in Athens, that he's to come to Rochester at once. Have the boy give your address and have the captain tell Doctor Forbes that Wyatt Livingston is at death's door. He's to drop everything else and come. Do you understand, do you have it straight?" Impatiently, she shook her head. "No. Bring me pen and paper, I'll write it out. At once!"

Uppity young miss, Mrs. Campbell thought. But there was an authority in Roxanne's voice and manner that made her move quickly.

Roxanne wrote the message, forcing herself to take time enough to write clearly so that there could be no misunderstanding. Lord, Lord, let Galen get here fast! "Send a boy with this, and as soon as he's left, I want blankets, and hot bricks." How was she to keep Wyatt warm, in this unheated room that had neither a stove nor a fireplace? He should be in a better house, in a better room, but she knew that it was impossible to have him moved, she'd just have to do the best she could. He wasn't going to die, she wouldn't let him die! Death would have to walk over her own dead body to get him.

Her mouth grim, Mrs. Campbell brought the blankets. They were thin and shabby, but they were clean. Roxanne piled them over Wyatt, tucking them in. "Hot bricks!" she demanded. "Didn't you hear what the doctor said?" And he'd better know what he's talking about, she thought! Personally, she'd never been able to understand why a person who was already burning up should be made even hotter.

The air in the room, as chill as it was, was stale from lack of ventilation and the odors that always accompany a seriously ill person. Roxanne pulled her coat more closely around her and pulled the one chair in the room close to Wyatt's bed where she could watch to see that he didn't throw the blankets off.

Under the blankets, which were weighing him down, Wyatt stirred, his voice fretful. "Thirsty."

"I'm sorry, darling. The doctor said you can't have any water." Roxanne slipped her hand under the blankets and groped until she found his. She held it tight, willing the strength of her own body to enter his. "Try to sleep."

"Mother, I want a drink."

"Hush, Wyatt, hush."

He was burning up, his skin felt like fire when she put her other hand on his forehead. How much time had passed since that half-witted doctor had left? She got up and found Galen's pocket watch on the bureau, but it had stopped, whether today or yesterday she had no way of knowing.

She went out into the hallway and called as loudly as she could, but there was no response, so once more she had to hurry down the stairs. Her face tight with tension, she went through the door at the end of the hall and found herself in a dining room, off which was a dark and gloomy kitchen where the landlady was stirring a kettle of salt pork and cabbage.

"What time is it?"

"Coming on to five-thirty, suppertime." The landlady's voice was curt.

"Exactly what time is it?"

"Look at the clock in the parlor. And close the door afterwards."

The mess in the kettle smelled nauseating, but Roxanne gritted her teeth. "Bring me a plate of that when it's ready. And coffee. A whole pot of coffee."

"That will be five cents."

"I don't care if it's five dollars!" Roxanne exploded. "Unless you have something decent to bring, instead. In that case I'd pay extra." She was afraid that the pork and cabbage would make her sick if she ate it, but she had to have nourishment. She'd been too frantic on the packet to more than nibble at her dinner, and if she was to watch over Wyatt she had to keep up her strength. At least the coffee would help no matter how vile it might be.

She'd gone only a few steps back up the stairs when the front door opened and a burly man, his rough clothing proclaiming that he was some sort of manual worker, entered.

"Well, well, what have we here?" The exclamation burst from him, and his heavy, less than intelligent face took on a leer that was meant to be a compliment. "What's a beauty like you doin' in this rattrap? I got it! You're lookin' for work at Belle's! I can put in a good word for you.''

He'd caught up with her before she'd gone five more steps, and then his hand was on her arm, preventing her from going any farther.

"Let go of me, you oaf!"

"Now, that ain't any way to act! A pretty piece like you, you'll be needin' all the help you can get in this town, and—"

Roxanne resisted the impulse to hook her foot under his ankle and topple him backwards down the stairs, a trick she'd learned during her days on the canal with her father. She could have done it, but the landlady wouldn't like it, and she couldn't afford to waste time explaining, or the risk of being asked to leave. So she drew herself up to her full height. The expression on her face would have been enough to make even this lout quail, even without the words that accompanied it.

"If you don't remove your hand, and keep away from me, my father will teach you better manners. Have you ever heard of Earl Fielding?"

The hand on her arm dropped off as if her arm had suddenly turned red-hot. The man's face went blank with slow-dawning comprehension. Everybody'd heard of Earl Fielding, and everybody knew that Earl Fielding had a beautiful red-haired daughter. The lust that had churned in him seconds ago turned to ice water in his veins.

"Beg pardon, Miss. I didn't mean no harm."

"Then see that you keep on meaning no harm!" Roxanne's voice was sharp. The man stared after her as she continued climbing the stairs. If she was fooling him, if she'd just said that she was Earl Fielding's daughter, he'd feel like a fool, but he didn't dare to take the chance no matter how unlikely it was that Earl Fielding's daughter would be in a rooming house like this. All the same, if she was fooling him, he'd find a way to get back at her.

Wyatt had thrown the blankets off when she regained his room, and she covered him again, trying to keep him from threshing around. "Water," Wyatt begged. "Mother, Addie, I want a drink."

It was only a quarter of six in the evening. Galen wouldn't get her message for two days, and then he'd have to get here. The terror that Roxanne had been fighting ever since she'd arrived and seen how ill Wyatt was came a step closer. How soon would her father get here? He'd said he'd come to check on Wyatt himself, but New York was a very long ways away. Even if he'd already started he couldn't get here any sooner than Galen. There was no one to help her; if Wyatt were to live she'd have to do it herself.

She squared her shoulders, and her face set in lines of determination. If she had to do it herself, she would. Wyatt wasn't going to die, because she wasn't going to let him.

Wyatt was tossing again, his eyes blank. Roxanne recovered him, using her own considerable strength to make him lie still.

"Wyatt, you must be quiet. I'm right here. I won't leave you, I'm going to take care of you. Galen Forbes is coming. He'll make you well again."

She didn't think that he understood a word she said, but her voice soothed him and he subsided.

Six-thirty. The night stretched endlessly before her. She'd lighted the oil lamp on the bureau when she'd returned to the room. Its smoky chimney made flickering shadows on the walls, the paper a faded dingy brown. Now the smell of the oil was added to the other stale odors of the room, and Roxanne's stomach objected. She was used to fresh air, to plenty of space around her. She'd never been confined like this, in a small space with a man who was sick enough so that he might die. Her man, the man she loved.

Mrs. Campbell's footsteps were heavy on the stair treads as she carried up Roxanne's supper, and she shouldered the door open without knocking.

"Worse, is he?" the landlady asked.

"Of course he isn't worse! He's going to get better, he's going to be all right."

"He doesn't look any better to me. If you were a proper wife, you'd have been with him, not letting him go traipsing around the country alone. Theatrical people, are you?"

"No, we're not." Roxanne took the plate and poked at the soggy mass of cabbage and pork. Resolutely, she put a forkful of it in her mouth, and nausea churned in her stomach. She swallowed. It didn't want to go down but she forced it down, and took another forkful. Mrs. Campbell waited, but Roxanne volunteered no further information. Thoroughly miffed, the landlady left the room.

"You'll have to carry the plate and the cup down when you're finished. This house doesn't furnish maid service."

Roxanne didn't bother to answer her, she was too busy trying to pretend that she wasn't eating cabbage and salt pork while she continued to lift the fork from the plate to her mouth.

She didn't throw it up. She refused to throw it up. When she'd finished almost all of it, she set the plate outside the door. It could stay there all night. She wasn't going to leave Wyatt, and she wasn't going to have what was left stay in the room, adding its nasty smell to all the others.

"Mother?"

She stroked his forehead, and he subsided once more. But twice that night she had to hold him down by main force as he tossed and threshed around in the bed, out of his head with fever. Roxanne thought that dawn would never come, and when it finally did, eons afterward, it brought no relief to her anxiety. It was just another long, gray day to be got through without letting Wyatt die.

The doctor came back at a little after ten, and he frowned when he saw Wyatt's condition.

"I'll have to bleed him. I was afraid of that, so I came prepared. If you'll hold the bowl for me, young lady, we'll get on with it, I have other patients."

Watching Wyatt's blood trickle into the small bowl were the worst moments of Roxanne's life.

15

Galen was at the smithy when the messenger sent by the captain of the Six Day Line packet found him. Ever since he'd come to Athens, he'd been drawn to the blacksmith shop and Lester Peterson. The good, clean smell of horse, the acrid odor of a hot shoe on a horse's hoof, the heat and smoke from the glowing charcoal, all brought him back to his own young years, when he'd worked at his father's smithy.

Besides, he liked Lester Peterson. The man was the best blacksmith he'd ever known, and more intelligent than most of the highly respected businessmen of Athens. Galen liked to talk to him, even to discuss medical matters with him. Peterson himself knew a little about doctoring, even if it was horses he doctored, and it was safe to discuss anything with him because the man was as closemouthed as a turtle.

They'd been hashing over Philo O'Brian's gashed leg. "Sounds like it's coming along all right, Galen. Mind you keep on with the whiskey, I like whiskey better than rum for wounds like that, I don't hold with the sugar in rum on open wounds."

"Neither do I. And it's whiskey I'm using, to Philo's delight. His only complaint is that it isn't Irish whiskey, but he manages to control his prejudice sufficiently to down an amazing amount of it. I've had to take in an extra bottle, because it's hard to hang onto enough of it to clean the gash before it all goes down his gullet."

It was safe talking to Peterson about Philo. Lester Peterson wouldn't give Herndon Livingston the time of day. He'd take care of the mill owner's horses, and do his best for them, but he had no use for the man himself. Ever since Herndon had sold that pretty little daughter of his to Henry Maynard, his aversion for him had strengthened.

Now Peterson laughed. "The whiskey won't hurt him. I never knew any Irishman who couldn't drink any other man living under the table, and still walk away without staggering. It's a blessing that the Emersons took him in. It strengthens my faith in the human race. As long as there are people like the Emersons, even the Herndon Livingstons of the world can't completely ruin things."

Peterson was closemouthed, and he liked animals better than he liked people, but his reluctance to engage in conversation didn't extend to Galen. The young doctor was different. He had common sense for one thing, and he knew about horses and blacksmithing for another, and it never entered his mind that because he was a doctor and Lester was a blacksmith that he was better than Lester.

"Doctor Forbes?"

Both men looked up as a third man entered the smithy.

"Here. Is someone sick?"

"I don't know. I was told to give you this." A letter was handed over, and Galen read it quickly and felt as if his stomach had turned upside down. Thank God the man had had the sense to follow instructions and deliver the letter to him personally instead of leaving it at Harding's office where Harding might have read it. If he had, the fat would have been in the fire.

Not that the fat wasn't already in the fire. Roxanne Fielding in Rochester, without as much as having taken Mary MacDonald with her to give this whole impossible affair a modicum of propriety! And Wyatt sick, very sick, Roxanne had written. Likely to die if he didn't get there as fast as he could.

He had to lie to Harding, there was no other way. He told the older doctor that he'd had a message from his father that his mother was ill, and he had to go to her immediately. Harding didn't like it. He made it clear that he wasn't paying Galen to go chasing off to care for his mother, when there were doctors in his hometown available. But professing to be a good Christian, there was no way he could actually refuse his permission.

Galen's next stop, after checking his medical bag and

throwing a change of clothing into his satchel, was at the Fielding house, where he asked for Mary. Mary's face went from an excited flush to pallor when he told her that she was to join Roxanne in Rochester. If Roxanne was foolhardy enough to insist on staying with Wyatt, and Galen knew that she was, having Mary there as her companion was essential, as late as it was to mend the bridges that Roxanne had left in a shambles behind her.

The idea of traveling all the way to Rochester was enough to frighten Mary out of her wits. All that way, on a fast packet, when she'd never been farther from the farm where she'd been born than Athens. But she wasn't going to be frightened. Miss Roxanne needed her and she was going. She'd have done anything for Miss Roxanne, who'd helped her when she hadn't known where to turn. She was grateful to Geneva Burton, and grateful to Mr. Burton, who'd convinced the judge that there was no case against her because she hadn't given that food to Mr. O'Brian, Ed Hanney had. There was no way to prove that she'd been going to give it to Mr. O'Brian. She could have been taking it to feed a stray dog.

"Pack what you'll need for several days' stay," Galen told her. "I'll be back to take you to the packet as soon as I check to see when the next one is due."

Galen had one more call to make, after he'd ascertained that there'd be a Six Day Line packet late that afternoon. He knocked at the door of the Burton house within minutes of checking on the schedule.

"You'll be wanting to see Miss Geneva," Nelly said. "She's in the library with Mr. Burton, helping him with his book."

Both of their faces registered surprise when Galen was ushered in. He never called during the daytime, and he'd been avoiding them entirely except for his and Geneva's necessary trips to the Emerson farm every evening. They'd been trips that were accomplished in a formal, uncomfortable near silence, the only conversation between them pertaining to Philo O'Brian and how fast he was recuperating.

"Wyatt Livingston is in Rochester, very ill, and Miss Fielding's gone rushing off to take care of him. She's sent for me. I'm afraid that I'll have to ask a favor that will be a great imposition. Miss Burton has watched me dress Philo's wound several times now. She'll be able to do it herself if she'll consent. She knows what to look for, but I don't anticipate any trouble. I just want to be sure that it's properly cared for. Not by hands that have been handling shovels and pitchforks around horse manure."

"Of course I'll do it. Poor Roxanne, all alone in Rochester, with Wyatt so ill. She must be frantic! You just get there as fast as you can, and leave Mr. O'Brian to me."

Marvin had brightened up. As dear to his heart as getting this book of his written was, sometimes the hours of work involved became tedious.

"Geneva's right, Galen. Don't give it another thought. I'll just tell her mother that I'm taking her with me to chase down some more research on the book, and I'll drive her out there myself. Not that Cora can't be trusted, but she has a lot of friends and she might let something slip if she knew what was actually going on. I'd like to talk to O'Brian anyway."

"Thank you. I'm taking Mary MacDonald with me, to stay with Miss Fielding. I don't know when I'll be back. You'll certainly have to take several trips to the Emersons' farm."

"Don't let it worry you. We'll take care of it." There was a twinkle in Marvin's eyes. "You have no idea how much research is necessary for a book like mine! And naturally I'll have to take Geneva with me, to take notes. No one will think a thing of it."

Galen's mind was considerably relieved. Now to pick up Mary, and they'd just be in time to board the packet.

It wasn't until Galen boarded the packet with her that Mary realized that she wasn't to make this journey alone. He was going with her! Her heart began to beat against her ribs like one of the drums in a Fourth of July parade, and for a moment she was afraid that she was going to faint. All the way to Rochester, on a packet, with Dr. Forbes! She pinched herself, not sure that she wasn't dreaming. It was not only the most wonderful adventure of her entire life, but she was going to share it with Galen Forbes! Dear Lord, she prayed silently, if I should die before I wake, thank you for this, anyway! Her smile was so radiant when she looked at him that Galen was startled.

She's a pretty girl, he thought. Prettier than I'd realized.

Jim Yarnell was a lucky man, and here Galen came near to a twinge of jealousy. The lineboat captain and the little mechanic would have a happy life together, once Mary made up her mind to accept him. He realized, startled again, that he himself could be happy with a girl like Mary, who'd make no demands on him. A girl like her would never expect him to compromise his dedication to treating the people who need him the most, just because there was more money and prestige in being physician to the wealthy.

Yes, Jim Yarnell had chosen well. But that was neither here nor there. All that mattered right now was to get to Wyatt Livingston as fast as this packet could carry him there.

Mrs. Campbell's face was forbidding as she regarded the two people who were standing on her doorstep. "Doctor Forbes? All the way from Athens?" Her glance, filled with suspicion, went to Mary. "I wasn't expecting another person, I was only told that a Doctor Forbes would be coming."

"This is Miss MacDonald, Miss Fielding's companion. She'll be staying on for as long as it's necessary for Miss Fielding to remain here."

Mrs. Campbell's face registered outrage. "*Miss Fielding!* I was given to understand by the young lady who is nursing Mr. Livingston that she was Mr. Livingston's wife! This is an outrage! I run a respectable house—"

That tears it, Galen thought. The scandal he'd been hoping to bypass by bringing Mary to stay with Roxanne would explode all along the Erie Canal, and Athens itself would be rocked to its very foundations. It was bad enough that Roxanne had come rushing off to Rochester to take care of Wyatt in the first place, but to pass herself off as his wife! It took an effort to keep his face impassive.

"I'll see my patient now, if you please. And if you happen to have an empty room, I'll doubtless remain the night. If not, I'll find some place else."

"Then you'll have to find some place else. This town is bursting at the seams, Mr. Livingston only got his room because I had to put a man out less than an hour before he arrived, for being noisily intoxicated. I do not put up with intoxication on my premises, Doctor Forbes, *nor* do I put up with indecency! *Miss* Fielding will be asked to remove herself from my house at once!" Her back stiff with indignation,

Mrs. Campbell led Galen and Mary up the two flights of stairs and tapped, not gently, on the second door on the left.

"Who is it?"

"It's me, Miss Fielding. Galen Forbes, and Mary's with me."

"Oh, thank God!" Roxanne's voice sounded strangled, and an instant later, when she unlocked the door, Galen's incredulous exclamation and Mary's gasp told her how dreadful she must look. She'd tried to keep her hair in decent order, but her face was hollow-cheeked with fatigue and the shadows under her eyes looked like bruises.

Even before he stepped inside the room, Galen's ears picked up the ominous rale in Wyatt's breathing. He stripped back the blankets and laid his ear against Wyatt's chest, and what he heard wasn't reassuring. Still, Wyatt was by no means beyond saving, with a little luck and a lot of expert care.

Roxanne had held herself together by sheer force of will, up until this moment. But now that Galen was actually here, she broke.

"I think I've killed him. I've been giving him water. But he's so hot, and he was so thirsty! Galen, what have I done to him? He couldn't drink very much. He'd beg and beg and then he could only take a swallow or two. But I gave it to him!"

"Did he throw it up?"

"No. He hasn't thrown up at all. How could he, he hasn't had anything to eat but a little horrible broth off the messes Mrs. Campbell brought up for me."

"Good." Galen nodded. "As long as he didn't bring it up, the water and broth won't hurt him. We'll give him all he can take, he needs nourishment to build some strength. You've been bathing his hands and face?"

"Yes. I couldn't think of what else to do. The doctor Mrs. Campbell sent for bled him, and left some medicine that hasn't done any good at all. Galen, is he going to die?"

"Not if I can help it. Roxanne, I want you to rest. Your estimable landlady told me there's no other room in the house, but I'll find a cot for you if I have to tear this town apart. Mary can watch Wyatt while you get some sleep. After that you can take turns. And I'll stay till the crisis comes."

Roxanne didn't know how it happened, but she was in

his arms, her shoulders shaking with uncontrollable sobs. Galen held her close. Lord, but she was beautiful, even in her present state. His heart twisted. Poor girl, all alone, afraid that Wyatt was dying! He had a very good idea of what she'd been through, and he forgave her for rushing off to Rochester to find Wyatt. It was a pity that Athens, and the country at large, wouldn't take as lenient a view.

"Keep cooling his face, but keep him covered. Get a little fresh air in here, the room's enough to stifle even a healthy person. Mary, open the window just an inch or two. I'm going out to scare up a cot, and something decent for both you and Wyatt to eat. I'll be back as soon as I can."

He patted her shoulder, and then, feeling that that wasn't enough, he kissed her cheek. "All right, now. It's all right. You aren't alone anymore."

"The other doctor said he shouldn't eat."

"The other doctor can stick his head in the canal," Galen said.

Watching him, Mary worshiped Galen for a few brief seconds before she ran to open the window, just two inches, as he'd bidden. For a moment she had almost died with jealousy when he'd kissed Miss Roxanne, but Miss Roxanne was in love with Mr. Wyatt, and it had been a brotherly kiss anyway. It had, hadn't it? She was going to stay right here, with Dr. Forbes and Miss Roxanne and Mr. Wyatt, until Mr. Wyatt was well. She'd see Dr. Forbes almost all of the time, and no matter how hard she had to work helping take care of Mr. Wyatt, it would be almost as good as being in heaven.

"Good girl, Mary," Galen said. "I know I can count on you. I can't tell you how glad I am that you were willing to come with me."

Mary corrected her last thought. She was already in heaven.

It was a beautiful day for a drive, and having her father with her only added to Geneva's pleasure. She made no pretense to herself that she wouldn't rather have been with Galen, but her father was the next best thing. She set her mind on the beauty of the drive, knowing that worrying about Wyatt and Roxanne could do no good. She simply had to have faith that Galen would save Wyatt. As for what would happen after Roxanne came back to Athens, it would have to be dealt with when it happened. At least Roxanne would have her, and her mother and father and Bobo, to defend her, even if everybody else turned their backs on her.

"You'd better rack your brains for some notes for me to take down, just in case Mother asks us about what we learned," she remarked. Once again, they'd decided not to confide in Cora Burton. If there was any slipup, God forbid, and it became known that Geneva and her father not only knew where Philo O'Brian was but had actually aided and abetted him, they didn't want Cora involved.

"I remembered to bring along paper and ink. And no doubt the Emersons, particularly the father, will be able to supply me with some local history, or at least a folktale or two that we haven't come across before. If they can't, we'll just use our imagination." Marvin Burton, too, was enjoying himself.

"I hope that the Emersons haven't tried to change the dressings themselves, when Galen and I didn't arrive last night." There was a trace of worry in Geneva's voice. It had been too late to set off on a data-gathering expedition after Galen had left them, and this morning Mr. Maxwell, Bob Maxwell's father, had come to the house with an involved legal problem regarding the disposition of his property in case of his death, and had stayed on and on, until Geneva had felt ready to scream. But as the proprietor of Maxwell's Emporium, a man who saw everyone in town in the course of a given number of days and who would rather talk than anything else except make money, they hadn't risked making an excuse to get away.

"Don't fret, Geneva. I've a whole bottle of my best whiskey with me to wash the wound, but as likely as not they didn't touch Philo. Sam Emerson is trustworthy, and intelligent."

"Here's where we turn. The farmhouse is only a little way now." Geneva drew a deep breath that tingled in her lungs. Some people thought that spring was the most beautiful season of the year, and others preferred full summer. Geneva had known people who went into raptures over autumn, as she herself did, with its crisp, cool weather and the flaming colors as leaves turned. Only a few expressed a preference for winter. But Geneva loved them all, every season as well as any other. "The air is like wine. It will be winter before we know it."

The elder Mr. Emerson's face relaxed into relief when they drove into the farmyard, and then wrinkled with concern again when he saw that Galen hadn't come. Geneva reassured him as he led the way into the house.

"I know my way up," she said. Carrying her little bundle of fresh bandages and the whiskey, she left her father to pick Mr. Emerson's brains while she tended to Philo.

"Well, it's about time! I'd begun to think you'd deserted me. Where's the doc?"

"He couldn't come. You'll have to put up with my treatment," Geneva told him.

A beatific smile lighted up Philo's bulldog face. "How lucky can an old warhorse get? What man in his right senses wouldn't prefer your lily-white hands to do the pokin' and probin'?"

The wound, when Geneva had uncovered it, looked none the worse for not having been tended the night before. Nearly all of the inflamation had disappeared, and it looked clean, with no trace of infection.

"This is going to hurt," she warned.

"And doesn't it always, bless your heart! And the good doctor, saint that he is, insistin' on wastin' that good whiskey on that little nic in me leg, instead of lettin' me put all of it where it'd do a lot more good! You'll spare me a nip, now, bein' the angel you are?"

"Let me take care of the redressing, first," Geneva laughed. "Then you can share your little nip with my father. He came with me, and he wants to see you."

"In that case, it'll be a pleasure to wait. Seein' your beautiful face will make me forget the pure agony." Philo screwed his face up and went through a pantomime of being half killed while Geneva cleaned and redressed the wound, no doubt in hopes of being allowed more of the whiskey afterwards than she might have thought he needed. "I know how lucky I am to have you to take care of me. You'll not hear a whimper out of me. Ouch! That burns like fire!"

Geneva's fingers were as deft as Galen's own from having assisted him those other times. There was no getting the little Irishman down. If he got himself killed doing the risky work he'd chosen for himself, she'd not only miss him, but the world would be the poorer without him.

Her father tapped on the door, which already stood half-open, and poked his head in. "Ready for company?" he asked.

Philo's face beamed. "Well now, an occasion like this calls for a drink! It isn't every day that Philo O'Brian gets to talk with a great man like Marvin Burton! Mavourneen, pass me that bottle. Seein' as me visitor is of such importance, maybe you'd best run down to the kitchen and fetch up clean glasses. It wouldn't do at all at all to ask Lawyer Burton to drink from the bottle!"

Laughing, Geneva did as he asked. When she returned with two clean glasses she found her father and Philo already deep in conversation.

"I know the good you're doing, but what intrigues me is what motivates you to take such chances when you know that all the forces of our present-day society are against you," Marvin was asking.

Philo made a great ceremony out of pouring Marvin a drink and offering it to him, insisting on doing the honors himself because when else would he be privileged to offer a famous lawyer a drink, even if it was the man's own bottle?

"Then you've never been hungry, Mr. Burton." Philo's face screwed up in concentration as he strove to explain. "But me, now, hunger was me twin brother. In Ireland it was, you understand. The potato blight ruinin' the land and starvation starin' us all in the face, and the landlords puttin' us off our land and tearin' down our cottages so we couldn't go back. I expect you've heard something about it."

Marvin nodded. He'd heard a great deal about the greed of the absentee landlords, most of them English but not all. Irishmen as well had turned their own people out to starve.

"And not bein' compatible to starvin', I came over on one of the death ships. The floatin' coffins. Only I didn't die because I was too stubborn. But me mither and me sister died, back there in Ireland before I could get a cent of me wages back to them to keep their souls in their bodies. And magnificent wages they were, Mr. Burton, eight dollars a month. I was one of the bogtrotters who inched that canal of yours through the Montezuma marshes, after every other breed of man they tried sickened and died or walked off the job.

"Eight dollars a month, standin' thigh-deep in the muck from first light till dark, wearin' nothin' but our shirts because it rots a man's trousers and shoes off him if he was foolish enough to wear 'em. We slept in huts you wouldn't stable a goat in. Ate what was furnished us, and it wasn't much better than starvin', and we dug that ditch for eight dollars a month and glad for the work. Then, when it was done, and they didn't need Irish bogtrotters anymore, it was look for other work, and I ended up in a textile mill."

Marvin nodded. "Which wasn't much better, except you didn't have to stand all day in muck up to your thighs, in nothing but a shirt." He raised his eyebrows in lieu of asking if he was right.

"It was better, don't ever doubt it," O'Brian answered. "But the owners were phasing out the men, you see, because girls and women and children work cheaper and don't eat as much. Man, woman, and child, all overworked and underpaid. It isn't right, and it never will be right. I came over here, and thousands like me, to what we thought was a land of freedom and opportunity, and didn't it turn out that the poor and helpless are treated just as bad here as they are in Ireland. But it wasn't meant to be that way. I've read the Constitution, and all of those great speeches by Patrick Henry and Thomas Jefferson and Tom Paine, the lot of 'em. I couldn't read when I got here, you understand, but I found ways to learn. And they never meant it to be like it is. As long as they're not still around to change things like they did in the Revolutionary War, then somebody else has got to do it. That's my way of thinkin' whether you agree with me or not."

Marvin looked at him, and he felt respect rising warm and satisfying, respect for this little Irish fighting cock who didn't know how to give up, who'd go on fighting until he drew his last breath. And with that thought came another that saddened him. The way things were now, Philo O'Brian's last breath might come sooner than anyone knew.

Downstairs in the kitchen, Sam Emerson was brewing a pot of fresh coffee to offer his guests before they left. He pricked up his ears when he heard his own farm cart being driven much faster than it should have as it came clattering into the farmyard. Both his boys were out cutting the winter's supply of wood in the woodlot, and they shouldn't have started back for at least another hour.

Luke burst into the kitchen, with his brother Donald right behind him. "There's men coming this way, two of 'em! I think one of 'em's Ed Hanney, the constable. We saw 'em from the rise at the bend of the road. They're looking for Mr. O'Brian, for sure. What're we going to do?"

"Donald, you take the Burtons' horse and buggy and drive it into the woods where it won't be seen. Luke, help me carry Mr. O'Brian downstairs. Donald, you make sure you get Cato far enough away so Hanney won't hear him if he nickers. We'll have to get Mr. O'Brian into the hayloft, it's the only place."

He and Luke thundered up the stairs, and together, accompanied by the choicest of Irish cursing from O'Brian, they managed to carry the wounded man down.

"Hurry, please hurry!" Geneva begged. She and her father were already in the hayloft in the barn, and she knelt to help her father grasp Philo by his arms to help haul him up the last rungs of the ladder, with Luke boosting from lower rungs.

"Burrow in good. Luke, you and me's goin' to be unloading that wood when our company arrives," Samuel said in a terse voice. "You get started on it whilst I hide any traces that Mr. O'Brian was ever in that room over the kitchen."

Geneva and Marvin helped Philo burrow into the hay, piling more and more on top of him and then burrowing in themselves. If some neighbor had happened to notice that Geneva and Galen had been calling on the Emersons at night and reported it to Hanney, finding Geneva and her father here would be as good as an admission that Philo was here too. Marvin's face was grim as he thought of what some men would do for a monetary reward.

The hay prickled Geneva's skin and the dust they'd raised made her want to sneeze. She seethed as she lay there, scarcely daring to breathe. Like her father, she wondered how anyone could turn in another human being. But there were people like that, and they probably went to church every Sunday and prayed more loudly than their neighbors! Ed Hanney mustn't find Philo, he just mustn't! She did some praying herself. That Hanney and his deputy wouldn't insist on searching the barn and hayloft if everything in the house appeared normal to them.

She broke her prayer off as she heard Hanney's buggy turn into the farmyard, and then Sam Emerson's voice raised in greeting. "You men drummers? I ain't in the market to buy anything. Oh, it's you, Mr. Hanney. Sorry, I didn't recognize you at first."

"We're going to search your house. I've had a report that you're harboring a dangerous fugitive."

"Nobody in the house. Me and Luke's been in the woodlot all day, as you can see. Dunno where my boy Donald is, off chasing that hired girl from the Swenson's place, most likely, drat his hide. Luke, you keep working, we got to have this wood unloaded before dark. I'll show these folks around the house so they can see for themselves there ain't no one here."

Deep under the hay, Geneva heard the sound of the kitchen door opening and closing, and then there was silence. The silence went on for a long time. Ed Hanney and his deputy must be searching the house from cellar to attic, she thought. She had to sneeze again, and she wondered if her father and Philo were having the same difficulty, and if hauling the organizer around the way they'd had to had done his wound any harm. She'd have to dress it again, before she and her father left, that was certain. It would have to be thoroughly cleaned again, and more whiskey poured over it, and wouldn't that make Philo angry, all that good whiskey wasted in one day. She'd have to stop her ears if she didn't want to learn words that she'd never heard before.

At last! It had seemed like an hour, but she realized that it probably hadn't been anywhere near as long, but Mr. Emerson and Mr. Hanney and the other men were back outside, heading toward the barn.

"We'll just take a look in here," Hanney's voice came out in an angry tone. "He's in the loft, most likely, we shoulda looked there first."

No! Geneva's body stiffened. It was all over, they were going to be found! Philo would be put back in jail and starved. Her father would give Mr. O'Brian all his pocket money to buy food, but it would soon be used up, and Herndon Livingston would do his utmost to see that Philo didn't come to trial until long after the money was gone. The fact that both she and her father would be charged with aiding and comforting an agitator and a fugitive hardly crossed her mind, although she quailed to think of what would happen to the Emersons for hiding Mr. O'Brian.

The idea, born out of desperation, had barely flickered into her mind before she giggled, a high, shrill, very feminine giggle. "Don, you stop that now! You just stop it!"

"Aw, com'on. Who's gonna know?" The voice sounded nothing in the world like Philo O'Brian's. There was a nasal twang in it, without the least trace of the Irish accent that ordinarily could have been cut with a knife. "Lemmie. . . ."

"Oh, oh!" Geneva squealed. "Donald Emerson, you dasn't!"

Working with furious haste, Geneva managed to get her shoes off. Just as Hanney started up the ladder to the loft, brought to a halt by the voices above him, Geneva worked one leg, the skirt and petticoats drawn up to her knee, out of the hay. It was that leg, shapely and undoubtedly belonging to a young lady, that stopped the constable in his tracks.

His face as red as a summer beet, Hanney backed down the ladder. "I reckon you know where your other boy is now, Mr. Emerson." Filled with disgusted indignation at the derelictions of the young, he motioned to his deputy. "We might as well get back and tell Mr. Livingston it was a false trail. Leastways he'll save the reward."

Samuel Emerson rose to the occasion. "Donald Emerson, you git yourself decent and git down outa that hayloft, and haul that hussy down with you! You think I want you havin' to marry her? I ever catch you up there with a girl agin, I'll take every inch of skin off your back!"

Very distinctly, there was the sound of a girl's muffled sobbing. Under the hay, Marvin Burton clapped his hand over his mouth to suppress a chuckle. Geneva had missed her calling, she should have been on the boards, an actress bringing down the acclaim of the most discerning of theatergoers.

An hour later, after Philo had been hauled and manhandled back to the room over the farmhouse kitchen, and Geneva had cleaned and redressed his wound, her father and Mr. Emerson had decided where to send the still white-faced man who had borne the additional pain without flinching. Well concealed by bushel baskets of potatoes and corn and other farm produce, Luke and Donald were to drive him, as carefully as possible, to Mr. Emerson's cousin's farm some fifteen miles away. Geneva and her father would go to tend him there, every day, until Galen returned and pronounced him fit.

Marvin Burton was content. Intrigue, especially in the matter of justice, tickled his fancy and gave savor to his life.

"Now that you've settled me fate, after half killin' me to save me life, I think I'm deservin' of another drink," Philo complained.

Meeting her father's eyes, Geneva laughed. "You know, I think you do. And I'm going to have one too. After all, it isn't every day that I have to compromise my honor in the interests of saving a rapscallion's neck!"

The level in the bottle went down considerably, although Geneva decided after sampling her one drink that she could do without another, before she and her father left. Geneva had no doubt that by tomorrow, it would all be gone.

"Father, if Mr. O'Brian doesn't get well soon, it's going to make a healthy inroad on your cellar."

"And who deserves my whiskey more than Philo O'Brian?" Marvin demanded. He flicked the lines, and as Cato stepped out eagerly, anticipating home and his oats, he broke out in song, an Irish ditty with naughty undertones that Geneva had had no idea he knew. Because she knew the words through Roxanne, who knew every ditty along the Erie Canal, Geneva joined in. And didn't they make a pretty picture, father and daughter, bowling along a country road singing at the top of their lungs for all the world as if they were both dead drunk!

16

Earl Fielding arrived in Rochester in a towering rage. Word of his daughter's latest escapade had reached him before he was halfway there, after he had finished his business in New York and boarded one of his own packets. The word, which had brought blood mottling to his face, had made him do something utterly unprecedented. At the first opportunity, he had left his own packet and boarded one of the Six Day Line in order to get to Rochester, and his erring offspring, more quickly.

Earl was so well-known along the canal that as soon as he debarked and started striding toward Mrs. Campbell's boarding house, groups of men parted to let him pass, and fell back to give him a wide berth. In the mood he was in, it was the wisest thing to do. Few dared even to speak to him, but as he forged ahead out of earshot they muttered to each other, grinning.

"Wouldn't be in young Livingston's shoes right now for a thousand dollars."

"Wouldn't be in his daughter's, neither."

"There's going to be more fireworks in Rochester than there was on the Fourth of July. Wish I dassed to amble over there to see it!"

"He'd yank your head off and throw it in the canal. Best stay clear."

All the same, they drifted, as rapidly as they could walk, to the vicinity of the rooming house, near enough so that they could hope to hear the shouting voices but far enough away to take to their heels in case Earl caught them listening. The whole town knew about Roxanne Fielding and how she'd come pelting to Rochester to move in with Wyatt Livingston, and had been there ever since. It was a scandal the like of which they'd never heard before or were likely to again. There might even be a killing tonight.

"Is he toting a gun? I couldn't see."

"Don't reckon so. But Earl Fielding don't need a gun to deal with any sissified young Corinthian, much less one who's still ailing. He'll tear the whippersnapper apart with his bare hands and scatter the pieces so far we'll have a hard time gathering up enough of 'em for a decent burial."

Mrs. Campbell, formidable as she was, nonetheless blanched when she answered the knock on her door that threatened to split the wood. She recognized the glowering man who towered over her, by reputation if not by sight.

"I've come to see my daughter. Where is she?"

"Third floor, second door on the left," Mrs. Campbell managed to gasp before she scurried back to her kitchen. In a moment, however, after she'd caught her breath and reminded herself that this was her house and she had a right to know everything that went on in it, she quit the kitchen and climbed up to the middle of the flight that led to the third floor. That was as far as she cared to go, she'd be able to hear from here, and still have a head start back down if the raging man came bursting out at her. Her face was a study in satisfaction. At last, that uppity young miss was going to get what was coming to her!

The action started even before she'd thought it would. His room also on the third floor, from where he'd done all the spying he could without being caught at it by the young doctor, Chad Richards had just placed his foot on the first step down when he came face-to-face with Earl coming up. Like Mrs. Campbell, Chad recognized Earl, and his satisfaction was even greater than his landlady's. That fine young lady who'd treated him like dirt the day she'd arrived would now have to face the music!

"She's in there," Chad said, smirking. "Still living with Wyatt Livingston."

His answer was a fist like a block of granite that landed squarely on his jaw. Chad didn't fall, because Earl's other hand held him up by his shirtfront. He didn't fall until Earl lifted him bodily off his feet by that same shirtfront and tossed him down the stairs. Mrs. Campbell barely had time to flatten herself against the wall to keep from being bowled off her own feet as Chad came hurtling down at her, his face filled more with terror than with pain. The man bounced three times, managed to stop his unorthodox descent by grasping the banister, got to his feet unsteadily, and limped the rest of the two flights down. He closed the front door behind him, deciding that he wouldn't come back to pick up his clothes and satchel until Earl Fielding had left town.

Without the courtesy of knocking, Earl flung open the door of the first room to the left. Roxanne rose from where she was bending over Wyatt's bed, giving him a drink of water.

"Father! Where have you been all this time? I expected you at least two days ago!" Watching her, frightened half out of her wits, Mary couldn't help admiring her benefactress-cum-mistress, who dared to open the attack when it was obvious that Mr. Fielding was out for blood.

"What do you mean by your half-witted, foolhardy behavior?" Earl roared. Mary quaked, glancing at the ceiling to see if his voice had cracked the plaster. Outside, the growing group of men huddled together, their faces lifted to Wyatt's window. Chad Richards, battered and bruised, yelped, "Didn't I tell you? He damn near killed me, and all I did was say that his daughter was in there! He'll probably beat that girl of his, and then he'll start in on Wyatt Livingston, and the poor critter won't live through it!"

A rough nudge in his ribs cut off his flow of self-important talk, as Earl's voice rose again.

"Whatever possessed you to come busting off to Rochester, all alone? The whole State of New York is buzzing with it. You're ruined, you realize that, don't you?"

"Yes, and I don't give a hang! Wyatt's alive, and he wouldn't be if I hadn't come! He'd have died, Galen himself said so."

"And it would have served you right!" Earl stood there glaring at Roxanne with blood in his eyes, until a voice from the bed against the far wall made his head jerk in that direction.

"Well, thanks. I didn't know you were that fond of me." Wyatt was better, so much better that the irony came to his lips without thinking. "I suppose you'd rather she'd waited for you so that you both could have arrived in time to attend my funeral.''

"Damn it, Wyatt, what the devil were you doing in Rochester, anyway? I expected you'd be hunting a job in one of the New England textile mills.''

"There aren't any jobs in the New England textile mills. Not for someone like me. An opening might come along eventually. They know I'm qualified, but in the meantime I had to live, without eating up every penny of my capital. I was hunting for work here, any kind of work, on a canalboat or building houses or clerking in a store, where my father would never think to look for me.''

"You damned young ass, if you needed a job, why didn't you come to me? You should have known I'd have use for a man who can handle figures.''

"I didn't care to ask my friends for charity, if I dare presume that you are my friend.''

"I was, or I would have been, but I damned well ain't now! Do you know what you've done to my daughter? She won't be able to hold her head up in public until you're married, and even then it'll be hard! I ought to break you in two!''

"I didn't ask her to come.'' Wyatt's voice was reasonable. "And I wasn't in any condition to throw her out once she got here. I didn't even realize it was Roxie, the first two days. By the time I might have handled the situation, if anyone could have handled your daughter when her mind was made up, Galen and Mary were here to give things a semblance of respectability.''

"Days too late! How long do you think it takes to blacken a young woman's name? One night would have been enough, or one hour behind a closed bedroom door!''

"Why, Father, do you think it would have taken me a whole hour, if I'd been of a mind to seduce him? You underestimate me.''

Mary's hand flew to her mouth, her eyes wide with disbelief. Lord have mercy! How did Miss Roxanne dare to talk to her father like that?

"I'm going to blister your bottom, for all you've turned twenty! And then I'm going to see you married to this young fool, if I have to hold a gun on both of you while the parson makes it legal!''

"You can't force me to marry him. Maybe you can herd me to the altar with a gun in my back, but you can't make me say yes when the crucial moment comes."

"Roxanne—" Wyatt's voice was apprehensive now. He wasn't well enough, or strong enough, to cope with this.

"You keep out of this! I'll handle my father. No one else can, when he's being this bullheaded."

"Bullheaded!" This time Mary was certain that plaster would fall, and she flinched. Out in the street, every breath was bated, and Chad Richards decided that he'd take the first packet out of Rochester, without his luggage, no matter which direction it was going. New York or Buffalo, it made no difference, as long as Earl Fielding wasn't there. "You call me bullheaded? But I've brought it on myself. I should have tanned the hide off you when you were young enough to handle!"

"You loved spoiling me and letting me have my own way, and you know it. You doted on it!" Roxanne challenged him. "Now lower your voice. You'll make Wyatt sick again."

"I'm already sick again," Wyatt mumbled, to no one in particular.

It was at this point that Galen had the misfortune of entering the room, having gone out in search of a decent meal.

"Mr. Fielding! I'm certainly glad you've come."

"You are, are you? You answer me this, Doctor Galen Forbes. Why didn't you send this girl of mine packing back home the minute you got here?"

"I intended to. I even brought Mary along to accompany her, provided that she'd go. Only she wouldn't go, and I'd anticipated that, so it was all the more important for me to bring Mary to stay with her while she remained here." Unflinching, Galen regarded the angry bull of a man who looked as if he were ready to fell him with a single blow. "Have you ever tried making her do something she didn't want to do?"

Earl chose to ignore that. "What I want to know is, is Wyatt recovered enough to get married?"

"No. It'll be a few more days. Congratulations, Wyatt. And best wishes, Miss Fielding. It's settled, then?"

"Of course it isn't settled!" Roxanne said impatiently.

"It's settled." Earl's face was grim. "I let you get away

with one escapade, that time you came home with Wyatt after the revival meeting at the crack of dawn. And it cost me to do it, knowing that the whole town was talking about you and counting on their fingers. You managed to carry it off that time, with my help, but this is something entirely different. No girl in the world, not even you, could help but be ruined for the rest of her life, after running away and spending days nursing a man, alone in his bedroom in a rooming house! I give Wyatt the intelligence to know that, even if you don't. You're marrying him, and as soon as he can stand on his feet.''

Even Roxanne, who knew her father better than anyone else, had never seen him look as he looked now, and she realized that for once in her life she'd met her match and been bested. She'd have to marry Wyatt, and she didn't know whether to laugh with elation, or cry. Whichever it was, it was settled, just as Earl had said it was.

''And now, dammit, Roxie, you put on your outdoor duds and come out to dinner with me. We're going to the best place this town has, and we're going to hold our heads up and act as if nothing out of the ordinary has happened. I'm damned if we're going to skulk around hiding, as if we had something to be ashamed of!''

''For once, I agree with you. Where are we dining? From all I hear there isn't anything in Rochester to compare with Miss Jewel Southern's place in Buffalo. It's too bad that Wyatt didn't choose Buffalo to get sick in, so we'd be able to find something fit to eat. I've heard so much about Miss Southern that I'd love to meet her.''

For a moment, Mary thought that Roxanne's father was going to strangle. Apparently Galen thought the same thing, because he began to pound Earl's back.

''How'd you find out about Jewel?'' Earl finally managed to splutter.

''I have big ears,'' Roxanne told him, her voice sweet. ''Well, do I get to meet her sometime, or don't I? Now that I'm a fallen woman too, there's no reason why I shouldn't. I've been dying to see if I think she's good enough for you. Maybe we could go on to Buffalo, after Wyatt is well, before we go back to Athens.''

''Some day,'' Earl said, his voice dangerous, ''you're going to go too far.''

Roxanne's expression was as sweet as her voice. "Why, Father, I thought I already had!"

But when they stepped out onto the street a moment later, Roxanne's hand was linked under her father's arm, and she was smiling up into his face. The men gathered in front of the house made way for them, their faces filled with astonishment. Earl Fielding hadn't beat his daughter, or killed Wyatt Livingston. In the center of the group, Chad Richards made himself as small as possible, in order to escape Earl's notice. There wasn't any justice. The uppity young society snob was going to get away with it!

Now that Earl had arrived, things changed. For Earl Fielding, there was no such thing as there not being rooms available. He moved Roxanne and Mary to a pleasant bedroom in a better rooming house, and engaged another for himself in the same house, after persuading the former occupants that they could find suitable accommodations elsewhere, with money to spare after what he gave them for their inconvenience. Galen went back to Athens the next day, again on a Six Day Line packet. He'd already been away long enough for Stephen Harding to be thoroughly disgruntled, and now that Wyatt was well on the way to recovery, nothing more was needed to restore him to full health except rest and good nursing care.

There were half a dozen places that Earl needed to be, but he didn't let that influence him to budge from Rochester as long as his daughter insisted on staying. Messages went out, and men came to him. Post-riders were sent galloping in all directions. For the moment, the center of his empire was in Rochester.

The men he did business with, and others who were acquainted with him, treated him with wary caution until they saw how the land lay. The way the land lay was that Miss Roxanne Fielding was beyond censure. They were careful to express none by either word or facial expression. The safest course was to pretend that they had heard nothing of the scandal. That suited Earl, although he seethed whenever he thought of how tongues would be wagging in Athens. Roxanne wouldn't have a shred of reputation left.

Roxanne herself couldn't have cared less. As long as Wyatt was alive, and getting well, she'd have allowed herself to be stood on a platform like Hester Prynne and condemned to wear a scarlet letter on her breast.

"Wyatt, you don't have to worry. I can still refuse to marry you. Father can't force me to marry you if I dig in my heels," she told him. She had a sinking feeling that her words were sheer bravado. From where she stood, Earl could and would force the marriage. All the same, if Wyatt was against it, she intended to try.

Wyatt was already convinced of that, but that didn't mitigate his own feeling of responsibility. Ruining a girl's name was a serious matter. The stigma could very well follow her all the rest of her life. Roxie had come charging to his rescue, and there was no doubt that she had saved his life.

How could he repay Roxie by letting her suffer the consequences of her rash errand of mercy? There was no place in the whole eastern part of the country that she could go where her reputation wouldn't follow her. All of Earl Fielding's money and power would be useless in protecting her. He didn't blame Earl at all for insisting that they must be married, and as soon as possible.

"I think we could make a go of it," Wyatt told her. It was what he'd told her that other time, when he'd brought her home at dawn after the revival meeting, when he'd been so drunk and sick that she'd had to keep him out all night until he'd recovered. But that amounted to nothing, compared to her staying alone with him in a room in Rochester, much less having told Mrs. Campbell that they were married!

Wyatt doubted that even Jebbidiah Tucker would concede that the Blood of the Lamb could wash her clean. Public confession, a plea for salvation at the next revival meeting, might win her a grudging acceptance as far as attending church was concerned, but nearly the whole female population of Athens, except for Geneva Burton and his own sister Addie, would still draw their skirts aside when she brushed too close to them.

Now that his first rage had been spent, Earl was a good deal more factual, and he didn't spare her. "Roxie, can't you get it through your head that Wyatt'll be ruined just as much as you are, if you don't marry him? He'll never be able to find a decent job, no respectable mill owner or any other man will hire him. And you can bet your Sunday boots that no other girl will marry him, even if she wants to, because her folks wouldn't let her. Is that what you want for him?"

"He's a man. It can't be that bad, for a man."

"The blazes it can't! You've lived in this world long enough to know how merciless Christian people can be to anyone who doesn't follow their rules. You couldn't have done a better job of ruining Wyatt's life if you'd tried. There's a chance that some fortune-hunting scoundrel would marry you, if you were fool enough to have him and sick enough of being an old maid, but Wyatt's broken with his father, so even a fortune-hunting hussy wouldn't marry him. That's the way it is and nothing's going to change it and you might as well accept it."

"I can't force him to marry me. What kind of a marriage would that be? He'd be miserable."

"He'll be more miserable if you don't marry him. What ails you, girl? You've loved him ever since you got out of pigtails, you've never looked at anyone else! You want him so bad it sets your teeth on edge and you know you'll never be happy without him. And now you can have him, and you say no!"

Roxanne wasn't nearly as insouciant as her outward facade suggested. Her father was right. She wanted Wyatt, she wanted him so bad she could taste it.

Alone in her room at night, except for Mary, who suffered agonies of sympathy for her, Roxanne paced up and down. Sometimes she yanked at a strand of her hair in hope that the pain would help her to think.

Why shouldn't she marry Wyatt? It wasn't as if Geneva would take him back. Roxanne knew that Geneva's heart had been caught by Galen Forbes. And outside of Geneva, who else would make Wyatt as good a wife?

She had so much to offer him! Not only her beauty, but she had fire, passion; she could satisfy him as no other woman could ever satisfy him. She doubted that even Geneva could have offered him what she could offer him. She'd be a perfect hostess for his guests, a perfect mother of his children.

They could go far together. Just thinking about it made her breath catch. Earl's empire was large and growing larger; he'd be one of the wealthiest men in the country in a few more years. Wyatt had the brainpower and the ambition to go right along with him. Earl could use him, and actually needed him.

He could teach him every phase of his far-flung enterprises, and groom him to step into his shoes when he became too old to hold the reins in his own hands. They could found a dynasty together. One that the world would have to reckon with.

But in the end, it was Mary who made up her mind for her.

"You love him, don't you? Then isn't *that* all that matters? People are always telling us girls that it doesn't matter if we don't love the men we marry, that we'll learn to love them afterwards. Well, isn't the same thing true for men? Mr. Wyatt likes you, I know he likes you a lot. I can tell. If you were married, he'd have to love you, because he wouldn't be able to help it, he'd just grow into it."

He'd better, Roxanne thought. And he would, because she'd see to it that he did. She'd be a wife to him that no man had ever dreamed of. He was hers, she'd known that from the first moment she'd seen him. She was only taking what was her own, but she'd be giving as much as she took, and a whole lot more.

It galled Wyatt to think that he'd have to work for his father-in-law, that the job would go with the marriage, but like Earl, he knew that his life wouldn't be worth living if he didn't marry Roxanne. Geneva was lost to him. Wyatt was a normal man with normal needs and desires, and the need for a wife and children, for a permanent and significant place in the scheme of things, was strong in him.

Every man he knew would envy him, and with reason. But there was one, nagging, bitter thought that he kept under the surface, refusing to acknowledge it. Roxanne and her father had always been determined that Roxanne would become Athens's uncrowned queen. Now they would have their wish.

Earl was satisfied. His daughter would be done right by. She'd have the man she wanted, and he'd have a son-in-law to train up the way he wanted him. Wyatt would pull his weight. It remained to be seen if he'd make Roxie as happy as she deserved to be, but if he didn't he'd better find a good place to hide because Earl would break him into pieces and throw them to the dogs.

"We'd better be getting on home," Earl said when they'd been in Rochester for ten days and Wyatt was on his feet. "Even a small wedding with just a few close friends will take some planning. You and Wyatt could be married here in Rochester, right now, but I wouldn't want to give the gossips that much satisfaction. I'll arrange for a couple of competent nurses to look out for Wyatt till he's fit to come back home. You can start planning the wedding."

"Small wedding my foot," Roxanne said. "It's going to be the biggest wedding Athens ever saw, and it isn't going to take place in a hurry. Well, not much of a hurry! We're going to show them what a wedding should be like. I hope you have plenty of cash on hand, because this is going to cost you!"

"The sky's the limit," Earl told her. A grin began to spread across his face, from ear to ear. Maybe he was nothing but a self-educated, rough canaller who'd pulled himself up by his own bootstraps, but this daughter of his was a thoroughbred!

There never had been a wedding like this one in all of Athens's history, probably not in the county or adjoining counties. For a start, Roxanne had completely done over the house on North Street, throwing herself into the project with all of her energy the moment she'd arrived home from Rochester.

The furniture, the rugs, the lamps and oil paintings and drapes and everything else her father had been so proud of when he'd furnished the house, all had to go. It had been all right for a rough canaller and his daughter, but it wouldn't do for Wyatt Livingston and his wife, who would automatically take their places as the king and queen of Athens.

The dining room was repapered with scenic silk that had come from France, and the drawing room with imported paper from Italy. The maroon window hangings were replaced with ivory satin. The massive and garish furniture was replaced with delicate pieces with classic lines, the products of the best cabinetmakers in London. It cost Earl Fielding a fortune, but he never said a word, any more than he said a word about being dragged off to New York City to purchase the new doodads at the same time that Roxanne had herself fitted for her wedding dress. He just paid the bills and clamped down a little more strongly than usual on his cigars.

As it would be a winter wedding, the dress was of the heaviest satin, its snug bodice embroidered with seed pearls. Its rounded neckline, rounded puffed sleeves, and voluminous skirt, were all the epitome of fashion, which decreed that the entire effect should be of rounded femininity. Knowing that her hair was her greatest beauty, Roxie insisted on the smallest of coverings. The lace encrusted with pearls made a delicate frame before it cascaded over her shoulders. The couturiere went into raptures over her figure and her mass of flaming hair. Any father but Earl would have gone into shock at the price tag. Earl paid it, and smiled.

Looking at him, Roxanne grinned. "Never mind, Father. As we won't be taking our honeymoon until late spring, you'll have time to recoup your losses before you have to buy me a trousseau. I'll make do with what I already have, until then."

Earl didn't return her grin, but his eyes twinkled. What she already had would have stocked the couturiere's shop. As long as Roxanne was happy, it would be worth it if it took every cent he had.

Any other girl would have been exhausted after the whirlwind trip to New York, getting everything ready for the first day of January, the day Roxanne had set for her wedding. Earl had to admire this daughter of his. New Years Day! Whoever had heard of such a thing? Leave it to Roxanne to be different, to give Athens something else to clack its tongue about!

If the tongues of Athens had clacked when Roxanne had run off to Rochester to take care of Wyatt, they almost stilled from sheer awe as the day of the wedding approached. The church was to be banked with hothouse flowers. In the dead of winter, a church full of flowers!

Mrs. Henry Maynard, who'd been Miss Adelaide Livingston, was to be the matron of honor, and Miss Geneva Burton the chief bridesmaid. As only eight bridesmaids were to be in the wedding, the other seven places were vied for so fiercely that several family feuds developed, and half a dozen girls swore that they'd never speak to each other again. All the best families, who'd agreed that Roxanne should be shunned as though she carried the plague, waited on pins and needles to receive their invitations.

At the Livingston house on Elm Street, Lillian Livingston faced her husband.

"I am going to attend the wedding," Lillian said. "Wyatt is my son, and I am going to be there to see him married."

"I forbid it!" Herndon told her. "As they have not seen fit to call on us, or made any move toward a reconciliation, as it is Wyatt's place to do, there is no way that you can go."

"I am going," Lillian told him. "I've already ordered my dress. It is nearly finished and you'll receive the bill for it in due course."

Herndon looked at her, and wondered where the meek, obedient woman he had married and lived with for twenty-five years had gone. For weeks now, ever since Lillian had found out how he'd tricked Adelaide into marrying Henry Maynard, she had slept in Adelaide's old room, with the door locked. And she'd visited Adelaide, but Adelaide still refused to receive her father. Now his son had turned against him. None of them knew what was good for them. He was a maligned and misunderstood man, turned on by his own family from whom he should have been able to expect complete loyalty. Being excluded from this wedding was the last straw. For Lillian to appear without him would make him a laughingstock.

"You are to obey me," Herndon told Lillian.

"And you can go to hell!" The word, which never before had passed Lillian's lips, finally got out. "Which is where you will without any doubt end up eventually, anyway."

"You are aware, of course, that it's within my rights to chastise you," Herndon warned.

"And you realize that if you do, I'll see to it that the story gets all over town, complete with a showing of my bruises to my female friends. Why do you think I've dared to lock you out of my bedroom all this time? Wife-beating may be legal, but you can't bear to have your image tarnished. Not the great Herndon Livingston! For appearance's sake, if you want to take a trip to some other town, I'll tell everyone that your absence from the wedding was unavoidable because of the press of business affairs. Nobody will believe it, but you'll be able to hold your head up the next time you walk down the street."

First Methodist was jammed to the doors on the day of the wedding. Those who had not received invitations gathered outside the church to catch a glimpse of the bride and groom when they arrived, and stayed to watch them leave. Herndon Livingston was conspicuous by his absence, having been called out of town at the last moment on mill business. As Lillian had predicted, only the most naive believed the story.

Roxanne was radiant as she walked down the aisle on Earl's arm. She'd even browbeat her father into wearing clothing of her own choosing, not the flamboyant things he ordinarily affected in the belief that they were in the height of fashion. Today, the most important day of her life, he could have passed as a gentleman.

But Roxanne wasn't thinking about her father, or about Herndon Livingston's absence, as she walked down the aisle. For her, no one except Wyatt existed. The murmurs of the guests, gasping at her beauty, were lost on her.

She scarcely noticed how lovely Geneva looked, or Addie's haunted eyes as she acted as matron of honor, or the way Bobo's face tightened when he saw Addie's telltale face and tragic eyes. And she was completely unaware that Jim Yarnell, whom Wyatt had asked to be, along with Galen, the ushers, led Mary MacDonald to the front of the church and seated her where she'd have an unimpeded view of the ceremony, ignoring the matrons who looked askance at an ex-mill-mechanic having a better vantage point than they did.

Geneva's eyes prickled with unshed tears as she stood beside Roxanne, watching her friend and the man whom she herself had once thought she'd marry, exchange their vows. Galen, looking at Geneva rather than at the bride and groom, felt an unaccustomed tightness in his chest. He tried to fight down his sudden, overwhelming elation that it wasn't Geneva standing there in a bridal gown, being married to Wyatt.

The reception at the Fielding house on North Street, directly after the ceremony, was an event that the guests fortunate enough to have received invitations would never forget. Marvin and Bobo were amused at the amount of champagne that Earl had provided. Cora Burton, keeping protectively close to Lillian Livingston, looked at the four-tiered wedding cake as though she couldn't believe her eyes.

"I hoped it would be Geneva," Lillian murmured. "But Wyatt looks happy, doesn't he?" There was such wistfulness in her voice that Cora winced.

"I'm sure that Roxanne will make him happy. She loves

him very much.'' Both women looked at Addie, whose husband, fairly bursting with importance, was hovering over her as if he were afraid that someone might spirit her away from him. Cora bit her lip. If Wyatt was happy, it was evident that Addie was not, and it was a black crime. She was glad that Herndon hadn't attended the wedding, because if God cared anything at all about people, He'd have made the roof of the church cave in on Herndon for what he'd done to Addie, and that would have spoiled things for everyone else. As for herself, she would never speak to him again, or as much as nod to him at Sunday morning services.

Roxanne and Wyatt slipped away before the reception was over, to drive a few miles to a coaching inn that had been famous since pre-Revolutionary days. There they would spend two days in lieu of a real honeymoon. They'd decided against the Exchange Hotel in Auburn, not only because it was too far away, but because neither of them wanted to stay in a place where Addie had been forced to stay on her wedding night, faced with the horror of being married to Henry Maynard.

Wyatt watched Roxanne with something like awe, as she consumed every morsel of the excellent dinner he'd ordered, and asked for a second dessert. No wedding-night trepidations here, no shy tremblings, real or feigned. Roxie had every intention of keeping up her strength for what lay before her. It was going to be a long night, if she had anything to do with it.

In her nightgown, the only new thing she'd bought to wear except for her wedding gown, Roxanne looked at her husband. Her hair, loose around her shoulders, caught the light from the lamp and shimmered like flame. The nightgown was of a rich, cream-colored satin, and it was cut so skillfully that it revealed rather than concealed the promise that lay underneath it.

"Just because this was the next thing to a shot-gun wedding doesn't mean that we can't enjoy it," she told Wyatt. "I won't disappoint you. I intend to give value received, and that's a lot.''

She wasn't going to beg him to love her. He already liked her, and that gave her a lot to build on. It was up to her to be such a perfect wife that he'd fall in love with her, and that included the best sex that a man had ever had. And having grown up on the Erie Canal, Roxanne knew a lot more about sex than most girls of her age and a great deal more than her father thought she knew. There'd been nothing wrong with her hearing when she'd traveled on the canalboats, and what she'd overheard as the crew and some passengers discussed their amorous affairs had been an education in itself.

She welcomed Wyatt into her open arms, her mouth turning to fire as he kissed her. Her body was a living flame against his. If Wyatt had loved her, if he hadn't harbored that small corner of resentment because he felt that he'd been trapped, he would have thanked God for his blessings. Roxanne was beautiful, and he was a normal young man whose banked fires had smoldered to the point of explosion, and now Roxanne's passion consumed him.

He knew that no other man had touched her, but she seemed to know instinctively every caress and movement to send him to the heights of rapture. Her cry as he entered her was more of triumph than pain, and then she pressed herself against him, drawing him even closer into herself until their bodies seemed to one living, throbbing entity. She gave herself completely, her love for him drowning out the pain of her first sexual experience. When they drew their last, shuddering breaths after a completion that most people only dream about, Roxanne sighed, Her hand stroking his hair.

"It's going to be a good marriage, Wyatt. I promise you that it is."

Wyatt kissed her, and was thankful that she had no way of knowing the bleakness in his heart. She'd given value received, and more, and she'd go on giving it, but he didn't love her, and he doubted that she loved him anywhere near as much as she loved the idea of being Mrs. Wyatt Livingston.

17

Roxanne was both surprised and pleased when Addie came to visit her late in March. It was a day on which the warm spring weather had backlashed into cold. The sky was so leaden that it foreboded snow.

Since her marriage, Addie had gone nowhere at all except to those affairs that required her presence along with her husband's, and Henry had virtually dropped out of social life since he'd acquired his young bride. No matter how hard Roxanne and Geneva had tried, she had grown away from them, quiet and withdrawn and discouraging their attempts to see her. Roxanne had remarked that she looked like a wax doll, one fashioned by an artist who had forgotten to draw on a smile.

"Are you happy, Roxie?" Addie asked her when Roxanne had drawn her into the parlor and had Freda bring in tea. Her hand trembled as she lifted her cup, and a little of the tea spilled over into the saucer. She put the cup down, and as she did so Roxanne noticed that her hand was so thin and white that it almost seemed transparent. The shadows under her eyes were even more prominent than they'd been the last time she'd seen her.

Addie's question was a difficult one for Roxanne to answer. By all rights, she should have been the happiest young married woman in Athens, perhaps in the whole country. She had Wyatt, she had this beautiful house, furnished so that all her friends were green with envy, she had all of Athens's society dancing to her tune.

She had Wyatt, yes. Legally, she had him. But was Wyatt really hers?

Outwardly, he gave every evidence of being a contented husband. He'd thrown himself into learning to handle the part of Earl Fielding's business that had been delegated to him, and he was doing well at it. At home, or when they went out together socially, he was attentive, smiling, as though he didn't have a care in the world.

But something was lacking. Wyatt made love to her expertly, he brought her to the heights of ecstasy, satisfying his own bodily needs at the same time. But there was a mechanical quality to his lovemaking that left her dissatisfied and apprehensive. It was as though he were performing his duty with good grace, living up to what was expected in a husband. The fact remained that they'd had to get married, even if there'd been no reason to have the ceremony immediately after she'd rushed off to Rochester to nurse him through his illness. Without that action of hers, the marriage would never have taken place, because he never would have asked her.

He didn't love her. He respected her intelligence and wit, he admired her beauty, he was able to satisfy his physical needs with her, but he still loved Geneva and he probably always would. And underneath everything else, Roxanne sensed that he harbored a resentment because he had been compelled by common decency to marry her.

Was she happy? The answer was no. But she couldn't tell Addie that, Addie had enough to contend with without adding her own troubles to her burdens.

"Happy enough. I suppose marriage is never the dream of bliss we imagined it would be when we were starry-eyed little girls. Addie, you don't look well. Are you going to have a baby?" The question was too blunt, but it was the only way to find out. They'd been friends for so many years that Addie shouldn't be offended.

"What?" Addie was so startled that she almost knocked over her cup. "Oh, no. No, I'm not pregnant. It doesn't seem to happen."

"Then what is it? For goodness sake, Addie, talk to me! It's me, Roxanne! I can't bear to see you like this. Does that old fool you married mistreat you?"

"No. Yes." Addie's face was so pale that for a moment Roxanne was afraid that she was going to faint.

"It's either yes or no. You might as well tell me, because now that you're here I'm going to drag it out of you if it takes all day!"

"I c-couldn't tell you, before. You weren't married, I couldn't tell anyone, there was no one I could ask, I can't talk to my mother about things like this—"

"Things like what?"

"The things he does." Addie's voice was so faint that Roxanne had to strain to hear her. She began to cry, her shoulders shaking, and the sound tore at Roxanne's heart.

"What does he do?" Roxanne demanded. She handed Addie a handkerchief, considered for a moment, and then went to the dining room sideboard and came back with a glass of sherry. "Here, drink this."

Addie drank it, and a little color came back into her face, but Roxanne thought that she still looked like death warmed over.

"Now tell me. From the looks of you, it's something you should have told someone a long time before this."

"He does things. He says it's all right, that a husband has a right to do anything he wants with his wife. He—"

"Unnatural things?" Roxanne felt anger surge through her, hot and dangerous.

"I don't know. How do I know if they're natural? I don't know things like that. Only I can't bear to think that my father did things like that to my mother, or that other men do things like that to their wives, or make their wives do things like that. If it's true, then no girl would get married, she'd rather die."

Roxanne held her anger in check so that it wouldn't distress Addie even further. She probed, insisted, demanded, and piece by piece, she learned what Henry Maynard did to Addie in the privacy of their bedroom, and the things he made Addie do. When she had learned the last bit, she felt like retching.

"That bastard. That perverted old monster! He ought to be tarred and feathered and ridden out of town on a rail. No, it isn't natural. He's sick, he ought to be put away. You don't have to stand for it even if he is your husband. Love isn't like that! What happens between a husband and wife is supposed to be beautiful. So beautiful that life wouldn't be whole without it."

Roxanne was fully aware that any woman unfortunate enough to be married to a man who mistreated her did have to put up with it. Both convention and the law stipulated that the husband was the complete master. But Roxanne didn't give two hoots in Hades for either convention or the law. In Addie's place, she'd have killed the old bastard if she couldn't control him any other way.

"Roxie, what am I going to do? I can't stand it any longer, I'll kill myself, I've thought of killing myself, to get away from him."

"You're leaving him," Roxanne said flatly. "You're never going back to that house. You're going to live here with Wyatt and me. Wyatt will see about bringing your clothes. Unless you'd rather not ever wear anything again that you had to wear when you lived with Henry?"

The tremor that went through Addie's body answered her question.

"All right. We'll get you all new clothes. As soon as we get something else for you to wear we'll even burn what you're wearing now!"

"He'll come after me. He'll make me go back."

"Wyatt and I will see about that! Come on, darling, I'm going to put you to bed, and you're going to sleep for hours. You'll feel better when you wake up."

To be in bed, any bed, alone, without a pawing, slobbering, abusing man sharing it with her! Addie drew a deep breath, and for the first time since the hotel bedroom door had closed behind her on her wedding night, a glimmer of hope filtered into her eyes.

Roxanne helped her undress, her movements as efficient as her hands were gentle. She drew one of her own nightgowns over Addie's head, and tucked her into bed in one of the extra bedrooms, drawing the fleecy blankets up under her chin. "You go to sleep, honey. I'll pull the drapes, to keep the light out. Get a good rest and don't worry about a thing."

She paused as she started to draw the heavy draperies across the windows. It was beginning to snow, and from the looks of the sky, lowering and black, it would probably turn into a blizzard. She could feel the cold air through the window panes, and she blocked it out by drawing the drapes the rest of the way across. She touched one of the newfangled wooden matches to the kindling and paper that was already laid in the fireplace, then laid another log on the fire and placed the fire screen in front of it to guard against sparks.

"Roxie, you won't let him in, will you?" Addie whispered from the bed.

"Just let him try to get in!" Roxanne's voice was grim. "Go to sleep. Wyatt and I are going to take care of you now, you don't have a thing to be afraid of."

Except that Wyatt would kill Henry Maynard, she thought, as she went back downstairs.

As she waited throughout the rest of the afternoon for Wyatt to come home from the office that Earl had virtually turned over to him on Canal Street, Roxanne wished that her father were at home. But Earl had made himself scarce since the day she and Wyatt had returned from their two-day wedding trip, claiming that demands of business would keep him away from Athens most of the time. Roxanne knew that it was because he wanted her and Wyatt to have the house to themselves, and she blessed him for it, but it would have been nice to have him home now, to help deal with Henry Maynard if the man had the temerity to demand that Addie return to him. Wyatt could handle Henry, but Wyatt's temper was liable to get out of bounds, and it could turn into something downright nasty that would be further damaging to Addie.

There were several inches of snow already on the ground when Wyatt came home a little after six. Addie was still asleep, so exhausted by her long ordeal that she would probably sleep for several more hours.

"Addie?" Wyatt's mouth fell open with surprise. "What on earth is she doing asleep here?"

"She's asleep because she's tired." Roxanne helped him as he shrugged off his greatcoat, and hung it on the hall tree, where it dripped a puddle that she ignored. She drew him into the parlor and closed the sliding doors. She'd told Mrs. Casey that supper would be half an hour late tonight, so that she'd have time to tell Wyatt what she had to tell him.

Wyatt's face became whiter and whiter with anger as he listened, and just as Roxanne had feared, he shouted, "I'll kill him!"

She clapped her hand over his mouth. "Be quiet! Do you want to wake her up? And you aren't going to kill him, that would make it even worse for her! To say nothing of the fact that I'd be a widow almost before I was a wife, because you'd hang. But she isn't going back there, Wyatt. I don't care what kind of pressure Henry brings to bear, she isn't going back."

"You're damned right she isn't!" Wyatt's jaw was clenched so that a muscle jumped near his mouth. "She's staying right here, where we can protect her! Damn my father, damn his black soul to hell! I ought to go over there and beat him to a pulp for marrying Addie off to that pervert, and then I ought to beat Henry Maynard for good measure!"

"No beatings," Roxanne told him, her voice sharp. "It's going to be hard enough on Addie as it is. Whoever decided that it was disgraceful for a woman to leave her husband, anyway? Men, I'll be bound! Just because they're bigger and stronger, they think they can treat their women like slaves!"

In spite of the fury that consumed him, Wyatt couldn't help grinning. He'd like to see any man in the world try to treat Roxie like a slave. If he tried, he'd be the sorriest man who ever walked on two legs. Provided she left him any legs at all to walk on!

There was a soft tap on the door, and Roxanne crossed the room to open it a crack. Mary peered in, her eyes filled with curiosity.

"She's awake. Shall I take her a tray?"

"Yes, Mary, you do that. And tell her that Wyatt and I will be up to see her in a moment. After that, Mrs. Casey can dish up."

Addie's face was still pale and filled with anxiety when Roxanne and Wyatt entered her room a few minutes later. But although there were still purple shadows under her eyes, Roxanne could tell that the rest had done her good. Her face twisted when she saw Wyatt, and then flushed as embarrassment swept over her.

"Dammit, Addie, I'm your brother! You don't have to be shy with me, even if you are in one of Roxie's sexiest nightgowns!" Then he had Addie in his arms, pressing his face against her hair. "Addie, why didn't you come to me? I'd have done something, short of killing the bastard, I hope."

"I couldn't. I didn't know whether Henry was within his rights or not. And there wasn't anyone I could ask."

"I knew it would be bad for you, but even I didn't think that Maynard would dare go as far as he did. You're his wife, not a hired whore! And no self-respecting whore would put up with what you've had to put up with from him, I can tell you that."

"He'll try to make me go back to him."

"Don't worry about it. You aren't going back." Wyatt could feel his sister trembling, and his fists clenched.

Addie's face was drenched with tears as sobs shook her. "Even if I don't have to go back, what have I left to live for? I'm still his wife, and Matt's lost to me. He thought that I married Henry because I wanted money, all the things Henry could give me. I'll never forget his face, that first Sunday we were back after I was married. I dream about it every night, it haunts me. . . ."

"Hush, hush. There's no use tormenting yourself about something that's over and done with. You'll forget, in time." Wyatt felt like a hypocrite. Would he ever forget Geneva? Would even being married to Roxie, who was more than holding up her part of the bargain to make him as happy as possible, ever be able to wipe the emptiness of losing Geneva from his heart?

"Here's Mary with your supper." Wyatt plumped up the pillows behind Addie's back and took the tray and set it over her lap. "Just eat as much as you can, and then try to get some more sleep."

They left Mary with Addie, and Wyatt's face was once again set in grim lines as they went back downstairs. "She looks terrible," he said, his voice filled with worry. "Do you think we'd better call Galen to have a look at her?"

"No, I don't. She'd die of humiliation. All she needs is a lot of rest and the assurance that she never has to go back to that monster."

"And I'll lay you odds that we'll have a visit from that monster before the evening is out. By this time he'll be combing the town for his missing plaything."

"Let him come! I can't wait to face him! If he doesn't know what he is now, he will before I get through with him!" Roxanne's voice was venomous.

They went through the motions of eating, too angry to taste anything, and then the meal was cleared away. They went into the parlor to wait for Henry Maynard to descend on them.

He was there less than fifteen minutes later. They didn't need Freda to answer the door to find out who it was; they knew it was Henry by the way the sound of the brass knocker reverberated through the house.

"Wyatt, go and make him stop that racket! Addie'll shake herself out of her skin."

Wyatt was already striding into the hallway, with Roxanne right behind him. He opened the door and snapped, "Henry, you don't have to break my door down! And if you want to know if Addie's here, she is. Now you might as well go on home because you aren't going to see her."

"What do you mean, I'm not going to see her?" His face was more red with indignation than with the bitter cold that had intensified since the sun had gone down. Henry tried to push his way past Wyatt into the house, but Wyatt put his arm across the doorway and barred him from entering. "Wyatt, let me in this instant! And tell Adelaide to get her coat and bonnet, I've come to take her home."

"You," Wyatt said, his words spaced to give them their full effect, "can go to hell. Addie's staying here. Don't bother to come back tomorrow, either, because it won't do you any good."

"Now you just see here, young man! You have no right to keep my wife from me. Every law of the land says that I can take her home where she belongs and see that she stays there. After this disgraceful episode, I'll see to it that she's never allowed to visit you or see you again!"

"Bring the law into this, and I'll break every bone in your fat neck. But before I do that I'll spread the whole story of how you've mistreated her, with no detail deleted."

"And I'll see that every woman in town makes her husband boycott your bank!" Roxanne put in. "Geneva Burton will help me, and by the time we get through with you you'll wish you'd never been born!"

"Boycott my bank! Young woman, don't be ridiculous! It's the biggest bank in town." Henry was shaken, but he was by no means through bluffing, even though Wyatt's murderous face made his blood run cold.

"It is now." Roxanne's voice was as sweet as treacle. "But my father will be happy to withdraw his money and use the smaller bank, and Marvin Burton has plenty of influence as well. He'll withdraw his money and see to it that all of his friends and clients do the same! If we have to do that, you might as well resign yourself to starving because we'll drive you out of the banking business so fast you won't know what hit you.''

"You can't do this!" Henry spluttered. "I'll go to Herndon—"

He broke off, staring past Roxanne and Wyatt. They turned to see Addie coming down the stairs. She was still in her borrowed nightgown, without even a robe to cover it, and her feet were bare. Her loosened hair streamed over her shoulders, and her face was so pale that the contrast of the purple shadows under her eyes made her seem more like a spectre than a human girl.

"I won't go back, I'll never go back, I'll kill myself first! I'll kill myself, do you hear?" She stopped beside Wyatt and her hand reached out for his, seeking comfort and courage. But her eyes remained fastened on her husband, with such intensity that Henry flinched. "Only I'll kill you first," she hissed. "I swear I will. I'll stick a knife in your heart while you're asleep, and then I'll use it on myself!"

She was hysterical, her body trembling so hard that Wyatt put his arm around her to support her. Roxanne moved closer to her, reaching out her own hand to touch her.

"Addie, go back upstairs. You'll make yourself ill."

"I can't make myself sick. I'm already sick, sick to the core from the things Henry's done to me. I'm so sick I could die of it. I might as well really be dead as to have to go back to him."

"She's insane!" Henry bellowed. "She's crazy, I'll have her committed, I'll have her put where you can't get to her to put these insane ideas into her mind, that she can leave me, her lawful husband! Stephen Harding will certify her. I'll have her out of this house before the night is over!"

"You come around here again and you'll get a bellyful of buckshot!" Wyatt shouted. "Now get out, get the hell away from my front porch before I forget myself and tear you apart without waiting to get my shotgun!"

All along the street, doors opened and people stepped outside to see what all the shouting was about. Across the street, Marvin Burton stepped out onto his own porch, with

Geneva right behind him. Marvin made to lay a restraining hand on Geneva's arm but she shook free of him and began to run, calling out through the rapidly increasing blizzard, "Roxie, what is it? Is that Addie with you? Get her back inside before she catches her death!"

She was with them in seconds, running ankle-deep in the snow, and then her arms were around Addie and her voice, gentle but commanding, urged her back into the hallway so that Roxanne could close the door.

"Wyatt, go and bring Mr. Burton over here." Roxanne was shaken by the scene that had just taken place, but she was Earl Fielding's daughter and her mind still functioned just as Earl's would have done. "Geneva, help Mary get Addie back into bed, while Wyatt and I find out just how many of Henry Maynard's threats he can carry out! And don't you worry, Addie. Geneva's father will know how to protect you legally, if Wyatt's fists aren't enough to keep that skunk away from you!"

And she added as an afterthought, "I think you'd better send for Galen after all. Addie's going to need something to calm her down. Whoever would have thought she had it in her!"

Henry Maynard was retreating, but he turned back to shake his fist at Wyatt. "I'll be back! I'll be back tonight! You can't keep my wife from me, even Earl Fielding isn't powerful enough to do that!"

Houses on both sides of the street chilled as front doors remained open while neighbors drifted back and forth, asking each other questions, shaking their heads, unable to comprehend what was happening in their peaceful, moral neighborhood. There hadn't been this much excitement since the revival meeting last summer. And then, as they realized that they were prying, not acting as proper ladies and gentlemen, they drifted back into their houses to speculate with their own spouses on what was happening.

Lordy, lordy, Roxanne thought, leaning against her own door. We've got us a regular Roman circus here. Everybody's gathering around to be in at the kill! They were in for it, all of them. This would be the worst scandal Athens had ever known. It would put her own running off to Rochester to nurse Wyatt right out of the running. It would be a long time before the town got back to normal.

She pushed aside the curtains that covered the window, straining to see through the snow that by now was like a curtain between her and the other side of the street. At last! They were coming. She could see Wyatt and Mr. Burton. Marvin had taken the time to put on his boots and coat and hat. She'd better go upstairs and give Geneva some dry, warm clothes. Two storms in one night, she thought. Her face reflected her eagerness to join battle. From the looks of it, the blizzard wasn't going to be half as bad as the human storm.

Henry climbed up into his buggy and clucked to the horse. It was standing with its head lowered, shivering in the cold. He was the only man in town who thought it was beneath his dignity to walk even around the corner, and always used his horse and buggy, to emphasize his importance. He gave the animal a vicious cut with the buggy whip, but although he whipped it again and again it couldn't make fast headway through the snow that was piling up in drifts, swept by a wind that cut to the bone. Any vehicle that moved after tonight would be on runners. It was a good thing that the Livingston house was directly across from his own. He'd put the horse in its stable and walk across. Horses were valuable, and he didn't want to lose the animal.

A drink, that was what he needed. He'd stop for a drink before he crossed the street, a good stiff tot of brandy. He wouldn't be offered any at Herndon's. The mill owner frowned on alcoholic spirits, not only in public, among his churchgoing neighbors, as Henry did, but in his private life as well.

The horse safely stabled and given a quick swipe with a piece of sacking, Henry let himself into his house and headed for his study where he kept a bottle locked in a desk drawer, away from the servants' prying eyes. His hand shook as he lifted the bottle to his mouth, not taking time to fetch a glass. In his haste he swallowed too much too fast, and choked, spluttering while tears came into his eyes. It was too much, it was altogether too much! Herndon had better make that son of his knuckle under, even if they were at odds. He'd have Adelaide back, and he'd have her back tonight! He'd make Herndon have his sleigh hitched up to fetch her. From now on he'd make sure that Adelaide never left his house without him even if he had to lock her in her room until she came to her senses.

Yes, and he'd have a court order served on Wyatt Livingston and that brazen wife of his. The red-haired bitch! They'd never give shelter to his wife again! A man had his rights, and absolute domination over his wife was one of them.

His choking eased, and he swallowed more brandy, relishing the soothing effect as it hit his stomach. Regretfully, he recorked the bottle. He had to have his wits about him when he talked to Herndon, it wouldn't do to go over there half drunk, as much as he'd have liked to feed his righteous anger with more brandy.

The wind was stronger when he left his house, driving the blinding snow with brutal force. He pulled the fur collar of his coat closely around his neck, lowering his chin, as he started down the porch steps. The wind-driven snow blinded him, and he missed the first step, skidding on the snow as he fell. He landed heavily on his hip, and felt the bone snap even as his head struck the edge of the riser. Pain exploded behind his eyes before blackness settled in. He lay there, unconscious, while the snow continued to pile up until his body was covered.

A stray dog, seeking any kind of shelter, stopped to sniff at the snow-covered mound at the foot of the steps, and lifted its head and began to howl. The eerie sound reverberated above the wind, and across the street Herndon lifted his own head from the sheet of figures he was studying, and frowned. Something must be done about those curs that wandered the streets, he'd have a word with Ed Hanney tomorrow, tell him to round them up and dispose of them. It was a nuisance that could not be tolerated.

18

For three days after Henry Maynard's body was found, Addie lay in her bed in Roxanne's house, her face white and still and her eyes seemingly seeing nothing. She didn't speak, and she ate nothing but a little broth and tea that Roxanne and Geneva literally forced between her lips.

Galen had come twice every day, and he was worried. "She's in shock," he told them. "It's all been too much for her. Keep her warm and comfortable, try to coax her to eat and to talk. Right now, unless I want to dose her with laudanum, which I don't, love and kindness is the best treatment. She's young, she'll come out of it, given time."

All the same, Roxanne and Wyatt could see that he was worried, and they were frantic. "Damn Henry Maynard!" Wyatt burst out. "He's still tormenting her even now that he's dead!"

"Wyatt, you mustn't damn a dead man. Besides, it isn't necessary." The corners of Roxanne's mouth twitched in spite of her worry about Addie. "Go on to the office. There isn't a thing you can do here. Geneva's coming over again this afternoon to help Mary and me watch over Addie."

Geneva had come every day, only watching to make sure that Wyatt was out of the house before she crossed the street. Always perceptive, she knew that her presence troubled Wyatt, and she was deeply sorry. Roxie was a wonderful wife to him. Why couldn't he be happy with her?

It wasn't fair to Roxie, and Geneva didn't want either of them hurt. Roxie loved Wyatt so much! She deserved a husband who loved her as much as she loved him. Sometimes

Geneva wondered how human beings managed to make such a coil of their lives.

The storm had worn itself out late in the night that Henry had come to try to force Addie to return home with him. The temperature, however, remained cold, and there were still several inches of snow on the ground.

"I hope the ground hasn't frozen too deep," Roxie said as she and Geneva drank tea in the parlor. "I feel sorry for the gravediggers."

"So do I, but all the same, it's better that we can bury Henry now, rather than have to wait until later. The sooner it's over, the sooner Addie will begin to get better. Mother always says that bereaved people can't begin to recover until the funeral is over. Until then, their minds refuse to accept that whoever passed away is really dead."

"That won't hold true for Addie, because there's no way she can go to the funeral. If your mother is right, it's a pity. Shock or no shock, there's no way Addie wouldn't have to feel better, seeing Henry Maynard covered with six feet of earth and realizing that there's no way he can ever get at her again."

The morning of the funeral dawned cloudy and damp, with another threat of snow. The services were to be held at two o'clock in the afternoon, hopefully the warmest part of the day for the convenience of the mourners. At one o'clock, Addie rose from her bed and asked Mary to help her dress.

Frightened by Addie's stony determination, Mary ran to call Roxanne and Wyatt. They weren't any more able to persuade Addie to go back to bed than Mary had been.

"I'm going to the funeral. Henry was my husband. I'm going to see him buried."

"Addie, don't you realize that nearly the whole town will be there?" Roxanne argued. "All of them filled with curiosity, remembering or having heard of the quarrel right before Henry died. There's no reason for you to put yourself through that. Everyone knows that you're ill."

"I don't care about the people. Mary, please run over to Mr. Maynard's house and fetch me back a black dress and bonnet and gloves, and my black shawl. Lucy will get them for you." As cold and seemingly as calm as ice, Addie sat down at the dressing table and began to brush and plait her hair.

Roxanne and Wyatt gave up. It might be more dangerous

to cross her than to give in. They'd be right beside her if she should collapse, and Galen would be at the funeral so he could follow them home and dose her.

Addie didn't say anything else until they were entering the church. "I won't sit by my father. Wyatt, don't let him try to sit near me."

"I'll take care of it," Wyatt said. His voice was so low that even those nearest him couldn't hear his answer, although both he and Roxanne were sure that several of the mourners who were already seated had heard Addie. One more ember for the fire, Roxanne thought. The blaze of this scandal would burn brighter and higher. She hoped that Addie would be able to control herself during the services and not add any more fuel to the flames.

If anyone had come to the funeral in hopes of adding some excitement to their lives by seeing Addie collapse, they were disappointed. Those so mentally deficient that they were forced to draw on other people's misfortunes to bring color to their lives had to be content with the way Addie ignored her father when he attempted to speak to her. It happened as he and Lillian left their pew with the other mourners to make their way to the cemetery.

Herndon was thwarted, not by Wyatt, who had stood aside so that Addie and Roxanne and Geneva could pass him, but by his friend, Eric Fleming, who interposed his huge bulk between Addie and her father. He stood there, his face blandly impassive, until Wyatt's group was out of the church. Even a Herndon Livingston stood no chance of getting past Eric. One woman giggled nervously, and then clapped her hand over her mouth at the shocked silence that followed.

If the deceased had been anyone of lesser importance than the banker, Jebbidiah Tucker might have cut the graveside services short, owing to the overcast chill of the day. As it was, he left no word out. The mourners tried to keep the stamping of their feet against the cold from being noticeable. Addie herself, with Wyatt on one side of her and Roxanne on the other, Geneva and Eric standing next to them, was erect and motionless until it was over. When it was time for her to drop the first clod onto the coffin after it had been lowered into the grave, she stepped forward and discharged her duty with no visible sign of emotion.

At the back of the crowd, one woman nudged her

neighbor. "I'll swear she isn't shedding a tear, even if we can't see her face under that veil!"

"Shock," her neighbor murmured, her voice filled with false sympathy. "I've seen it happen, she'll cry when she comes out of it. There's nothing like a good cry to start the healing after the loss of a loved one."

Leaving the cemetery, Addie nodded to her mother and looked straight through her father. Once again, Eric's bulk prevented Herndon from getting close to his daughter, and more tongues clacked. But at least the ordeal was over, and Roxanne breathed a sigh of relief as Wyatt helped Addie into the sleigh and tucked the buffalo robe around her knees. She only wished that the worst part of this day were over. Now there was the gathering of close friends and neighbors at the deceased's house to sympathize and mourn and eat the funeral food that these same friends and neighbors had brought in until the kitchen and dining room tables groaned under the weight of the platters and dishes. She was afraid, as were Geneva and Galen, that having to enter her husband's house again would be too much for the frail girl who had already lived through more horror than most people dream of.

They needn't have worried. Addie, her shoulders still squared, drank hot tea and nodded in all the appropriate places. Her face was pale but composed, as one after another came forward to offer their condolences.

"She's all right, isn't she?" Geneva asked Galen.

Galen frowned. "I'm not so sure. She's a little too composed. I'd rather see her cry or have hysterics. It would be more natural."

"I don't think she's going to cry. What does she have to cry about? She's free, Galen! And Roxie and Wyatt will take care of her. I'm only glad that Herndon Livingston didn't have the gall to show up here."

"It wouldn't have done him any good. Earl Fielding and Jim Yarnell are watching the door." In spite of the inappropriateness of the situation, Galen couldn't help a near chuckle, and Geneva had to control her impulse to chuckle right along with him.

From his chair across the room, Bobo's eyes never left Addie's face. Outwardly calm, he was battling his fury. There was no way that he could take Addie in his arms and comfort her, tell her that now that she was free, he intended to spend the rest of his life making it up to her for every moment of agony she had lived through. His longing to enfold her in his love was a physical thing, but this wasn't the time or place. Decency demanded that he give her a little time. So he had to sit there and suffer through it until the right time came.

He hung onto the fact that she was free, that now, at last, nothing stood in his way except a few weeks of time. How he loved her! He'd never forgive himself for ever having let this happen, for not having made her fall in love with him before Matthew Ramsey had ever come to Athens, or her father had forced her to marry Henry Maynard. If he hadn't been a blind fool, none of this would have happened.

But he wasn't a fool now, and this time, he was going to make sure that Addie would spend the rest of her life in happiness. They belonged together, and once they were able to marry, all of this would be blotted out as if it had never happened.

The partakers of the funeral feast began straggling away in twos and threes, and finally the last of them were gone. Only Geneva and Galen remained after Bobo finally drove himself to go.

"It's time we got on home, honey," Roxanne told Addie. "Wyatt, get her things. We have to get her back into bed."

"I'm not going back with you, Roxie." Addie's voice was low but firm, and her eyes were clear with no trace of indecision or weakness. "Thank you for being so kind to me during all these days, but I'm all right now."

"But you can't stay here, all alone! Wyatt! Galen! Tell her!"

"Of course you can't, Sis. You'll stay with us for at least several more weeks. There's no way we can let you stay here by yourself."

"I won't be by myself. The servants are here. I have to come home some time, and it might as well be now."

"Galen?" Roxanne appealed to the young doctor.

Galen took Addie's wrist and counted her pulse. It was normal and steady. Her color, although pale, was good. He studied her for a moment, and then nodded.

"I think she'll be all right, Mrs. Livingston."

"Mrs. Livingston!" Roxanne stared at him. "I'll be double-blasted! Don't we know each other well enough yet so you can call me Roxie? You do it when you aren't thinking! And I think you're off your rocker, *Doctor* Forbes! How can she possibly be alone!''

"I can stay with you, Addie," Geneva offered, slipping her arm around Addie's waist. "I'd like to."

"Thank you, Geneva, but no." A faint smile quirked at the corners of Addie's mouth, the first smile that any of them had seen on her face since she'd married Henry Maynard. "Just as Doctor Forbes, as *Galen,* says, I have to start adjusting. I promise I'll send for you if I need you."

They didn't like it. Even Galen wasn't sure if his decision was the right one. But in the face of Addie's determination, what could they do but leave? Addie was a widow now, not a young girl, and her decisions were her own. The servants would watch over her, she'd be all right. Galen hesitated for another moment, debating with himself whether to persuade her to take a sleeping potion, but he decided against it. She was all right, and in spite of a nagging at the edges of his consciousness, he could detect no sign that she needed to be dosed or nursemaided if she didn't want to be.

And so they left, and now that she was alone, Addie instructed the two hired girls to go about their cleaning up, and ascended the stairs. She entered the room she had shared with her husband, but she stayed there only long enough to gather up her night things and toilet articles before she crossed to a bedroom across the hall. It was a room delegated for the overnight guests who had never come. The bed was made up, as it always was, the furniture free from dust. A fire was laid in the fireplace ready for the match that would set it to blazing to take the chill from the room.

She sat in a low chair by the fire for a long time, holding out her hands to its warmth. Then she undressed and got into her nightgown, and brushed and replaited her hair before she got into bed. She slept, but her sleep was light. She opened her eyes and checked the clock she'd set running before she'd gone to bed.

When she woke for the fifth time, at four o'clock in the morning, she got out of bed. Ignoring the cold that had settled in again now that the fire was dead, she slipped into a robe and left the room, carrying a candle, its flame shielded by her hand. Her slippered feet made no sound as she avoided every board that might squeak under her weight. She slipped down the hallway toward the back part of the house until she came to the chamber they called the trunk room. She eased the door open half an inch at a time to make sure that its hinges wouldn't creak and alert the servants who might be sleeping with one ear open, worrying about her, in spite of having been up late cleaning up after the funeral feast.

She wanted only one of the smallest boxes, something small enough so that she could carry it herself with no trouble.

By five o'clock the box was packed with everything she would need. She carried it downstairs and set it outside the house, under the shelter of the skeletal bushes that hugged the foundations.

Her feet icy, her hands blue, she rebolted the front door and crept back to her bed, where her eyes closed the moment her head touched the pillow. She smiled in her sleep. Her face in the dim lamplight looked as young and innocent as it had before her father had sold her to Henry Maynard.

Carrie Flagg, the older of the Maynards' two hired girls, tiptoed in to check on her mistress half an hour later, just as she'd tiptoed in before she and Wilma had finished the clearing away and washing up last night. Carrie's face, under the nightcap that covered her graying hair, softened. She'd just let her mistress sleep, and go back to bed and get some more sleep herself.

It was a blessing that the young widow had taken the death of Mr. Maynard so well, and it was a double blessing that now she and Wilma would only have her to do for. She'd be a good deal easier to work for than Mr. Maynard had been.

She'd heard things during the night when Mr. Maynard was alive that had made her quake in her bed. After seeing the young bride's face in the mornings, she'd come near to quitting, except that she hadn't wanted to leave the unhappy young lady. She'd been hired to see nothing and to hear nothing, and she'd done what she'd been hired to do. That hadn't meant that she'd liked it. Things would be different now. Carrie smiled as she went back to sleep.

At seven-thirty Wilma carried a breakfast tray to Addie, and reported to Carrie that Addie had eaten everything on it. "All the porridge, every spoonful! And two cups of tea. And the pie! Even the crust!" Wilma said. "Doesn't look like she's doing much grieving, does it, at least not enough to spoil her appetite!"

"She's young, and the young get hungry," Carrie said, her voice sharp. For all that Wilma was twelve years younger than Carrie, and supposed to have sharper ears, Wilma always slept like the dead and she'd never heard the noises that had disturbed Carrie's sleep while the banker was alive. "And all to the good. It's easier doing for a healthy body than a sick one."

"She ain't sick, that's for sure." Wilma nodded several times. "But all the same, it don't hardly seem decent."

"Wash up them dishes," Carrie told her shortly. "And mind your own business, unless you want a box on your ears."

It was eight o'clock in the morning when Addie appeared downstairs, composed in her widow's black, and dressed for the outdoors. She found Wilma in the parlor, giving it its usual dusting and polishing. "Wilma, I'm going to walk over to Mrs. Livingston's. I'll probably spend the rest of the day there."

"You sure you're dressed warm enough? Would you be wanting me to walk over with you?"

"I'll be fine, and there's no need for you to come with me. It's practically around the corner. Just go on with what you're doing." Addie gave Wilma no time to protest. She walked, her step brisk, to the parlor door and out into the hall, where Wilma heard the front door close behind her.

Once more the housemaid shook her head, her face registering disapproval. Not a sign of grief on Mrs. Maynard's face. Her eyes weren't even red and swollen! And going visiting, even to see her sister-in-law, when by all that was decent she should be in her bed, prostrated, and her friends coming to her! Still, mindful of Carrie's admonition to mind her own business, she shrugged and went back to her polishing, intent on bringing up a good shine. If the young widow wouldn't notice if she shirked her duty, Carrie would.

One glance at the front windows was sufficient for Addie to see that Wilma wasn't watching through the curtains. Her eyes rested for a moment on the black-ribboned wreath on the door, and then she retrieved the box she'd packed before dawn. She began walking, not toward Roxanne's house, but toward the center of town and Lester Peterson's smithy and livery stable.

Les's face registered more expression than it usually did

when Addie made her request. She'd been lucky during her walk down. She hadn't met anyone at all on the streets except for a few children too young for school, and although they'd looked at her with fleeting curiosity they'd immediately gone back to their games, grown-ups being of no interest. The men were all at their work, the women still busy with their housework before they'd venture out to do their marketing.

"A sleigh, Mrs. Maynard? How far are you going, and who's going to drive you?"

"I don't know exactly how long I'll be gone. I'm going to Lyonsville, to visit friends. And I can handle a horse and sleigh, Mr. Peterson."

"Lyonsville! Ma'am, that's twenty miles away! You can't go driving alone all that distance. It wouldn't be safe!"

"I'm sure you have a docile horse that won't give me any trouble. And I'll make sure that you're well compensated."

"I'm not worried about the money. I can't let you go off all by yourself, is all."

Addie hadn't foreseen this hitch, and she began to grow desperate. "I'll double your usual fee," she said, trying to sound authoritative.

"Bound and determined to go, aren't you? Well, then, you wait here, and I'll find you a driver. I have a good man in mind. You'll be safe with him." Lyonsville! Les was uneasy. He thought he knew why Adelaide Maynard, née Adelaide Livingston, was going to Lyonsville. Everybody in Athens knew that Lyonsville was where Matthew Ramsey had found a church.

By rights he ought to go over to the Fielding house and let Wyatt and Roxanne know what Wyatt's sister was up to. On the other hand it wasn't any of his business, and if the young widow had it in her mind to hunt up the man she loved now that she was free, it was her right. Only he'd make sure that she got there safe and sound, his conscience would bother him otherwise.

"Mr. Peterson, you aren't going to—"

"I'm not going to do anything but get you a driver. You wait inside, out of the cold." And out of sight, he added mentally. No use in setting tongues wagging any sooner than need be.

Jim Yarnell was startled when the blacksmith banged on

his door at his rooming house, but he'd been up and dressed and had his breakfast an hour since, so he opened it at once.

Jim, along with Ike, had taken quarters in town during the winter months when the canal was frozen solid. The barge captain would admit it to nobody, but he'd stayed in Athens to be close to Mary.

"Jim, I have a chore for you to do, if you're minded," Peterson told him. "Adelaide Maynard's got it in her mind to go to Lyonsville, and she needs somebody to drive her. She was all set to go alone, but I told her I wouldn't let her unless she let me find her a driver."

"Good Lord!" Jim stared at his friend. "She's chasing off to Lyonsville, alone? Do you think that Wyatt and Roxanne Livingston have any idea what she's up to?"

"Nope. And I don't reckon it's my place to tell them. The young lady has a right to do what she wants as far as I'm concerned. She'd a widow now, not a young miss. Will you take her?"

"If she's set on going, of course I'll take her! But don't you think we should tell the Livingstons? The young Livingstons, of course, not her father. If they'll let her go at all, at least Mary ought to go with her."

"No, I don't. They'd try to stop her, like as not. And from the looks of her, she isn't about to be stopped. She'd find another way to get there, and without you to look after her. If she can make it up with young Ramsey, I'll be happy for her. After being married to Henry Maynard, she deserves every chance she can find at happiness."

It only took Jim a moment to decide that he agreed with Les. Tongues were going to wag, that was for sure, but there wasn't a man, woman or child in Athens who'd dare to think, much less to say, that Miss Addie wouldn't be as safe with him as she would be in her own parlor. If there was going to be another scandal, it would be because she was chasing after Matthew Ramsey, not because she'd gone with Jim with no lady chaperone.

"Take some money. I don't reckon she thought to bring any with her and you'll have to eat along the way," Peterson advised him. "From what I knew of Henry Maynard, he wouldn't have let her have any cash in her possession, and she hasn't had a chance to get any since he died. She knew I'd trust her to pay me later."

"Right." Jim was already struggling into his coat. He stopped only to write a note to Ike, who was out looking for what amusement he could find in Athens on a weekday morning. He still didn't like it, but Les was probably right, he thought, as he followed Peterson out into the cold. If Addie was determined to go, she'd find a way, and her reasons for going alone were her own affair.

Addie's face flushed when she saw who it was that Les Peterson had brought to be her driver. She would have rather had someone she didn't know, but she didn't dare take the time to protest. If he was willing to take her, it was probably for the best, because she knew that Wyatt liked and respected the canalboat captain. The thing was to get away before anyone could stop her and try to talk her out of it. She didn't care if she wasn't acting like a lady. After she'd found Matthew and they were married, it wouldn't matter anyway. Nothing would matter except that they'd be together at last.

With Jim driving, Peterson had no need to hitch a docile animal to the sleigh. He led out the best horse he had for hire. They made good time as the day was clear and crisp, and the snow on the roads was well packed, making easy going for the runners.

Addie's face was flushed as much with excitement as with the cold as the horse's hooves threw up an occasional snowball. Her mouth parted in a smile as one of them was thrown so high that she had to duck. Jim marveled at how good she looked; nothing like the lifeless wraith she'd been ever since that father of hers had decided that her worth to him as Henry Maynard's wife was worth more than her own happiness.

They stopped at an inn at noontime, where their horse was given a measure of oats and a chance to rest in a warm stable, while Addie and Jim ate a hearty meal. Once again Jim had to marvel as Addie ate everything on her plate. Mary had kept him informed about Addie's lack of appetite, how they'd all been worried half out of their minds because she wouldn't eat. The food wasn't even that good, but she ate it as if it was a feast.

"Can't we start on now?" Addie finished the last bite of her pie and wiped her fingers on her handkerchief, the inn not boasting such niceties as table napkins. Jim looked at his watch and shook his head.

"It's not even been an hour. Best to let the horse rest another half hour. We'll make better time in the long run." He wished that he'd been able to bring Mary along with them, not only because it would have looked better, but because Mary would have been almost as excited at the adventure as Addie was.

When they started out again they made good time. They crossed a covered bridge where a lad was shoveling snow onto the planks so that the runners would have a good surface, a task generally tended to by boys during the winter. Too heavy a load of snow on a bridge was dangerous because of the weight, so someone had conceived the idea of covering them with pitched roofs, but that made it necessary to shovel in enough snow for the sleigh runners. Addie waved and smiled at the boy. His ears, already red from the cold, turned several shades brighter as he gaped at the beautiful girl whose smile was like that of a joyful angel.

"Do you know exactly where you're going, when we get there?" Jim asked her.

"No, but it doesn't matter. Everyone will know where the Methodist church is, and the parsonage."

Right, Jim thought. There wouldn't be any problem. If Lyonsville had been on the canal he'd have known where they were himself, but they could find what they were looking for with no trouble.

On the way to the Methodist church they passed a livery stable. "You can let me off at the parsonage and have the horse taken care of there," Addie said. "Tell the liveryman where you'll be, and I'll find you when I want you to take me back to Athens." Her face was alight as Jim helped her out of the sleigh.

"Are you sure you don't want me to wait here?"

"I'm sure. Go on along. You'll be wanting to find some place to get in out of the cold. It looks like it's going to snow again."

Jim himself had been keeping a wary eye on the sky for the past hour, but he hadn't wanted to dampen Addie's spirits by mentioning that it looked as if they were in for some bad weather. If Addie had come alone, as she'd wanted to, and been caught in a snowstorm on the way back, she'd have been in trouble.

"If I were you, I wouldn't stay too long. You're right about it looking threatening."

"It won't take me long." Addie, her smile so filled with pure happiness that it made Jim's heart lurch, walked up the path to the front porch of the parsonage and lifted the knocker.

Jim waited until he saw a young woman open the door and Addie enter the house. Then he got back into the sleigh and turned to go back to the livery stable just as the first flakes of snow began to fall.

Addie was so elated at having reached her goal that she scarcely noticed the young woman who admitted her to the parsonage. She was probably in her late twenties, with soft brown hair plaited severely around her head and drawn into an uncompromising bun in the back. Her face was quite plain and a little pinched.

"I'm looking for Matthew Ramsey. Is he at home?"

"Yes, he is." The young woman led Addie into a shabbily furnished parlor and indicated a chair. "He's in his study, I'll call him. Who shall I tell him is calling?"

"Adelaide Liv . . . Adelaide Maynard. He'll know who I am." Adelaide didn't take advantage of the chair that had been offered. Her body was wound up like a coiled spring as she waited, her eyes glued to the doorway the young woman had gone through. Her breath caught as she heard footsteps, and as Matthew stepped over the threshold her hands reached out to his, her face uplifted and radiant.

"Matthew, I'm a widow! My husband died, I'm a widow, I'm free! Oh, Matthew, I thought I'd die when I had to marry Henry Maynard. Father tricked me into it. He lied to me, and I'd rather have been dead, but Henry died instead and I'm here . . ."

Something was wrong. Matthew's hands were abrupt as he disengaged them from hers, and his face, when her tear-blurred eyes cleared enough so that she could see, was pale.

"Mrs. Maynard, please control yourself." His voice, the voice that had sent her into raptures every time she had heard it, rasped in his throat as if he were having difficulty in speaking. Addie looked at him, her smile fading, not understanding, and a cold dread crept into her heart and left her trembling.

The young woman had followed Matthew back into the

parlor, and she came forward quickly, her face filled with concern. "Are you all right? Can I get you something, some hot tea? It will only take a moment."

Matthew found his voice again. "Nothing, my dear. Mrs. Maynard, this is my wife, Helen. Helen, Mrs. Henry Maynard. She only stopped in to apprise me of her husband's death, as we were acquainted back in Athens."

"Oh, my dear! I'm so sorry to hear of your bereavement!" Helen Ramsey was polite, but her eyes betrayed her uneasiness to Addie. "You must sit down and let me bring you some tea." Her gaze searched her husband's face.

"Thank you, no. I must be leaving." Addie turned and walked out of the room, through the hall and outer door, and then she was outside. She walked away from the parsonage, her face as white and blank as if she were dead.

19

Roxanne stared at Jim, her face filled with disbelief. "Why didn't you bring her here? After a terrible shock like that she shouldn't be alone. You should have brought her to me instead of taking her home!"

"I know that, Mrs. Livingston. I tried to talk her into letting me bring her here, but she wouldn't let me. But she didn't tell me not to come and tell you that she's back, so I did."

"Lyonsville! Wyatt and I almost went out of our minds. Carrie told us she thought Addie had come here, so we combed the town looking for her. And all the time she'd gone running off to Lyonsville, looking for Matt Ramsey!"

Jim was standing with his back to the fireplace, soaking up the warmth after the long, cold trip back to Athens. "And she found Matthew Ramsey, and he's married, only I didn't know that until I asked the liveryman if Matthew Ramsey was still at the Methodist church. I thought maybe he'd gone to some other town, or had died, even, the way Mrs. Maynard looked."

"You great silly oaf, you had no business taking her to Lyonsville without telling us!" Mary burst out, her face flushed with anger. "Ma'am, shall I fetch your wraps? You'll want to go to her right now, won't you? Shall I come with you?"

"Yes, yes, come with me. I may need to send you to fetch Galen Forbes, if she's as bad as Jim says. And to see if you can find Wyatt, he'll still be looking for her."

It took Roxanne and Mary only moments to get into

their coats and bonnets. Jim waited in the sleigh as they knocked on Addie's door, and disappeared inside when Wilma answered it. He waited for twenty minutes, his coat collar pulled up around his neck, wishing somebody would come out and tell him that the girl was all right.

There was Mary now, running down the front steps. "It's all right, she hasn't tried to kill herself or anything." Mary was breathless, her cheeks flushed. "Miss Roxie says I can go back home, and thank you for waiting."

"I'm glad she's all right."

"Well, maybe she is and maybe she isn't. It doesn't seem natural to me."

"What doesn't seem natural?" Jim clucked, and the horse moved out. He had his hands full for a moment turning it to go back to the Fielding house instead of turning to get back to its stable.

"The way she looks and acts, just like you said. As if she's somebody I never saw before. Cold and hard and not caring about anything, but you can feel the fury in her, you can feel the air shake with it. It's scary, that's what it is."

"It's probably shock. Mrs. Livingston will probably send for Galen, that would be the thing."

"I don't think so. I don't think it's anything that Ga . . . that a doctor can do anything about. It has Miss Roxie spooked, too, but she said for me to go on home, that she could handle things. Thanks for bringing me, I could have walked as well as not. I'm sorry I yelled at you, when you came to tell us. Only I still think you should have told us before you went chasing off to Lyonsville with Miss Addie."

"I probably should have, but I didn't. Nobody can live their entire life without making a mistake. Miss Mac-Donald—Mary—I'd like to know how things turn out. I feel responsible because of my part in this. Would it be all right if I called on you tonight?"

Mary hesitated. She wasn't afraid of the captain as she had been when she'd first known him. In spite of being a canaller he was a decent young man, or else Roxie and Wyatt wouldn't like him as much as they did. Even Geneva Burton and lawyer Burton and Geneva's brother Bobo liked him. It was as obvious that he'd like to court her, but she didn't want that, because even if she ended up an old maid, she couldn't ever love anybody but Dr. Forbes. Only this time she didn't know how to say no, and it wouldn't be like he was calling on her, exactly. Roxanne and Wyatt would be there, and he'd only ask after Miss Addie.

"All right. After supper? We eat at six-thirty."

Jim jumped out of the sleigh and hurried around to lift Mary down. It was the closest physical contact he'd ever had with her and the blood raced through his body. He had to exert every ounce of his willpower not to crush her in his arms and kiss her right out here in the street, with all the neighboring housewives peeking at them through their curtains. Blast it, his hands were shaking, as if he were a schoolboy with a crush on his first girl. Reluctantly, he took his arms away, and Mary skittered away from him like a frightened hare with a hound on its trail. He'd frightened her again, why couldn't he learn not to frighten her?

"About seven-thirty?" was all he could think of to say.

"That'll be all right." Mary paused only long enough to fling the words over her shoulder before she was up on the porch and through the door.

Cursing himself, Jim turned back to the sleigh. He was going to court Mary all the same, and go on courting her; and win her, if it took him all the rest of his life.

In Addie's front parlor, she looked at Roxanne over the rim of her teacup. Her face was composed, even if it did seem cold, with an eerie anger that made Roxanne's flesh crawl. What in thunder had got into her? Why didn't she cry, or scream and throw things, the way any other girl would if this had happened to her?

"Henry was a wealthy man, wasn't he, Roxanne?"

"Of course he was. And you're a wealthy widow. You can do anything you like. Why don't you travel? Not until spring decides to come, of course, but you could go anywhere. Mary can go with you, she's a good girl and she knows how to make herself useful and you'd probably rather have her than some middle-aged matron."

Addie's eyes were unflinching. "I won't be traveling. How much do you think Henry left?"

"I don't know. Wyatt can find out for you. All you have to do is appoint him as your representative, or something. I think it's called a proxy. He'll take care of everything for you, you know that. Find someone to run the bank for you, you can hardly do it yourself, or if he can't, my father or Geneva's father will know who to get. You won't have a thing to worry about."

"I'm not worried. I just wanted to make sure that there was money, a lot of money, and that it's mine and I can do whatever I want with it."

"It's yours. Good grief, Addie, you own a bank! Henry didn't have any family, there was nobody else he could leave it to. And the bank never had any directors or anything; he was the whole shebang because he wouldn't trust anyone else. Addie, are you sure you're all right? Don't you want to pack a few things and come over and stay with Wyatt and me for at least a few days, while Wyatt and Mr. Burton straighten everything out so you'll know exactly where you stand?"

"Thank you, no. I'm going to be busy."

"Busy! Busy doing what?"

Addie smiled, and once again Roxanne felt her flesh creep. There was something about that smile that sent shivers up and down her spine. What ailed Addie, anyway? Roxanne didn't like it. Maybe she should go and find Wyatt, or call Galen in, after all. Only Addie had said no, she'd said it so positively that Roxanne hesitated to go against her wishes.

"You'll see. I'm not ready to discuss it with anyone, but you'll see, soon enough."

Roxanne slammed her cup down into its saucer. "Addie, you're getting me worried."

"Don't worry about me. You can see that I'm perfectly all right. It's just that I'm going to be busy, very busy, so if you'll excuse me, I have to make some plans."

Dismissed like a child! Roxanne thought as she left, seething and still feeling spooked. She'd give her eyeteeth to know what was going on in Addie's head. Maybe Wyatt could get it out of her tonight. If he couldn't, then nobody could.

But Wyatt, when he went to see his sister that evening, had no more success than Roxanne. Addie assured him that she was perfectly all right; she instructed him to look into her assets and see that she'd be able to draw on them when she was ready. She refused to make him proxy so that he could handle her affairs. He was only to show her how to go about doing things. Defeated, Wyatt returned home to down a stiff drink.

"Roxie, has Addie gone crazy?"

"I don't think so. I think she's dangerously sane."

They looked at each other, but neither of them had any workable suggestions to make. After a moment Roxie got up and poured herself a glass of sherry. She'd have rather had brandy, but addling her brains wasn't going to help matters.

"We'll just have to wait and see," she said.

Morosely, Wyatt was forced to agree with her.

While they waited, one or the other of them went to see Addie every day, because she wouldn't come to them. Geneva was also a regular visitor, and used her powers of persuasion to try to find out what Addie had in mind. And Bobo went to see her, accompanied by Geneva, because it would have been improper for him to go alone although he had an idea that it would have been easier to pry Addie's secrets from her if no one else had been with him. Bobo had always been very good at teasing and jollying and coaxing any information out of anyone he wished.

None of them met with the least success. Addie greeted them, friendly but aloof, as though they were casual acquaintances rather than friends she'd grown up with and known all her life. She offered them refreshments, but kept her own council.

"Damn the girl!" Wyatt burst out to Bobo after one of their fruitless visits. "I know she's up to something, but what in the name of heaven could it be? What can she have up her sleeve that could give me this feeling that whatever it is, we aren't going to like it?"

"I haven't the faintest idea, but something tells me that it's going to be mighty interesting, when it happens." Bobo's grin hadn't changed a whit since he'd been a small boy shinnying up a farmer's apple trees. He was fully capable of convincing the farmers, when he was caught, that he'd only been picking the apples for them, in order to save them work. And he had picked them for them. He'd always brought baskets with him, although he'd chosen the dark of the moon for his adventure, when honest people would hardly be abroad picking other peoples' apples, so that he could deliver them to the farmers' doorsteps.

Bobo's idea had never been to steal, but only to see how much he could get away with by the use of his golden tongue. Everyone who knew him agreed that he was one of the devil's own, and everyone who knew him liked him and would have sworn on a stack of Bibles that on the day he died, he'd go to heaven in the fastest golden chariot Gabriel was able to send for him.

But now even Bobo had a worried look in his otherwise laughing eyes. He was more uneasy about Addie than he wanted to admit. If she hadn't been so recently widowed he'd ask her to marry him without waiting for the official year of mourning to be up, but so far, he hadn't even had a chance to begin courting her. It wouldn't have been decent, let alone the fact that he hadn't yet had a chance to see her alone.

He accepted the drink that Wyatt poured for him, but only drank half of it. "Don't fret yourself to a frazzle. Whatever she's up to, we're here to bail her out of any trouble she might get into. After all, what could she do, here in Athens?"

Spring had finally come. The Erie Canal had been bottomed out and cleaned, the banks repaired of any breaks caused by winter freezes and snow, and the canalboats were running again. It was just four days after the first runs had started that Addie came to see Roxanne.

"Roxie, I have to go to New York City. Would you lend me Mary to go with me?"

"New York!" Roxanne's mouth fell open. "Why on earth do you have to go to New York? You don't know anyone there."

"I'm going to redecorate my house, completely refurnish it, and I want to buy the things in New York because they'll have the best selection."

Roxanne closed her mouth. At least redecorating her house and refurnishing it was a step in the right direction. It would keep Addie busy for weeks, maybe for months, and redecorating is therapeutic for any woman. Getting rid of every trace that Henry Maynard had ever lived there would be good for Addie. And when it was done, Addie would probably be so proud of it that she'd begin entertaining, in order to show it off, and that would be the first step toward getting her back into the stream of life.

"What a wonderful idea! Addie, why don't I go with you? I'd love to be turned loose in the New York stores."

Addie's face stilled, but her voice remained normal. "I'd rather just take Mary, if you don't mind. Besides, you wouldn't want to leave Wyatt for so long. I'm going to take my time, I'll be gone for quite a while.''

Wouldn't she like to leave Wyatt alone for a while! The relationship between herself and Wyatt had deteriorated through these last weeks. Not outwardly, not anything she could put her finger on, but Roxanne felt a coldness encroaching on her heart every time they made love. Her physical desires were satisfied but her heart wept because she knew that Wyatt was only going through the motions.

She'd done her best to make Wyatt love her. She'd done everything she could think of, everything she'd ever heard of. But the fact still remained that Wyatt resented having had to marry her, and Roxanne was miserably certain that he never would love her because he still loved Geneva. It didn't matter that he couldn't have had Geneva, that Geneva had turned him down. No one knew better than Roxanne that you can't turn love off just because it isn't convenient. Pretending that she was happy, that nothing was wrong, was getting to her, until sometimes she felt like screaming. Going to New York with Addie, being away from Wyatt for a while, would give her time to think and to sort out her emotions.

But a look at Addie's face convinced her that Addie really didn't want her. Maybe Addie, too, needed to get away from all familiar associations for a time, throw herself into something new with nothing to remind her of the past.

But if she felt like that, why didn't she move away from Athens entirely? She could afford to live any place she wanted—Boston, Albany, New York, or any place up or down the eastern seaboard. In Addie's place, Roxanne would have showed Athens her dust long since.

"Of course you can have Mary. She'll be so excited there'll be no holding her. When are you planning to leave?''

"I thought I'd take a packet on the Six Day Line the day after tomorrow.''

Roxanne thought for a moment. "Are you in all that much of a hurry to get there? I had an idea it would be nice for you to go on Jim Yarnell's lineboat, give him a chance to see something of Mary.''

"I am rather in a hurry, Roxie. I want to get started. But we can take Captain Yarnell's boat back, along with the furniture I'll buy.''

"If you're bringing it back with you, you'll want

everything out of your house before you get here." Roxanne jumped at the chance to find something to keep her busy. "Are you going to make a clean sweep? Every last stick?"

"Yes, I am. Everything—furniture, hangings, carpets, pictures, I want the house completely bare so I can start over." Addie's tone was definite.

"Then I'll take care of that for you while you're gone. And you can bet that I'll get the best price for everything. Or hadn't it occurred to you that furnishings have value, even if they're secondhand?"

"I'd appreciate it, Roxie. Thank you. It will make it easier for me, if you're sure you don't mind."

"I'll love it! I'll have an auction. I'll have posters made right away and put one in every store window and on every fence in town! Bobo can be the auctioneer, it's right up his alley, and people will fight to buy things from the banker's house, you'll see. They'll be agog to see what's going on, and come out of curiosity, and by the time Bobo and I get through with them they'll stay to buy. Unless—" Roxanne hesitated, ". . . you don't want that much publicity."

Addie's face was enigmatic. "I don't mind."

"And what," Roxanne thought as Addie rose to leave, "does she mean by that?"

As Roxanne had predicted, Mary was so excited that she could hardly contain herself. This was an adventure she had never dreamed of, twice as exciting as the time she'd gone to Rochester to stay while Roxanne had nursed Wyatt through his illness. New York City, and to travel first class!

There hadn't been time to outfit her properly, but she'd had her pick of Addie's clothes. Addie had told her to take whatever she wanted. "I won't be wearing any of them again, so you can have them all, except for what I'm packing for the journey."

Mary couldn't believe her good fortune. To think of anyone giving away all these perfectly good, expensive clothes, without a sign of wear on them! It smacked of being wicked, even if Adelaide Livingston Maynard was rich. Still, Mary didn't hesitate about talking herself into it. Beautiful things like this would turn her friends Dorothy Monroe and Nancy Steele green with envy, to say nothing of Agnes Barlowe, who never failed to make some derogatory remark about Mary's being a servant when they came into contact with each other. As if there were anything degrading about being a servant! Besides, she wasn't a servant, exactly. Roxanne said that she was a companion. Taking care of Roxanne's clothes and helping her with her hair and things like that didn't mean that she was a servant.

So she chose what she wanted for herself, and when Addie assured her again that she could have them all, she put aside some of the dresses for Dorothy and Nancy. If they didn't fit, the girls could make them over, and wouldn't that make Agnes froth at the mouth!

Once they'd boarded the packet, Addie found a secluded place for herself and didn't mix with the other passengers. As she was still dressed in mourning, her seclusion was respected. But she told Mary to enjoy herself, to mix and mingle all she wanted to and not miss a thing.

Dressed in Addie's blue dress, her hair in ringlets that she'd spent an hour coaxing into just the right frame for her face, her bonnet trimmed with ribbons and roses, Mary had never felt so pretty. As she sat on one of the benches on the upper deck, she was deliciously conscious of the admiring glances that were sent her way. What a pity that Dr. Forbes couldn't see her in all this finery!

The entire trip was so enjoyable that she refused to let the thought of having to make the return journey on Captain Yarnell's lineboat dampen her spirits. With Miss Addie with her, it shouldn't be too difficult to keep Captain Yarnell from backing her into a corner. The fact that the thought of his backing her into a corner made shivers of pleasurable delight run up and down her spine was something that she chose to ignore.

They stayed at the City Hotel on Broadway, which filled up the whole block between Cedar and Thomas streets. The establishment was far from ornate on the outside, but inside it was well furnished and comfortable. Addie had chosen it because it had a ladies' dining room, where they could take their meals without being stared at or accosted by gentlemen who might think that two unescorted ladies might welcome their attentions. Roxanne had known about the hotel and recommended it. Although it wasn't elegant according to some standards, to Mary it was no less than a palace.

Addie herself had no interest in either her surroundings

or in sight-seeing. She'd come for one reason only, to purchase furnishings for her house. Together, she and Mary visited every available outlet, and Mary's eyes grew round with the elegance of everything that Addie wrote out drafts for at figures that would have made other people quail.

Everything Addie chose was so beautiful that Mary could hardly believe it. She hadn't even known that furniture and accessories like this existed. Why, they were even more elegant than the things Miss Roxanne had in her house! Mary wouldn't have believed that was possible until she'd seen it with her own eyes.

The shopping expeditions took a long time, and everything had to be crated for shipping, but even with the crating, Mary was disappointed that the time went by so quickly. She could have stayed in New York City for weeks, never tiring of riding the horse cars and gaping at buildings that were so tall that she wondered how they'd been put up. The jostling, bustling crowds held no terrors for her. She smiled at every urchin who begged alms, and emptied her reticule for them, not caring that it left her nothing to buy remembrances for herself, but only inexpensive lockets for both Nancy and Dorothy. Children shouldn't have to beg or go ragged. It wasn't right. But even the begging children failed to depress her, because they were so quick to grin in response to her smiles.

Captain Yarnell himself came to the City Hotel to escort them to the *Undine*, where the crates and boxes were already stowed. Jim's face was alight with pleasure at this opportunity to spend so much time in Mary's company, and on his own ground, where he was sure of himself and his worth. Ike's face was almost as shining. The young driver had a fondness for pretty ladies, and although he still thought that Roxanne Fielding—Roxanne Livingston now—was the most beautiful woman in the world, Miss Adelaide Livingston, who was now the widow Maynard, was almost as beautiful and Mary Mac-Donald had a prettiness that was sweet and wholesome and all her own. Besides, getting them home safely would be a service to Roxanne, and like any young knight of yore, Ike was eager to do service for his unattainable lady.

As she had on the trip to New York, Addie kept herself apart from the other passengers on the trip back. Seeing her desire for seclusion, Jim saw to it that at mealtimes she was seated with Mary on one side of her and himself on the other, making it virtually impossible for any of the other passengers to try to strike up a conversation with her. His duties kept him busy a good deal of the time, but he still managed to get Mary alone, on deck, that first evening, with Ike set to guard Addie's privacy.

"Tell me about your stay in New York. Did you have a good time?"

"Oh, it was wonderful! I never dreamed that a city could be that big!" Mary breathed. The moon was almost full, so that Jim could see her face clearly, shining almost as brightly as the moon and stars themselves. "I'd have been scared out of my wits if I'd been alone, and I'd never have been able to find my way around."

"There are other much larger cities in the world. London, for instance," Jim told her.

"That doesn't count. It isn't even in this country."

Mary's voice was decisive, dismissing London as of no importance. "And the furniture Miss Adelaide bought, you've never seen anything like it! She's going to have the most elegant house in Athens!"

"And she deserves it, after all she's been through," Jim said. He hoped that Adelaide would be happy, now that she was finally free of Henry Maynard. It wasn't likely that he'd ever get to see the inside of her house, social distinctions being what they were, but anything that gave Mary pleasure gave him pleasure too. Adelaide, and Geneva and Roxanne, had been good to Mary for all that they were the elite, and he loved them for that.

Then he forgot about Adelaide and her new furniture, because Mary was looking up at him, her face as beautiful as an angel's in the excitement of telling him about New York and the things that Adelaide had bought. Her lips were slightly parted as she waited for him to make some comment, and without thinking, Jim threw all caution to the winds and pulled her into his arms and kissed her.

Everything he felt for her was in that kiss, all his love, all his longing, all his passion. For a brief second, Mary stiffened and made to pull away from him, and then she melted against him, returning his kiss, filled with the magic of her journey and being on the canal with the moon and the stars.

And then Jim had to spoil it all. Of its own volition, as if it had a life of its own, his hand was drawn to her breast under the snug-fitting bodice. He'd rather have cut his hand off before he'd have let it happen, but it was done before he knew it. Mary started as if she'd been burned, and began to struggle free.

"Mary, I'm sorry! I didn't mean . . . I love you, Mary! I love you and I want you marry me. You know I'd never do anything to hurt you. . . ."

His answer was the sight of Mary's back as she ran from him, and a muffled sob. Damn himself for the world's biggest fool! He'd done it now, he'd lost her. She wouldn't trust him again for a long time, maybe never. He felt like throwing himself overboard and drowning himself. Now he'd have to start all over again, and it would be twice as hard. If she never spoke to him again it was nobody's fault but his own.

Huddled into a corner, her fingers pressed against her throbbing mouth, Mary was trembling. Waves of emotion surged through her, feelings that filled her with shame; but more, that filled her with a yearning, throbbing excitement that she had never known before, even when she was near Galen Forbes.

I'm brazen, Mary thought, her eyes filling with scalding tears of shame. I'm a brazen hussy, because I enjoyed having the captain kiss me! What if Dr. Forbes found out, what if the captain told him? She'd die of shame, she'd never be able to look at him again! All the pleasure had gone out of her adventure, and she only wanted to be safely at home again.

The auction that Roxanne and Bobo had held, to sell Addie's old furnishings, had been a complete success. Just as Roxanne had predicted, nearly the whole citizenry of Athens had come, and even people from nearby farms. Some had come to gape and surmise and wonder, but others had come to buy, and Bobo had driven the price of each piece up and up again, expert at getting the bidders to vie with each other.

Everything had been sold. Not one piece was left to be stored in the attic, and only the things from the servants' rooms had been left in place.

And now the house was furnished again, but Roxanne still hadn't seen it. Addie had made it clear that no one was to see it until every stick of furniture, every carpet and drape and mirror and picture was in place.

Tonight was the night. Roxanne and Wyatt were to be the first to view the new splendor of Addie's home.

They arrived five minutes before Addie had told them to come, but she was waiting for them. It was dusk outside, nearly dark, and every lamp was glowing, making the parlor they entered almost as bright as day.

Roxanne was struck speechless by what met her eyes. The draperies were of red velvet, decorated with gold tassels and fringe. The furniture was also red, settees and the upholstery on gilt side chairs matching the draperies. The carpet was beflowered, the mirrors on the walls were in heavy gilt frames and decorated with romping cupids. The paintings depicted scenes of cavorting nymphs and satyrs, of voluptuous women draped in flimsy robes that revealed a great deal more than they concealed.

Addie waited for their reaction, but not for long.

"Addie, what in blazes got into you?" Wyatt burst out. "This isn't a home, it's a bordello!"

"And a fine one, don't you think? Everything of the best. Henry told me all about them, the ones he'd been in, the really good ones, when he traveled. I knew exactly what to buy. Don't you think I did a good job?"

"Have you lost your senses? Why? In the name of heaven tell me why!"

"Because it *is* a bordello," Addie told him, her voice perfectly calm. "My father sold me to be Henry Maynard's whore, didn't he? So if he wants me to be a whore, that's what I'm going to be. A very expensive whore. Well, not a whore, exactly. I'll be the madam, and they don't usually entertain the clients themselves, I understand. But Father won't know that. His daughter's bordello, the best bordello in the State of New York, is going to be right here across the street from him for as long as he lives!"

20

"Addie, be sensible! You've had your fun, you've made your point, you have your father in fits, so now stop this destructive idea of revenge and marry me. We'll live anyplace in the world you want so you'll never have to see him again, or even think about him again."

"No," said Addie.

Bobo's face was white. "You can't do it! Don't you see that you're ruining your own life? Didn't you ever hear about cutting off your nose to spite your face?"

"I haven't time for this, Bobo. My girls will be arriving any minute, so if you don't want the honor of being our first client, you'd better leave."

"Your girls! And where did you find them, if I may ask?"

"Why, right here in Athens! I've been busy, Bobo. They're all young, all pretty, and they're going to be clean and beautifully dressed. No man is going to be allowed to abuse them. I've hired a guard, a . . . bouncer, do you call them? His name is Art Franklyn, he was a canaller but Captain Yarnell sent him to me. You've probably seen him around. He's a big man, really burly. He'll be able to keep order and see that none of the gentlemen get out of line.

"My girls will be well treated and well paid. They'll be better off than they've ever been since they decided to pursue their current careers because of hunger and deprivation. They'll have servants to look after them. Carrie's staying on as our cook, even though Wilma left when she heard what this house is to become. But I've hired another girl to take her place, a plain girl who was discharged from my father's mill for contumacy and blackballed so she can't find any other work. As a matter of fact, three of my girls were discharged from my father's mill for the same reason; for daring to protest against starvation wages and inhuman hours, and their present work is the only way they could find to make a living.''

His hands in his pockets so that he wouldn't be tempted to wave his arms as if he were addressing a jury, Bobo paced the floor to try to keep his temper in check. "I can understand how you could do a thing like this to your father, but haven't you given a single thought to what it will do to your mother?''

"Yes, I have. Of course, I have! I visited Mother when Father wasn't at home, and told her that she'd better move in with Roxie and Wyatt. But she wouldn't do it. She said they have a right to their privacy, and besides, she wouldn't miss being right there to see Father squirm. I'm beginning to know where I got my spunk, even if it was a long time coming out, the same as it was for her. I never suspected it, I guess nobody did, but she has it and she can use it when it's needed. Father had her cowed all of her married life, till she found out what he did to me, and then she turned on him and she's going to enjoy watching him suffer. Mother will be all right. She doesn't care a fig for social life and if her friends snub her because of me, then they aren't worth having.''

"You'll be arrested. You'll be read out of the church.''

"Read out of the church, probably. But arrested? Who's going to arrest me, unless Father tells them to? And he won't, because he wouldn't be able to stand the public scandal of having his daughter hailed into court as the proprietress of a house of prostitution.

"As for the church, being a so-called Christian didn't keep my father from lying to me and selling me, did it? And it didn't keep Henry from being what he was—something less than human. I'm not very bright about such things, but it occurs to me that I'll be a better Christian, taking those girls off the streets and giving them a good home and all the protection they need, than my father is or than Henry was. I'm going to let them keep all they earn, except what it costs to feed them. They'll be able to save it all, and stop being what they are anytime they want to. I'm furnishing their clothes and everything else, so they'll have no other expenses. And I've already sent three girls I interviewed back to their families. I paid their way and gave them enough extra to help out for a while. The ones who accepted didn't want to go home because they wouldn't be welcome after what they've become.''

"All right, you're an angel of salvation! All the same, you don't have to do this. You can afford to pay your girls off, or if you can't, if you've spent all your ready cash furnishing this . . . this . . .''

"Whorehouse?''

"Addie, dammit, you stop that! I never thought I'd hear a filthy word coming from your mouth! If you can't afford to set them up, I'll borrow the money from my father.''

"It's no use, Bobo. I'm going to stay right here. I'm going to make my father wish, every day he has left to live, that I'd never been born.''

It was all there, twisting around in her heart, all the reasons she had for hating her father and having to do the worst thing she could to punish him. His betrayal of her, the ugly, degrading, unending months she'd been at Henry Maynard's mercy, the look on Matt's face when they'd attended church that first Sunday, and worst of all—far worse than all the rest—the look on Matt's face when she'd gone to tell him that she was free, and found him married. Stricken, white, stunned!

She didn't blame Matt for marrying. There'd been no way he could have known than Henry would die and set her free. And it was virtually impossible for a minister not to be married. His vocation called for it. Helen Plimpton was the Reverend Plimpton's daughter, and when her father became ill and a new minister was needed to assist him and eventually take over the church, it was only natural that Matt should choose her for his wife.

Looking at her, Bobo took his hands out of his pockets and ran his fingers through his hair, further rumpling it from its already unruly state. It wasn't any use. Addie was set on the most excruciating revenge that she'd been able to think of. She lived for it, she breathed it. She was as hard as the marble that topped the gilded table that held that obscene lamp with its red shade and its prancing cupids cavorting among pink roses.

Not Bobo, or her brother Wyatt, or Roxie or Geneva or

anyone else, would ever be able to talk her out of it until she was satiated with revenge, until the taste of it turned to dust in her mouth. Defeated, feeling like cursing and crying at the same time, Bobo left her. He was glad, at that moment, that he wasn't in the habit of carrying a gun, because he'd have been tempted to go to Herndon Livingston's office and use it on him.

Instead, he went to Wyatt's office, by the canal, the office that Earl Fielding had turned over to him while he himself now made his headquarters in Buffalo where he could be near Jewel Southern. Wyatt's face held a momentary hope as Bobo entered, and then fell back into dejection as he saw his friend's expression.

"It didn't do any good. Even you weren't able to talk her out of it."

"No, I wasn't, and if you have anything to drink in this place, I'd appreciate it."

Wyatt's smile was thin. "I have, but I can warn you that getting drunk won't help. I've tried it."

"I'm not going to get drunk. I haven't been drunk since the night of Athens's most famous horserace." There was no accusation in Bobo's voice, no trace of resentment. He'd been drunk, Wyatt had been drunk, and there'd been an accident. It was no more Wyatt's fault than it was his own. It was just one of those things that happen and have to be lived with.

"How much do you know about Art Franklyn, this man she's hired for protection?" Bobo wanted to know as soon as he'd tasted the whiskey Wyatt poured for him.

"Enough. I asked Jim Yarnell about him. It was Jim's idea to send him. He has his orders from Jim, as well as from me. He'll do a good job or he'll wish he had. Bobo, isn't there anything we can do?"

"Not a thing, as long as Addie feels as she does. And if we're going to be honest, we'll both admit that we don't blame her. Only I wish she didn't feel compelled to wreck her own life, getting her revenge. The best we can hope for is that she'll tire of it, after enough time has passed, and then I'll spirit her away and we'll live happily ever after."

"You'd still marry her?"

"Today, or tomorrow, or next month or next year or ten years from now," Bobo said. He finished his drink and grinned at Wyatt. "In the meantime, you and I, and Jim Yarnell and the canallers he has so much influence with, to say nothing of Earl Fielding himself, can let it be known that no disturbances had better take place at 24 Elm Street.''

The town of Athens was almost rocked off its foundations by the unthinkable event that had taken place in its midst. Adelaide Maynard, née Adelaide Livingston, running a house of ill repute! Running it in Henry Maynard's old home, directly facing her father's house across the street.

24 Elm Street was a success the moment it opened its doors for business. With the exception of Wyatt and Bobo and Bob Maxwell, who abstained out of deference for Geneva and Roxie, Athens's Corinthians visited it in force, and came away with glazed eyes and beatific expressions on their dazed faces. Older, more stable men also visited, making sure that they weren't seen entering or leaving. Word got around, spread by the canallers, and there was a sprinkling of wealthy men from as far away as Syracuse and Albany and Troy. Addie's house became a place to visit for traveling men of substantial means, and it was clear that it would never lack for clientele that could readily afford its prices.

Herndon Livingston clenched his jaws until his back teeth ached, and stepped out of his house for his daily walk to his office at the mill. Although it was only a little before seven in the morning, he knew that he would not be spared today, as he was never spared, from the ordeal that awaited him on the sidewalk in front of his house.

There were two of them this morning. Sometimes there was only one, sometimes there were as many as three. Did the young ladies never sleep? Dressed in bright finery, extremely becoming and in the best of taste, the blond young lady and the dark young lady inclined their heads graciously.

"Good morning, Mr. Livingston."

Herndon's face turned a mottled red. He acknowledged their greetings neither by word nor gesture, but kept his eyes straight ahead of him as he walked past them, his back ramrod stiff. He would not for an instant consider leaving his house by the back door and cutting across lots to avoid these encounters. He would not acknowledge the existence of the young ladies or of their mistress. Sometimes she herself—Herndon never knew when it would be—appeared with one or more of her charges as he left his house, to nod her head at him and say, "Good morning, Father."

The third time this happened, Herndon's face contorted and he lifted his hand as though to strike her.

"I wouldn't, Father," Addie said, as Art Franklyn loomed up out of nowhere to stand directly behind Addie, his flint-hard eyes pinned on the mill owner. The lace curtains at the front window of the Livingston mansion moved, and Lillian's mouth curved into a bitter but satisfied smile.

The young ladies didn't solicit. Herndon had no grounds to ask Ed Hanney to arrest them for speaking to him. There was no law against saying "Good morning." Herndon took to having his dinner sent in to his office, but when he walked home again in the evening, one or more of the young ladies were invariably walking past his house, and there was no law against saying, "Good evening, Mr. Livingston."

Outside of having his daughter's establishment raided, there was nothing Herndon could do, and he'd never lay himself open to such ridicule. His only defence against the laughter, the scorn, the pointing fingers, was to ignore the fact that his daughter was running a bordello across the street from him. Once, just once, when he ranted and raved behind his own closed doors, and threatened to take steps against Addie, Lillian effectively threw a monkey wrench into the machinery.

"If you do anything at all to hurt Adelaide, I shall move across the street and assist her in her madaming." Lillian looked a little startled the moment she said it, because the word didn't sound quite right, but Herndon understood her meaning, and no action was taken.

Addie's girls worshiped her. Just as Addie had promised, they got to bathe with hot water every day, using scented soaps and drying themselves with soft, fluffy towels. Each girl had a beautifully furnished room of her own, with toilet articles on her dressing table for her own personal use. They were assured that they could leave anytime they wanted, to start a new life somewhere where they were unknown; Addie would give them enough financial help to do it. They chose to stay, because this was the most security, comfort, and luxury that they had ever known. Addie herself, forced out of her bedroom to make way for the girls, took over Henry's study, which she had furnished as a cosy sitting-bedroom, with none of the garish touches that now characterized the rest of the house. Art Franklyn was stationed in the formerly seldom-used front parlor, where he could keep an eye on the front door and admit the gentlemen callers to the house, screening them with all the astuteness he'd learned from his life as a canaller.

Athens watched, and Athens condemned; or was scandalized; or chortled with glee; according to individual character. In spite of the requests of a few respectable town leaders who were prodded by their wives, Addie was not read out of the church. Jebbidiah Tucker could scarcely read her out, when no person with reliable knowledge of her affairs had come forth to testify against her, and he himself, certainly, had no desire to investigate in person. For all he knew, Mrs. Maynard had several young lady houseguests, and Herndon Livingston must not be given any excuse to withdraw his support from the church by being displeased with the publicity that reading Addie out would be sure to bring. Addie set no foot in his church, and Jebbidiah set no foot in her establishment, thus retaining the status quo.

Now that Addie's house was off limits to respectable females, Roxanne and Geneva saw nothing of her. While they couldn't go to visit her, she in turn couldn't go to them. All they knew of Addie's affairs was what they could extract from Wyatt and Bobo. Their hearts ached for her, and like Wyatt and Bobo, they were dismayed because she was so determined to ruin her life in order to exact revenge on her father.

"There's nothing we can do," Bobo told Geneva, and Marvin Burton told her the same. "We can only hope for her to get tired of her game, and be here when she needs us."

Geneva felt no surprise at her father's statement. It had never entered her mind that the lawyer would turn his back on Addie. It was Bobo she was sorry for, because in spite of his smiling face and insouciant manner, she knew that he was suffering. But she knew, also, that he wanted no sympathy. Of all of them, Bobo was the one who was doing the most to help Addie. Marvin had found a good man to place in the bank, but Bobo, always a near-genius when it came to figures, spent two or three hours there every day, making sure that everything was in order. Geneva wasn't sure that Addie even knew it.

If only Addie hadn't done it! In a year, less than a year now, she could have married Bobo and they could have had a wonderful life together. As understanding as Geneva was, it was hard for her to understand how Addie could hurt Bobo so badly, and turn her own back on the happiness she could have found with him. Bobo was worth a dozen Matt Ramseys, and Addie must be blind not to see it.

It was in the middle of the hottest part of July that something happened to take Athens's mind off 24 Elm Street. Philo O'Brian had come back to town, and he came at the crucial moment to convince the mill mechanics that it was time for a turnout in order to force Herndon Livingston to grant them better working hours and higher pay.

Because of the loan he'd obtained from the bank that now belonged to Addie, Herndon had cut wages and once again lengthened hours in order to meet the monthly payments. Meet them he must, because through her new manager, Addie had let him know that if he fell behind, she would call in the loan and plunge him into ruin. So in order to guarantee that he would always have ready cash to meet the payments, Herndon extracted the extra that he needed from his workers' skins.

Philo chose a Saturday night to call a mass meeting, because even as fanatic an agitator as he was couldn't break the Sabbath by such an action without calling down censure on his head from even those people who were sympathetic to his cause.

The mill still closed at sundown on Saturdays, and although sundown came late in midsummer, he'd managed to send word through the rank and file of workers that he'd talk to them on the outskirts of town, where an abandoned barn would offer them shelter from prying eyes.

The barn was packed by an hour after sunset. Overworked, ill-fed, exhausted, the mechanics turned out in force. No nightmarm showed up, and no nightmarm noticed that all of her charges had scattered, all of them having come down with sudden sick headaches that had sent them to their beds, a ploy suggested by Mrs. Simms and readily accepted by the others. Philo stood on a plank that he'd laid across two kegs, to put him above eye level of the crowd and make sure that they could all hear him.

"How long are you going to stand for it? Are you human beings, free citizens of this country, or are you slaves? No man, not even Herndon Livingston, has the right to treat you like serfs, to own your body and soul and decide whether he shall work and starve you to death. If you stand together, he'll be forced to meet your demands! You all know that he can't afford to have his mechanics walk out in force. It would take too long to recruit and train replacements. He'd fall behind on his loan payments and be ruined. Now is the time, friends. Are you going to let it pass by without grasping it?"

"It's Adelaide Maynard's fault! If she wasn't clamping down on her father, we wouldn't have been put on overtime and had our wages cut again!" Agnes Barlowe shouted, her face twisted in an ugly grimace.

"You shut yer trap!" Nancy Steele shouted back at her. "We all know that Mrs. Maynard has a darned good reason! And it ain't her fault anyway, it's Mr. Livingston's fault for expanding when he didn't have enough money, and he didn't need to expand anyway, he was already makin' enough out of us without needin' to make more!"

"Ladies, ladies!" Philo held up his hands to restore order. "The reasons for your present troubles are of no importance right now. The only thing that matters is what you're going to do about it!"

"And how're we going to live, if we walk out? Answer me that, you Irish booby!" Agnes shrilled at him.

"You have friends in this town. There are several prominent men I needn't name who will dig down into their pockets to carry you until your demands are met." Philo hadn't confirmed that, and with his fingers crossed, he hoped fervently that his faith in Marvin Burton and Earl Fielding was justified. In the light of the single lantern that hung from a rafter above his head, his face gleamed with fiery determination. "Now is the time! They've done it in other places, and you can do it too! Now tell me, are you going to be at your looms on Monday morning?"

"No!"

Mary was there, even though she was no longer a mill mechanic. When she'd heard about the meeting, nothing could have kept her away. Roxanne stood on one side of her, and Jim Yarnell, who was laying over in Athens over Sunday, stood on the other. Roxanne had come because Wyatt was away from home again tonight, as he'd been for nearly every night in the week ever since Addie had opened her house. He was either helling around with the Corinthians, or seeing other women. She knew he was torn apart by Addie's actions, but the marriage that she'd thought would open the gateway to heaven had turned into the threshold of hell, and her dreams of making him love her had turned to dust in her mouth.

At the back of the crowd, Geneva and Galen Forbes stood together, with Marvin Burton a few feet away, his interest in the proceedings avid. Bobo was closer to the front, his face alight with admiration for the fiery little Irishman who was willing to lay his life on the line in order to bring justice to the downtrodden. He was glad that Mary had told Addie about this meeting, and that Addie had passed the word along, because he'd have hated to miss it.

"Stay away from your looms! Let no soul here tonight show up for work on Monday morning, or on any morning until your demands are met! You've been taught to believe that you can't exist without Herndon Livingston, but by the same token, there's no way he can exist without you! You may suffer, but you'll win. Without you, the workers, the wheels of commerce would grind to a standstill. It isn't the rich, the privileged, the employers who keep this country going, it's you, the workers! The bosses know that, they've just been keeping it a secret so that you wouldn't dare ask for your rights!"

Jim Yarnell looked down at Mary's face. Her lips were parted with excitement, and her cheeks were flushed. Except for the kindness of Roxanne Livingston, of people like Geneva and Marvin Burton, her face would be as thin and pale now as the faces of these other girls who'd been inflicted with the additional privations that Herndon Livingston had imposed on them. He ached to gather her into his arms, to hold her close and protect her from all the Herndon Livingstons of the world.

But she didn't need him, other people were taking care of her. And she didn't want him. What he'd done on the *Undine*, when she and Addie had been returning from New York, had lost him what little advantage he had gained over all these months, and made her afraid of him again. And now, a stab of fierce jealousy shot through his body as her eyes sought out Galen Forbes.

He'd seen that look in Mary's eyes before when she'd looked at the young doctor for whom Jim had so much admiration. She was in love with him, or thought that she was in love with him. And she was doomed to suffer for it, because anybody with only half an eye could see that Galen Forbes was in love with Geneva Burton even though for some unknown reason of his own he hadn't spoken for her.

His jaw muscles ached as he ground his teeth together. Mary was going to be hurt, and there was nothing he could do about it except to stand by and hope that she'd let him pick up the pieces when she shattered. If he didn't like Galen so much, he'd hate him. He was learning, this late in life, that jealousy was a burning and destroying thing.

"Miss Burton, do you think you should be here?" Galen asked Geneva.

"I came with my father and brother, so I'm not outraging convention. Of course I'd have come anyway, even if they hadn't. Mr. O'Brian is wonderful, isn't he?"

"He's a real man. And he has this crowd in the palm of his hand. He couldn't have chosen a better time for this rally."

"No, he couldn't have, and I hope the mechanics do walk out! Mr. O'Brian's right. Herndon Livingston will have to meet their demands. There's nothing else he can do."

Geneva hadn't seen Galen for some time. He hadn't come to the house to see her father and Bobo the way he used to. Geneva knew that she was the one he was avoiding, and it made her anger stir again, but now that he was here she had a question to ask him.

"Doctor Forbes, what are we going to do about Addie? I know she has cause—no one ever had better cause—but isn't her overwhelming desire for revenge unhealthy?"

"Of course it's unhealthy! If it goes on long enough, it could be disastrous."

"No pills for it, no tonics?"

"That's right. There's nothing except time, and a hope that her common sense will take over so that she can cure herself." Galen wished that he'd spotted Geneva and Roxanne before Roxanne had spotted him and beckoned to him to join them. Being in such close proximity to Geneva made him uneasy, put him on the defensive. What was she doing here, anyway, a wealthy girl with no personal interest in the mechanics? Once again, he told himself sourly, if without absolute conviction, that Geneva enjoyed the role of playing Lady Bountiful, that she was playing at being an intellectual with the well-being of the poor at heart. Give her another year or two, and she'd revert to type: self-centered, caring for nothing but her wealth and social position. Roxanne was a different matter; she had an earthiness, an innate integrity, that other young women of her social standing lacked.

On Geneva's other side, Roxanne had stopped giving her undivided attention to Philo O'Brian. She was already committed to his cause. She'd shout the justice of the mechanic's demands from the rooftops, if they turned out as she was sure they would. But she was thinking about Wyatt. Was it another woman who kept him away from home every night? Or more than one woman. Just any woman, as long as it wasn't his wife? What had she done to him by putting him in a position where he'd had to marry her? And just as important, what had she done to herself?

Outside the barn Ed Hanney, together with two deputies and a dozen men he'd recruited in haste when Carl Jakes had found out about this unlawful meeting, crouched in the darkness waiting for the exact time to charge into the barn. Herndon Livingston had made it plain that he wanted Philo O'Brian, who must by no means be allowed to slip through the net. But Mr. Livingston also wanted Nancy Steele and Dorothy Monroe apprehended, and as many of the other mechanics that they could lay their hands on. Let the other mechanics see what suffering Herndon Livingston's reprisals could bring down on their heads, and he'd have no more problems.

"You're sure you know all of 'em by sight? Leave O'Brian to Clem and me, you others grab the ones I told you and don't let them get away or you'll never find another day's work in this county. Mr. Livingston might decide you're in cahoots with them and treat you accordingly!"

They were armed, Ed Hanney with a sidearm, his deputies with shotguns, the recruits with clubs. The surprise when they burst into the barn would throw the gathering into such confusion that there should be no trouble carrying out Herndon Livingston's orders. Ed drew a deep breath. "Now!" he said.

The screaming of the terrified mechanics rent the night as Hanney and his cohorts burst into the barn, brandishing their weapons and making directly for the individuals they wanted. Jim Yarnell moved fast, drawing Mary over against a side wall, shielding her with his body, while he fought down the curses that rose to his lips. If he wasn't able to shield her, there was every chance that she might be trampled in the panic as the mechanics fought to gain the door and run for freedom.

As fast as Jim moved, Bobo moved even faster. Game leg or not, he scrambled up the ladder that led to the ruined loft, and shinnied along the rafter until he reached the lantern. Grabbing it from its hook, he blew it out and plunged the barn into darkness.

In the middle of the melee, Roxanne used her hands and elbows and her feet, kicking and hitting and on one occasion latching her teeth into the arm of one of the recruits she'd been thrown against when the meeting had been invaded.

"Scum!" Roxanne screamed at him, as the man howled. "You ought to be ashamed of yourself, frightening helpless little girls! Why don't you let Herndon Livingston do his own dirty work? Oh, I wish my father were here, he'd show you a thing or two!"

Her father not being there, Roxanne stood proxy for him, and even Earl Fielding would have had no reason to be ashamed of his daughter's ability to inflict punishment where she wanted it inflicted. Her victim's curses rose as he struggled to extricate himself from the clutches of the she-demon who was taking a toll of his flinching flesh. And he dared not retaliate, because he knew who he was up against and he knew that if he as much as laid a finger on her his life wouldn't be worth a plugged nickel. Earl Fielding would get him. There wouldn't be a hole deep enough to hide in, not if he dug it all the way to hell.

Jim Yarnell dragged Mary toward the door, shoving a way through the milling bodies, and thrust her outside. "Wait for me by the old well!" he shouted in her ear. "And don't you dare budge till I come back for you, do you understand?" He gave her a shove, and Mary's legs began churning as she raced for the well, her heart pounding. Then Jim plunged back inside. Most of the mechanics were out by now, except for four or five whom Hanney's recruits had latched onto. Even in the darkness, it was easy to tell the difference between a man and a woman, and two of the girls who'd been caught found themselves suddenly free as Jim's powerful arms picked the recruits up, one at a time, and threw them out through the door.

Mary was only halfway to the well when she slowed and turned around again. What was she doing, running away like this, when her fellow mechanics were in trouble? She, of all people, who knew what it was like to be in jail! She began running again, but this time back toward the scene of the action, darting between other girls who were running away as fast as they could.

She reached the door and darted inside, and immediately hurled her body onto the arm of a man who was struggling to hold onto a screaming, terrified mechanic. Mary's teeth sank into the man's arm and she clung like a rat terrier even when he tried to shake her off. A vicious kick to the man's shin, administered by Geneva Burton, added to his agonized howls. He bent over to nurse his injury, and his captive got away.

Geneva had lost her hat, and Mary's bonnet was hanging by its ribbons. They were both disheveled and out of breath, when Roxie groped her way toward them, her laughter ringing out.

"Oh, Roxie, don't laugh!" Geneva exclaimed. "I think they got at least three of the girls, in spite of everything Mr. Yarnell and Bobo and Galen could do."

"Where's Mr. O'Brian?" Mary demanded, her voice filled with apprehension.

"My father pushed him out and told him to skedaddle. He blocked Ed Hanney until Mr. O'Brian got away." Geneva had hardly stopped speaking when Marvin loomed up beside her, with Galen beside him, and Bobo, wiping perspiration from his forehead, right behind them.

"They're gone, the lot of them," Bobo said, his voice filled with elation. And then he sobered. "But you're right, Geneva. In all the confusion, I'm sure that two or three of the mechanics were dragged away before we had a chance to get to them."

Marvin Burton's voice was calm. "I have a feeling that Herndon Livingston has done himself a disservice tonight. If this doesn't persuade the mechanics to turn out, I don't know what will. And Philo got away. Herndon will be gnashing his teeth."

"I hope he gnashes them hard enough to break them, so he'll have to live on porridge the rest of his life!" Mary burst out before she clapped her hand over her mouth. She didn't sound like a lady at all, and there was Dr. Forbes, hearing her! But she didn't care. She did hope he'd break his teeth. Then he'd find out what it was like never to have anything good to eat.

"I'll see you two ladies home." Jim, hardly sweating, appeared beside them as they were grouped just outside the barn. He'd given chase to one last recruit, but as the man hadn't taken a captive, he'd given it up as fruitless and come back.

"You can see us home, but as soon as Mary's inside behind locked doors, I'm going to the dormitories and talk to the mechanics." Roxanne's jaw thrust out, and her eyes blazed. "They're probably scared out of their wits and they need somebody to tell them that this is the time to stand together and break Herndon Livingston's power once and for all."

"Good girl. Bobo and I will go to the jail, and see what we can do for the girls who were taken. Geneva, I want you to go home. If your mother's heard about this riot, she'll be worried. You're to tell her that we're all right. Galen will escort you."

At that moment, having had a long head start, Philo O'Brian was trotting through the residential streets of Athens. If he'd had any sense, he'd have made a break for open country, and holed up somewhere alongside the canal until a packet or a barge came along that he could drop onto, and got himself well away from the arm of Herndon Livingston's law.

But he didn't have that kind of sense. There was no way that he would turn tail and run now, at this crucial moment. He had to be right here, where he could do some good when the mechanics staged their turnout. They'd need him to keep heart in them, to keep them from knuckling under when the going became rough. If he was somewhere out in the country, there'd be no way he could make his way back into town without being seen and apprehended. The only thing to do was to find a hole somewhere in Athens itself, to make sure he'd be on hand come Monday morning.

He kept his eyes and his ears sharp as he trotted. Ed Hanney and his deputies would still be abroad, roaming the streets, looking for whatever stragglers from the meeting they might pick up.

The street he was on was one of the less prosperous, although the neatly kept yards and small, freshly painted houses attested to its respectability. There was little chance of finding a place of concealment here, and Philo quickened his pace, heading for a more likely neighborhood.

Philo's ears pricked up at the sound of footsteps behind him, heavy footsteps although they were still a long way away. It had to be one of Hanney's men; no one else would be out at this hour of the night. The brawlers, the canallers and the towpath riffraff would all be in the center of town, looking for whatever excitement they could scare up.

Philo looked behind him. He couldn't see the man who was behind him yet, but he was coming closer. His heart in his throat, the organizer looked around for someplace to hide, but no clump of bushes or tree afforded enough cover.

Two houses ahead of him, on the same side of the street, a door opened a crack. Philo had the distinct feeling, a sense that had never failed him, that he was being observed. His flesh began to crawl. An outcry from a householder would bring his follower running. Once he'd been caught sight of, the hue and cry would be on, and Hanney and his men would never stop until they'd caught him.

"Mr. O'Brian! Come quickly, hurry!"

Philo couldn't believe his ears. It was a woman's voice, filled with urgency. "Hurry!" she said again, as she opened the door a little wider.

He had no time to think about it. Any port in a storm, he thought with grim amusement as he broke into a sprint and fairly leapt up the porch steps and through the door, which closed behind him instantly to the accompanying sound of a bolt being shot.

"Whoever you are, thank you," Philo panted.

A hand on his sleeve guided him down a hallway to a room at the back of the house. The hand left his arm, and a few seconds later a candle flame flared, almost blinding him after the total darkness.

Philo goggled. There was no other word for it. His rescuer, dressed in a long nightgown and robe, her hair in curl papers and an expression of terror mixed with determination on her face, was Miss Minnie Atkins, who had charge of the Athens Reading Rooms.

"They're after you. I wasn't able to sleep. I heard about

the meeting, and I overheard two of the mill girls whispering about it as they passed me while I was on my way home this evening.''

"They're after me, all right." Philo's voice was grim. "Are you sure you're wanting to do this, Miss Atkins?"

"Yes, I am sure. I never make a habit of doing things I don't want to do. Herndon Livingston is a wicked man, and I want you to lead those unfortunate mechanics to a better life.''

"Your reputation will suffer, if I'm discovered here, you're after knowing that, aren't you?''

Minnie Atkins paled, and her mouth quivered, but her voice was strong and her eyes didn't waver. "Then it will have to suffer. After all, only God has any right to judge me, and I've made my peace with Him long ago. If the disciples could suffer for us, then I can suffer for the mechanics.''

I'll be dogged, Philo thought. Aloud, he said, "Miss Atkins, lady dear, you are a real martyr.''

"Come. I've a bed for you. No one will dream of looking for you in my house. Are you hungry? I can bring you up some tea and pie.''

"I'd be grateful. Running is hungry work, and so is exorting. Mind you keep the shades drawn. We wouldn't want Ed Hanney or any of his bloodhounds peepin' into your windows and seein' you in your nightgown, fixin' a late snack. It might set him to wonderin'.''

Marveling at his good fortune, still stunned by this unexpected source of succor, Philo followed Minnie up a steep flight of uncarpeted stairs. Here he was alone with a woman, and him so woman-hungry it didn't bear thinking about never having the time to follow his natural inclinations. But there wasn't a thing he could do about it, because Miss Minnie Atkins was a lady as well as his salvation angel. Well, a man couldn't expect to have all the luck. Having Miss Minnie Atkins look out of her parlor window right when he'd needed her was luck enough for any man, and he wouldn't try God's patience by asking for anything more.

A broad grin stretched his mouth from ear to ear as another thought struck him. He'd purely like to be at the next camp meeting out at Chestnut Grove, if Miss Minnie felt impelled to confess that she'd had a man in her house overnight.

Walking back to the Burton house, because no one had taken a horse and buggy to the rally for fear of attracting notice, Galen resented having to escort Geneva home. He resented it because of the pleasure that walking her home gave him. Inch by inch, he could feel himself losing ground in his fight to steer clear of her and all she stood for.

Beside him, Geneva gave an almost inaudible gasp as her weight came down on her left foot. Somehow, she'd managed to turn her ankle in the melee she'd taken such a delighted part in, and now it was beginning to hurt.

"What's the matter?"

"It's nothing. I turned my ankle, is all. It will be all right." Geneva took another step forward, and flinched.

Damnation! Galen's voice was gruff as he said, "You'd better let me look at it. Take your shoe off, so I can see if there's any damage."

"Here?" Geneva's voice was incredulous.

"If it's hurt, I'll have to carry you. Walking on a sprained ankle can injure it even more."

He had to let her hold onto his arm for balance as she worked her slipper off, and then there was nothing he could do but catch her in his arms when he let go of her and she lost her balance. She turned her face up to his, her eyes dark and questioning, so desirable, so forbidden, that Galen held her even closer. Before he could stop himself, his head bent and his mouth closed over hers.

The kiss went on for an eternity, while the world spun wildly on its axis and threatened to go flying off into space. Her body was pressed close to his. He could feel its softness and its strength, he could feel his desire flame out of bounds. Her arms crept around his neck and she strained against him, unable to help herself, only knowing that this was the most wonderful moment of her life, that nothing else could ever match it.

The moment was shattered when Galen thrust her away, his face cold. "A very pretty trick, Miss Burton, but isn't it a little stale? Girls have used the same trick for centuries! I can see there's nothing wrong with your ankle, you're standing on it now with no evidence of discomfort."

Damn him! Oh, damn him! The insufferable conceit of him, the unbearable arrogance! Geneva's hand ached to strike him. So he thought she'd pretended the sprained ankle! He thought that she'd tricked him!

She wrenched away from him, and without bothering to retrieve her slipper, she whirled and ran, clenching her teeth against sobs of fury.

"Wait for your shoe. I still have to escort you home, your father delegated me to the task."

"Don't bother! I know my own way!" Geneva flung back over her shoulder. "Nothing's going to hurt me, you're the only polecat I know that's still out tonight!"

She ran all the way home, limping both because of her ankle and because she was wearing only one shoe. By the greatest effort, she shed no tears. When her mother met her at her door, and exclaimed, "Why, Geneva, where on earth is your other shoe?" She said, "I lost it at the rally."

And that wasn't all she had lost. She'd lost her faith that she'd find the happiness she ached for, with the man she loved. Damn him again, she'd never forgive him, not for as long as she lived!

21

The potbellied stove in Earl Fielding's office on Canal Street glowed cherry red in its efforts to combat the chill that crept in through every crack and crevice, and that radiated from the windows on which wind-driven snow hissed as it struck the glass panes.

Marvin Burton accepted the glass of whiskey that Earl handed him, and studied the other man's face. At a table on the other side of the room, Wyatt was toting up figures, but his ears were attuned to what Marvin and Earl were saying.

"Is the news good or bad?" Marvin asked, before he took his first sip from his glass.

"Good," Earl told him. He lifted his own glass to admire the color. "The Canal Fund commissioners voted to issue another loan to the banks, so that they can keep up their interest payments and keep things from sliding even farther downhill."

In this winter of 1837, a depression had swept across the entire country. Businesses were failing, banks were defaulting on their obligations, crops had failed over widespread areas, and the outlook for an early recovery was far from promising.

"It's a good thing for the country that the canals have made so much money, and taken care of it. As bad as things are, it would be a lot worse if it wasn't for the commissioners digging into the Canal Fund to keep things going. I hate to think what would happen without their loans. You've had a large hand in that, I understand."

"They listen to me. Have you been hit hard, Marvin?

I've been so busy trying to keep things afloat that I haven't had time to ask.''

"Fortunately, I took your advice when you told me as early as last fall that this depression was likely to hit us. I got out of everything shaky, not that much of my assets were invested in shaky enterprises. You know I own a good deal of real estate and farmland. They aren't going to be showing any profits for a long time, but they'll still be there when this depression is over, and there's hard gold put away, too.''

"Gold's a comforting thing to have, at a time like this.'' Earl's grin was wry as he refilled Marvin's glass. "Unfortunately, the common workers, especially the mill mechanics, don't have any.''

"Yes, they've been hit the hardest. It's a terrible thing to have happened to them, after they gained so much last summer after that to-do at the barn when Hanney and his men tried to quash any chance of a turnout. They got nearly everything they asked for, when the turnout materialized.''

"Largely due to your advice and help.'' Earl's glance at the lawyer was filled with respect. "The girls who were arrested were freed first of all, and given their jobs back, along with the promise of no reprisals. Shorter hours, better food, fires in the dormitories before they got chilblains, a small raise in their salaries. It hit Herndon hard but they had him by the short hairs. There was nothing else he could do unless he wanted to lose the mill.''

"Don't forget Philo O'Brian's part in it. Without him, the turnout never would have had a chance to happen. He's some man, is our Philo. I still can't get over Minnie Atkins hiding him, in spite of the damage to her reputation.''

"And she didn't even bare her soul of that sin at the late July camp meeting!'' Earl shook his head, chuckling. "I made it a point to be in town for that, but I was disappointed. When Carlton Booth himself challenged her after she felt called upon to get herself saved for the umpteenth time, she said there'd been no sin and God knew it, it was other sins she was asking forgiveness for.''

Marvin's eyes crinkled at the corners as he chuckled. "And now Philo's courting her and giving her no peace, claims that she's the noblest woman God ever put on earth and that he can't live without her. And she's acting like a skittish schoolgirl, dying to say yes but afraid of the consequences. In her mind, marrying a Catholic is as good as jumping into the flames of hell on purpose, but not marrying him will make her life unbearable. It's a dilemma.''

It was a good thing that there was something, even something as unlikely as the romance between the Irish organizer and Athens's number one spinster, to take people's minds off their troubles in this depression winter. As worried as they were, sometimes even suffering actual privation, people could still dredge up a smile at the sight of short Philo O'Brian trotting down the street behind tall Miss Minnie for all the world like a beseeching puppy, dogging her footsteps every time she ventured out of the Reading Rooms or her house.

''My money's on Philo.'' Marvin smiled. ''If he could beat Herndon Livingston, he can win over one spinster lady, no matter how convinced she is that marrying a Catholic would mean losing her soul.''

Earl himself had suffered little through this depression that had seemed to come out of nowhere. It was true that his vast real estate holdings in Rochester and Buffalo had plummeted in value and no longer brought in the profits that they had, but he still owned the property and he had the means to hang onto it. Like the lawyer, he was in no danger of losing everything he had.

''I'm glad that I didn't invest in that railroad stock I was thinking about,'' Marvin remarked. ''Thanks to you.''

''Don't sell the railroads short, my friend. Depression or no depression, and as unlikely as it seems with the canals growing in importance with every year that passes, the railroads are the shipping and transportation lines of the future. A few more years, and you'd be wise to buy as many shares in them as you can lay your hands on. That's what I'm going to do. Even buy in, own a line myself, if I can manage it.''

Marvin whistled. ''You believe in them that much, then?''

''I do. They're coming, and not hell nor high water's going to hold them back. But that isn't what you came to talk to me about, is it?''

Marvin shook his head. ''I'm worried about Geneva. She's working herself to death trying to keep the out-of-work mechanics fed, and anyone else who's down and out. She's at the soup-cellar every day, or nursing people who've fallen sick from lack of food and fuel. I was hoping that you'd ask Roxanne to reason with her. Every word I say falls on deaf ears. And Bobo backs her every step of the way. He's out right now, with Cato and the light sleigh, combing the farms, trying to buy fuel and food, or beg it, or get it any way he can, to help keep the soup lines going.''

''I know how hard she's working. Roxanne, too. I've raised hell with her and raised hell with Wyatt for allowing it, but she pays no attention.'' Earl's face changed, became grim. He wasn't about to discuss Roxanne's problems with Wyatt, especially with Wyatt right here, even with Marvin. Most especially not with Marvin, whose daughter was the thorn in Wyatt's side that drove him to other amusements. If Roxie would have stood still for it, he'd have given Wyatt cause to mend his ways, but Roxie had told him to mind his own damned business and let her mind hers. But their childrens' troubles had no bearing on his friendship with Marvin, and he dredged up a smile again.

''I'll tell Roxie you're worried, Marvin. Maybe she'll be able to do something. I hear that your wife puts in more than her share of time feeding and clothing the hungry and cold, too. We can be proud of our womenfolk. It seems to me that it's always the women who pitch in and do what has to be done when things get bad. Maybe it's because they've always had to be the practical ones, while men spend their time dreaming of how to make things better, instead of contending with what's facing them at the moment.''

Neither of them mentioned 24 Elm Street, and what was going on there to better conditions for the poor, but it was in both their minds. Their admiration for Addie Livingston Maynard's spunk had gone up several more notches.

24 Elm Street was a beehive of activity, little of which had anything to do with its original purpose. The parlors, the dining room, half of the bedrooms including the servants' quarters, had been filled with cots as close together as they could be placed and still leave room to walk between them. The cots were occupied with mill mechanics who had been laid off because of the depression.

Every day Addie went out onto the streets to seek out still more girls. The depression had wiped out all of the advantages the mechanics had gained through their turnout. Nobody was hiring. The whole country was laying off help, there were no jobs to be had. Those workers fortunate to still have employment were only too willing to see things go back to the way they had been before, in order to earn barely enough to survive, no matter the conditions. Hours had been lengthened, and then lengthened again, wages had been cut, and there were still two mechanics ready and eager to step into the place of any girl who was still working.

Desperate, starving, a good many of the girls who had no place to go, no family who could afford to take them back and support them, were forced to turn to the world's oldest profession. Only the soup cellars, and women like Geneva and Roxanne and Cora Burton and Adelaide Maynard Livingston, stood between them and either starvation or a degradation from which they'd never be able to recover.

Nancy Steele occupied one of the cots at 24 Elm Street, Dorothy Monroe another. They'd been among the first to be discharged. Agnes Barlowe had also been discharged, but she had not come nor allowed herself to be persuaded to come to Addie's house for succor. No one knew for sure how Agnes managed to survive, and to survive well, as was attested by her well-rounded figure which had lost not an ounce of its voluptuousness, and the new, bright, gaudy clothes that she flaunted when she walked down the street with money in her pocket to spend in the stores.

"She always has money, all she needs and to spare, not that she spares any of it for the girls she used to work with!" Nancy Steele said, her voice laced with anger. "I saw her at Maxwell's Emporium just yesterday, when Mrs. Maynard sent me to buy more sheets and blankets to cut down to fit the cots. She was buying a shawl I'd almost sell my soul for, and the one she was already wearing was something she couldn't afford unless she was doing you-know-what to get the money. And she must be doing it with some man whose pockets are well lined, because ordinary men couldn't afford to hand out that much these days. I wonder who it is?"

"One of the Corinthians, probably," Dorothy surmised. She smoothed the sheet that had been cut in half so that it would fit the cot, and tucked in the ends and corners. "Or one of their fathers, more likely. From all I hear, even the Corinthians have had to pull in their horns when it comes to spending money."

Nancy reached into her pocket and drew out a small, square piece of leather and tossed it into the air. "Money! And this is what Mr. Livingston was giving us for our wages, instead of real money, before he gave us the sack!" The tokens, as they were called, had been substituted for cash money early in the first days of the depression. They could be spent in Herndon's company store, or not spent at all because no one else would honor them.

"How come you kept it? I spent mine, all of them, the day we were laid off. Keeping it was just like making a present to Mr. Livingston!"

"It got stuck in my reticule, and I never noticed it till this morning. But I'm not going to the company store to spend it, I'm going to keep it to show my children how Mr. Livingston treated us. It'll be a keepsake! I don't need to spend it now that Mrs. Maynard's taken us in."

"Mrs. Maynard's wonderful, I don't care if she is running a . . ." Dorothy's face turned red, and she went on without naming what it was that Addie was running. "She's an angel, that's what she is!"

"Even the *girls* are nice!" Nancy's chin went up, as if she dared Dorothy to deny it. "They're chipping in everything they earn toward feeding us, did you know that?"

"No, I never!" Dorothy's eyes widened. "Are you sure? How'd you find out?"

"Carrie told me, this morning, when I was helping with the breakfast dishes. They're chipping it all in, every penny, and they're taking part of what they've saved out of the bank to chip in if we run short. Not that Mrs. Maynard wouldn't pay for our food herself, but Carrie said that they love Mrs. Maynard so much that they don't want her to go broke feeding us. They help so it won't all fall on her. Even if she does own a bank, banks are having a hard time these days, just like everybody else."

"Who'd ever think that that sweet, little, young thing was a missus, and a widow to boot! Let alone a . . ." Dorothy clamped her mouth shut again. She wasn't going to say the word even if it was true, not about Adelaide Maynard. "I mean, who'd ever think that she could be Herndon Livingston's daughter, he's such a bast—"

"Go ahead and say it. He is, so why not say it? Do you

think Mrs. Maynard will go out again tonight, looking for girls to bring back? If she brings many more, the house is going to collapse from bulging at the seams!''

Addie did go out on the streets again that evening. Her hood pulled close around her face, her fur-lined cape warm enough in spite of the bitterness of the weather, she started on her nightly quest for girls who hadn't come in off the streets of their own accord, for whatever their reasons might be. Once in a while she encountered a girl who wouldn't come, who thought that she might earn enough to be better off working the streets than she would be at Addie's house. But tonight, it was so cold, and snowing too, that if any girl happened to be out, she'd probably let Addie take her home.

Taking girls off the street had become Addie's mission in life, second only to her continuing revenge against her father. The thought of any girl having to sell her body, to suffer any abuse men wanted to inflict on her, was so abhorrent to her that she would have crawled on her hands and knees over broken glass to rescue even one of them. She kept a sharp lookout as she walked, and her passion for what she was doing kept her from noticing the cold. But behind her, Art Franklyn grumbled and cursed under his breath. It was bad enough to have to keep his hands off all the delectable young flesh under Addie's roof, and to keep his drinking and his temper under control, but walking the streets every night, in weather like this, was more than any man should be asked to endure.

Still, he endured it. He knew he'd better, if he didn't want to get Jim Yarnell down on him. Besides, he had a sneaking admiration for Mrs. Maynard, and the work was steady and the wages were good. His accommodations were comfortable, even if he had had to move into a cubbyhole up in the attic when all those mechanics had moved in. And most of all, Carrie had taken a liking to him. A big woman herself, she liked men who were big enough to make her feel feminine. She hadn't had the opportunity to meet many like that, and Art Franklyn filled the bill. She was always ready to slip him an extra piece of cake any time he wandered into her kitchen between meals.

Nevertheless, coming out on a night like tonight was fool's business. No girl in her right mind would be soliciting on the streets tonight. Even the most raucous of the canallers, to say nothing of more respectable men, would be under shelter, not out looking for girls eager to sell their favors.

Apparently Addie had come to the same conclusion, because after an hour and a half she stopped and turned around, heading back toward 24 Elm Street. And about time, too, Art thought. His feet and his nose felt as if they were on the verge of being frostbitten. He waited until Addie had passed him, and then quickened his pace to keep close behind her, visions of Carrie's warm kitchen, a cup of steaming coffee and a man-sized slab of apple pie making his present discomfort bearable.

Deep in his anticipation of warmth and food and Carrie's company, Art didn't notice Addie stop as she stared at a man who was walking toward them from the opposite direction. He turned to mount the outside staircase of the Waterman's Haven, a tavern that canallers and other traveling men frequented. The Waterman's Haven rented rooms on the second floor, with access to them via the outside staircase.

"Wyatt!" Addie called.

Art caught himself as he almost bumped into her. She started forward again, opening her lips to call her brother's name a second time. What on earth was Wyatt doing, going into such a place? But no matter what he was about, Addie ached to see him, she wanted to talk to him. Her fondness for him, the adoration she'd felt for him since her earliest childhood, had not abated even though she'd cut herself off from her family and all of her old associations.

Art clamped his hand on her arm, rough and demanding. "No, Miss Addie. Don't."

Addie looked at him, her face filled with surprise.

"But it's Wyatt, and I want to talk to him!"

"You don't want to talk to him now. He wouldn't appreciate it." Art's voice was as rough as his grasp on her arm.

"What in the world are you talking about? Of course he'll want to see me! I only want to talk to him for a moment."

Art's face flamed. Madam of a bordello or not, Miss Addie was still a lady. He'd never in his life had occasion to tell a lady that her brother was on his way to meet his mistress, a woman he kept in a room at The Waterman's Haven so that he could avail himelf of her company at any time he liked.

Addie was becoming impatient, tugging to free herself. There was nothing for it, but to blurt it out.

"He's going to see a friend," Art said. "A lady friend, Mrs. Maynard. I don't think he'd want to talk to you right now. If you need to talk to him, I'll go down to his office in the morning and tell him you want to see him. Come along now, it's cold. You'll get a chill and then Carrie'll have my hide."

A lady friend! Addie's breath caught. Wyatt, with a lady friend, a mistress, when he was married to Roxie who loved him so much! Hurt stabbed through her. She'd always looked on Wyatt as being perfect, as having no flaws at all. She bit at her lower lip, railing at herself. How could she have been so naive, so blind! Wyatt was a man, wasn't he? All the same, she blinked to hold back tears of disillusionment, and the one that escaped to roll down her cheek froze before it had traveled halfway.

"Come along, now." Concerned for her, pitying her as her stricken face looked at him blindly, Art urged her forward. "There's nothing you can do about it. Let's get you home and warm."

"Do you know who she is?"

Art's mouth clamped shut. He knew, but he wasn't about to tell. It wouldn't serve any purpose and it would only hurt Addie more if she knew that Wyatt's mistress was common and coarse and had no pretensions of being a lady.

Addie started walking beside her protector, her feet moving automatically, and Art breathed a sigh of relief. He'd tell Carrie to bring her some tea laced with brandy. She looked bad, she did, like she'd had a shock. Of course she'd had a shock. Likely it had never entered her mind that that brother of hers was human, although even Art couldn't conceive of any man turning to a woman like the one he kept in the room above The Waterman's Haven, when he was married to a stunner like Roxanne Fielding.

He consoled himself thinking about Carrie. He hadn't got her to let him between her sheets yet, but he was working at it. And she'd be an armful, too, for all she wasn't as young and pretty as Wyatt's doxy. What the hell, he wasn't any wet-behind-the-ears tad himself, he was still in his prime but he was crowding forty. He'd settle for Carrie if she'd only make up her mind that she'd settle for him.

He'd have Carrie take Addie that tea laced with brandy,

and he'd tell her what Addie had seen that had given her such a shock, and it would make for interesting conversation, something for them to have in common. There'd be a little of the brandy to spare for their own tea, and maybe tonight would be the night.

In the second-story room at the back of The Waterman's Haven, Wyatt stood looking at the girl who was brushing her hair. She lay on top of the bed, admiring herself in the mirror she held in her left hand while her right drew the brush through her long, dark, shining tresses with sensual pleasure. She was wearing a dressing gown with nothing under it, and her voluptuous curves under the satiny fabric left little to the imagination. But the dressing gown had been a mistake. Wyatt had paid a pretty penny for it, but now that he saw it on her he realized that he must have had Roxanne in mind when he'd bought it. The soft green that would have been so lovely on Roxanne brought out a sallowness in Agnes Barlowe's complexion. It did nothing to complement her rather pale blue eyes.

Growing impatient, Wyatt took the brush and mirror from Agnes's hands. She looked at him, pouting, her face a little sullen.

"I wasn't finished."

"You're beautiful enough. Besides, what's the point of brushing your hair now, when I'll have it tangled like a magpie's nest in a few more minutes? Stand up, I want to look at you."

Agnes smirked. She got off the bed and stood in front of him, thrusting her breasts forward so that they all but spilled out of the low-necked dressing gown. She liked to be admired. She liked having a man's hands stroke her shoulders and arms, as Wyatt's were doing now. Having a man's hands on her, caressing her, made her purr like a kitten. And having Wyatt Livingston as that man, the handsomest man in Athens, even if he wasn't the richest anymore, was something that she had only dreamed of back when she'd been a mechanic working at Wyatt's father's cotton mill.

Agnes had no idea why he'd turned to her the night she'd flaunted herself at him outside the Cayuga after this depression had started. She'd been sacked and had to either sell her favors or take refuge in Addie Maynard's house, along with Nancy Steele, and Dorothy Monroe, and all those other girls who'd been catty to her just because she was prettier than they were.

She hadn't had to think about it for very long. Having a roof over her head and food on her plate wasn't compensation enough for having to go on living with Nancy and Dorothy, and being beholden to any Livingston, even Addie. It had been the best decision she'd ever made, because look at her now! Landing a fish like Wyatt Livingston was success beyond her wildest dreams.

Still, it wasn't so strange once she stopped to think about it. Wyatt could hardly go to 24 Elm Street if his wife didn't satisfy him, not with his own sister running it. And Agnes had found out right at the onset that Wyatt relished her coarseness, her vulgarity. And if that was what he wanted, she had it in plenty to give him.

Wyatt's hands tightened on her shoulders, and then slipped the dressing gown off of them to reveal her breasts, large and firm and thrusting, swelling under his hands as he closed over them, the nipples standing erect under his seeking fingers. Her full mouth was passionate and moist when he bent his head to kiss her, and she raised her arms to grasp his hair in her hands, holding him to her.

"Oh, I like that, I like it!" Agnes breathed, undulating her hips against him. "You're a man, you are. You're a real man. You give me what no other man ever did! I'll never be satisfied with anyone else, you've spoiled me!"

"You'd better not try to be satisfied with anyone else!" Wyatt growled. His hands tightened on her breasts, making her squeal, but it only served to heighten her excitement and she undulated against him again, harder and more insistent.

"You're a witch!" Wyatt's breath came short. "You're a common, vulgar witch, and I'm satisfied with you, too."

It was true, if not the entire truth. She gave him what he wanted—plain, common whoredom, with no pretense at anything else. She had a commodity to sell, and he bought it; it was as honest as that. Having Agnes, debasing himself in her commonness and vulgarity, somehow eased the raw, throbbing wound in his ego that had developed and grown ever since he'd married Roxanne. He'd married her and now he was a kept man, a male whore, performing on command because that was what Earl Fielding's money paid for. He was a male whore, and Roxanne was a female whore, because she'd sold herself, just as he'd sold himself. She'd sold her body, her beauty, all she could give him through her father, for the prestige of being Mrs. Wyatt Livingston, the queen of Athens society.

It didn't matter that he earned his pay in Earl Fielding's employ. He wouldn't have the job unless he'd married Roxanne; he'd be working as some underpaid clerk or foreman, living in a rented room, facing years of hard work to climb up the ladder again to some rung reasonably near that he'd left behind when he'd broken with his father.

He blanked out his thoughts, lifted Agnes, and threw her onto the bed, falling on top of her, intent on taking her, wiping clean the slate that mocked him with the facts of his life and his marriage. Forget Roxanne, forget Geneva . . .

Geneva! Groaning, Wyatt tore at his clothing until he could enter the writhing body under his own. He thrust hard and deep, until his rising tide of passion overwhelmed him, and left him drained, and unsatisfied.

"Wyatt, Wyatt . . ." Agnes's voice was a moan. "There's nobody like you, there never could be. You're wonderful."

His face grim, Wyatt rolled off her and got to his feet, heading for the bottle of fine brandy that he kept for when he visited his paramour. The fire of it burned his throat, settled in his stomach. He considered having another, but replaced the bottle on the bureau instead. Brandy wouldn't help the sickness inside him, and Roxanne wouldn't look lightly at it if he returned home drunk. She wouldn't complain to her father, either, damn it. She was too proud to complain to her father, or to complain to him. Or she just didn't care. That was more like it. That was the way it really was. She'd got what she'd wanted, she'd *bought* what she'd wanted. It was a mutual bargain and she had no reason for complaint, any more than he did.

"Wyatt, I'm sick of this room. Why can't you rent me a house, even a little one?"

"There's a depression, or haven't you heard? Later, maybe, when things get better."

"How much later? And I need a new dress. I haven't had a new dress in more than a month, I'm tired of everything I have."

Wyatt threw a handful of bank notes onto the bureau top next to the brandy bottle and gathered up his clothes. Tired of everything she had—a girl who'd owned only three dresses when he'd picked her up, who'd never had more than one new dress every two years since she'd grown up! She didn't mind asking him for what she wanted, that was part of her vulgarity.

He went to the washstand and washed himself before he got dressed. Watching him, Agnes's mouth curled with amusement. He always washed himself like that after he'd been with her. She didn't mind the smell of sex, but it offended his aristocratic nose. She had no idea, it never entered her mind, that Wyatt was so much of an inborn gentleman that he wouldn't dream of returning to his wife with the odor of another woman on him.

Roxanne was still up when he let himself into his house. *Her* house. She was seated at the beautiful mahogany table in the parlor, making out a list of some kind. She looked up when he entered, and she lifted her face so that he could kiss her. Her mouth was cool and sweet and yielding under his, turning warm before he drew away.

"What's that you're doing?"

"I'm going to give a party. A big party, that will make Athens's eyes pop out."

Wyatt frowned. "Roxie, times are hard, even if your father does have all the money in the world. Don't you think a lavish party would be in poor taste, right now?"

"It's because times are hard. I'm selling tickets to this party. Oh, I won't put it in any such a vulgar way, of course. I'll merely ask for subscriptions, for donations for the soup cellar fund. But nobody's going to be invited unless they kick in. It'll be the chance a good part of Athens has always wanted, to come to a party in this house, to rub elbows with Geneva Burton and Bobo Burton and even with me. They'll pay through the nose for the chance."

"You're your father's daughter, all right."

"You bet I am, and I'm darned proud of it. A lot of the people I'm inviting haven't given one penny toward the soup cellar fund, and now they'll have to, because if they aren't here everyone will know that they didn't give."

"Blackmail."

Roxanne grinned. "Certainly it's blackmail. Why not,

the customers. Value given for value received. As my father would say, honesty is the best policy, because people tend to remember when they've been cheated and then you don't get another chance to get your hand in their pocket. Geneva and I are going to wear our fanciest dresses, we're going to give them their money's worth. And you and Bobo and Marvin Burton and my father, and all your Corinthians, are going to come in evening clothes and be very attentive to the ladies. Geneva and I, and the other young ladies I'm recruiting, will be very attentive to the gentlemen. We'll make enough to keep that soup cellar going for another three months, or my name isn't Roxanne Fielding."

That was a mistake, a slip of the tongue that made her feel like biting the offending tongue off. But she wouldn't apologize, that would only make matters worse. Instead, she changed the subject.

"Addie's doing wonderful work, Wyatt. All of Athens is talking about it. She started out to disgrace your father, and now if she isn't careful she'll end up practically sainted for what she's doing for the mechanics who've lost their livelihoods. I'm so proud of her I could cry. Damn society, anyway! If the men weren't so desperate, I wouldn't give this party when she can't be invited, but even Roxanne Livingston couldn't get away with that and have anyone show up. Besides, she wouldn't come anyway. Have you seen her lately?"

"Not as lately as I should have. I'll take the time to stop and see her tomorrow."

"Try to talk her out of working so hard. She always was small and delicate. She can't carry the whole burden of this depression on her own shoulders, single-handed."

"I'll tell her, but I doubt if it'll do any good. I think I'll turn in now, it's been a long day."

Watching him leave the room, Roxanne bit her lip. Who was the woman he'd come from tonight? There was a woman, she was sure of it. She had a great deal of pride, but not so much that she wouldn't like to know who it was, so she'd know what kind of competition she was up against.

She bent her head again to her list. She wrote slowly, using up all the time she could, so that Wyatt would be asleep when she slipped into bed beside him. That way he'd be saved when she slipped into bed beside him. That way he'd be saved the embarrassment of not wanting her tonight, so soon after he'd come from that other woman.

22

Roxanne had never been more beautiful, more radiant, more the epitome of the queen of Athens's society, than she was on the evening of her charity ball. Her head high, laughter bubbling from her lips and her eyes shining, she was the hub around which the party revolved and all eyes went back to her again and again, either in envy, admiration, or aching acceptance.

The Fielding house—people couldn't break the habit of calling it that even though Earl Fielding now put up at the Cayuga whenever he was in Athens—was packed shoulder to shoulder with not only the cream of Athens's society, but with all the less prominent citizens who had never dreamed of entering its door. The wide doors between the front and back parlors had been pushed back, so that the two rooms became one. Most of the furniture from them had been carried up into the attic to make more room, and the rug had been taken up from the front parlor so that there could be dancing to the music of a string quartet.

The dining room table had been extended to its full length, and was laden with refreshments. Roxanne had begged, borrowed, or confiscated every small gilt chair she could locate to line the walls in the double parlor. She'd promised to give her guests their money's worth, and that was exactly what she was doing, but all of the other attractions notwithstanding, the very privilege of seeing her in all her radiance made the price the donors had paid well worthwhile.

Mary MacDonald, in a blue silk brocade dress, provided by Roxanne for this occasion, was so excited that she could hardly keep from dancing, even without a partner. There was only one fly in Mary's ointment on this most glorious of all evenings. Carl Jakes had come to the ball. As much as Herndon Livingston's former recruiter for the mill was disliked, he'd gone to Wyatt's office and donated twenty dollars, a princely sum in these depression days, and Wyatt had given him an invitation. By all rights Wyatt should not have given out the invitation, because even though the ball was supposed to be for everyone who donated, it was still accepted that a certain class of people would not attempt to attend. Wyatt did it more out of a sense of humor than anything else. If Roxie was determined to turn their house into a carnival, and flaunt her social position by virtually blackmailing people into coming, it served her right to have Jakes appear at the door armed with an official invitation. If she was going to be all that democratic, let it be all the way! Besides, Wyatt thought that Jakes would find himself so uncomfortable rubbing shoulders with his betters that he'd leave almost as soon as he came.

But Jakes had no intention of leaving. Dressed in his flashiest best, he spent no time trying to mingle with the other guests, but rather hovered as near Mary as he could, never taking his eyes off her. If most of the guests had come to see Roxanne, Jakes had come to see Mary, in a place where she couldn't snub him or run away from him.

It gave Mary the creeps every time she saw his eyes on her, looking as if he wanted to devour her whole. But he couldn't do anything to her at a party like this, right in the Fielding house with all these people around. All the same, he had his nerve coming here, where he was as out of place as a pig at a dinner table. Even Herndon Livingston had had the good sense not to attempt to show up. You'd think that his minion would have had that much sense too.

Across the room, Wyatt was acting the perfect host, giving men with whom he ordinarily had no contact the impression that he valued their comments about the cause and cure of this depression, no matter how idiotic their views were. When his gorge rose at one particularly asinine opinion and he was in danger of telling the man that he was an ass, he excused himself and asked Mrs. Maxwell to dance.

Mrs. Maxwell preened, all one hundred and sixty-three pounds of her. The feather plumes she'd attached to her ringlets, at least half of them not her own, shook and quivered with her elation.

"What a lovely gown you're wearing!" Wyatt said, his eyes melting with admiration. "It enhances you, ma'am, it truly does."

Inside, he was seething. Every man in the room was looking at Roxie, admiring her, lusting after her, and she was eating it up. She loved every minute of it! If her dress had been cut any lower in front she would have spilled out of it, and he had an idea that half of the men were holding their breaths waiting for it to happen.

His eyes fell on Geneva and Bob Maxwell, and he couldn't force them away. The young Corinthian was in seventh heaven as he danced with Geneva, his face moonstruck, his adoration for her exuding from every pore. Geneva was smiling at him, a smile that broke into a delighted laugh as he whispered something to her.

Idiotic young nincompoop! Wyatt thought as he smiled at Mrs. Maxwell and complimented her on how light she was on her feet. Knowing that Bob wasn't a nincompoop made him all the angrier. Bob Maxwell had a head on his shoulders, and his shoulders were broad and manly. He was handsome, he had a thoroughly nice personality, and a quick sense of humor. In fact, Bob Maxwell would make an admirable husband for Geneva, something that he was determined to do. Tonight it looked as if he'd finally found an inside track.

And there was Roxie again, dancing with Galen Forbes, and even Galen looked bemused as she laughed up into his face. Didn't she have any sense of decency? She knew that Geneva was interested in Galen, why did she have to go all out to charm him, and thus aid and abet Bob Maxwell in his pursuit of Geneva? Roxie couldn't help trying to bedazzle every man with whom she came in contact. It was in her blood, she'd never change, she had to be the queen and every male her subject.

And then, in spite of the dourness of his mood, his expression relaxed and he actually smiled as he saw Philo O'Brian piloting Minnie Atkins around the dance floor. Philo was beaming, his feet breaking into a jig that had nothing to do with the waltz. He was so happy to be here with his dream woman that he couldn't control himself. Minnie's smile was a trifle forced. She was convinced that dancing was a sin in the first place, that dancing with a man's arm around her was a double sin, and that dancing with a Catholic would put her forever beyond the pale of all decent Christians.

Just as Wyatt had despaired that it never would, the number came to an end. He escorted Mrs. Maxwell back to her husband as quickly as he could without being impolite, and cornered Philo.

"How's the world treating you, Philo? You look hale and hearty."

"It's the good food I've grown used to," Philo told him, unabashed. "Miss Minnie thought I needed feedin' up, and she's been seein' to it."

Minnie's face turned red, and she tried to make her expression severe.

"Mr. O'Brian was run-down from all that running and hiding he had to do. It was my Christian duty to see that he was nourished until he regained his strength."

"Clean sheets on a soft bed, instead of havin' to sleep in ditches and haymows hasn't hurt, either," Philo said cheerfully. "I'd almost forgotten about clean sheets and featherbeds, Wyatt me lad. The Waterman's Haven isn't elegant, you understand, but for the likes of me it's a palace. I hope I can go on affordin' it a little longer. I'm afraid I'll have to be lookin' for honest work if I want to keep on enjoyin' them. With this nasty depression, the bottom's fallen out of the organizin' business. I haven't had a day's work since the canal closed for the winter, so there's no more loadin' and unloadin' and such to be picked up. If it wasn't for Lester Peterson, bless the man, who calls me to help him with his horseshoein' and muckrakin' now and again, I'd be in a bad way."

Wyatt knew all about Philo's odd jobs with the blacksmith, because he himself chipped in to pay him, along with Marvin Burton, while Peterson himself made up the rest so that the Irishman wouldn't either go hungry or be forced to accept charity, which would have been as bitter as gall to him. Donations to keep him going while he fought for the rights of the common working people were one thing, but donations to fill his belly for its own sake was something entirely different.

"Come spring, there'll be work bottoming out the canal, and when that's done there'll be something for you on one of the barges. Earl Fielding thinks highly of you, and he'll see that you have a berth.''

"Now that's good to hear. Did you hear that, Miss Minnie? I'm goin' to be an honest workin' man, so you won't need to be ashamed to be seen with me."

Minnie's voice was stiff and formal and just slightly miffed. "No Christian is ever ashamed to be seen with anyone, no matter how unfortunate his circumstances."

Philo winked at Wyatt. "I'm parched. Head me toward the potations. I'll be careful not to eat and drink more than my donation was worth."

"You eat and drink all you want. Roxie flimflammed most of it without laying out a cent. She has a genius for making people give till it hurts."

"Your wife is looking lovely tonight, Mr. Livingston," Minnie said. "Of course, she always looks lovely. You must be very happy."

"Ma'am, how could it be otherwise?" Wyatt offered her his arm. Minnie felt almost as beautiful as Roxanne as she let him lead her to the refreshment table. Mr. Livingston accepted Mr. O'Brian as an equal. And if Mr. Livingston accepted Mr. O'Brian as an equal, knowing that he was a Papist, maybe her soul wouldn't be forfeit for having befriended him.

Mary had watched the little exchange with a sparkle in her eyes. She thought that Philo O'Brian was adorable. He was so short, but so full of spirit and fight. And she liked Minnie Atkins, who was always nice to her when she went to the reading rooms.

She started, jerked out of her reverie as a hand touched her arm with a great deal more familiarity than it should have. "Miss MacDonald, would you do me the honor of granting me the next dance?"

Carl Jakes! Mary recoiled, jerking her arm away. She wouldn't have believed that he'd have the audacity to approach her here, where she was so well protected. Jakes saw the revulsion in her face and his own became ugly. The malice in his eyes, mixed with his avid, disgusting lust for her, frightened her more than she'd ever been frightened before.

She looked around wildly, seeking a means of escape, but no one was paying any attention to her and she couldn't make a scene and spoil Miss Roxanne's party, it would be unforgivable. Reluctantly, her flesh crawling, she let him lead her into the front parlor and put his arm around her as another waltz began.

"I don't really know how to dance," she said. "Maybe we'd better leave the floor."

"You'll catch on in no time. A smart little girl like you can do anything she wants to do." Jakes drew her closer, so close that it went completely beyond propriety, and his face was very nearly pressing against her cheek.

"You're holding me too close!" Mary hissed. "Stop it this minute!" She missed the beat of the music and stumbled, but his grip on her didn't relax.

"Not half as close as I'd like to hold you! Mary, I could do a lot for you. You just say the word, and you won't have to go on being a servant in Mrs. High-and-Mighty's house anymore. I'll take you out of here as quick as a wink of an eye! I'll rent us a house, and I'll treat you right, and you won't have to be beholden to anyone anymore. You'll be my woman, and queen it just as good as Mrs. Livingston queens it!"

"Let me go! I wouldn't go with you if I'd hang for it if I didn't!" Mary whispered, and her whisper was as fierce as a shout. "I don't even want to dance with you, much less be your woman! Take me off this dance floor this minute, and then leave me alone. Don't you ever come near me again!"

Carl released her and gave a slight bow, offering her his arm. Her head high and her face flaming, doing her best to appear as if nothing was out of the way, she let him lead her from the floor. But instead of taking her to the row of gilt chairs, or back into the dining room, he clamped his arm close to his side so that her hand was caught, and steered out into the entrance hall, deserted now that the ball was well underway. There was no way that she could free herself without making an ungodly scene.

She was backed into a corner now, her back pressed to the wall, as Carl released her hand only to put his own on her breast, his other clamping her against him as he lowered his head and tried to kiss her. Mary shook her head violently, twisting it from side to side.

"Come on now, be nice to me!" Carl hissed. "You won't regret it, you've known for a long time that I'm crazy about you. You don't belong in a place like this, you belong with me!''

Mary kicked him. Unfortunately, her soft kid slippers, expressly made for dancing, had almost no effect as her foot landed on his leg; she might as well have been barefoot. Drat it all! It looked as if she was going to have to scream after all, and then everybody would come rushing out here and she'd be disgraced and Miss Roxanne's party would be ruined.

But if it had to be, it had to be. Mary opened her mouth, but before the scream could come out her eyes widened as Captain Yarnell loomed over Jakes. The next instant, Jakes's feet left the floor as Jim spun him around and lifted him by the back of his coat and the seat of his pants.

''Open the door, Mary,'' Jim said.

Her eyes as round as saucers, Mary opened the front door. A blast of icy air came in, almost blowing her off her feet. Another instant, and Jakes went out, his exit unorthodox as he sailed through the air to land sprawled, bottoms up, in a snowbank.

''You can close the door now,'' Jim said. ''You're cold. A good turn around the dance floor will warm you up.'' Before she could protest, Mary found herself back where she'd started, only it was Captain Yarnell's arm around her this time, his hand barely touching her back, just as it should have been, with plenty of space between them.

''Thank you for rescuing me,'' she managed to get out.

''It's a privilege I'd be delighted to have every day, except that I don't like to see you frightened, especially by the likes of Carl Jakes. Does he bother you often? Just say the word, and I'll see that he leaves you alone.''

''How could you do that? He's always lying in wait for me whenever I go out!''

''Well, the canal's frozen over right now, so I can't drown him. I suppose I could break his neck and bury him in a snowbank. The cold would keep him till spring, so he could be buried.''

''Captain Yarnell! It isn't funny. You shouldn't talk like that, anyway.''

''I didn't intend it to be funny. If you asked me to kill the skunk, I'd do it without a second thought, as much as I'd dislike to dirty my hands on him. But if you're so concerned, I'll take it out in warning him off.''

"I'd appreciate it." As big as Captain Yarnell was, way taller than she was, and so broad in the shoulder, Mary marveled that he was so light on his feet. Dancing with him was easy even though she hardly knew how. She'd only practiced with the other mechanics at her dormitory when she'd worked at the mill. Mrs. Simms had allowed it because she said that all ladies should know how to dance if a social occasion arose that called for it. But dancing with Nancy Steele and Dorothy Monroe wasn't anything like dancing with Captain Yarnell. She realized that she was shivering even if she wasn't cold anymore.

In the dining room, where Galen Forbes was being attentive to Mrs. Baker, whose husband owned the feed and grain store and who was so awed by being here that she was almost paralyzed, Freda returned from answering a knock on the door, and touched his arm.

"Doctor Forbes, I'm sorry but there's a man at the door asking for you; he says his son is terribly sick."

As much as he hated the thought of anyone being terribly sick, much less a child, Galen was almost relieved at the summons that would take him away from Roxanne's gala. Geneva's presence here seemed to surround him. Wherever he looked she was there, with half a dozen young men dancing attendance on her, Bob Maxwell in the lead. She'd never looked more beautiful, and her face was as serene when she looked at him as if they hadn't parted so angrily, after the rally in the deserted barn, way back last summer.

Galen had avoided all of the Burtons ever since that night, even though he missed Bobo's company, and Marvin Burton's. He'd come too close to losing control of himself, to committing himself to a girl he wanted nothing to do with. Her little trick of pretending to have sprained her ankle had almost worked, he'd almost been caught in the same kind of trap that had caught David Harshey. He'd come so close to telling her that he loved her, and asking her to marry him, that it still sent him into chills to think about it.

It took him only a moment to find Roxanne and explain that he had to leave.

"But you'll come back, after you've seen your patient? Remember, you're one of the star attractions, half the women here are dying to dance with you."

"If it isn't too late."

"It won't be too late. This affair will go on forever. Promise you'll come back, Galen. I need you for moral support."

Because he knew that he couldn't go on avoiding the Burtons forever in a town the size of Athens, Galen promised. And then he was gone, pulling his coat collar up around his chin as he set out with his guide in the bitter night.

For Wyatt, the hands of the clock on the parlor mantel seemed to crawl. He was sick of smiling, sick of dancing with socially inept women he had to compliment even if they were as plain as a barn door. And most of all, he was sick of seeing Roxanne surrounded by hordes of admiring people, doing homage to her and drinking in her beauty.

Look at her now, dancing with Emery Ledbetter! Emery's round face was a picture of worship. Had she no shame at all?

And then it was even worse, because Roxanne went from Emery's arms to those of Mr. Baker, and the man—old enough to be her father—was positively drooling over her! As Wyatt watched, he was sure that he saw Mr. Baker's hand stray too close to Roxanne's breast, and linger there. And Roxanne went right on smiling into the ass's face, her eyes filled with admiration as if she thought that he was the most fascinating man in the world.

His jaw set in a grim line, Wyatt shoved his way through the dancing couples. "Pardon me. Would you mind very much if I danced with my wife?"

Mr. Baker's face turned red. He stammered as he released Roxanne to Wyatt, and wiped his forehead with his handkerchief as he hurried off the floor.

"You're making a spectacle of yourself! Do you have to flirt with everything in trousers?"

"Wyatt, for goodness sake! What's got into you? I'm only being a proper hostess, I can hardly refuse to dance with any man who asks me!"

"You don't have to let them paw you!"

"Nobody's pawed me! I think you're drunk."

She was very nearly right about that. Wyatt had visited the refreshment table once too often during the course of the evening to fortify himself for going on acting the perfect host.

"He did paw you. If he comes near you again I'm going to punch him in the nose. I'm damned if I'm going to have a bumbling lout pawing my wife in my own house. I think I'll throw him out as a matter of principle, before he has a chance to paw you again!''

"You're jealous!" Roxanne's heart leaped. Oh, Lord, let it be true!

Wyatt's reply was shattering. "Don't flatter yourself. It's simply that my self-respect demands that my wife be more circumspect. I have a reputation to uphold in this town."

The music stopped, and Wyatt, his face reflecting his cold anger, started walking toward Mr. Baker who was standing beside the gilt chair that held his wife. Roxanne was panic-stricken. Marvin and Cora Burton were in the dining room, Bobo was dancing with a girl, making a joke out of his limp, and didn't look her way. Wyatt couldn't throw Mr. Baker out, he just couldn't! They'd be laughingstocks, she'd never be able to hold her head up again! And even worse, all the tradespeople in town would turn against them, when Earl and Wyatt and she herself had always been so friendly with them.

Like a miracle, she caught sight of Jim Yarnell escorting Mary from the floor, and she sent him a glance filled with appeal. Jim caught the message; indeed, the look on Wyatt's face sent out alarm bells, and he quickened his step, and an instant later his hand was on Wyatt's arm.

"Wyatt, I've been looking for you, I want to talk to you," Jim said.

"Later. I have something to do right now."

"Come on, Wyatt." Smiling, giving the impression that this was a friendly exchange, Jim put his hand on Wyatt's arm and headed him toward the dining room. "And I'm parched after all that dancing. It's hard work for a canaller. I'd like to sample that punch, and so would Mary." Somehow, without Wyatt being sure how it happened, they ended up in the kitchen instead of the dining room.

"Jim, stick with him till he cools off," Roxanne pleaded. "He's had too much to drink."

She wondered if she should send her father or Marvin Burton to help Jim keep Wyatt under control. But she knew instinctively that that would be the worst thing she could do as far as her relationship with Wyatt was concerned. Tomorrow, he'd resent her having called in the older men, even more than he'd resent it tonight. Besides, she didn't want to take Bobo from the girl he was paying so much attention to. It would be wonderful if he'd really get interested in some other girl than Addie, whom he couldn't have. Jim could handle things, he was already asking Mrs. Casey for coffee for both himself and Wyatt.

She took Mary back to the party, and directed her attention to seeing that everything was going smoothly. The gala was an enormous success. Thank God that Jim Yarnell had been at hand to keep it from turning into a disaster!

Left to herself, Mary was too shy to try to smile at men she didn't know well. She took her place at the dining room table to help serve the people who drifted in for refreshments. Lordy, but she hoped that Captain Yarnell would be able to keep Mr. Wyatt from making a commotion! During lulls, when she wasn't helping people to punch or cold sliced ham, or turkey, or cake, she sampled the punch herself and it was so delicious that she sampled it again, and then again. Oh, this was a lovely party! She was actually tingling.

The first person Galen saw when he returned half an hour after Mary had taken her first sample of punch was Geneva Burton. It was between dances, and as he entered the front parlor she smiled at him and said something to Bob Maxwell, who was still hovering over her as if he couldn't bear to let her get more than two inches away from him. Then, to Galen's dismay, Geneva started to walk toward him.

Having no way of knowing that Geneva only intended to ask him who was sick and how serious it was, Galen turned his back on her and went into the dining room. There was Mary, as sweet as sugar and spice and just as pretty. She was alone, and the music had started up again.

"Miss MacDonald, will you do me the honor?"

Mary literally floated into his arms. If she had been tingling before, now she literally vibrated. Her head was in the clouds, her heart was on her sleeve, and the rest of her body was in heaven. To dance with Dr. Forbes, with Galen! Dancing with Captain Yarnell had been fun, even if she didn't like him that much, especially after the way he'd acted on his lineboat last spring when she and Addie had been coming back from New York, but dancing with Galen Forbes was the stuff that dreams were spun from!

And the dream went on and on, because Galen asked her for the next dance and the next, never leaving her side. He took her back into the dining room and poured her still another cup of punch, which had turned into ambrosia while her back was turned, and then they danced again.

People were looking at them and smiling, nodding approval. It was true that Mary had been a mill mechanic, but her association with Geneva Burton and with Roxanne had polished her rough edges, and she came from a decent farm family. Even if she was reaching a little high, going after a young doctor who had yet to make his way wasn't too high to be tolerated, and they all liked Galen. If he chose Mary for his wife, they would accept it, and not turn their backs on the young couple. After all, the social elite among them wouldn't have to mingle with them at many affairs in a year, and the lesser citizens were glad to see one of their own better herself.

Mary didn't notice the attention they were receiving. She was only aware of Galen. Galen noticed it, and he felt a moment's dismay. And then he shrugged wryly to himself. Why not? There wasn't a nicer or a sweeter girl in the world than Mary. She was healthy, she'd bear beautiful children, and she'd be a wonderful mother. He'd have had to be a fool not to realize that she was in love with him.

It was a damned shame about Jim Yarnell. The canalboat captain loved Mary with a single-mindedness that had made a deep impression on Galen. But Jim had told him, only a short while ago, that he didn't have a chance, that Mary wouldn't have anything to do with him as far as romance was concerned. And Galen himself had been unable to make Mary see that Jim would make her a perfect husband, although he'd tried.

"We might as well face it, Doc," Jim had said. "Mary only has eyes for you. She isn't ever going to have me, so if you find yourself falling in love with her, don't let me hold you back. I won't hold it against you. I'll be happy as long as she's happy. Well, as happy as I can be, not ever being able to have her for myself!"

At the time, Galen had tried to encourage Jim to go on trying, but remembering that conversation now, he knew that nothing stood in his way if he should decide to ask Mary to marry him. As young as Jim was, he'd be bound to get over Mary in time, and find someone else. Nature, Galen knew, had as much to do with love as the heart.

So he held her a little more closely, and Mary decided that if she should die at this moment, she'd die happy. He'd noticed her at last, he liked her, he wasn't paying attention to any other girl, only to her. Only she wasn't going to die, she was going to live, she was going to live happily ever after just like in the novels that Mrs. Simms had read to the mechanics during their cultural hour.

"It looks like we have a romance among us," Bob Maxwell said to Geneva.

Her heart feeling like solid lead, Geneva smiled. "It does, doesn't it? I'm happy for Mary." And she was, because Mary deserved the best that life had to offer. Only why did she have to be happy for Mary at her own expense?

She smiled at Bob, and stepped into his arms to dance again. If she had a brain in her head, she'd take what was offered, offered with a devotion that any other woman in the world would envy. Bob's heart swelled. Something told him that he was going to get her yet.

On the dance floor, Galen momentarily forgot where he was. There was a bleakness in his eyes that would have dismayed anyone, had they but noticed it.

Diphtheria. Timmy Grimes, nine years old, had diphtheria. If Athens wasn't extraordinarily lucky, in a bitter winter like this, with people going cold and hungry, there'd be a full-scale epidemic.

23

"No," Valerie said. "You girls from the mill aren't going. Every one of you is a good, decent girl, and maybe you'll have a chance to get married and have children. But it won't matter that much if us others go and catch it, we don't have any of your chances anyway."

Valerie looked at her sisters in profession, and although Ethel May and Flossie's faces were pale as the implications of what Valerie was asking them to do sunk in, they nodded. The mill girls shouldn't go to nurse the sick in the hospital. The risk was too great. But for themselves, for Miss Addie's girls, even though their status at 24 Elm Street had elevated them almost to the point of being ladies, they had a great deal less to lose.

Until they'd come here, to 24 Elm Street, they'd run the risk of hunger, of exposure, of being mistreated by the men they picked up, or contracting diseases from them. Even more likely, was the chance of contracting something else that wasn't a disease but that lasted for nine months and then left you saddled with a responsibility that you had no chance of carrying out.

But here, all of those risks had been removed, except the last one, and that had been cut down to almost nothing since Dr. Galen Forbes had told them ways to protect themselves, just as he made sure that they were free of other diseases. He did it because he liked Addie and because he liked them, and he never asked for a fee.

Since Addie had opened this house and they'd become

Addie's girls, everyone had helped them. Now it was their turn to help somebody else in return.

"Miss Geneva says we're needed. And I say that if Doctor Forbes needs help, then we give it to him."

"It won't be pleasant," Geneva warned them. "From what I know of diphtheria, the risk of contagion is high. And the nursing itself will be hard, and probably disgusting. I appreciate your volunteering, but I think you'd better give it a lot more thought."

Geneva had come to 24 Elm Street this morning to ask the out-of-work mechanics to canvas Athens for sheets, blankets, or anything else that the Athens hospital could use during this epidemic.

The epidemic had swept through Athens with appalling swiftness. Most of the stricken were being cared for at their own homes, but there were some among the very poor, the derelicts, and a few canallers, who had no one to take care of them. These cases were shunted to the hospital, but the hospital didn't have anywhere near enough help or materials to handle the cases.

She herself was going to the hospital to nurse the victims there as soon as the canvasing for what was needed was organized. Galen didn't know it yet. He'd find out when he made his daily visit, and if he didn't like it, there wasn't a thing he'd be able to do about it because he himself had stated, positively and with near violence, that strict quarantine should be enforced.

She was in little danger of contracting the disease herself, as she'd had a mild case when she'd been a child, and she'd never heard of anyone having diphtheria twice. If she hadn't had it, her father, as permissive as he was about anything she wanted to do, would never have allowed her to go to nurse the sick. As it was, he'd capitulated to her arguments that someone with both ability and sense should be in there, besides the rum-sodden old man and the blowsy, gin-soaked woman who constituted the regular nursing staff. Nursing, in a hospital, was not a respectable profession, and so the dregs of humanity had to be accepted in lieu of anything better.

"We don't have to think about it," Valerie said. A vivacious, dark-haired girl, whose greatest attraction was her contagious smile and unfailing cheerfulness, Valerie lifted her chin. Goldie, whose hair had earned her her nickname, tossed her head and seconded Valerie's statement in spite of the fact that she was scared half out of her wits.

"You can't know how much I appreciate having your help. All of you girls are being wonderful. It isn't going to be easy to collect things from people when times are so hard, but don't take no for an answer unless the families are really poor. My mother has already bought all she could from Maxwell's Emporium, but Mr. Maxwell doesn't carry a large enough stock to fill our needs, so we have to scrounge up everything we can from private families."

"I'm going with you, Geneva." Addie met Geneva's eyes, her own filled with determination. "If you can do it, so can I."

"But you can't," Geneva told her. "You have to stay here and run this house. You have all these girls under your charge and they need you. You're doing enough. You've already done so much that it makes me ashamed that I haven't done more. Everybody's talking about how you've taken all these girls in and are supporting them out of your own pocket. Addie, you're wonderful, and I love you to pieces." She threw her arms around her friend and kissed her, her eyes smarting with tears.

"I know you do. I love you too. Only we can't be friends anymore, Geneva." Addie's face was pale but she met Geneva's eyes without flinching.

"Addie, you can stop what you're doing! You've already made your point, you've made your father suffer. From now on all you're doing is hurting yourself and those who love you. Don't you have any idea what you're doing to Bobo? He's eating his heart out for you." Bobo's brief attention to the girl at Roxanne's party had ended when the guests had left, just as Geneva had been afraid it would. Bobo was a one-woman man.

"Then he'll just have to stop, and find someone else, someone who can love him as he deserves to be loved. Even if I stopped running this house, I couldn't marry him. You know how I felt about Matt, how I still feel about him! It's too late, anyway. Do you think that anybody will ever forget what I've done? How could Bobo marry an ex-madam of a bordello, even if I loved him!" Addie turned her face away, and Geneva clenched her fists until her fingers ached, so filled with anger and pity that she could hardly bear it.

Herndon Livingston had done this. Every time she thought about Herndon Livingston she seethed until she was ready to explode. The suffering he had inflicted, not only on Addie but on his mill mechanics, was enough to condemn any man to damnation.

Herndon's greed, his overwhelming need for self-aggrandizement, had ruined Addie's life. Geneva was sure that the suffering he'd caused never entered his mind. Why, if her father were penniless, he'd still be a great gentleman and Athens's most respected citizen! But if Herndon Livingston were the richest man in the world, he'd still be hated, he'd still be damned in the eyes of humanity.

But she didn't have time to think about that now. There was work to be done. There was a devilish twinkle in her eyes as she wondered what Galen's reaction would be when he visited his patients at the hospital and saw his new staff of nurses. To say nothing of his reaction when he found her working right beside them. It would be a mercy if the place didn't burn to the ground from the sparks that were sure to fly. She'd better make sure that all the water buckets were kept full, just in case.

A pesthouse, Galen had called it, although the more civic-minded citizens of Athens proudly called it a hospital, and congratulated themselves that their Christian charity had provided a place for the indigent to go and die when they were fatally ill and had no one to fend for them.

Pesthouse, Geneva told herself. The outside of the building was unprepossessing enough—a square, wooden building with peeling paint and sagging steps that needed repair. Its windows were so dirty that they could hardly be seen through.

Valerie grinned at her. "You shoulda seen it before we cleaned it up. The patients were wallowing in their own filth. We told off that old crone and that bewhiskered sot, I can tell you. It's a good thing you weren't here to hear what we called them! Miss Addie would have been horrified. She's taught us to act like ladies. But you shouldn't of come here, Miss Burton. This is no place for a lady like you. Me and the girls coulda managed."

"Valerie, watch your grammar. Addie isn't going to be happy if you go back to her talking like guttersnipes."

"You shouldn't have come, Miss Burton." Valerie put

one hand on her hip and simpered, mocking the society matrons she'd seen, her mouth pursed but imps in her eyes. "My friends and I could have managed."

Geneva grinned. "That's better. Now, let's see what needs to be done."

"We've changed all the beds, but they have to be changed so often you wouldn't believe it. It isn't all diphtheria patients in here, you know. We have some old derelicts who can't control themselves. We try to get the patients to eat, and we hold them up when they cough so they won't choke. Doc Forbes says there isn't much to be done, except try to get nourishment in them, and keep them comfortable, and let them know that they aren't alone. And keep them clean, of course. You should have been here when Doc walked in this morning and saw this pigsty cleaned up. It was a real treat. First he cussed, and then he cried."

Geneva tried to swallow the lump that rose in her throat. "Cried?"

"Cried. Tears. He just stood there and cried. He's so tired, Miss Burton! It's all too much for him. You know that old Harding won't set foot in this place. He says it's Doctor Forbes's responsibility, that he brought him to Athens to take over 'a certain element of the practice.' Doctor Harding wants to devote his full time to his more respectable patients. Anyway, Doc Forbes said we're angels, that we've earned our way into heaven. He said a lot of things. And he kissed us, every one of us."

He kissed me once, Geneva thought, a dull ache in her heart. And then he said unforgivable things, he called me a cheat, and he never came near me again.

"Maybe you'd better talk to those two who were taking care of things. They're raising the devil because we've got them scrubbing down the walls and floors."

"I'll speak to them."

"You'll have to use rough language. They don't understand anything else."

"I think I can manage that." Geneva had heard very little rough language in her life. Certainly she never heard any at home, but she'd been around Roxanne when Roxie had exploded, and the words that had come out of Roxanne's mouth had been enough to make a canaller's hair curl. She thought she remembered enough of it to make herself understood. She was speaking to the slattern and the bewhiskered sot when Galen arrived for his second visit of the day.

"Miss Burton!"

"Hello, Galen. You now have a staff of seven nurses, and two washer-uppers. You'd better look at Mrs. Kirby first. She seems worse off than her little girl."

"What the devil are you doing here?"

"What the devil do you think I'm doing here? I'm here because I'm needed here. Roxanne is on top of keeping food and supplies flowing in, and you can bet that she'll see that they get here. Addie's mechanics are collecting from door to door. Roxanne's buying, where things can't be begged, just as my mother did." She paused to nudge the bewhiskered sot with her foot. "Do you call that clean? Do it again."

"You little idiot!" Galen exploded. "Don't you know that I can't let you leave here, now that you've been inside?"

"Of course I know it. But why we ordinary folk carry contagion more than you doctors is still a mystery to me. Go and look at Mrs. Kirby. None of the diphtheria patients seem to be running very high fevers, yet they're so ill! I can't understand it."

"It isn't the fever we have to worry about, it's the membrane that forms over their throats." He walked her over to one of the patients. "Look here, I'll show you." Gently, he opened the elderly woman's mouth. "It's yellowish. Do you see? And it adheres strongly to the mucous membrane. The throat is ulcerated and bleeding." Thank God Geneva'd had diphtheria, he thought. He'd have sent her home even if she *had* been in here, if she hadn't. Marvin Burton must have been out of his mind to allow her to do this.

"I see," Geneva said. Her face was calm, her eyes filled with understanding. Galen could tell that she was highly intelligent. Having her here would be a godsend. She could be trusted to watch the patients, to know whether they took a turn for the worse. He needed her here.

"Miss Burton, go home," he said. "And when you get there, have your housekeeper burn the clothes you're wearing, and take a bath and wash your hair."

"In the middle of the winter? What do you want me to do, catch pneumonia?" Dimples appeared at the corners of

Geneva's mouth, dimples that Galen had never noticed before. They made her look like a mischievous little girl. She was joshing him; he knew that she washed her hair in the winter, just as she bathed, although the large share of ordinary citizens held that it was courting death to do either. "You're wasting your breath. I'm here and I'm staying."

Galen gritted his teeth. "Do you know how to take a pulse?"

"No. But I can learn."

He placed Geneva's fingers on his own wrist. "Do you feel it? Can you tell how strong and steady it is?" Damn it, it was strong, but it wasn't steady, it was racing at the feel of her fingers on his flesh. "Flossie, Ethel Mae! Come here, please! I want all of you girls to practice on each other."

Geneva looked perplexed as she took Flossie and Ethel Mae's pulses. Galen's had been so much faster! Was there a difference between a man's pulse and a woman's? There was only one way to find out, and that was to ask.

Galen's face flushed, and Geneva kept hers straight. There wasn't supposed to be any difference, and that could only mean that Galen was affected by her presence. But her elation died a quick death. Galen belonged to Mary MacDonald now, it was an accepted fact that they were affianced. Mary's shining eyes and radiant face attested to how happy she was. Galen's pulse was fast because he was angry that she was here, where he'd have to see her every day. Why did he hate her so? Once again, the question tore at her heart.

He gestured at a patient. "Now try Mrs. Kirby's. It's small and fast."

Galen went on talking, with all seven of the girls giving him their intense attention. I'm running a ten-minute medical course, Galen thought irritably. How to become a qualified physician in one easy lesson! But he went on speaking, his face betraying none of his feelings. "The grayish white specks in the throat spread rapidly, until they turn into the thick, yellow, false membrane that can cut off intake of air. Bits of the membrane are often coughed up and expelled, leaving bleeding spots. The throat is very sore, making it difficult for the patient to swallow or take nourishment."

"What I want to know is, how many of them are going to die?" Fifi asked bluntly.

Geneva winced, glancing back at Mrs. Kirby, but

thankfully Galen had moved them well away from the row of cots, and Fifi had had the sense to lower her voice.

Galen's answer, in an equally low tone, was also blunt. "Too many, unless we're uncommonly lucky. But you can be assured that a great many more would die, if you weren't here to give them proper care. The patient can weaken very rapidly, the pulse grow faint and rapid, bodily strength fail. You're going to have your hands full. But I want you to know that I'll be in your debt all the rest of my life. Miss Burton, why the devil did your father allow you to come here?"

"He doesn't like it, but he knows that when there's something to be done, someone must do it. He'd have volunteered himself, except that he's never had diphtheria, and like most men he's all but useless in a sickroom. So he's going to try to pound it into our city fathers' heads that Athens needs better facilities for caring for the indigent sick, and more funds for food and all the other necessary supplies. It'll be like trying to get blood out of a turnip. The people who pray the loudest in church are likely to be the same ones who contend that less fortunate people deserve their misfortune and therefore don't merit any help, especially if it affects their own pocketbooks.

"All the same, he'll come up with donations or I don't know him. He and Earl Fielding are going to lead it off with enough to keep us going through this epidemic, but they want to be sure that when something like this happens again, the hospital will be equipped to handle it."

For the second time that day, Galen felt like crying. But unlike the first time, this time he controlled himself. Thank God for men like Marvin Burton and Earl Fielding! And thank God for girls like these. That last he put into words.

"Thank God for girls like you," he said.

"*Young ladies*, Doctor Forbes!" Valerie made a tut-tutting moue at him. "My colleagues and I are *young ladies*, or else Miss Addie's been wasting her time."

Galen bowed to them. "Young ladies, you have my gratitude, and my heartfelt thanks. And if I catch even one of you pursuing her old profession after this is over, I'm going to blister that young lady's posterior until she can't sit down. I happen to know that you've been offered enough money to start over in some other town, and within a year of the day you're free to walk out of this pesthouse, I want to hear that every one of you has married a good man."

"But we like it at 24 Elm Street!" Annabelle protested. Slender and willowy, Annabelle had honey blond hair and blue eyes so large and innocent that a man could feel that he was drowning in them. All of her clients wanted to rescue her from her life of degradation; it was an asset that she was astute enough to play for all it was worth.

"I don't give a hang if you like it there! You're not going to cheat half a dozen good and decent men of the best wives they could ever have!" With that, Galen clapped his hat on his head, picked up his bag, and banged out of the door.

On her cot beside her mother, little Lollie Kirby began to whimper. Geneva hurried to her side and held her in her arms, soothing the eight-year-old child with gentle murmurs. The little body was so thin! Geneva could feel the child's ribs through the clean nightgown, one of the ones that Cora Burton had had made up from material she'd bought from Maxwell's Emporium.

Watching Geneva, Annabelle spoke to Ethel Mae. "She's a real lady," Annabelle whispered, her voice filled with awe. "Miss Addie says we're ladies, but we're not. Maybe we will be some day, if we manage to do like Doc Forbes said, but we'll never be the kind of lady Miss Geneva is. She's special."

"So is Miss Addie."

"Miss Addie isn't a lady anymore," Annabelle replied. "She used to be a lady, but she can't ever be again because she's a madam and madams can't be ladies."

"She's a lady to me," Ethel Mae retorted.

"She'd be a lady to this whole stinking town if people had a lick of sense, but they don't. Doctor Forbes is right. When this is over with and I can walk out of here, I'm going somewhere else; to Auburn, maybe, or Syracuse, or Troy. And I'm going to find me a husband. I'll miss living at 24 Elm Street. I liked doing what I was doing, I like the gentlemen, but I think I'd rather be a lady."

"It'ud be awful hard to leave Miss Addie. We owe her a lot, and 'sides, I love her," Fifi broke in.

"If you love her, you'll leave her," Annabelle said. "Because if Miss Addie loses all us girls, then she won't be a madam anymore. And then she could move away too, and be a lady again. If she moves far enough away, nobody will have heard about her.''

''Then I'll go, but I don't think I'm going to like it,'' Fifi said dolefully.

Across the room, Geneva inspected the floor that the bewhiskered sot had finally finished scrubbing. ''That's very good. As a reward, you may have a small glass of your whiskey. After supper.''

''Bossy bitch!'' the old man muttered. For thanks, he felt Valerie's hand across his mouth, directed with such force that it split his lip.

They worked and slept in shifts. They took pulses and checked throats. Another diphtheria patient was carried to the front of the hospital. The men who carried him set his stretcher down in the snow and hurried away, not willing to wait even until the door opened and the suffering victim was carried inside. It took four of the young ladies to lift and carry him, because he was a full-grown man, a canaller, who weighed over 180 pounds, all of it deadweight.

That was the day after Geneva had arrived. On the second day, two more were brought in, and on the third, another two.

Except for Galen's twice-daily visits, they had no contact with the outside world. The supplies that Addie's mechanics and Roxie gathered were also set down in the snow in front of the hospital. The men Roxie had browbeaten into carrying them were afraid to get any nearer.

''Cowards!'' Valerie fumed. ''We could use some help in here, but will they help us? Fat chance! They're too scared of getting sick. You just wait, when I get out of here, I'm going to hunt them up and beat them over their heads with a broom! I know who they are, I have a good memory, and I'll find them!''

''And you'll land in jail for disturbing the peace,'' Geneva said, grinning at her. ''And it's harder for a lady jailbird to become a lady and find a husband than it is for a—''

She broke off, wanting to bite her tongue off. But Valerie took no offence.

''I expect it is. All the same, I'll take my chances. What really worries me is how people are going to take the way you've come in here and worked right alongside of us girls. I know this town. They're apt to say that now you're tarred with the same brush, or birds of a feather flock together, or some such nonsense. The old harridans won't want you to associate with their daughters because you might contaminate them after being in contact with us."

"I'll take my chances." Geneva's face was bland, unworried. And Valerie thought, once again, how Geneva Burton was a real lady.

24

Nancy Steele burst into the sitting-room-cum-dormitory at 24 Elm Street, her eyes fairly popping with excitement. She was out of breath, her face bright red from having run all the way back from the mill, where she'd gone to wait for the mechanics to get off work. It was Saturday, so the mill closed at sundown, and Nancy had wanted to talk to some of the girls she used to work with, and bring back all the freshest gossip to Addie's house.

"Mr. Livingston has laid off a quarter of the mechanics he had, and cut the wages of the ones that are still on, and told them that if they want to go on working, they'll have to get the orders out even if they have to stand at their looms eighteen hours a day! There's a crowd gathering, everybody's making a beeline for the mill. You never saw anything like it!"

Dorothy Monroe gasped, her mouth falling open. "Let's go see! Sacked more of them, has he, the old devil? First he works *us* most to death and now he's *really* goin' to, work the ones that're left to death, as well as throwing all those others out on the street!"

Addie came into the room, drawn by the excited babble of voices. "What's all this? What's going on, Nancy? Did I hear you say something about the mill?"

Nancy's face reddened even more but she stood her ground, even if it was Addie's father who was being so wicked. It wouldn't surprise Addie any; she already knew that her father was a devil, else she wouldn't have turned this house into what it was, or what it had been before all of her girls had gone to the hospital to nurse the diphtheria cases.

"Your father's laid off a lot more girls, and cut the wages and lengthened the hours of the ones that're left. We're all going down there to see what's happening."

Addie's face paled, but she kept it expressionless. "I don't think that you should get mixed up in it. It's already after dark, and if there's trouble, you shouldn't be out on the streets."

"There's going to be trouble, all right. And me and the other girls want to see it! It's time Mr. Livingston learned that he can't treat people like they were cattle or slaves just because he happens to be the one with the jobs to hand out!"

Trouble! As much as Addie would like to keep her own ex-mechanics away from it, she herself was drawn to go and see what was happening. All of her old fury at her father rose up in her, so that she hoped that there would really be a riot, enough of a riot to cause him a great deal of trouble. Her need to see what was happening overrode her conscience about her mechanics, and she ran to fetch her own coat and bonnet as they snatched up theirs, and poured through the door.

They were all out of breath by the time they reached the activity directly in front of the mill. At first glance, things weren't as bad as Nancy had led them to believe. There were knots of people in front of the mill gates, and more were joining them as word got around of what had happened, but so far they were relatively quiet, with only shaking of heads and an occasional raised voice.

Dorothy Monroe reached for Addie's hand and held it tight as though for comfort. "I wish Philo O'Brian was here! I'll bet he'll come, soon as he hears of it. He'll know what they should do. What a time for another turnout, a real turnout with every single mechanic quitting! Only I guess the ones that weren't sacked are so afraid of losing their jobs that they mightn't turn out even for Mr. O'Brian."

"Times are hard," Addie agreed. She returned the pressure of Dorothy's hand as she saw Ed Hanney, with both of his deputies, patrolling the growing crowd. "It would take a lot of courage for the rest of the girls to turn out." A turnout right now, if it lasted long enough, would ruin her father. And she'd like to see him ruined, trampled into the dust so that he could never rise again. Nothing left in her life would give her that much pleasure. "Do you think they would listen to me, if I told them that I'll pay for sending them back to their families, and manage somehow to squeeze in the ones with no place to go?'' It would take just about all she had, ready cash wasn't that plentiful, and she'd already stretched her resources to the limit caring for the mechanics she'd already taken in, but she'd find the money somehow.

"They'll listen to me! Let me tell 'em, Miss Addie! I can talk louder than you can.''

It was Nancy who spoke, and the light of battle was in her eyes. "I'll yell it out so's every one of 'em will hear me, and if that doesn't make them turn out, I don't know what will! We'll squeeze in the ones that don't have anyplace to go, somehow, even if we have to sleep on the floor!''

Nancy pushed and shoved her way to the front of the crowd, and she hadn't been exaggerating about being able to talk louder than Addie could.

"Listen to me, all you mechanics! Listen to what I have to say!'' Nancy screamed. "Are you just going to stand around and let that devil make you starve? And we all know what it's like to put in hours like he wants now, and try to live on what he'll be paying!''

"What can we do?'' a pinched-faced girl asked her. "See the constable and those men with him? If we as much as whisper that we don't like it, we'll end up right in Ed Hanney's jail!'' Her voice was bitter and hopeless.

"But you aren't going to starve! Miss Addie Livingston will see to that!'' In her excitement, Nancy forgot to call Addie by her proper name, Mrs. Maynard. "She's promised that she'll pay for getting all of you home that have folks to go to, and take the rest of you in just like she did me and Dorothy Monroe and all the others that live at 24 Elm Street now! How about it? Old Livingston can't hold out if every one of you walks out! You'll never gain anything if you keep on knuckling under every time he cuts wages and tacks more hours onto your working day! Are you going to go on being slaves to that old devil, or are you willing to risk a little to gain a lot?''

Philo would have been proud of her. Nancy was on fire with her determination to do something about her lot and the lot of all the other mechanics who were at the mercy of the mill owners.

Adelaide was so enraptured by what Nancy was saying that she jumped when she felt a touch on her arm.

"Addie! I just heard. Isn't that one of your girls up there, one of the ones you took in?"

"Yes, it is. Isn't she marvelous?"

Roxanne's face was grim, and she said a word in connection with Herndon Livingston that made Mary MacDonald, who'd come with her, flinch even if she did agree with it.

"They're listening to her," Roxanne added. "Philo O'Brian himself couldn't do better. They're going to turn out, or I miss my guess!"

"I'll have a time taking in the ones with no place to go," Addie told her. "But I'll do it somehow."

Roxanne's eyes took on a sparkle. "I'll throw my house open for as many as it'll hold." She stood on tiptoe and screamed, "That's the girl, Nancy! Tell them!"

Addie looked at her, startled. "Do you think Wyatt will like it if you turn your house into a dormitory?"

"I don't give a hoot if he likes it or not," Roxanne snapped. "He isn't home enough to notice, anyway." She couldn't help the touch of bitterness that seeped into her voice. Wyatt came home every night, she had to admit that, but it was often nearly midnight, and there had been too many times when she'd known that he'd been with another woman. She'd caught the faint scent of her perfume on his clothing. It was a scent that was too blatant to be worn by a lady, something that only a street girl would wear. And even without the scent, she would have known because he always came to bed as quietly as he could so as not to wake her, while she pretended to be asleep. And he didn't draw her into his arms, wanting and needing her.

Their marriage was a farce. She'd failed miserably in her determination to make Wyatt love her. She knew it, Wyatt knew it, her father knew it. Earl had asked her if she wanted him to talk with Wyatt, but she'd told him to keep out of it, that she'd handle her own marriage in her own way.

Only, to date she hadn't thought of any way to handle it. Accusations, recriminations, would be worse than useless, they would only serve to widen the rift between them. So she spent her time acting the contented young wife, the active social leader, presenting a serene face to everyone except her father and Geneva, before Geneva had shut herself up in the hospital for the duration of the diphtheria epidemic. And now Addie, who was looking at her with troubled eyes.

We're a fine pair, Roxanne thought. The two richest young women in Athens, and the two most miserable. She wished she could hit something, strike out to relieve her feelings. If there was going to be trouble tonight, she intended to stay right here and be in the thick of it. Maybe she'd get a chance to slug Ed Hanney or one of his deputies.

Her chin thrust out, she began to elbow her way through the crowd toward the front where Nancy was still exhorting the mechanics. "Let me through, darn it! Get out of my way!" More than one man's shins were bruised before she gained Nancy's side.

"If you girls know what's good for you, you'll listen to Nancy! There are people in this town who'll take care of you until you get your rights! I'm one of them, I'm promising you that right now. All you have to do is stand together!"

Carl Jakes circulated through the crowd, keeping a sharp eye on the situation. If he was in Ed Hanney's place, he'd haul both those girls to jail and lock them up until things were under control, even if Roxanne Livingston was one of them. Herndon Livingston would back him; nothing would please Herndon more than having his estranged son's wife arrested and jailed.

But he wasn't Ed Hanney, and this time Carl was on the other side. If the mechanics turned out and ruined Herndon, Carl would chortle with all the malicious glee that was in him. He'd done Livingston's dirty work for years, enticing girls to sell themselves into virtual slavery in the Livingston mill. Now, just because there was a depression and the mill was firing instead of hiring, Carl found himself short of work and short of cash. Herndon had refused to carry him, refused to advance him anything on the girls he'd bring in again after this depression was over.

He wasn't destitute, by any means. With only himself to support, he'd managed to save a little, and he could get by for a while. He'd decided, only this afternoon, that he was going to get out of Athens. He was sick of this town, there was nothing for him here, it was time he moved on and tried his luck someplace else.

His satchel was already stowed in the wagon, crammed full of all his worldly possessions. He'd gone to the bank before he'd packed, and drawn out all of his savings. The bank notes made a comfortable buldge in his inner coat pocket. He'd only been waiting to leave town under cover of darkness, when nobody would notice that he was leaving: he owed his landlady for two weeks rent, and there was another debt or two that he'd as soon not have to pay. There wasn't enough snow on the roads to keep him from getting through to Syracuse, which was turning into an up-and-coming town, what with the canal and the salt fields.

His breath caught sharply as his eyes came to rest on Mary MacDonald, who was standing beside Roxanne Livingston as Roxanne went on helping Nancy Steele try to convince the mechanics to turn out. It went against his grain to think that he'd never been able to get close to her, to break through her defences. And now she was fixing to marry Galen Forbes, and he'd never have another chance, even if he decided to come back to Athens some day.

As he watched, Adelaide Maynard beckoned to Mary, and Mary left Roxanne's side and made her way back to Addie. Addie pointed at something, and said something, and Mary shook her head, but Addie spoke to her again, and reluctantly, Mary began to edge her way toward the outskirts of the constantly growing mob while Addie went in the opposite direction, toward Roxanne and Nancy Steele. Without conscious thought, Carl began to edge in the direction Mary had taken, keeping her in sight.

What Addie had said was, "Mary, look how Ed Hanney's looking at Roxanne and Nancy! He's about to move in on them, he's going to arrest Nancy for sure even if he wouldn't dare try to arrest Roxie! I'm going to try to stop him, and I want you to go home right away and start getting ready to take in as many girls as Roxie's house will hold. Tell Freda and Norah that they're to help you, that Roxie said so."

"You can't go trying to stop Mr. Hanney all by yourself! Let me go with you!" Mary protested.

"No, I want you to do as I say." Addie wanted Mary out of this. There might be real trouble and she, like Roxanne, felt a special responsibility for Mary. "Go on now, you can help us more by getting ready for the influx of mechanics than you can here."

The moment Mary turned to obey her, Addie plunged ahead. Rather than hindering her, her smallness made it easier for her to get through the press as she ducked under people's arms or darted around them through spaces that a larger person couldn't have managed.

As she came abreast of Hanney, who was having considerably more trouble in forcing a passage for himself, she seemed to stumble. Her foot flew out, right in front of Hanney's leg, and the constable went down as Addie clutched at him as though trying to keep her balance. An instant later Hanney was sprawled face down in the trampled, dirty snow, and Addie, her own footing completely gone, fell none too gently on top of him and landed sitting on his head.

"Oh, my goodness! Why didn't you help me and stop me from falling? What kind of a gentleman are you?" Addie burst out.

"Lady, get offen me!" Hanney spluttered as best he could, his face still pressed into the snow.

"I'm trying, I just can't seem to get to my feet! If you'd been watching where you were going this wouldn't have happened!"

Now Roxanne stood over them, her eyes dancing, choking back laughter which threatened to strangle her. "Take my hand, Addie, I'll pull you up," she said. "I saw the whole thing, it was an accident, I'm sure, but Mr. Hanney isn't being very polite about it, is he?"

Addie grasped Roxie's hand. Under her, Hanney was struggling, trying to get to his hands and knees and regain his own footing. Roxanne began to pull Addie to her feet, but she too lost her footing and went down on top of them both, adding her own weight to Hanney's burden. They scrambled and struggled there in the snow, with Hanney doing his best not to give vent to the expletives that he dare not express in the presence of Mrs. Roxanne Livingston, who was not only a lady but Earl Fielding's daughter.

"You clumsy ox! Stop that wriggling or we'll never be able to get up!" Roxanne's hand came down on the back of Hanney's neck with a force that made the constable gasp with pain. "Oh, I'm sorry! Did I hurt you? Addie, are my petticoats showing? Dear me, what a contretemps!"

"Lady, cussing won't do no good! You gotta get offen me!" Hanney yelped.

"Cussing! Are you implying that I'm using indecent language? Be still, you imbecile, you've put me off balance again! Addie, are you hurt, has this half-witted lout injured you?''

"He kicked my ankle," Addie said.

"Then we'll bring him into court to answer for it." Roxanne's voice was decisive. "My husband will see to it." To her side she saw that Nancy Steele had melted into the crowd, safe now from Hanney's intent to arrest her. It should be safe to let the man up in a minute, and besides, more exciting things were developing.

The temper of the mechanics had been set off like tinder by Roxanne and Nancy's exhortations, and they had begun to wave their arms and scream while the townspeople were either egging them on with shouts of encouragement or, in a few cases, crying "Shame! Ungrateful! Your duty is to your employer, to the mill. You'll gain nothing by this unlawfulness!"

A fist swung here, another fist there, and what had been an orderly gathering turned into a mob as tempers flared and exploded. With a whoop of delight, Roxanne scrambled to her feet and plunged into the melee, striking out at every townsman's hostile face within her reach. Smug, conceited men, filled to bursting with their own importance just because they got to wear trousers! If she had anything to do with it, there'd be more than one black eye before this night was over, and she'd thoroughly enjoy inflicting every one of them!

At the extreme edge of the crowd, Mary fought against her desire to throw herself into the fray. If Miss Roxanne and Miss Addie could have all that fun, why did she have to trot along home like a good little girl, and count out blankets and pillows? She'd like nothing better than to take a poke at Ed Hanney herself, to pay him back for throwing her in jail where she'd probably still be if it hadn't been for Miss Roxie and the Burtons.

She paused for another second, looking back over her shoulder, before she sighed and decided that she'd better do as Addie had told her, her loyalty to Roxie and Addie overcoming her desire to get in on the fun. And besides, if she were to take part in a riot, and actually enjoy it, what would Galen think? It wouldn't be ladylike, not a thing that the future wife of a doctor would do.

She had only a fleeting glimpse of Carl Jakes's face before

his fist struck her on the side of her chin and plunged her into darkness.

Tired from their long day of scouring the countryside for firewood for the needy families of Athens, Jim Yarnell and Ike Oldham knew nothing of the excitement down by the mill. They'd been out since daylight, and they'd had to range for miles because the farmers who lived near Athens had just about run out of charity and patience.

They headed for Les Peterson's smithy and livery stable to return the wagon and team that Les had lent them, their minds filled with visions of a hot, hearty meal at the Cayuga and then a good night's sleep.

Les was nowhere to be seen when they got there, although the livery barn was unlocked. "He must have had a call to tend an ailing animal," Jim speculated. "Well, there's nothing for it but to rub down the team ourselves, and bait them. We'll leave the wood on the wagon until tomorrow."

Every muscle in Jim's body ached. The thawing snow, too little of it left for runners, had turned the low spots into mud, and the wagon had bogged down three times. He'd had to use every ounce of his strength, and Ike's as well, to get it moving again. Looking at Ike's sagging shoulders, which he knew ached as hard as his own, Jim softened.

"I can take care of the horses myself, Ike. You scoot on over to the Cayuga and grab us a table and tell Joe Moody to ladle out the best supper he can scare up." Jim gave Ike a swat on his skinny rear to send him on his way. "I'll be there as soon as I've finished up here."

Ike scooted, his stomach growling at the prospect of food. He felt a little guilty about leaving the captain to take care of the team himself, but Jim liked horses, he wouldn't mind, and he'd rather have his meal on the table waiting for him when he got to the inn than have Ike stay to help.

The streets seemed awfully empty. It didn't seem natural. And then a woman's head popped out of a door and she called, "Do you know anything about the riot down by the mill?"

Riot! Ike hesitated, torn between hunger and fatigue and wanting to find out what was going on. His curiosity won. At his age, the choice between supper and a riot was a foregone conclusion. You could eat any time, but riots weren't all that easy to come by.

"No, ma'am!" he yelped, and broke into a run. His heart pounded against his ribs. He came to the corner of Mill Street. Now he could hear the sounds of the mob and he ran even faster until he saw something that made him skid to a halt.

There was a black, enclosed wagon by the side of the street, its horse hitched to the hitching rail. And a man coming toward it, fast, carrying something. It only took Ike an instant to see that what he was carrying was a woman, lying limp in his arms. Fainted, most likely. Women were likely to faint if there was any excitement.

Then his heart gave a great lurch as he recognized the coat the woman was wearing, a green coat with a fur collar. There weren't many coats like that in Athens, for not many women could afford them. It was Miss Roxanne's coat, or had been, until she'd given it to Mary MacDonald when the cold of the winter had set in.

His breath came out again with an explosive sound, because now he recognized the man who was carrying Mary. It was Carl Jakes. Even as he yelped out Mary's name, Jakes threw Mary into the back of the wagon, yanked the lines loose from the hitching rail, and jumped into the driver's seat. He laid across the horse's back with the buggy whip.

"You there, Mr. Jakes! Hold up! Hold up, I say!"

Instead of holding up, Jakes whipped the horse into a gallop. The horse and wagon bore down on Ike at full speed as he jumped into the road and waved his arms in an attempt to stop them. Agile as he was, he was barely able to leap out of the way at the last instant to avoid being run down.

Ike fairly turned a somersault in midair as he leaped for the wagon and held on, clinging like a monkey. Jakes cursed, his lips drawn back over his teeth, and lashed at him with the whip. Ike yelped as pain tore through his face and hands, but he didn't relax his hold. Jakes cut at him again and again, cursing a blue streak, leaving off only to whip the horse to still greater speed. The horse's ears lay back, its panic at this treatment sending it into its fastest possible stride, and the wagon rattled down the street.

Ike closed his eyes and hung on, but Jakes struck at him again, just as the horse struck a rut that made the wagon lurch violently. Ike lost his grip and tumbled off, half stunned as he struck the road.

He didn't know how long he lay there before he was able to crawl to his hands and knees and then stagger to his feet. There was no sign of the horse and wagon now. Carl Jakes, with Mary in the wagon, had disappeared.

His jaw set, his eyes blazing with a fury that made him ignore his dizziness, Ike turned back the way he had come. He had to get to the captain and tell him that Carl Jakes had Mary.

Jim himself, having finished rubbing down and feeding the horses, had looked into the Cayuga and found it inexplicably empty. He'd turned his footsteps toward the commotion down by the mill, confident that that was where he would find his errant towpath driver. He wasn't angry with Ike. Any boy would head directly for any trouble that was in the offing, but he'd just as soon find him and keep a tight rein on him so that the lad wouldn't get himself involved in whatever it was that was going on.

He quickened his pace, uneasy at the thought that Ike might get himself into trouble. He was as fond of the boy as if Ike had been his younger brother, and he didn't want anything to happen to him.

There was Cato, hitched to the Burtons' buggy. The beautiful animal pawed the ground with one forefoot, its ears pricked forward toward the sound of angry and shouting voices in the distance, but there was no sign of Bobo. Without a doubt Bobo had left the horse and buggy here, well out of the vicinity of the riot for safety's sake, and gone ahead on foot.

He paused to stroke Cato's nose. "You're better off where you are, boy. Just be patient," he advised the animal. Well, Les Peterson talked to horses, so he guessed he could too because nobody had ever accused Les of being addled. "I wish you could talk back to me, I'd like to know if you've seen anything of Ike."

Cato wiggled his ears and whinnied, for all the world as if he was saying something. And the next instant, Jim jumped half out of his skin, because Cato was looking at something over Jim's shoulder, and it was Ike, but a totally different Ike than the boy Jim had last seen trotting off in the direction of the Cayuga Inn to order their supper.

Ike was breathing so hard that he could hardly gasp the

words out. "Mary," he croaked. "Carl Jakes has got her, he's carrying her off in that black wagon!"

It took a moment for it to penetrate, because Jim was occupied with Ike's appearance. The boy's face and hands were welted and bruised, and his coat was torn. "Mary?" Jim asked, struggling to understand. "Mary MacDonald? Ike, what is it?"

"He's got her. Jakes has got her. I tried to stop him, I hung onto the wagon, but he kept hitting me with the buggy whip, and then the wagon bounced and I fell off. Cap'n, we gotta do something, we gotta get her back!"

"Which way did Jakes go?"

"He was heading west, right on this street. I'm coming with you—"

"No, I don't want any extra weight in the buggy, because if you don't know how much of a head start they have, speed's going to count. Go find somebody to patch you up." Jim jumped into the buggy, flicked the lines over Cato's back, and turned him in the middle of the street. Cato whinnied once more and then broke into the long-strided trot that had made him a champion. "Get up there, Cato! Lay into it!"

Before he got out of town, Jim had eased Cato down into a steady, mile-eating pace. If Jakes had headed this way, then he'd likely be headed for the Old Mill Road, the only major road that this street connected with. He knew that he'd catch up with him sooner or later. The wagon was heavy, and the horse Jakes was driving was a work animal, built for strength and durability rather than speed.

His jaw set, Jim held Cato to his steady pace in spite of his urge to set him into a gallop. Mary, in Carl Jakes's hands! The thought was enough to make cold sweat spring out all over his body. The man must have lost his mind! But sane or insane, Jim was going to get her back from him, nothing in the world was going to stop him.

A watery moon shed a faint light over the countryside, and familiar landmarks were approached and passed. Cato's pace never faltered. He had his wind, and his legs moved like pistons, never missing a beat. The dirt road moved like a ribbon underneath the buggy's wheels. The muscles in Jim's jaw tightened, his narrowed eyes squinted into the distance ahead of him, straining for the first glimpse of the enclosed wagon.

Mary! Once again, Jim fought down his raging impulse to urge Cato to a faster pace. Steady did it. They'd catch up, there was no doubt about it, and he knew that he was on the right track because the tracks of Jakes's wagon were plain in the muddy spots in the road. No farm horse could maintain a lead over Cato's relentless trot. Just keep it up, Cato, just keep going, it won't be long now!

In the back of the black wagon, Mary had regained consciousness with a throbbing head and the distinct impression that she was somehow on a boat that was being tossed around on an angry ocean. She rolled and bounced from one side of the wagon to the other. She moaned, and braced herself with her hands on a bench, and managed to crawl up on it. Her head was killing her, but snatches of the moments just before she'd lost consciousness came back into her mind. There'd been trouble at the mill, the mechanics were angry, there'd been the beginnings of a riot. And Addie had told her to go home, and then . . . and then . . .

Carl Jakes's face swam into her mind's eye. He'd been there, she'd looked around and he'd been there, right at her shoulder.

She knew where she was, now. She was in the wagon, Jakes's wagon, the same wagon that had carried her from her parents' farm to Athens. Carl Jakes had her, and God only knew where he was taking her.

Her terror sent a surge of adrenaline through her veins. She stood up to wrench at the door at the back of the wagon. It was bolted from the outside; there was to be no escape by jumping free even if she would have dared to risk breaking her neck. And even though she knew she'd have jumped if she could have opened the door, how long would it be before Jakes realized that she was gone, and came back looking for her? If she'd hurt herself, broken a leg or something equally dire, she'd have even less chance of escape than she might have when Jakes stopped the wagon. He'd have to stop some time, the horse couldn't go on pulling it into eternity.

Her mind darted frantically into every corner, exploring every possibility. Her reticule was still looped over her arm, but there was absolutely nothing in it that she could use as a weapon. The interior of the wagon was equally bare, nothing but the bare floor and the benches. A few desperate tugs at one of them convinced her that there was no way to pull a part of it free to use as a club. She had only the natural weapons that every woman possessed, her fingernails and her teeth.

Galen, she whimpered. Oh, Galen! Like Jim, she knew for what purpose Carl Jakes had abducted her, because there couldn't be any other. If she couldn't get away from him before he'd had his way with her, she'd never be able to go back to Athens and Galen, because she'd never be able to hold her head up again, much less marry a decent man.

I'll kill him, Mary thought. I'll find a way! I'm strong, I'll fight him. I'd rather he killed me than do what he's bound to do. He'll have to kill me first, but maybe he isn't that crazy. If I fight hard enough, there might be a chance. She racked her brain for things she'd heard Roxanne talk about, the fights along the towpaths. Go for his eyes, blind him, sink your teeth in his ear and tear it off; go for another place with all your strength, that brings such pain it makes a man helpless.

The wagon struck a rut and lurched, and nausea welled up in her. She had to clap her hand over her mouth to keep from retching. She'd never had to fight while she was racked by nausea, while her head was throbbing until she saw flashes of light in front of her eyes, stabbing through the darkness inside the enclosed wagon. But I'll fight him anyway, she swore, as she controlled her dry gagging. Maybe I can't win, but I'll hurt him. He won't have any pleasure of me, I swear it! But oh, Galen!

Behind her on the road, Jim's breath whistled between his teeth with a sound of intense satisfaction. There they were, up ahead. "Keep going, Cato!" he said. "We've got the bastard now!"

Jakes heard the sound of the oncoming buggy, coming at a clip so fast that he knew that it had to be after him. Someone had seen him take Mary, and now the pursuit had caught up with him! Cursing fate, he hauled up on the lines and drew an oversized pocketknife from his pocket and snapped it open. Its blades were razor-sharp, because he never knew when he'd need it.

He wasn't going to be stopped now! A glance behind him had shown him that there was only one man in the buggy. His rage knew no bounds as he realized that his plans for Mary would have to be thrown away. He'd try not to kill whoever it was who had caught him, but just disable him, so that he'd have time to get clear away. If they got Mary back unharmed, and if the man were only injured, not dead, they wouldn't have as determined a hue and cry after him.

He cursed again, lashing out at the fates that had thwarted him at the very moment of his triumph. It wasn't as if he'd been going to hurt Mary. Take her, yes, so as to make sure that she wouldn't go running away from him, back to Athens and her friends and Galen Forbes. She'd be too ashamed to go back. Any sensible girl would accept his alternative. He'd marry her, and he'd treat her right. She was so pretty, so sweet and fresh and clean. With a wife like her, he'd have settled down, worked hard, no more drinking too much or chasing after other women. He had a longing eating at his insides to be respectable, to have his fellow men respect him, to have children, a son who'd look up to him . . .

The buggy was alongside the wagon now, forcing it off the road as Cato responded to Jim's pull on the lines. A past master of infighting, Jakes didn't hesitate. He launched himself off the wagon seat and catapulted onto Jim, the force of his descent knocking them both into the road. As quick as a cat, he raised the knife and plunged it downward. A gash opened on Jim's arm, but his hands had grasped Jakes around his neck and he didn't release his hold.

Then Jim was on top of Jakes, and Jakes had just time to strike again, this time driving the knife deep into Jim's shoulder. Blinded with fury, bleeding, feeling nothing of his wounds through his rage, Jim knelt on Jakes's chest as his uninjured fist lashed downward. It was all over. Jakes's eyes rolled back and his body lay as limp as an empty grain sack in the road.

Jim shook his head to clear it. He eased himself off of his fallen adversary and struggled to his hands and knees, shaking his head again. Cato had trotted a short distance ahead, but now he'd stopped and was looking back to see what on earth those humans were doing. The heavier cart horse stood in its tracks where it had stopped, too phlegmatic to bother trying to bolt in spite of the battle that had taken place almost under its feet.

Inside the wagon, Mary was pounding against the door with her fists so hard that her knuckles were bruised. She screamed to be let out. "Darn it! What's going on? Open this door!"

Jim staggered as he reached the rear of the wagon. He had to lean against it for a few seconds before he could find the strength to throw the bolt, both of his wounds throbbing now, pain lashing through him. His knees felt weak and bile rose up in his throat.

"Mary? Are you all right?" His voice was no more than a croak.

"I'm all right. Open the door, dang you!"

The door swung open and Mary, caught off balance as she was starting to pound against it again, tumbled out into Jim's arms. Her weight toppled them both, and she cried out in horror as she felt warm blood flow over her face and hands.

"Captain Yarnell!" she gasped. "You're hurt! Oh, glory, you're hurt!"

"I'm bleeding a little," Jim conceded when he was able to draw a breath. "Maybe we'd better see if we can slow it down."

Her heart in her throat pounding fit to choke her, Mary's hands tore at her petticoats ruthlessly. Her face streaming tears, she pressed a wad of the rags against Jim's shoulder. Oh, Lord, if she only had four hands! Captain Yarnell's arm was bleeding too, and she daren't take the pressure off the wound in his shoulder because that was the worse, but she'd give everything she ever hoped to have if she only had those extra hands!

Necessity being the mother of invention, it took her only a few seconds to solve the problem.

"Lie down," she commanded. "Flat." And when Jim complied, she promptly sat on the wad of cloth that was stemming the bleeding in his shoulder, leaving her two hands free to rip more material from her petticoat and wrap it around his arm. If God hadn't seen fit to give people four hands, then it was a mercy He'd given them some brains to think with.

"Don't you go dying on me, do you hear?" she scolded. "Don't you dast! I won't have it!"

Dear Lord, maybe he would die, and what would she do then? She looked at his face, his dear, familiar, strong face, all white in the moonlight and his eyes closed as if he were already dead! She wanted to shake him, to order him to open his eyes, but she had to go on sitting on him while she fastened the bandage around his arm before she dared move off his shoulder.

When she was able to get off, she began to cry great, choking sobs, because his chest moved up and down. He was still breathing, he wasn't dead yet. But what was she going to do now? She couldn't lift him into the wagon or buggy to get him back to town, he was too heavy, and if she went tugging and hauling on him it might kill him. So she sat there, applying pressure, her tears washing his face until it was as wet as her own, and she prayed as she'd never prayed before.

Let him live. God, send somebody, anybody, I don't care who just so they can help. Don't let him die!

The bleeding seemed to have been stemmed, but now there was another danger as Jakes moaned and stirred. Mary bit her lower lip, and decided that she had to do something, because if Jakes came to and found Jim and herself helpless, it would be all up with them.

Farm-born and bred, it took her only a moment to undo the buckles of the cart horse's lines. With the leather straps, it took her only another moment to truss Jakes up like a turkey ready for the oven. She wasn't gentle about it, but she was quick. And then she knelt beside Jim again, her hands pressing against the wad on his chest, and resumed her praying.

That was how Les Peterson and Ike Oldham found them. With both Marvin Burton and Bobo at the mill, trying their best to talk the unruly crowd into dispersing peacefully instead of burning down Herndon Livingston's house, as some of them were determined to try, Les had started on back to his livery stable, mindful that Jim Yarnell and Ike should be back by now and that there'd be a tired team to take care of. Let the lawyers handle the crowd; he'd go back after he'd seen to the horses. If the Burtons needed some brawn to help them bring order, he'd do what he could, but the horses had to come first.

He'd met Ike staggering toward the scene of the trouble, intent on finding someone to go after the captain and help him. It had taken only a few minutes for Les to hitch up a buggy, and Ike had been right with him in spite of the stitch in his side and the burning of the whip welts on his face and hands.

The smithy's strength made nothing of lifting Jim into the Burtons' buggy. Ike drove it back to town, while Mary continued the pressure against his shoulder. The cart horse he tied to the back of his own buggy. It would slow down his return to town, but he wouldn't have been able to keep up with Cato in any case, not with the way Ike was tooling him along, urging all possible speed out of him.

"Just keep him steady, don't go winding him!" Les shouted after Ike, and the boy, his face so white that the freckles stood out even in the moonlight, understood.

Les lifted the still trussed-up Carl Jakes into his buggy, told him in a deceptively mild voice to behave himself, and started out after Ike. He wasn't too worried about Jim, he knew enough about wounds to be reasonably certain that once Galen Forbes got his hands on him, his friend would pull through. He wondered, as he drove, if Marvin and Bobo had had any luck in controlling the mob. When he'd left to tend his borrowed team, it had looked like there was going to be a full-scale riot. It was turning out to be quite an evening.

Far ahead of him, Mary was pounding both her fists on Galen's chest.

"You save him, Galen Forbes, do you hear me? Don't you dast let him die! Do something, hurry! Why are you just standing there?"

It took only a few moments for Galen to be able to assure her and Ike that Jim wasn't in danger of dying, that he'd only lost too much blood and would be laid up for a while until he regained his strength.

"Thank you, Galen. I mean, thank you, Doctor Forbes. And I'm sorry, but I can't marry you. I hold you in the highest esteem and I'm sorry if your heart will be broken, but I love someone else."

Galen's voice was dry. "I'd already gathered that. Ike, we'll take him to the Burton house. And Miss MacDonald, you could use a bath, if you don't mind a man you aren't engaged to anymore telling you so. Mrs. Burton will take care of you, and see that Jim gets the nursing he's going to need. Ike, you go along too. I'll take a look at those welts when we get there."

A wide grin spread from his mouth to his eyes as he added, "Bobo will be glad to get Cato back. Somebody told him he'd seen some man driving him off. From what I heard, he's been swearing to string whoever it was up to the nearest tree, after that riot calms down."

25

Philo O'Brian was missing out on all the excitement for a highly unlikely reason, considering that he was an Irish Catholic. All the time that the crowd had been gathered outside of Herndon Livingston's mill gates, Philo had been attending a prayer meeting-cum-hymnfest at the home of Mr. and Mrs. Applegate, who lived four doors down from Minnie Atkins's house on Prine Street.

It wasn't that Philo had wanted to go, it was that Minnie had insisted that he go if he wanted to continue seeing her socially, with courtship in mind. How could she continue her relationship with him, innocent as it was, unless she made an effort to bring him to the light? Marian and Walter Applegate were among the most avid of First Methodist's members, and Minnie's closest friends, and they had helped Minnie recruit a dozen other reproachless members of the congregation to help them in this effort to bring in another sheaf.

As Prine Street was one of Athens's backwaters, far removed from the center of town and its activities, no inkling of what was going on outside the mill reached the group. They alternated loud and lusty singing of such old standbys as "Rock of Ages" with prayers delivered in voices almost as loud, the faithful Methodists combining their utmost efforts to save this misguided soul that had wandered into their midst.

Philo entered into the hymn-singing with gusto. For a man of his size, his voice was remarkably powerful, probably because he had used it for so many years exhorting workers to rise up against their employers. During the prayers, he bowed his head and asked the Holy Mother to tell her Son that he hadn't had any choice but to be here unless he wanted to lose the only woman he'd ever loved, feeling sure that the Blessed Virgin would understand and intervene for him. It wasn't as if he had any intention of forsaking the Mother Church; and since it was unlikely that any children would be involved if he had the sublime good fortune to convince Minnie to have him, the sin wasn't all that black. And there was always the chance that once they were married, Philo would be able to bring Minnie into the proper fold. To Philo's way of thinking, it was worth taking the chance.

The meeting had started promptly at six-thirty, but as Philo had been subjected to a nearly two-hour lecture by Minnie, in Minnie's house, before it had started, aided and abetted by the Applegates who'd come not only to assist her but to protect her reputation, he had no inkling that he was missing out on something he'd have risked his soul to get in on. He, Minnie, and the Applegates had had a hasty supper at Minnie's and then walked the few steps to the Applegates' house where the meeting was to take place. Marian Applegate's parlor was larger by half than Minnie's and better able to accommodate so many people.

And they were nice people, Philo had to admit it. Their hearts were in the right place, it was their souls that had become lost somewhere along the way when their remote ancestors had had the misfortune to be influenced by Martin Luther's heresy.

The meeting broke up at eight o'clock. These were all working people who rose early and retired early so as to be able to rise early again the next day.

It was while they were saying good-night outside Minnie's house, a rather protracted procedure because Minnie was insistent on learning whether or not Philo's heart had been touched by the praying and singing, that Verne Baldwin, inflamed as much by liquid spirits as by the spirit of fair play for the mechanics, came staggering down Prine Street in search of the one man in Athens who had no right to be absent from what was happening at the mill.

"Gol darn, Philo, where the blazes you been?" Verne demanded. "This's the third time I been here lookin' for you. I promised everybody I'd fetch you. Don't you know there's a riot goin' on down to the mill? Herndon Livingston done laid off a whole lot more of the mechanics, and they're fixin' to tear things apart. Com'on now, yer missin' all the fun!''

"Holy Mother!" Philo gaped at Verne. "I'm coming, man! You'll have to sprout wings to keep up with me!"

"Philo O'Brian, you aren't going anywhere! I won't have you mixed up in unlawful violence, do you want to spend the rest of your life in prison?''

"They need me, Minnie me darlin', they need a leader. If I'm martyred, then I'll count it well worth the cost. Martyrs have a special place in heaven, as you ought to know, as pious as you are even if you're misguided." With that, Philo turned on his heel and began trotting off after Verne, who'd already started back to the scene of the action.

It took Minnie only seconds to dart around to her back stoop and snatch up a bucket that she used to scrub her floors, and then she was after him. The middle-aged spinster, half a head taller than Philo and with longer legs, cut down the distance between them with surprising rapidity even though she hadn't run since she was a girl.

"Mr. O'Brian, you come back here!"

Philo looked over his shoulder and increased his pace. Minnie's stride lengthened, even though it wouldn't have seemed possible. Then she caught up with him, and the bucket came upside down over his head, effectively blinding him and stopping him in his tracks. Relentlessly, Minnie began to pull him backward, step by step.

"Woman, leave me go!" Philo's voice boomed and echoed inside the bucket as he struggled to remove it from his head.

"You're coming back with me!" Minnie shrilled. "You're coming back this instant, or I . . ." She faltered only for a moment, and then she burned her bridges behind her. "Or I won't marry you!"

"What did you say?" Philo finally succeeded in removing the bucket, being stronger than Minnie even if he was shorter. "Did you say you'd marry me?"

"If you come back." Minnie's voice was firm in spite of her gasping for breath after her sprint after Philo.

"Then I'll come back." Obediently, like a tractable puppy, Philo trotted after her as she reversed her direction.

The front door closed behind them, and Philo looked at

the love of his life, his eyes shining. Then his face fell, and he shook his head.

"Martyred I'll be, then, and double-martyred, because I can't do it, Minnie, even for you. I'm sorry, but I'm needed." With that, he grasped her by her arms and dragged her, struggling and screeching, up the stairs and pushed her into her bedroom and locked her in, almost catching his hand in the door as he snatched the key from the inside and slammed the door. He barely got the key turned in the lock before Minnie was pounding on the panels.

"Mr. O'Brian, I'll never forgive you!"

"I know it, woman dear," Philo shouted as he pelted back down the stairs. "And it's sorry I am, but this is the way it has to be!"

Verne Baldwin had outdistanced him by so far that Philo only caught a glimpse of him at the edge of the crowd in front of the mill gates. Philo's heart lodged in his throat when he heard the ugly shouts and saw the torches that were flaring in more than a dozen hands.

"Let me through!" he bellowed. Using his head as a battering ram, he managed to work his way toward the front. Added to the smell of smoke from the torches, there was another, more ominous smell that sent alarm stabbing through every inch of him. Tar, melted tar. "What the divil's goin' on here?"

Bobo Burton grasped his arm, his eyes glittering in the torchlight. "Thank God you're here! Maybe they'll listen to you. The fools are set on dragging Herndon Livingston out of his house and tarring and feathering him, and there are a few maniacs who insist that they're going to fire his house for good measure!"

The crowd was already milling around, reversing direction, readying themselves for the march to the Livingston mansion. Philo's heart sank at the expressions he saw on those dozens of set faces. He could hear Marvin Burton's voice as Marvin tried, in vain, to stem the tide.

"Why don't you listen to the man, you spalpeens?" Philo bellowed. "An honest turnout is one thing, but takin' the law into yer own hands and inflictin' bodily injury, and destroyin' property, will only land you in prison!"

"He's got it coming to him, it's long overdue!" someone shouted. "Get out of our way, Mr. O'Brian, unless you want us to walk over you!"

Roxanne appeared at Philo's right side, Addie at his left. Their faces were pale, although Roxanne's eyes were still alight with excitement. "Philo, they won't listen! Mr. Burton and Bobo have talked themselves hoarse, and Nancy Steele and I all but lost our voices shouting at them that all that's needed is a turnout! I had no idea that things would go this far when I helped Nancy convince the mechanics that it was time to take a stand."

They were being pushed along by the sheer force of the numbers behind them. Philo saw everything that had been gained over the last grinding, heartbreaking years about to go up in smoke. If this mob had its way, the cause of labor would be set back for more years than he'd live to see.

It was into this mad scene that Les Peterson came driving his buggy, pulling up just before it ran into the foremost of the crowd. Even despite its present mood, the sight of the bound man beside Les stopped the mob in its tracks.

Les stood up in the buggy and hauled Carl Jakes to his feet beside him. "This piece of scum kidnapped Mary Mac-Donald a little while ago, right out from under your noses," Les said. He didn't have to shout, everyone was listening. "He put her in his wagon and was making off with her when young Ike Oldham saw him, and told Captain Yarnell, and the captain gave chase and caught up with them, and got himself well carved up by Jakes's knife while he was stopping him. Jim's going to be all right, no thanks to Jakes, and Mary wasn't harmed except for a clout to her head. Where's Ed Hanney? He has a prisoner to throw in jail."

"Jail, hell!" It was Verne Baldwin, still so drunk that he could hardly stand on his feet. The town reprobate was jumping up and down, windmilling his arms to keep his balance. "Lynch him!"

Philo saw his chance, his only chance. At the risk of overturning the buggy, he clambered up to stand beside Les.

"No lynching! That's murder, me friends! But now we've got a use for that tar and feathers, and if evir a man deserved to be tarred and feathered and ridden out of town on a rail, it's Carl Jakes!"

The crowd hesitated, some of the diehards reluctant to relinquish their original purpose. Philo, with expert timing, followed up his opening.

"I say we march this spawn of Hades to Herndon

Livingston's house, and tar and feather him where Herndon can see it happen! Let's get going, me friends, before that tar gets cold!''

In their present mood, the mob wanted a victim, and here was a victim who not only deserved what they were going to do to him, but on whom they could vent punishment without fear of reprisal. And if seeing his minion tarred and feathered didn't throw a scare into Herndon Livingston, as well as finding out that come Monday morning not one soul would pass through his mill gates to work his looms, they didn't know what would. They had Livingston in a forked stick, and tonight was the night they were going to throw the fear of God into him!

''Throw me that torch, man!'' Philo said to a torch-bearer at the front of the crowd. ''Les, you turn this rig around, and we'll lead the procession!''

Les pushed Jakes back down onto the seat, sat down himself and turned the horse. Philo continued to stand, his torch held high, his heart filled with elation. The danger to his lifework had been averted. The mob would disperse after Jakes had got his just deserts and Herndon Livingston had seen the handwriting on the wall. Most of them would go home, satisfied with a good night's work. Others would repair to the various taverns and spend what was left of the evening celebrating, as long as their money or their credit held out.

The procession wound its way down Seneca Street, and turned onto North and then around the corner onto Elm. Householders who had not hurried to the scene of the excitement earlier in the evening looked out of their windows or stepped out onto their front porches, their mouths hanging open at the sight of this torchlight parade. Boys who hadn't managed to elude their parents earlier were hauled back into their houses as they tried to make a break. And at the tail end of the procession, Ed Hanney, nursing various bruises he'd picked up during his encounter with Roxanne and Addie, trailed along, knowing that to try to stop the mob would mean being torn limb from limb. Several houses before they reached the Livingston house, he turned around and headed back to the safety of his jail, where a bottle of rum, locked in a cupboard, would comfort him as he wondered what reprisals he'd have to face from the mill owner and the more substantial city fathers come tomorrow.

Walking beside his father, Bobo forgot about his limp. Neither he nor Marvin had any inclination to try to stop what was going on. Jakes deserved what he was getting, and they, like Philo, were only relieved that nothing worse was going to happen.

"If Jim wind-broke Cato, I'll flay him alive," Bobo said.

"There's no chance of that," Marvin said. "Jim Yarnell has better sense than to ruin a horse. He knew that Cato would catch up with that wagon without being pushed. Just be glad that Mary MacDonald is all right. It's a miracle that young Ike saw Jakes take her, else God knows what would have happened to her by now."

"I am glad. I've a good mind to help with the tarring and feathering."

"No, you haven't. You'd get tar all over yourself, and how would you go about explaining it to your mother? Not that she won't approve of Jakes's punishment, but she has the idea that lawyers are supposed to be dignified. Besides, tar's the very devil to get off. We'll satisfy ourselves by making sure that it isn't hot enough to inflict burns."

"Little chance of that. In this weather, it's already cooled enough so it'll be hard to spread. We'll have to keep Philo from actually riding Jakes out of town on a rail. It's too cold for him to be dumped somewhere, and he'll need attention."

"Maybe Les will let him spend the night in his loft," Marvin agreed. "In the morning he'll be able to ride his cart horse out to where his wagon was abandoned, and make tracks for parts unknown, and I'll be glad to see his back."

Inside his mansion, Herndon was annoyed when his wife entered his study where he was going over the latest figures pertaining to the expansion of his mill. Every total he reached underlined the fact that if his mechanics failed to report for work on Monday, and stayed out for any length of time, he'd be a ruined man. He'd been kept apprised about what was going on in front of the mill, up until an hour ago, when Arnold, his butler, whom he'd sent to keep an eye on the situation, had failed to report back. He had no way of knowing that Arnold, having been recognized, was now locked in the cellar of the Cayuga, with a bottle for company while he waited for his release after the mob's mission had been carried out.

"Herndon, there are some persons in front of the house. A good many of them," Lillian told him. "They have torches, and they seem to have a large iron kettle and some pillows. And Mr. Jakes is there, all tied up in Mr. Peterson's buggy. Mr. O'Brian is with them."

One glance from the front window confirmed what Lillian had told him. The size of the mob surprised him, even though he'd known that there was a large number of people gathered at the mill. Herndon opened the window a crack so that he could hear as well as see, and the pungent smell of the melted tar flowed in along with the cold air. Beside him, Lillian's voice conveyed interest rather than apprehension.

"I've never seen anything like this, but I'd surmise that they're going to tar and feather someone. Do you suppose it could be you?"

"Nonsense! I'll soon put them to rout!" Whatever his other faults, Herndon was not a coward, and a few seconds later he was on his front porch, addressing the crowd with a voice filled with authority, fully expecting to be obeyed.

"Take that paraphernalia away immediately, and take yourselves with it!" Herndon ordered.

He was answered by a hail of clods and insults, small stones and something worse, horse droppings not being hard to come by. There was no course open to him except to retreat behind his closed door, his blood pressure soaring.

"They aren't going away," Lillian observed. "Herndon, your eyelid is twitching. You'd better be careful, my father's eyelid twitched like that right before his stroke."

"Go to your room and stay there!"

"I'm staying right here. I want to see the excitement. Do you think they'll break down the door?"

"They wouldn't dare. This is a law-abiding town. Whatever they're up to, they'll be punished for it, I assure you of that. The ringleaders will go to prison, and the others will be blackballed and never find another day's work." And Mr. Hanney will be looking for another means of livelihood, come next election, he added mentally. Such dereliction of duty could not be tolerated.

Outside, the crowd, filled with anticipation, had fallen

silent. Philo turned to the female mechanics and to Roxanne and Addie, who were staying close to them, giving them moral support.

"Ladies, you'd better leave now. This isn't going to be any sight for such delicate eyes. But you can trust us men to do our duty, never fear."

"We're staying put!" Nancy Steele shrilled. "We wouldn't miss seeing Carl Jakes get what's coming to him for a year's work at twice the regular wages!"

Inside the house, Herndon caught sight of his daughter standing with the mechanics, and his eyelid twitched more spasmodically than it had before. Traitoress, whore! Turning on her own father!

Lillian watched him with a clinical eye. "You're going to have a stroke if you don't control yourself." Then, as a shout arose outside, she turned her attention to the window again.

Jakes's face was livid with fear. All of his bravado had vanished.

"Let me go! I didn't hurt the girl! I swear before God I didn't! She's all right, Les Peterson himself told you so! Let me go and I'll leave town and I promise I'll never come back!"

"You'll leave town all right, you blackhearted sinner!" Nancy Steele screamed. "And you'll be lucky if you aren't mistaken for a bird, with all those feathers sticking to you!"

"Nancy, me love," Philo chided her, "and is that any way for a lady to be talkin'? Hush up, like a good sweet lass, and let us men get on with the business at hand." Philo was protracting the moment as long as he could, because the longer and better the show he put on for the would-be arsonists, the more likely they would be to disperse peacefully and be content not to harm Herndon Livingston or fire his house. "Is the tar ready? Who's goin' to rip open a pillow? No, only one! There's no use in bein' wasteful. Your wives will be glad to get the others back, and so will you when you go to rest yer weary heads this night."

"It's ready! Let's get on with it!"

"Easy now, boyos. We don't want to go ruinin' the man's clothes, do we now? We'll peel him down, but leave his long johns on, mind, there's ladies present. Be careful, don't go tearin' that coat, some poor soul can make use of it, a man who never had the fortune of earnin' good money like Jakes has. He can afford to buy another one but there's plenty here in Athens that can't.''

The peeling down tickled the crowd's fancy. No longer a mob, it was more like an audience at a stage play. They waited with bated breaths for what would happen next. The two men who did the peeling down made the most of it, taking their time, stripping Jakes of his outer clothing with exaggerated care and taking their time about it.

"I'll take the coat!" Verne Baldwin squealed. "I wuz the one saw Les bringin' him in, an' I'm 'titled to it!''

"Agreed," Philo said. He handed over the coat, and Verne squirmed into it. It hung almost to his ankles, and the sleeves were so long that his hands were hidden. He snuggled himself inside of it, hugging it around his skinny body, and then he squealed again with delight, as he reached inside and pulled a roll of bank notes from an inner pocket.

"Lookee here! I'm rich, I'm rich!"

Philo reached over and relieved him of the money. On second thought, he peeled one note from the outside of the wad and gave that to Verne. "We aren't thieves, now are we? Blackhearted as he is, the man will have to live till he can find work." Thoughtfully, Philo counted off half of the bills and handed them to Les Peterson. "You'll be so kind as to return this money to Mr. Jakes, after we've finished with him.''

Roxanne, delighted, called out, "And what about the rest of it?''

"Why, Mr. Marvin Burton will hold it, to be sure, until it can be used to buy food and fuel for the needy." Making a flourish of the movement, he handed the remainder of the money to the lawyer.

In nothing but his long underwear, stripped even of his shoes that another man pounced on, Jakes stood shivering, his face white, near to fainting.

"And will you look at the man!" Philo said, his voice filled with wonder. "He's not much of a ladies' man now, is he, lads? I don't see him struttin', and givin' the girls the eye, and flashin' his roll to entice 'em into givin' him their favors! Maybe he'll be more attractive to the ladies after we've prettied him up a little. Let's start with his face. A little bit of tar here, a little bit of tar there, smear it on! That ain't enough, we can still see who he is. Now the neck, and the shoulders, spread it even, lads, we want enough to cover him all over."

Jakes stood in the middle of the circle of people, who left plenty of room for the volunteers to cover him with tar. "You're missing his hand! His left ear doesn't have any! How about his feet, get his feet!"

"And now for the feathers. Give somebody else a chance, me boyos. Who wants to put the feathers on him?"

"I do!" Nancy Steele burst into the cleared space. "An' Dorothy here, and some of the other mechanics. He's the one recruited us, telling us lies that musta earned his way into hell the minute he said 'em! Let's cover him good, girls, let's cover him so good that some farmer will think he's some monster hawk after his chicken coop, an' take a shot at him!"

Inside the house, Herndon watched as the girls snatched handsful of feathers from the ripped-open pillow, and plastered them all over Jakes's body. Savages! He made a careful note of who the girls were. He had a phenomenal memory for names and faces. There was scarcely a mechanic in his mill that he couldn't name at first glance.

"They're doing a good job," Lillian, who was standing slightly behind him, remarked conversationally. "My, he does look strange, doesn't he? I never did like the man. If it wouldn't have been unseemly, I'd have gone out and offered to help them. I'm glad that Addie didn't get in on it, though. It would be a shame to soil that lovely dress she's wearing."

Herndon's eyelid twitched again, but he didn't favor his wife with an answer.

When the girls had finished with Jakes, Roxanne turned to Addie, almost doubled over with laughter. "He does look like a bird, Addie, I swear he does! A rare bird indeed! Come on, I've seen enough. Let's go home and see if everything's ready to take the mechanics in. We still have a long night ahead of us."

An hour later, after he'd supervised picking the feathers off the victim at Les Peterson's livery stable, and removing as much of the tar as possible with turpentine, Philo also set off to finish his evening's work. He walked with a great deal less buoyancy than Roxanne and Addie, because making his peace with Minnie, after he'd let her out of her bedroom, was going to be the hardest night's work he'd ever have to face. If he hadn't known that Minnie would never have forgiven him if he did, he'd have repaired to the Waterman's Haven with the men who urged him, to bolster up his courage first.

But women aren't apt to be reasonable, more the pity. The Lord had made them soft and beautiful, so He'd probably thought that there was no need for them to be reasonable as well.

Sighing, he thought again of what he'd likely thrown away by going to that damned Livingston's rescue. Well, too much of a good thing was apt to spoil a man, and lessen his chances of going to heaven.

26

During the night's excitement, little Lollie Kirby was going through her crisis, and Geneva all but lost her. Galen had shaken his head when he'd seen her early that evening, and told Geneva, well out of earshot of both Lollie and her mother, that he was afraid that the child wouldn't live through the night. If he hadn't been compelled to tend to another desperate case, Mr. Maxwell's fourteen-year-old nephew, who was even worse off than Lollie and had less expert nursing at home, he wouldn't have left the little girl. As it was, he had to trust Geneva and Addie's girls to do everything that could be done, which was so little that it moved him, not for the first time, to despair.

Geneva had refused to accept his verdict. They'd lost five patients since she and Addie's girls had come to nurse the stricken. Lost them although they'd fought as hard for them as one human being could fight for another. Geneva had taken each death as a personal defeat. She'd grown thin, until it hurt to look at her.

But she refused to let Lollie die. She remained at the child's bedside the entire night, coaxing each breath, swabbing her throat, fighting the disease that was as determined to take the little girl's life as Geneva was to save her.

And this time she had won, although the victory had left her drained. When Galen had come in, before dawn, he'd found her still holding Lollie in a half-sitting position to ease her breathing, her arms numb and her face drawn with complete exhaustion. But Lollie was still breathing, her breathing a little easier than it had been the last time Galen had seen her. He'd called Goldie to take over and ordered Geneva to bed.

"You saved her, Miss Burton. I don't believe anyone else could have done it. Lollie's going to get well, and she has you to thank for it. Now I want you to stay in bed for at least twelve hours. Eat something first, and then sleep. The other girls can manage. All of our other patients are on the road to recovery, the epidemic has run its course. There haven't been any new cases for over a week."

It grated on Geneva that Galen still persisted in calling her Miss Burton, even though they knew each other so well and they'd been working so closely together. Her lips firmed as she told herself not to think and act like a silly schoolgirl with her first crush. Galen had made it plain, from the first time she'd met him, that he had no use for her. It was Mary he'd fallen in love with, Mary he was going to marry, and she hoped that both he and Mary would be happy. If it hadn't been in the cards for her to win, at least she could be a good loser, and stop flinching every time Galen addressed her as though she were no more than a casual acquaintance.

To divert her thoughts from her aching hurt, she changed the subject. "What's going on in town? Did the mechanics really turn out, and are they going to refuse to go back?"

"It looks like it. Oh, I'm sorry, Miss Burton. I forgot that you're so isolated here. Yes, the girls are going to stay out. Addie and Roxanne are taking care of all of them who had no place to go, they're packed in like herrings in a barrel but they're doing all right. And Jim Yarnell is recovering nicely, he'll be on his feet in a day or two, and nobody knows where Carl Jakes went after he left Athens the morning after he was tarred and feathered."

It never entered his mind to tell Geneva that Mary had changed her mind about marrying him. In fact, he himself was so tired that he scarcely thought of it. He'd had his doubts about marrying Mary ever since she'd jumped to the conclusion that they were engaged, even though he was inordinately fond of her. The fact that she'd have made him an admirable wife wouldn't have been enough to make up for the fact that he didn't love her. Love and fondness were not the same thing. He'd been afraid that he'd hurt her, which was the last thing in the world he wanted to do. And he himself would have always been aware of the lack in his life, the lack of an all-fulfilling love. He was both happy and relieved that Mary had finally realized that she loved Jim Yarnell. Jim would be a good husband to her, he'd take care of her and make her happy, and they both deserved the best.

Geneva's pale face jerked him back to the present. "Go on to bed, Miss Burton. There's nothing to worry about. Sleep for as long as you can. We can manage perfectly well without you."

And haven't you always, Geneva thought, bitterness creeping in in spite of herself. Except here at the hospital, of course. Here, where she had been so desperately needed while the epidemic had raged, she had at least proved that she was needed, that in spite of being the daughter of a wealthy man who had allowed her so much latitude to do as she pleased, she was capable of making herself useful.

She kissed Lollie's forehead, drank two cups of hot tea and forced down a bowl of cereal. Then she took off her apron and dress, and without even bothering to take down her hair or remove her underclothing and get into a nightgown, she lay down on her cot in the partitioned-off alcove that she and Addie's girls shared as a makeshift bedroom. She was so tired that she was asleep the moment her head touched the pillow.

"Miss Burton, Miss Burton, wake up!"

She struggled up from sleep, her unconscious fighting against waking. It was Flossie, shaking her shoulder. "Hurry, do hurry!"

"Lollie? Is she worse?" Geneva sat up, still disoriented but already swinging her feet over the edge of the cot while she reached for her dress.

"No, no, it isn't Lollie, it's Valerie! She's sick, she can't get up, she's awful sick!"

Geneva forgot about her dress and stumbled to Valerie's cot. Valerie's blanket was rumpled, her hair was disheveled from tossing, her face was flushed. It didn't seem possible. Valerie had been her usual, irrepressible self only last evening before Geneva had sent her to bed. Or had she? With Valerie, it was hard to tell, because she was so expert at hiding any tiredness or illness she might feel, determined to keep everyone else cheerful by her own cheerfulness. Feeling as though she were in the depth of a bad dream, Geneva put her hand on Valerie's forehead and told her to open her mouth.

"Turn your head, Val. Turn it so I can see your throat."

Her heart sank when she saw the telltale spots. Galen had said that the epidemic was over, that there were no new cases! Valerie couldn't have diphtheria, it wasn't possible! She had to fight against crying, against the despair that threatened to sap the last of her strength and leave her useless.

"I got it, ain't I?"

"Haven't I," Flossie said. "Miss Addie wouldn't like you to say 'aint.' Ain't you ever paid attention when she told us to talk like ladies?"

It almost undid Geneva. She had to turn away, so blindly that the room blurred.

"Flossie, bring a basin of water. We'll sponge her, try to make her comfortable. Don't worry, Val honey. We'll soon get you well."

"O' course you will. I'm too tough to be sick. Ain't nothing ever got Valerie Hopkins down, I'll be better by tomorrow, you wait an' see."

"We won't have to tell you how to take care of yourself," Geneva said, fighting to keep her voice light. "You're a nurse now, you know as much about the treatment as a doctor does."

"Drink all the water you can. Take nourishment. Keep breathing," Valerie croaked. "That's the most important part, keep breathing." She grinned, the grin as saucy as ever, but it was a weak effort for all that. Valerie was very ill, and Geneva had a premonition that she was going to be a lot worse.

Stop it! she told herself. Valerie's just another patient now. You have to remember that. You can't go to pieces just because she's your friend, because you've come to love her, as much as you love Addie and Roxie and Mary.

Somehow, she managed to keep her hands from trembling as she sponged Valerie's feverish body and helped her get into a clean nightgown. "Try to rest. That's the best thing," she urged, and miraculously, her voice was steady, too.

"Don't you worry, Miss Burton. No old diphtheria's going to get the better of me. There, I said that right, didn't I?"

"You certainly did. Addie would be proud of you." Geneva got the few words out as she pulled her dress over her head and left the alcove. An instant later her face crumpled and the tears burned and stung her eyes as they broke through the barrier she'd raised against them.

"Aw, now, Miss Burton! Com'on now! You can't go goin' to pieces on us, not now you can't!" Flossie begged her, her eyes wide with fright. "She'll be all right. Like she said, she's tough!"

Geneva groped for Flossie's hand and squeezed it. "Of course she'll be all right. I'm just a little tired, I expect."

"An' why wouldn't you be tired?" Flossie demanded indignantly. "There ain't one of us has worked as hard as you have, 'cept Valerie! Honest, Miss Burton, you can go back to bed for awhile. I'll sit with Val."

Geneva shook her head. She wouldn't be able to sleep, she'd be better off keeping busy. She went to check the ward, and found Lollie sleeping, a natural sleep that made her breathe a prayer of thankfulness. There was little doubt now that the child was going to be all right. All of the patients who remained in the hospital were going to be all right, it was only Valerie who was desperately ill. The thought struck her that if Valerie had had to be stricken, it was a blessing that it hadn't happened until she could devote her entire time to nursing her. The other girls could easily cope with the few patients left.

Addie's girls, Addie's brave, wonderful, spunky girls. Every one of them had been willing to risk her own life to help the diphtheria victims, while women who were considered far above them wouldn't have dreamed of exposing themselves to the grueling work and the danger of contamination. And Valerie was the pick of them all, Valerie was the one who had rallied them to volunteer, who had kept their spirits up, who had been indefatigable when the rest of them, Geneva included, had been ready to drop.

"Hey, whyn't you go to bed?" Valerie asked her when she went back to the alcove.

"I just thought I'd sit and talk to you for a while. We haven't had much chance for that, have we?"

"We've been pretty busy. But we done . . . we did good, didn't we?"

"You've done wonderfully well! No one on earth could have done better!"

"And now it's almost over, and we'll all be able to leave

this hospital and make new lives for ourselves. We can do it, I know we can, just like Doctor Forbes and you said we can."

"Of course you can do it! I've never doubted it for a moment."

"I think I'll go to Albany. That oughta be far enough away so's nobody there'll know about me. And if any gentleman does, I'll bet he won't tell. The gentlemen liked me, Miss Burton, they liked me real well even if I ain't as pretty as Flossie or Ethel Mae. I'm gonna set myself up in some kind of business, maybe makin' hats. I always loved fancy hats. And I'm gonna be a lady, and some day I'll get married to a good man and raise some children. I'm gonna be a lady. Maybe I'll even belong to the Wednesday Afternoon Sewing Circle, an' sing in the choir. I ain't been to church since I was sacked from the mill, there wasn't any way I could go, not doing what I was doing in order to stay alive, but I'd like to go to church again if you think the Lord wouldn't be mad about it."

Geneva swallowed, and her own throat felt sore, but it was from the tears she was fighting back, not from diphtheria. "Valerie, the Lord will be so happy to see you that there'll be rejoicing in heaven! Don't you remember that the Bible promises us that He forgives us all our sins, no matter how dreadful they are?"

"That's right. Go an' sin no more!" Valerie's hoarsened voice was triumphant. "It does say that. So I'll join a church. My voice is pretty good, maybe they'll let me sing in the choir. I'd like that."

"Try to get some sleep now, Val. The more you rest, the sooner you'll get well and be able to start that new life." Geneva smoothed Valerie's ruffled hair back from her forehead.

Valerie closed her eyes obediently, but she opened them again and winked at Geneva. "I'll have to watch my grammar, though, won't I? I've been makin' a lot of mistakes right now, but it's 'cause I don't feel so good. But I can do better, Miss Addie kept at us and kept at us till we can all talk right . . . correctly."

She slept at last, but it was a feverish sleep, restless and tossing. Geneva stayed with her, soothing her with a gentle hand and murmured words when she became too restless. Ethel Mae brought Geneva something to eat, a soft-boiled egg and a slice of buttered bread and some coffee. She ate, because she knew that she had to if she wasn't going to risk collapse, but the food was tasteless. Ethel Mae should have saved the egg for Valerie when Val woke up. Hens weren't laying well in this cold weather and they weren't easy to come by. How Roxie managed to collect so many to send to the hospital was something of a miracle in itself.

"Go and rest," Ethel Mae urged her, her brown eyes filled with concern. "I'll watch her for a while."

"No, you go and rest. I haven't been doing anything but sitting here, I'm fine."

She was still sitting there when Galen came for his afternoon hospital check.

"I can't believe it!" Galen's voice was filled with frustrated anger. "I thought we'd seen the last case now that the Maxwell lad and Lollie are better, and now poor Valerie has it!"

"I can't believe it either, but she has it." Geneva watched Galen's face as he examined Val, and her own diagnosis was confirmed even before he spoke. Valerie not only had diphtheria, but she had a very hard case.

Galen's own fatigue and his rage at this newest development made his voice harsh. He turned on Geneva, snapping at her with angry impatience. "Will you for the Lord's sake go to bed and get some rest? You look like the devil! It's bad enough having Valerie down sick, without your getting sick too just because you're too damned stubborn to take care of yourself!"

"You needn't concern yourself about me." Geneva's chin lifted, and her eyes regarded him with no hint of the hurt that she felt at his uncalled-for tone.

"I'm responsible for you! If I'd had a grain of sense I'd have sent you packing the first day you came here to the hospital. What am I supposed to tell your father and mother, if you collapse?"

"I'm not going to collapse, so you don't have to worry about it."

Galen's face hardened, and he turned on his heel and left. Damn the girl! He had to get out of here, or he'd make the biggest fool of himself the world had ever known. Why couldn't she remember who she was, that she had no business here in the first place? He'd better get to his own bed and get some rest, he was just about at the end of his tether.

Valerie tried to eat the coddled egg that Geneva spooned into her mouth at suppertime, fighting against the pain of her throat. She swallowed sips of warm tea, but even that didn't go down easily.

"Never mind, it won't hurt me to lose a coupla pounds, anyway. I'll be able to lace myself into a smaller waistline when I get to Albany."

At eleven o'clock that night Geneva finally allowed Fifi to sit with Valerie. Her body felt leaden as she lowered herself to her cot. Every ounce of her flesh and blood cried out for rest. She could have slept the clock around, but she was up at first light, her worry about Val refusing to let her go on sleeping.

Valerie was worse. Fifi, who was still sitting with her, knew it. She'd been crying, and her eyes were red and puffy.

"She's got it bad, Miss Burton. I'm scared."

Geneva's heart constricted when she looked closely at Valerie. She'd seen that look in patients before, that particular look of impending death. Her throat felt tight and aching as she motioned for Fifi to go and take her turn sleeping. Then she took up her place and steeled herself to wait.

Galen came in at nine o'clock. "There's nothing we can do now except try to keep her as comfortable as possible." His face was bleak, and he avoided looking at Geneva. Geneva knew without asking that there was no hope.

But still Valerie put up a fight. She was determined to live, determined to go on to the life that Geneva and Galen and Addie had promised her. Of all of Addie's girls, Valerie was the one who'd always had absolute faith that it could be done.

"I ain't gonna let it lick me," she whispered through cracked lips, her breath rasping painfully as she struggled to draw air through her raw and lacerated throat. "I'm . . . not . . . going to let it lick me. You wait an' see. Bring me another of those soft eggs, will you, Miss Burton? I gotta keep my strength."

She couldn't eat the egg. Geneva turned away blindly until she was able to compose her face and smile when she turned back to her again. "You don't need much nourishment just lying in bed. We'll try again a little later."

"Sure, we'll do that." Valerie closed her eyes, but then she opened them again, her expression different and almost sheepish.

"Miss Burton, if I don't make it, do you think I might be buried from the church, from First Methodist?"

"Don't talk like that! Of course you're going to make it!" Geneva's heart was breaking.

"But if I don't, do you think I could? I never wanted to go to any other church, I was raised Methodist. I got myself saved at a revival meetin' when I was only fifteen. I had to make up a couple of sins to confess, but I was so bound an' determined to be saved that I said I'd had bad thoughts about boys, an' that I liked to dance better than I liked to do my chores, and the evangelist forgave me and everybody prayed over me and I worried for a year that lyin' about those sins mighta kept my bein' saved from takin'."

She stopped to rest and struggle for breath, and Geneva marveled to see mischief on her face before she went on. "It was all right, though. Come next camp meetin', I went forward again an' confessed that I'd lied an' the evangelist forgave me again. Only I fell from grace but good, after I got sacked from the mill, an' now I don't know if there's any way I could be buried from the church."

"Val, don't! That's all in the past, now. You've been forgiven, you've made up for it a hundred times over. Don't try to talk anymore, conserve your strength."

"It's all right. It don't upset me none. I was lucky, didn't any man mistreat me, like happens to some girls. An' then Miss Addie took me in, I was one of her girls, an' it was wonderful. But if I don't make it, will you ask Reverend Tucker if I can be buried from the church? You can tell him that if I'd lived, I woulda gone to revival meetin' come summer, an' got myself saved again."

This time when Valerie closed her eyes, she went to sleep.

Two days later she was dead. She'd never uttered another coherent word, she'd been delirious until death.

Geneva's face was stark with grief as she told Galen of Valerie's last request. Galen's face was almost as stark as he told her that he'd see to it.

His face was livid with fury when he returned hours later and told Geneva that the Reverend Jebbidiah Tucker had unconditionally refused to allow Valerie's funeral to take place in his church.

"He told me he'd think about it, to come back in two hours," Galen told Geneva, his voice choked with his fury. "But what he did was go to Herndon Livingston and ask him if it would be all right, and Herndon told him in no uncertain terms that if he conducted a funeral service for one of Addie's girls, he'd resign from the church and withdraw his support, and take all of the merchants and well-off businessmen with him. But don't worry. I'm going to see Luther Carruthers at the Baptist church, and if he says no I'll see Daniel Bradley over at Congregational."

"Just any church won't do. It's First Methodist she wanted to be buried from," Geneva said, her voice breaking. "But thank you for trying, Galen.. I think she'd have understood, if it has to be from another church."

By that evening, word of Tucker's refusal to bury Valerie, and the reason why, had penetrated to the farthest corner of Athens. At the hospital, Addie's girls were wild with anger. Her face grim, Geneva laid Valerie out in the soft blue dress that her mother had sent over, one of Geneva's best, so that Val wouldn't have to be laid to rest in a dress that she'd used in following her calling. If she could have left the hospital, she'd have gone over to Jebbidiah Tucker's house and blistered him so badly with her tongue that he would have thought that he was already being roasted in hell.

Geneva had no way of knowing it, but Roxanne was at that moment in the Reverend's parlor, doing exactly the same thing, and in terms of authority that Jebbidiah knew she could make stick. Both Marvin and Bobo Burton were with her, and Roxanne had sent a messenger, by fast horse, to get to her father in Buffalo.

"And don't ever make the mistake of thinking that he won't come!" Roxanne said. "And he'll do just as I ask him, which will be to withdraw his own support from your church, just as the Burtons are going to. Bobo already has every Corinthian in Athens lined up to walk out en masse, and most of them will be the town leaders in another few years."

"Don't forget the little people," Bobo put in, for once his face serious, completely lacking its usual good humor. "Every mechanic or ex-mechanic in Athens is against you, and the canallers are gathering on the street corners, making plans that I'd as soon not know about. Everybody in this town knows what Addie's girls have done for us during this epidemic, and outside of a handful of 'more righteous than thou's', they're solidly against you. Christian charity isn't tied up in the pocketbooks of a few stiff-necked bigots, Reverend Tucker. The common people make up the backbone of the church."

He was interrupted by the ominous sound of a crowd of people who were converging on the minister's house. His face pale and his mouth trembling, Jebbidiah looked out of his window to see as many as two hundred people outside. They were canallers, mechanics, small shopkeepers and ordinary householders. Philo O'Brian, who was busy during these earliest spring days in helping to bottom out the canal to ready it for reopening, led the procession, and almost beyond belief, Minnie Atkins was beside him.

Jebbidiah's face worked. "I have seen the error of my ways," he said. Looking at him, Roxanne and Marvin and Bobo didn't think that he was being a hypocrite.

Three days later, Valerie was buried from First Methodist Church. Every pew was filled and people overflowed the church itself to stand outside.

Jim Yarnell and Ike Oldham sat with Mary MacDonald between them, Jim still weak but able to stand on his feet. Marvin and Bobo Burton and Cora Burton occupied their own pew, with Lillian Livingston and Addie. All of the mechanics were there, while Geneva sat with Addie's girls because her place was with them during this heartbreaking occasion.

The service was beautiful. Marvin Burton had suggested the theme, that no man can have greater love than to lay down his life for his brother. Valerie would have been proud of the tears that were shed. She'd made it. She was a lady at last.

27

Agnes Barlowe was taking a bath. The tin tub stood in the middle of the kitchen of the little white clapboard house that Wyatt Livingston had rented for her on the outskirts of Athens.

Agnes sat in the tub, her knees almost up to her chin, and luxuriated in the warm water and the scented soap. Her hair, dark and thick, was piled in a loose knot on top of her head and her body was well covered with lather. Soap like this was a luxury, but Wyatt was generous with her, she could afford it; she could afford all sorts of things now.

As small as the house was, and as unpretentious, to Agnes it was the culmination of a lifetime's ambition. A house of her own, and enough money, and a closet full of expensive clothes, and never having to raise her hand to do a lick of work except to keep the place reasonably clean, because Wyatt was fastidious about that, as he was about her keeping her body clean.

They should see her now, all those other girls she used to work with at the mill! Been uppity with her, they had. None of them had liked her, but who was sitting in the lap of luxury now while they didn't even have jobs anymore! Why, they had to whore for a living!.

To be perfectly truthful, Addie wasn't running that kind of a house anymore. Annabelle had married a canaller she'd help to nurse at the hospital, and the others had gone away, financed by Addie and Roxanne and the Burtons. But Addie had been a madam, and the taint would follow her to her grave, the stupid, silly bitch.

Imagine her being crazy enough to do a thing like that, when she was rich and a widow, and could have done anything or gone anywhere in the world, and was still young and beautiful so's she could have found an even richer man to marry the next time? You'd never catch Agnes being that crazy. She'd have known when she was well off and she wouldn't have cared a fig about getting even with her father. She'd have been long gone from Athens and kicking up her heels in London or Paris.

Adelaide Livingston and Geneva Burton and Roxanne Fielding: how Agnes had envied and hated them for having and for being everything that Agnes would never have, and could never be! And look at them now. Addie a madam, or an ex-madam, and Geneva an old maid, skinny and scrawny from being crazy enough to go and nurse destitute people with diphtheria and getting no thanks for her pains. Out to catch Dr. Forbes she was, and he'd still have nothing to do with her. Why, the whole town was laughing at her!

As for Roxanne, for all that her father was Earl Fielding and had all the money in the world, what did Roxanne have? She didn't have her husband, that's what she didn't have, because Agnes had him, and Agnes was going to keep him. Every time she saw Roxanne on the street, she laughed herself sick.

Here she sat, in a tub of lovely warm water, with all the scented soap she wanted and bottles of perfume to splash over herself after her bath, and she didn't have to get out of the tub till she wanted to, and after Wyatt had visited her tonight she could sleep till noon. Right at the moment, Agnes was a contented woman, so contented that she made purring noises in her throat as she worked up even more lather from the scented soap just for the extravagance of it.

She paused with soap and sponge in midair, her senses suddenly alert. Was that somebody at the front door? But of course not, nobody ever came to this house, nobody except Wyatt and he only came in the evenings. Likely it was children playing around outside or a stray dog walking across the porch.

No. There was somebody there! Agnes listened for another few seconds, and then she shrugged. It didn't matter. The door was locked. She always kept it locked. And the kitchen door was locked too. No one could get in, even if someone was there.

Someone was there, because there was a sharp rap on the front door, and then another. Go away, Agnes thought. Or go on knocking, see if I care. Wyatt had his own key and there wasn't anybody else she wanted to see.

She heard the sound of footsteps now, leaving the front porch, and then walking around the house. But the kitchen window shades were pulled down. There was enough light without having them up and a lady didn't take a bath with the shades up. Maybe it was a traveling tinker.

There was a rap on the back door now. "Go away!" Agnes yelled. "Whatever you're selling I don't want any!"

A moment later there was a crash and a tinkle of broken glass as the kitchen window broke. A parosol poked through and knocked the shards away. Agnes's eyes bulged, and she struggled to stand up, to reach the towel she'd left on a chair beside the tub, but the tub was small and she slipped, all soapy as she was, and she sat down again, so hard that she hurt her bottom.

"Whoever you are, you get outa here!" Agnes yelled.

The parasol was withdrawn, and then Agnes's face blanched as Roxanne crawled through the window to stand regarding her with contempt flaring in her green eyes.

"Get out of that tub," Roxanne said.

"You see here! You got no business busting into my house. Breaking a window to get in, that's burglary that is!"

"It isn't your house. It's my husband's. He pays the rent. I said to get out of that tub!"

Trapped, Agnes decided that attack was the best course to follow. What could the bitch do, anyway? And wait'll Wyatt heard about this, he'd be furious with his wife, it'ud be just as like as not to break them up for good and that would be all to Agnes's advantage.

"You go to hell! And get outa here the same way you came in, or I'll get out of this tub all right and I'll throw you out!"

Her words broke off in a yelp of pain as Roxanne's hands closed in her hair and yanked. Agnes came to her feet as she was hauled out of the tub, still yelping and writhing and slipping. Roxanne let go with one of her hands, and while she still hung onto Agnes's hair with the other, she let go with a slap across Agnes's face that snapped her head back and brought up a fiery red mark that began swelling almost instantly.

Contemptuously, Roxanne shoved her, so that she went sprawling on all fours. "Now find your clothes and get out. You don't live here anymore. You don't live in Athens anymore."

"Is that so!" Goaded beyond endurance, Agnes scrambled to her feet and launched a counterattack calculated to either lay Roxanne out cold or to send her scurrying to safety, glad to escape with her life. "We'll just see who lives here!"

It was a shame to have to do it, Wyatt probably wouldn't like it when he found out that she'd had to rough up his wife, but she had to defend herself, didn't she? And she was strong, she'd grown up tough, it wouldn't take her more than a few seconds to make mincemeat of this rich society bitch, sending her screaming for mercy.

Agnes had made just one mistake. She was strong, but so was Roxanne. Agnes had grown up rough, having to fend for herself, but Roxanne had grown up on the Erie. She knew more about dirty infighting than Agnes had ever heard of.

The fight was lively, but brief. Roxanne ended up with her bonnet ripped off its ribbons, her hair disheveled, and one bruise on an unmentionable place. But Agnes ended up shrieking and bruised from head to foot, her eyes streaming with tears of pain, her head snatched almost bald. She was a devil, she was! Wyatt's rich-bitch wife was a devil!

"Now do as I said and get some clothes on, and get out. You won't be coming back. There's a fast packet leaving in half an hour and you're going to be on it. I have a horse and trap outside and I'll deliver you to it myself. And let me give you a word of advice. Go as far as your money will take you, so you won't be tempted to come back. Because if you do, I'll be waiting for you."

"You can't do this! It ain't right! I'll have the law on you!"

Roxanne laughed. "Not unless you want to crawl to Ed Hanney's jail on your hands and knees to report me, dragging two broken legs!" She lifted her hand. "Move! I've run out of patience."

Agnes moved. First she backed away, and then she turned and ran. Roxie was right behind her all the way up the stairs, standing over her while she scrambled into the first clothing that came to hand and crammed what she could into the satchel that was all the luggage she'd had when she'd moved into this house.

"Brush your hair a little. Here, I'll do it." Agnes's hands, bruised and swollen, made such poor work of it that Roxanne snatched the brush from her and swept Agnes's hair into a knot and then jammed a bonnet on top of it. "All right, let's get started. I wouldn't want you to miss the packet."

Agnes obeyed, thoroughly cowed, although she was still seething with hatred inside. She couldn't lick Roxanne in a fight, fair or otherwise, and she had no choice. But if that bitch thought she could force her to stay out of Athens, she had another think coming! She'd be back as soon as the bruises faded and she looked decent again, and then it'ud be Roxanne out in the cold and who knew? Maybe Agnes would end up living in the Fielding house! Maybe Wyatt would divorce the shrew, and then she'd see that he married her. Then who'd be the queen of Athens?

Beside her, handling the lines as the trap bowled toward the canal and the fast packet, Roxanne's lips curled. "If you're thinking of coming back, you might consider that you'll have to walk, because I'll see to it that no boat on the canal will carry you, or no stage line, either. It isn't that I'd mind teaching you another lesson about the perils of helping yourself to another woman's husband, it's just that it would take time that I have better use for. Consider yourself lucky that I let you take some of your clothes. I could have burned them instead. After all, they're mine by right, because my husband bought them."

Agnes's face turned white under the bruises. My God, what would she have done, without her clothes? They, and the few dollars she had in her reticule, were all she had, but they were beautiful enough and gaudy enough so's she wouldn't have any trouble latching onto another man till she got back on her feet.

The *Pride of the Erie* was ready to cast off when they arrived. Roxanne's hand under Agnes's elbow hustled her aboard. Roxie smiled at the captain, a smile calculated to make him her slave. "Miss Barlowe has met with an unfortunate accident. Take good care of her, Captain Baines. Her destination is Albany, unless she desires to go farther. If she does, you can bill me for the extra fare. It gave me a great deal of pleasure to meet you. It's a shame that you're so pressed for time that we won't have the chance to get to know each other better, but if you're ever laying over in Athens, my husband and I will be delighted to have you for supper.''

Captain Baines rushed to hand her back into the trap. ''Good afternoon, Mrs. Livingston. It's been my privilege to serve you.''

''Thank you. Mind that you take good care of Miss Barlowe.''

''Right, Mrs. Livingston, ma'am. Albany it is. I'll see that she gets there, you need have no worry on that score.''

''Good evening, Mary. Where is Mrs. Livingston?''

Mary paused long enough in helping to fill bowls and platters to look up and answer Wyatt's question. ''I don't know, sir. She went out, she didn't say where. Will you be wanting to eat your supper here?''

Wyatt kept his expression blankly polite. His house was still filled with out-of-work mechanics, and Roxanne was heaven knew where, running around playing at being Lady Bountiful. What looked and smelled suspiciously like boiled cabbage with moderate amounts of ham seemed to be his evening meal! His bedroom had been taken over by mechanics. He himself had been relegated to a narrow, hard bed in a small attic room, one of the two bedrooms designed to accommodate servants. It was a bed that Roxanne was invariably asleep in before he came home to retire for the night! Wyatt had no quarrel with Roxanne's determination to go on helping the mechanics for as long as it was necessary, but this was no way to live. Bile rose in his throat every time he thought of what his life had become.

Face it, he told himself as he told Mary that he'd find some supper elsewhere, you're just what you appear to be. A kept man, living on Earl Fielding's money, holding down a job that was manufactured for you so that his daughter's husband wouldn't be a no-good sponger with no visible means of support. The fact that he did his job well had no bearing on it. He was a cotton mill man, he'd been raised to fill that capacity. It was where his talents lay, not running a shipping office for a line of canalboats.

His anger grew as he turned his steps toward the white

clapboard house where Agnes would be waiting for him. It was even more bitter because he suspected—more than suspected—that Roxanne wouldn't care a fig if she knew about Agnes. Roxanne had what she wanted, what she'd always wanted ever since her father had brought her to Athens. She was a Livingston, Mrs. Wyatt Livingston. She was the undisputed leader of Athens's society because Geneva didn't bother about such things anymore, and because Addie had placed herself beyond the pale. Mrs. Wyatt Livingston, the most beautiful young matron in Athens, in the county, probably in the State of New York. Women aped and envied her, men admired and lusted after her, and she reveled in it.

He admitted, in his less bitter moments, which were becoming fewer and fewer, that Roxanne had held up her part of the bargain. She'd never cheated him in bed. She never made any allusion to the fact that he was one of her father's flunkies, just an unimportant cog in the machinery of Earl Fielding's growing empire. But the fact remained that he'd been bought and paid for, in return for the prestige of his name. The fact remained that Roxanne didn't love him, that Roxanne loved money and social position and being Athens's reigning queen.

His face took on an expression of distaste as he thought of what was waiting for him in the clapboard house. The rooms would be cluttered, poorly cleaned and dusted because Agnes had no inclination to keep it the way Wyatt had been brought up to expect a house to be kept. She'd make him a meal, but it would be even more unpalatable than the ham and cabbage he'd declined at home, and the plate she served it on would be poorly washed. And then there'd be the bedroom, and Agnes herself.

Her animal sensuality, created to attract men, was coarse and common. No matter how well groomed she attempted to be, there was always something that grated on his senses. And he had to remind her, every time he came, that he wanted the sheets changed.

But she was pretty, she was accommodating, and she was available. She was good enough for what he needed her for, as good as he deserved. But sometimes, even in the act of making love, he felt the gorge rise in his throat as he remembered Roxanne, who was always immaculate, always perfectly groomed, her skin fresh and as sweet as summer clover. He turned to Agnes out of the desperation of his soul, seeking oblivion, no matter how fleeting; seeking, even though Roxanne had no way of knowing it, a kind of revenge.

His unhappiness, his bitterness, was exacerbated by what his father had done to the mill. The turnout, instigated by Herndon's discharging even more mechanics and cutting the wages and increasing the hours of those who remained, was still in effect. Herndon had been convinced that the mechanics would be so desperate after a week or two of unemployment that they'd come back under any terms he offered them.

He had been mistaken. Not a loom was running, and the mill, and the Livingston fortune with it, was about to be lost. With the looms standing idle, there was no way for Herndon to meet the payments on the loan that Henry Maynard had given him in return for Addie's hand in marriage. And as Addie herself now owned the bank, there was no possibility of Herndon gaining extended time to get the mill in production again.

In the continuing depression, there was no place else that Herndon could raise the money to meet the notes. Those banks and businesses that were struggling out of the doldrums had nothing to spare to risk on a strike- and debt-ridden mill.

If only he had been in charge! If only his father had been a different kind of man who'd listen to the advice of another, even if it happened to be his son! If only Herndon hadn't sold Addie to Henry Maynard, and so driven Wyatt away, the mill might have been saved. But Herndon listened to no one, he never had and he never would. And because of what he'd done to Addie, there'd been no way that Wyatt could stay on.

There were no lamps burning downstairs when Wyatt let himself into the clapboard house. He frowned, his sense of frustration and anger growing. Agnes had known that he would come tonight, but the chances were that she'd taken a nap this afternoon and was still asleep, drowsy and untidy in a rumpled bed, the room stuffy because she had an aversion to opening the windows to let in fresh air. The prospect was anything but pleasing.

He made no effort to be quiet as he ascended the stairs. His appetite, what he had left of it lately, had disappeared. He'd still get what he'd come for, an hour's blotting out of the most unpleasant of his thoughts until, sated, disgusted, he'd leave her and fill his lungs with fresh air again as he walked home. Even if he couldn't rid his mind of its self-loathing. At least this way he'd feel no need for Roxanne when he got home. She could sleep in peace without having to feign response to his desires.

The bedroom was dark when he opened the door, the window drapes were tightly drawn across the panes. He fought down the impulse to step backward into the hall as the stale scents of Agnes's presence met him: the faint hint of perspiration and unwashed sheets, dust and spilled powders.

His eyes adjusted enough to the dimness to make out a form in the bed. He didn't bother striking a light, tonight he could do without seeing Agnes's ripe body. He'd already made up his mind that he wouldn't ask her to prepare him a meal. He'd go to the Cayuga, where Joe Moody would find something for him that at least would be fit to eat. And maybe Bobo would be there. He hadn't seen much of Bobo lately, and he'd enjoy talking to him, as much as he was capable, these days, of enjoying anything.

"Agnes? Are you awake?"

A mumbled murmur was his only answer. Disgusted, but not deterred, his general anger at life itself driving him on, Wyatt took off his coat and draped it across the back of a chair. He never hung it in Agnes's wardrobe, where it would pick up the cheap scents from her dresses; not so much because he was afraid that Roxanne would detect them, but because of his own fastidiousness. He hoped, even now, that there'd be hot water at home when he got there, so that he could give himself a good scrubbing before he went to bed. There would only be cold water in the pitcher and basin in this room to clean himself with after he'd left the bed, while Agnes showed her amused contempt.

"Agnes?" he asked again.

Once more he was answered by a sleepy murmur. His mouth a hard line, Wyatt continued to remove his clothing. Naked at last, he approached the bed and lifted the sheet.

A pair of slender white arms raised to him and clasped him around his neck, and a faint, elusive scent, completely unlike anything that Agnes wore, made the short hairs at the back of his neck prickle. Something was wrong. He pushed up on his hands and arms to look at the face under his own, narrowed his eyes.

"Surprise!" Roxanne said.

Wyatt tore himself free from the clinging arms, and an oath exploded on his lips. "Roxie! What the hell do you think you're doing? Where's Agnes?"

"Where you can't find her, unless you want to go to one heck of a lot of trouble." Roxanne propped herself up on the pillows, her hair falling around her shoulders and half covering her breasts. Under the sheet, she was as naked as Wyatt. "What's the matter, Wyatt? If you need a woman, won't I do?"

"You little bitch! So you want to play whore, do you?" Infuriated, feeling like a fool and reacting with blind anger, Wyatt grasped a handful of Roxie's hair and yanked. "How did you find out?"

"I'd have had to be blind, deaf and stupid not to know you had another woman! Did you think you could get away with it forever? I knew where to go for my information. I got it out of Art Franklyn, and then I made Addie admit that she's known it for a long time. What's the matter, Wyatt? Can't you work up any enthusiasm for taking your own wife to bed, or do you only like whores?"

His mouth hard and grim, his voice seething with fury, Wyatt let go of Roxie's hair and grasped her shoulders, forcing her down flat on the bed. Even in the darkness, Roxanne could see the glinting of his eyes. "Why don't we find out? If you want to play whore, you'll be treated as one!"

Roxanne gasped as he came down on top of her, thrusting, relentless, his hands rough and demanding as he held her down. Roxanne used all of her strength and a trick or two she'd learned on the canal to throw him off. In another instant she was off the bed, screaming at him, her voice dripping venom.

"If you think you can treat me like your bought woman, you've got another thing coming! I won't be manhandled by any man, even my husband! When I take a man it's because I want him, and for no other reason, and you've given me damned little reason to want you these last few months!"

Wyatt moved like a coiled spring to reach her, and then he had her by her shoulders and was shaking her. "You'll take me when I want you to take me! As you just pointed out so charmingly, you're my wife!" Lifting her, he threw her back on the bed and threw himself on top of her.

There was no escape this time, he was ready for her tricks. He took her with a savagery engendered by all the days and weeks and months of his frustration, his humiliation at being Roxanne's paid-for husband. Roxanne's head threshed against the pillows as she turned it from one side to the other, writhing, fighting, her teeth bared as she endeavored to get away.

But even her strength was no match for his, especially in his present temper. And suddenly, her own blood began to race through her body, as flame spread through her, enveloping every inch of her, consuming her. Her arms were around him again, holding him closer, pressing him down on her as she lifted herself to meet each thrust. This was rape, but it was a hundred times more satisfying than all the nights Wyatt had taken her gently and with consideration, performing magnificently, but lacking the undiluted passion that he was venting on her now. At least this time he meant it, he wasn't doing his duty, he was taking what he wanted because he wanted it. For the first time since their marriage, Roxanne felt completely fulfilled, completely a woman.

They climaxed together on a wave that thrust them up into eternity and left them to tumble back to earth exhausted, limp and spent. It was a moment before Wyatt could speak, and then his voice was rough and hateful.

"Did you like it? Was that what you wanted?"

"Yes, that was what I wanted! Damn you, Wyatt Livingston, at least this time I had all of you! And I won't ever settle for less again!"

"You're going to have to, because I'm through being your lapdog, your kept man! Whatever you got out of this tonight will have to last you all the rest of your life, because I'm calling it quits!"

Roxanne hit him. She used every ounce of strength in her body. "You are not calling it quits! If you think I'm going to give you up, you're crazy! I love you, damn you! My kept man, are you? Whoever said you had to be my kept man? Do you think I need what my father's money buys us, do you think I'm not woman enough to be your wife no matter how little we might have, how hard we might have to struggle?"

She paused for breath, but it was only for an instant. Wyatt didn't have time to get a word in edgewise before she was screaming at him again.

"Where do you want to go, what do you want to do? I'll go with you, you can't leave me behind because I won't stay! You can take any job you want, anywhere in the world, and I'll be right there beside you! If things are rough, I'll work too. I'll be a laundress, I'll run a boarding house, but I'll be with you! We'll take what we have and get out of here just as soon as you want. I'll sell my jewels to give us a start, they're my own and they'll bring enough so we won't starve until we find something else to live on. But I'd go with you even if we didn't have anything, and don't you think I wouldn't! We'll make it on our own, but it'll be together. Do you understand me, Wyatt Livingston? I'm your wife, and there's no way on God's green earth you're going to get rid of me!"

Wyatt's mouth closed, and he swallowed. He made a fumbling, groping motion with his arms, and then let them drop back to his sides. Was this Roxie, his beautiful, arrogant, spoiled wife, the queen of Athens society, the girl who was convinced that her father's money would buy her anything she wanted? He couldn't believe it. She'd married him for only one reason, for the prestige of his name, of the Livingston place in society.

Now Roxanne was on top of him, shaking him, her fingers digging into his shoulders. "When are we leaving, Wyatt? It won't take me half an hour to pack! We can be on the first packet in the morning, east or west, I don't give a darn which direction we go. Wherever we go, wherever we stop, you're going to be a success because we'll be together! Nothing's going to lick us, we're a team!"

This time, when Wyatt's arms moved, they closed around her, held her with a desperate agony of hope. "You mean it? Do you really mean it?"

"You fool, you stupid, unmitigated fool! What do you think I've been telling you? I love you! You aren't going to get away from me, I'll never let you go!"

Wyatt held her closer, his face pressed against hers. He was trembling, the tremors starting in his arms and growing until they enveloped his whole body. Then he was crying, the first time he'd cried since he was a boy. A pet had died, and he'd learned, then, that when something was gone there was no way to bring it back. The only way to go on living was to find something else.

This time, the something else was right here in his arms.

It had been there all the time, only he'd been too blind, too stupid, to see it. Roxanne loved him. She loved him for himself, not for any of the reasons he'd thought she'd married him.

Roxanne drew his head down to rest on her breasts. "It's all right, Wyatt. It's all right, darling. We're going to make it, wait and see."

Make it! They'd already made it. Nothing else, no triumph, no success he might ever hope to achieve, could equal this. The past was dead, but the future lay before them, beckoning, offering everything they dared to take from it.

They lay there, holding each other, their hearts and bodies filled to bursting, until they came together again, slowly this time, sure of each other, to find a completion that they had only dared to dream of. Tomorrow, they would decide what they were going to do with the rest of their lives. Tonight, they had each other, and that was all that mattered.

Earl Fielding leaned back in his desk chair and puffed on a long cigar, squinting against the smoke that swirled around his head as he got the tobacco going.

"This is better," he said. The cigar finally burning to his satisfaction, he fixed Roxanne and Wyatt with his eyes. "I thought I'd walked into some women's dormitory when I opened the door of what used to be my house. Every time I tried to take a step I fell over another out-of-work mechanic."

"They had to have some place to go." Roxanne met her father's eyes squarely. "And I'm afraid you're going to be stuck with having them in your house for a while longer, and supporting them, too. It's a good thing you can afford it, because Wyatt and I are leaving town."

Earl's face showed interest. "You mean you're giving me your notice?" he asked Wyatt.

"I'm afraid so, sir. We've decided to strike out on our own."

"Sink or swim, that's it?" Earl's thick eyebrows rose.

"That's about it. I didn't exactly enjoy being dependent on you for my livelihood, even if it was a darned good one."

"If a job was offered you right here in Athens, would you stay? Not working for me, that is."

Wyatt's answer was cautious. "It would depend on what it was. I'm not looking for any more charity."

"Nobody's asking you to take any. As a matter of fact, it's somewhat the other way around. That's why I came back, Wyatt. Marvin Burton's been in touch with me, and we have a proposition to make you. How would you feel about taking over complete management of the mill?"

"The mill's closed down," Wyatt said. "My father couldn't meet the interest on his note, and Addie wouldn't extend him any more time. She wouldn't have given him more credit even if she'd been able to, which she isn't. She's about cleaned out all of her available resources, helping the mechanics. From what I understand, the bank's about to go under. She'll have enough left to live on in moderate comfort, and that's about it."

Earl put his cigar in the ashtray and clasped his hands behind his head, rocking his chair on its two back legs. "The Canal Commission is ready to extend a loan," he said. "Marvin Burton and I have talked it over with them. They've kept a good many banks afloat through this depression, as I have reason to know. With Marvin's and my promise to keep an eye on things, and to put Bobo in there to run the bank, they're willing to put up enough cash to keep the bank open and to get the mill running again, providing that you'll go in as manager and run it the way it ought to be run. I convinced them that you're capable of doing the job."

Wyatt's smile was without mirth. "My father would have a different opinion."

"Your father has nothing to say about it. He's through, Wyatt. Without you to step in, he'd be bankrupt." He turned his attention from Wyatt to his daughter, who was leaning forward, her face filled with animation as her interest caught fire.

"You wouldn't be able to keep up your house. The profits will be almighty thin for a while. It would mean that you'd have to move in with Herndon and Lillian, and pare expenses even there right to the bone. I wouldn't blame you if you didn't want to take it on, Roxie."

"Don't you worry about Herndon! I can handle him with one hand tied behind me! And I can run that house on a quarter of what Herndon's been spending. I'm able-bodied, and I'll lay odds that Lillian's not above wielding a dustcloth and boiling a pot of water! You and Wyatt concentrate on pulling the mill through, and leave Herndon Livingston to me!"

"That's what I hoped you'd say. It won't be easy. There won't be anything left over for fancy duds, or parties, I'm afraid. The Queen of Athens is likely to go shabby, and lose her court."

"Ha! If the Queen of Athens gives a picnic, with nothing but lemonade and cookies, it'll still be the social event of the year!"

Wyatt was pacing. "The expansion will have to be dropped, left to stand where it is until things pick up. But if the Canal Commission will advance enough for us to get started, the mechanics can work reasonable hours at reasonable wages. Not as much as I'd like to offer them, at first, but if we put it to them the way it is, I think they'll come back. They'll be assured of roofs over their heads, and three wholesome meals a day, and we'll dispense with some of those archaic rules my father and the rest of the cotton-ocracy imposed on them."

"We're all having to pull in our horns," Earl said. "None of us came out of this depression as well off as we went in. The mechanics aren't stupid, they realize that. But if we pull together, we'll make it. I'm banking on it, and so is the Commission, or we wouldn't be making you this offer." Earl broke off to look at Roxanne's stomach, and Roxanne laughed.

"It doesn't show yet," she said. "Give it time."

Wyatt's face turned the color of putty. "Oh, my God! Roxie, you little idiot, are you insane? Why didn't you tell me? I'd never have . . . you might have lost . . ."

"And I might have lost you, too, but I didn't. Why do you think I took such drastic steps to get you back and keep you? I was darned if I was going to raise a baby alone, while you went chasing around with some other woman! A child needs two full-time parents, if there's any way possible. And it'ud take more than a mere man to make me lose any baby I wanted to keep, Wyatt Livingston, and don't you forget it!"

"God bless," Earl muttered, his eyes rolling toward the ceiling. "No, don't tell me what the devil this is all about. I take it that you two had a dust-up. Well, it was about time; sometimes it takes a storm to clear the air."

"And this one was a dilly." Roxanne's face reflected sweetness and light. "I hope to repeat it some time."

"A grandson!" Earl stubbed out his cigar and promptly

reached for another one, changed his mind and reached for the bottle of brandy that always waited in one of his desk drawers instead and poured three glasses. He started to hand the first to his daughter and then snatched it back.

"None for you. My grandson's too young for alcohol."

"Your granddaughter wouldn't want it anyway," Roxanne told him serenely. They glared at each other until Earl started to laugh. He tossed his brandy down his throat, beaming.

"Drink up, Wyatt. You and me're going to celebrate! It'll be your last chance to let yourself go, because after tonight you're going to be too busy to lift a glass to your mouth. What are you going to name him?"

"We're going to name her Adelaide, after Addie. If you want a son, marry Jewel and get one of your own, you aren't too old yet by a long shot."

"I might just do that! This depression has hit me, but it hasn't wiped me out. If you aren't going to supply me with enough grandsons to run the empire I intend leaving, then I'll just go ahead and get a son or two of my own to pitch in and help the ones you'll have when you get over this idea of having girls!"

"Will you two stop it?" Wyatt demanded. "If Roxanne chooses to present me with a daughter, I hope it's just like her. If it's a son, I'll be elated, but either one will satisfy me. Right now we have to concentrate on having something to leave him, or her, as the case might be."

"Them," Roxanne told him, grinning at him. "If you think I'm going to stop with one, you have another think coming. I was an only child, and while I can't say that it ruined my life, I'd like for my children to have brothers and sisters to fight with. It gets tiresome just fighting with your father."

"God help us!" Earl said, throwing up his hands.

28

Even though Bobo knew that Roxanne had cut down the staff at the Livingston mansion, he was still mildly astonished at the length of time that it took for the door to be answered. He dropped in early on this Saturday morning to find out firsthand how things were going now that she and Wyatt had taken over the helm. His astonishment burgeoned almost to the point of disbelief when Herndon himself answered the door.

"Cyril," Herndon said. His tone held a hint of the distasteful, as though he were not at all pleased to find Bobo at his door. Bobo's amusement evaporated as he saw that Herndon's face was set in lines of grim anger that gave every appearance of having been there for weeks.

"Is Roxanne at home?" Bobo asked.

Herndon moved aside with scant grace to allow Bobo to enter. "She's in. You'll find her and Mrs. Livingston and Mary in the kitchen. If you'll excuse me . . . " With no offer to lead the way or to call Roxanne, Herndon turned to return to his study. The doors to the drawing room were closed, and when Bobo passed through the huge dining room he saw that it gave no indication of having been used for some time.

In the kitchen, cavernous enough to have catered to an army, he found Roxanne standing at the huge cast-iron stove. As he stepped over the threshold from the butler's pantry, he seemed to have stepped into bedlam, although another second or two showed him that there was order at the core of the seeming chaos.

Pots and pans simmered on the stove; Lillian Livingston, her once ultra-fashionable body completely wrapped in a voluminous apron, sat at a table slicing vegetables; Roxie was stirring the contents of a caldron; and Mary MacDonald, her face puckered with concentration, was packing plates and cups and silverware into large baskets.

"What the devil! Pardon me, Mrs. Livingston, but you haven't started a soup kitchen in this house, have you? I thought the need for them was virtually over, now that we're well into summer."

Her face flushed from the heat of the stove, Roxanne pushed her hair back off her forehead and laughed.

"Something a deal more practical," Roxanne told him. She thrust a long-handled spoonful of stew toward him. "Taste this."

Bobo tasted. "It's good."

"It had better be. Dear knows we've worked hard enough making it. Mary, you can slice the bread now."

"You haven't answered my question. What's going on?"

"Dinner for the mechanics. We decided that we'd take over providing their meals ourselves. We can feed them better, and for less outlay, than having their meals catered. Right at this stage of the game every penny counts, but Wyatt's making the mill pay, even though at a profit that's been cut until Herndon's about to have a stroke."

"He won't have a stroke. He's too ornery," Lillian said, her voice so cheerful that if Bobo hadn't been looking directly at her he wouldn't have believed that it was she who was speaking. "A stroke would impair his speech, and he needs his voice to rant and rave about how Wyatt's leading us down the road to ruin."

"I'll be d—" Bob caught himself just in time. "Jiggered! When you start out to do something, you don't use half measures, do you?"

"Darned tootin' we don't." Roxanne grinned. "I'm having more fun than a barrel of monkeys. We all are. And Mary's an angel. She's sticking with us and working like a draft horse, even though she's going to marry Jim Yarnell."

Mary's eyes went soft as she lived again the evening that Jim had proposed to her. They'd been alone in Roxanne's parlor, right here in this house. Roxanne had threatened mayhem on anybody who dared to disturb them. Jim's face had been grim as he'd pulled Mary out of her chair and put his hands on her shoulders to hold her fast. She hadn't had a chance of getting away, even if she'd wanted to.

"Hang it, Mary, I've had enough shilly-shallying! I love you and I want you to marry me, and even if I am nothing but a rough canaller, I'll make you happy or die trying! Will you or won't you, I want to know right now!"

For one brief moment, Mary had toyed with the idea of telling him that she'd think about it. It was no more than he deserved, taking all this time after she'd practically thrown herself at him in front of the whole of Athens! But the impulse had lasted no longer than that. Her eyes shining like stars, she'd pressed herself against him so hard it was as if she were trying to crawl inside his skin.

"I will. Oh, Jim, I will! You know I will—"

She hadn't had time to say anything else, because his mouth had cut off her voice. For a moment there she'd thought she was going to die of happiness, and what better way was there to die, except there was so much in the future that she didn't want to miss!

Bobo's face brightened as he turned to her now. "I heard a rumor or two about that. When is the happy event to take place?"

"In the autumn, just before the canal closes down," Mary said. "We're going to have our honeymoon on the *Undine,* all the way to New York City, and stay at a hotel there for a few days. I didn't get to see anywhere near enough that time I went with Miss Addie, and Jim's promised me that we'll explore every corner. Then we'll come back here, because I won't want to live away from Miss Roxie and Miss Addie and Miss Geneva. We're taking a house on Vine Street, right around the corner from Minnie Atkins. And when the canal opens next spring I'll be traveling with Jim on the *Undine* a lot, until—"

She broke off, her face flushing scarlet.

"Bobo's heard of babies before," Roxanne told her. "You can say the word right out loud."

"Roxanne, stop teasing her. I think it's wonderful. Mary, you know I wish both you and Jim every happiness. He's a lucky devil to get you. And now that it's settled, do you mind if I tell you that there were times when I felt like shaking your teeth loose because you couldn't seem to get it through your head that you and Jim are a perfect match? But you finally chose the right man, and I know you'll be happy."

There was a deep, joyful shine in Mary's eyes that tugged at Bobo's heart. "So do I. I was just awfully silly, thinking I was in love with Doctor Forbes. I admire him an awful lot, but it's Jim I loved all along only I was too stupid to realize it."

"You're anything but stupid. You're a bright, beautiful girl and you deserve the best and I'm glad you've got it." Bobo crossed over to the table where Mary was slicing bread and buttering it generously, and kissed her cheek. "A friend's privilege, and Jim had better tag me for best man for the wedding. I suppose Wyatt will want that honor but it'll be safer to pick me because there might be an emergency at the mill and he wouldn't be able to make it."

What Bobo really wanted was to ask Roxie about Addie. He'd been trying to see her for weeks, but every time he'd called, Carrie Flagg, her hired girl, had told him that Addie wasn't at home, when he'd known perfectly well that she was. Yesterday, frustration and the need to get away from the scene to gain a better perspective had driven him to Lyonsville where he'd put Cato up against half a dozen trotters. Cato had shown them all a clean pair of heels in all three heats. Limp or no limp, he was as good a man as the next, and better than most, and he meant to knock the nonsense out of Addie's head and marry her before they were both too old to enjoy it.

If frustration had driven him to the trotting races, curiosity had sent him to the outskirts of Lyonsville where a summer revival meeting was in full swing. There'd been talk around the racetrack about the preachers; Carlton Booth was the headliner, of course, but Matthew Ramsey was also one of the speakers. What he'd seen and heard had made him forever thankful that Addie had escaped marrying the man, even if she'd had to pay such a terrible price for her escape.

Now, in the Livingston kitchen, he didn't have a chance to ask Roxie to intercede for him with Addie, before Roxie, her eyes sparkling, asked him if he'd heard the latest tidbit.

"Philo O'Brian and Minnie Atkins are going to be married. Minnie took a lot of persuading, because Philo's Catholic. She's forty-six, mind you, but she made a big thing of the Catholic church demanding that any children of a mixed union must be brought up as Catholics, can you believe it?

Philo had his hands full, I can tell you, but he finally wore her down. The whole town is laughing, but everyone is pulling for them. It's time they both found happiness and it's certain that they'll only find it with each other. This is the first romance for either of them, can you imagine?

"Even so, Minnie's going to quit running the Athens Reading Rooms because she's convinced that most of Athens's ladies will boycott the place because she's marrying a Catholic, and she doesn't want to deprive anyone of the opportunity to enlighten their minds with good books. Not that she'll need to work now; Philo's on steady with Father's canal-boats. She'll have enough to do just monitoring Philo's drinking. Bets are already being laid on how successful she'll be."

"With you laying odds on Philo, no doubt," Bobo laughed. "I'd back Minnie, only I don't have any spare cash to throw away gambling, at the moment. This depression has made people resolve their differences out of court, without benefit of legal council. There'll be a backlog of cases, as soon as things pick up a little more. In the meantime I'm making do with my salary for running the bank."

"You poor thing, you!" Roxie scoffed. All the same, she was proud of him. He was making his own way instead of splurging on his father's money. She pushed the huge iron kettle to the back of the stove, away from the direct heat, and when she turned to face Bobo again, her face had lost its gaiety and was deadly serious.

"Bobo, Addie's leaving town! I've done everything but snatch her bald-headed to talk her out of it, but her mind is made up. She says she can't stay here where she's nothing but an embarrassment to Lillian and Wyatt and me, even though all her girls are gone and her house is respectable again. I was going to go and see you tonight to tell you about it."

Bobo's face was stricken. "Good Lord! Good-bye, Roxie. It was a pleasure to see you, Mrs. Livingston, Mary." The words were hardly out of his mouth before he was on his way across the street to confront Addie.

Leaving town! Going away, alone, unprotected, never to come back! He wouldn't have it, he'd let her get away from him once, and he was damned if he was going to make that mistake again. He'd tried to see her, on half a dozen occasions, but she didn't want to see him.

Blast the stubborn girl! She certainly knew how to make

herself unavailable. She went nowhere, not even downtown to shop—Carrie took care of all her needs. But Bobo hadn't given up, he'd just been coasting until he'd got the bank's affairs straightened out, thinking that what Addie needed was time, enough time so that her wounds could heal and he'd have a better chance of talking sense to her. She couldn't remain a hermit forever. But now it looked as if his time had run out.

Carrie answered to his knock, her face startled and frightened by his battering on the door.

"Mrs. Maynard isn't in—" Carrie had her orders, no one was to be admitted, not even Roxanne Livingston anymore, or Geneva Burton. Bobo pushed past her and barged into the entrance hall.

"No, you don't, not this time! Where is she?"

Carrie's frightened eyes moved toward the stairs, and Bobo was up them two at a time in spite of his limp. "Addie? Dammit, answer me! Get out here, I want to talk to you!"

One of the bedroom doors opened, and Addie, her face pale, stood there looking at him. "Bobo, you shouldn't be here. It isn't fair to your parents or to Geneva for you to be seen coming to this house. Please leave, before you do any more damage."

"My parents are perfectly capable of looking after themselves, and they wouldn't care if I stayed here all day and all night or never left!" Bobo ran his fingers through his hair, so that it tumbled over his forehead and into his eyes, making him look younger than he was. Addie remembered how stubborn he could be as a boy, in spite of his good nature. "Well, what I mean is that Father and Geneva wouldn't give a hang, and Mother always thinks what they think. What's all this about you leaving town?"

"I have to leave. You ought to realize that."

"You don't have to! What do you intend to do, go running away from Athens with your tail between your legs, just because you made a mistake that everybody who's worth thinking about knows was justified?"

Addie's face went even whiter. "You don't seem to understand. You know what I was, you know that I can't stay here where I'm an embarrassment to my family and my friends. I know the women of this town better than you do.

I'll never be accepted again. I'm putting this house up for sale, and I'm leaving."

"You've hidden yourself away for so long that your brain has atrophied!" Bobo yelled at her. "What do you intend to do for the rest of your life, hole up in some strange place with one hired girl and a cat and your knitting? You aren't even out of your teens, dammit! You can't bury yourself alive! I've damned well had enough of this. Get your bonnet, we're going for a ride."

"I don't want to go for a ride." There were tears in Addie's eyes. Why wouldn't Bobo leave her alone! Didn't he know what he was doing to her? The thought of leaving Athens, leaving everything she had ever known, and striking out on her own was terrifying. She'd die of loneliness without Roxanne and Geneva, without her mother. The prospect of growing middle-aged, of growing old, holed up as Bobo said in some strange place, afraid to make friends because her past might come out, was appalling to her. But what other course was open to her? She'd hurt her mother and her friends enough, she couldn't go on hurting them by staying here, no matter what it would cost her.

"You're coming if I have to carry you out to the gig and tie you in it! It's a beautiful day, and it's damned foolishness to skulk indoors when you could be out in the fresh air, enjoying yourself. Well, are you coming, or shall I actually carry you?"

Addie swallowed. He'd do it, it was there in his face. He'd carry her right out of the house and everybody on the street would see them and it would be all over town within an hour, adding to the scandal that already hung over her and causing Wyatt and Roxie and her mother even more humiliation.

A few minutes later, Herndon rose from his desk when he heard Bobo's gig move away from the front of his house, and his eyelid twitched as he saw that his daughter Adelaide was with him. His mouth grim with fury, he smoothed the twitch with his fingertips, but his concentration on the figures he'd been toting up was spoiled.

The world had turned against him. Wyatt, with the connivance of Earl Fielding and Marvin Burton and the Canal Commissioners, had taken his mill away from him. He'd been reduced to living as a virtual pauper in his own house, with more than half of its rooms closed off because his daughter-in-law said they couldn't afford to keep them open. His impotence to do anything to salvage the situation ate at him like a cancer. And now, this final indignity. Cyril Burton, his son's friend, his enemy's son, having the gall to take his disgraced daughter out in his gig, in broad daylight, right in front of his own house!

Only it wasn't his house anymore, except for the name on the deed. Roxanne had taken it over. Roxanne, with Lillian's connivance, ran it to suit herself, and together they'd turned it into a meal-catering station for his own mill mechanics! Herndon let the curtain drop and sat back down at his desk. Wyatt had asked him to go over these figures and bring them to the mill later in the day. Herndon knew that it was a sop, a ploy to let him retain some vestige of self-respect in the eyes of the townspeople whom he had reigned for so long. Wyatt would go over his tallies, read his recommendations, and then do as he pleased.

Lately, in spite of a lifetime of total abstinence, Herndon had begun to wish that he were a drinking man. If he could go to bed with his head muddled and his eyesight blurred every night, at least he wouldn't have to see the contented smile on his wife's face as she turned into Addie's old bedroom and locked him out.

Cato bowled along the road to Lyonsville, head high and stepping out as smartly as if he were remembering his victory there yesterday and would like nothing better than another race. Bobo glanced at Addie, dismayed to see that her face was set and that she wasn't enjoying herself at all.

"Just look at that meadow! The grass is lush. We'll have a good harvest this fall. The depression's back will be broken. All of the farmers are optimistic. It'll seem good to have things back to normal."

"Yes, it will. I hope there's never another period of such misery for the poor people the depression hit the hardest." Addie's reply was perfunctory, without real interest.

"Have you heard from any of your girls?" There must be some subject that would interest her! "They must have written to you."

"Flossie wrote to me, and Ethel Mae. Fifi doesn't know how to write, but she and Ethel Mae have opened a dressmaking shop in Syracuse. Flossie went to Albany, and Goldie went to Buffalo and she's opened a restaurant and Flossie's going to join her to help her run it. Ethel Mae has a gentleman friend and doesn't want to leave Syracuse, she'll probably get married soon." For a moment Addie's face lighted up, and it tore at Bobo's heart. "I just knew they'd be all right, they're all good girls."

"Of course they'll be all right. Between you and Earl and my father, they had every chance in the world of making it. Look at that colt over there! He looks as if he might make a trotter."

"Yes, he does."

Bobo repressed a sigh. "We'll have something to eat at the Lyonsville Inn. The food is good. I ate there yesterday when I took Cato over to race. I don't suppose you've heard how we showed our heels to all the competition?"

"Carrie mentioned it. Congratulations, Bobo. It must have made you proud."

"Not really," Bobo said with false modesty. "I knew that Cato could do it. I just needed to get the smell of money and ledgers out of my nostrils. I wasn't cut out to be a miser, counting up my profits, there's more to life than that."

"I suppose there is."

Damn it, it wasn't going the way he'd thought it would at all. But he still had an ace up his sleeve, and after he'd played it, Bobo was ready to bet that Addie would change her tune. A rueful grin spread over his face. She'd change it, all right, but she might come out of this frightening apathy of hers only to turn on him and hate him for what he was going to do. She might never speak to him again as long as she lived, much less consent to stay in Athens and marry him and squeeze the last drop of happiness out of life, with all the zest he knew she was capable of if only he could get through to her.

The Lyonsville Inn was a comfortable place, not as prosperous as the Cayuga but more than passing. Bobo ordered the best meal available, but Addie only picked at her food. She was too thin. She must be starving herself. If she went on like this she'd waste away to a wraith and then there'd be nothing left of her at all.

"Eat your pie," he told her. "It's good. Are you sure you don't want a glass of wine?"

"No, thank you. I'm not very hungry."

"Then we might as well go." Outside, Bobo handed her into the gig, but instead of turning toward Athens, he headed out the other side of town.

"Bobo, I really ought to go back now. I have a lot of packing to do, and arrangements to make."

"There's some place I want to take you. It's a surprise," Bobo told her.

For a moment, when Addie saw the camp meeting, Bobo was afraid that she was going to jump out of the gig and run. Her face turned so white, so stricken, that he was almost sorry that he'd taken this last desperate gamble.

"Turn around. I want to go home right now!"

"No! I want you to see this." HIs own face set in lines of totally unfamiliar grimness, Bobo half forced her out of the gig. "Do it for me, Addie. Do it for old time's sake, back when we were friends."

There were people everywhere, all looking at the young couple: the man insistent, the girl with her face pale to the point of fainting and anger in her eyes. Addie couldn't wrench her arm from Bobo's grasp and take to her heels without making a public scene, and every ingrained sense prevented that because she'd been brought up to be a lady under any circumstances.

Her legs felt as if they didn't have any bones as Bobo forced her to keep step with him. In the preaching area, all of the benches were well filled, but Bobo, disregarding common courtesy, made a place for them in the second row. Addie was shaking, and the trembling took over her entire body as Bobo half pushed her down onto the bench and she saw that Matthew was on the platform, in one of the usual straight-backed chairs, waiting for his turn to preach. Looking at her, Bobo prayed that she wouldn't faint, because if she did, then his gamble was lost.

She didn't faint. She sat as still as a corpse, her eyes half glazed as they riveted themselves on Matthew. Bobo died a little inside. But he had to go through with it, for her sake as much as his own.

The revival meeting was a carbon copy of the ones that were held outside Athens, at Chestnut Grove, every summer. The outskirts, where the riffraff gathered to make a mockery of the salvation that was offered only a few steps away, was fairly quiet at this time of day; the real activities of such a large gathering wouldn't get well underway until after dark. But the preaching was the same. Carlton Booth himself was up on the platform, his noble head thrown back, his fists pounding the podium in front of him as he exhorted the sinners who faced him to come forward and throw themselves on God's mercy and be saved.

Booth's voice went on and on, and Addie's trembling increased rather than decreased. Bobo was afraid that she'd collapse. Should he give it up, and get her out of here?

No! In spite of her fragile appearance, more fragile now than it had ever been, Addie was stronger than that. She could bear it. For her own sake, as well as his, she had to.

For three-quarters of an hour, Carlton Booth never faltered. But at last he gave way and gave Matthew a chance.

Matthew stood up, his steps deliberate and his eyes piercing as he glowered at the congregation. Addie's breath caught and she felt light-headed; her eyesight blurred and then cleared as she noticed, hardly realizing that she noticed it, that Matthew was heavier, stockier even in the short time since he'd left Athens. And his hair—there was something different about his hair. It took Addie a moment to realize that it was receding, if only a trifle, from his forehead; that in another few years it would have receded even more, emphasizing the almost imperceptible heaviness around his jaw, a heaviness that she'd once thought strong and masculine but that now gave the promise of turning into jowls.

It was a strong face, but there was no compassion there, no allowance for human weakness. Pressed close because the bench was so crowded, Bobo felt her shudder, a shudder that went all the way through her.

"Sinners!" Matthew bellowed. "Sinners, sinners, sinners! There is not one among you who is not a sinner—a vile, miserable sinner in the eyes of God. There is not one among you who does not deserve to be cast into the fiery pit of Hades and burn for all eternity!"

Addie's mouth tightened. Matthew had said "you," he hadn't included himself in his condemnation of the sinners.

"And hellfire is what is waiting for you, each and every one of you, if you fail to see the error of your ways! There will be no mercy at the end of your days: you will die in darkness, be cast out into the outer darkness, none of your entreaties will be heard after your lifetime of sin! Beware of the flames of hell, before the pit opens to receive you! This night, this afternoon, this very hour it might be too late!"

Bobo touched her arm, jerking his head toward a row of seats on the opposite side of the aisle. Addie looked where his gaze indicated, and she recognized Helen Plimpton, or rather, Helen Ramsey, Matthew's wife. Helen, her face thin and her expression one of intense anxiety, was holding an infant in her arms. Her dress was brown, with no trace of ornament, with no saving grace of well-cut lines to keep it from being dowdy. Her bonnet was of an even darker brown than her dress, without as much as a ribbon to give it any attractivness. The ties were narrow and the bow under her chin the smallest possible.

The infant stirred and whimpered, the whimper rising as it stuffed its minuscule fist into its mouth, obviously hungry. Matthew paused in his exhortation and glared at his wife. Her face went white, and she whispered apologies as she stood up and made her way down the row of people to the aisle. She was frightened half to death of Matthew's disapproval. Just because she wasn't able to keep her baby quiet while the preaching was going on. The poor little mite had probably been here since early this morning!

Dear God, Addie breathed, but she wasn't praying for forgiveness for her sins. Dear God, was this what she had sacrificed? A lifetime with a man with no saving grace of warmth or of humor? A man so filled with his own self-importance that his wife was terrified of him, his own baby not allowed to whimper when it was hungry!

Matthew's voice boomed on, beating against her ears. Repent! Repent! But what had they done, these hardworking, honest country people, these simple shopkeepers and housewives? What dreadful sins had they committed for Matthew to shout at them as if the very sight of them was an abomination to his eyes? Most of them were too busy with the struggle for survival to have either time or inclination for sin.

She turned a glazed, stricken face to Bobo. "Take me away from here," she whispered.

She'd had enough. Bobo's heart leapt as he stood up and made way for them. "Pardon me. Pardon me. Sorry. Excuse us, please," he murmured until they gained the aisle. His hand under Addie's elbow was strong and firm, and she felt that she would have collapsed without its support.

Addie's knees buckled as they reached the gig. Bobo had to half lift her into it. "Are you all right?"

"I'm going to be sick."

"No you aren't. You'd rather die than heave up your dinner in public. Hang on, honey, I'll have you out of here in a minute."

Cato was ready and willing to go. His nostrils flared as he stepped out, anxious to get away from the unfamiliar noises and smells, and back to his own sweet pasture at home.

They trotted through the town, and Bobo pulled up in front of the Lyonsville Inn again. Addie opened her eyes, which had been closed, to protest. "Oh, no, Bobo! I couldn't go in there again, not the way I feel!"

"I'll only be a minute," Bobo promised her. "Just hang tight."

He was as good as his word. When he came out, he had a bottle in his hand. It gurgled as he climbed back into the gig. Addie hardly noticed, she only wanted to get home.

Bobo didn't speak, and neither did she, until they were well out into the country. Then Bobo guided Cato into a side lane and pulled him to a halt under a tree that cast a circle of shade to protect them from the heat of the day. He helped Addie from the gig and urged her to sit down on the grass, with her back against the trunk of the tree. Then he busied himself opening the bottle.

"Sherry," he told her. "A lady's drink, but I'll have some anyway, if you don't mind sharing it. Ladies first." He handed the bottle to her. "Go on, drink some, you need it and it'll make you feel better."

Her teeth clattered against the rim of the bottle, but she took three or four swallows. Addie Livingston, Addie Maynard Livingston, sitting under a tree out in the country and drinking from a bottle! If she hadn't been so torn up inside the thought would have made her laugh, it was so utterly beyond belief.

"How could I have been such a fool! How could I ever have thought I loved him!"

"Don't be too hard on yourself." Bobo took the bottle away from her and helped himself to some wine. "He wasn' that bad when he was in Athens. Oh, Geneva never liked him much, and I didn't think too highly of him either. The pom posity was there, only it was well hidden, and you were young and inexperienced. And don't forget that he set out to charm you, with his eye on the main chance, the prestige of marrying Herndon Livingston's daughter and the hope of money to carry him until his newly exalted social position got him the kind of church he wanted, a prosperous church with a congregation made up of the best people.''

"I still can't believe that he could have changed so much! In Athens, his preaching was so much more gentle, he made people feel that he really cared about them."

"His preaching in Athens was geared to impress you, Addie. There was a flaw in his character, a bad flaw. He was set on getting you and everything that your name would bring him, and when it fell through he turned bitter and vindictive. He isn't a man who can stand up to trouble or disappointment. Even if you'd married him, sooner or later something would have happened that would have brought his real nature to the surface, and you would have had to suffer the consequences. He doesn't have what it takes to be a good minister. He's too selfish, too intent on his own ego and advancement. It doesn't excuse what your father did, nothing could ever excuse that, but at least Henry had the grace to die and leave you free. I'll lay odds that Matthew will live to be ninety.''

Addie reached out her hand for the bottle. Her trembling had abated, but she still felt shaky, and now her tears spilled over. "Poor Helen! I'm so sorry for her, Bobo. She looks as if she's afraid of her own shadow."

"She's afraid of Matthew's shadow. You'd better thank God for sparing you, even if you had to go through another kind of hell before you were free."

"I'll thank you first, for dragging me here today. Otherwise I'd have gone on grieving for Matthew for as long as I'd lived. Now at least I can bury his memory. Wherever I settle I won't have to battle against a broken heart as well as loneliness."

"You're not moving away from Athens," Bobo said. "I forbid it." He took the bottle back from her and helped himself to another drink. "You're staying right in Athens, and after you've got over the shock of seeing what you might have been stuck with all your life, you're going to marry me."

"Bobo, don't be crazy! You know I can't marry you, I can't ever marry anybody. I'm what I made myself, an ex-madam, a woman to be shunned."

"You aren't even a woman. You're a girl. You'll be a woman after I've married you and taught you what being a woman is all about. A beautiful, adored, worshiped woman."

"Even if I loved you, I couldn't marry you. You'd be ruined, your name would be blackened, your family would be disgraced! And what if there were children? Oh, Bobo, it would be awful! We'd have to move away, somewhere where nobody had ever heard of me. Just like Fifi and Goldie and Ethel Mae had to go away, and even then someone would be bound to find out, and our children's lives would be ruined."

Bobo handed her back the bottle. "Have another drink. We aren't moving away, we aren't going to run. We're going to stay where we belong, in Athens. Blackened name—balderdash!" He took the bottle back. "Take it a little more slowly, honey." The bottle tilted as he had some more. "I hate that word—balderdash. It makes me sound a hundred years old, but it fits the occasion. Balderdash! The story of what you did is already turning into a legend. By the time we have children, it'll be something for them to brag about. Our friends aren't going to turn their backs on us, and they're the ones who really count in Athens. As long as my father and mother, and Geneva, and Roxie and Wyatt accept us, do you think anybody else will dare to look sideways at us? Not if they value their social standing, they won't! Here, have a little more, you still look shaky."

"You're insane. You're only trying to be kind. You don't want to marry me, you just feel sorry for me."

"I'll show you how much I feel sorry for you!" Addie had scarcely swallowed when he took the bottle away, corked it very carefully, set it aside, and caught her in his arms.

His mouth came down over hers. He held her so tightly that she couldn't breathe, he kissed her as she'd never imagined any girl could be kissed. Not a discreet, gentle caress, such as Matthew had bestowed on her, well within the dictates of decency before they were married; and a thousand miles away from the slobbering, slavering kisses that Henry Maynard had forced on her shrinking lips while she'd fought down nausea at his very touch.

It couldn't be true, there was no such thing as a kiss like this, there was no such thing as a man like Bobo holding her and kissing her and making her head swim. Making her forget everything she had to remember, that she was an ex-madam, that any association with her would ruin even a Burton.

She was trembling again, and this time it went all the way through to her core. Bobo was her friend. She'd grown up thinking of him almost as another brother, a funny, kind, always laughing and joking brother but never, even in her wildest imaginings, anything like this forceful man who was turning her bones and willpower to jelly.

Bobo let her up for air. Her lips were throbbing and swollen. Her heart was pounding and her blood was racing. She couldn't breathe.

"Damn it, Addie, don't you know that you're mine? Don't you know that I'll never let go? You might as well give up right now, because I'm going to have you. There's no way you're ever going to get away from me."

"Insane!" Addie whispered.

"If we're insane, then long live insanity!" Bobo caught her tight against his body again, and she felt herself melting into it.

"I can't. We can't!"

"You can. We can. And we're going to." Bobo retrieved the bottle, uncorked it, and handed it to her. "Have a little more, you've had a shock. I don't want to take you back to Athens all white and shaking. We're going back with our heads high and our banners flying and the devil take anybody who doesn't like it!"

"Bobo, you aren't being fair. I'm all confused."

"You don't have to think. Let me do the thinking. If you want to think, think how wonderful it'll be when we're married. Think how furious your father will be, when Wyatt and Roxanne force him into recognizing your existence again. Your revenge will be complete, and you won't even have any more reason to go on hating him and ruining your life trying to hurt him."

"That's a terrible reason to get married!"

"It is, isn't it? So we'll leave him out of it, and get married just for ourselves." Bobo looked at the bottle, hesitated, and then shrugged and tilted it again.

"You're getting drunk. How are we going to get home?"

"Cato isn't drunk, and he knows the way." Once again, Addie's protests were shut off as Bobo covered her mouth with his own and all the pent-up fires of longing and yearning flared into life in her body. Oh, God, she'd been so alone, but now she wasn't. And more, this was Bobo, her own, dear, familiar beloved Bobo. He wasn't ever going to let her go and she was glad. Maybe they were crazy but it was a wonderful kind of craziness and she hoped that she'd never be sane again. In all the world, there was nothing but Bobo—his hands on her body, his mouth bruising hers, the two of them melded together and soaring into the sky as if the earth had no power to hold them prisoner. Something wonderful had happened today. Today was the day she'd been born.

They returned to Athens in the last traces of a glorious sunset, the low-hanging, fluffy clouds on the horizon streaked with every shade of pink and red. Cato was still stepping high, and Addie was snuggled close to Bobo, his arm around her, her head on his shoulder.

They bowled down Seneca Street, and people turned their heads to stare after them, their eyes popping out as they were already forming words to describe this latest scandal to their friends who hadn't been fortunate enough to have seen it for themselves. Bobo Burton and Adelaide Livingston Maynard—both of them inebriated, if they were any judge, and behaving in a disgraceful manner right on the main street of Athens! Herndon Livingston would be fit to be tied, and what would Lawyer Burton have to say about it?

In an upstairs window of the Livingston mansion, Roxanne and Lillian watched as Bobo pulled Cato to a halt in front of Addie's house. He lifted her from the gig and walked hand in hand with her to her front door. Then he took her in his arms and kissed her. The kiss went on and on. Roxanne thought that it was—with the exception of the way Wyatt kissed her these days—the most thorough kiss she had ever seen.

"Oh, my!" Lillian said.

Roxanne hugged her. "And isn't it just about time!"

29

There was no way that Galen could get out of going to Addie and Bobo's wedding. He dreaded it because Geneva would be there. Being thrown into her company both at the wedding and at the reception afterwards would cause him even more mental distress than he'd been experiencing ever since she had left the hospital to return home.

Galen no longer tried to deny the truth to himself: he loved Geneva, loved her with a deep and abiding love that would exist for as long as he lived. There could never be any other woman for him, and therefore there would be no woman at all; because even if Geneva didn't hate him as he deserved to be hated after the way he'd treated her, what did he have to offer her? A struggling doctor with his income couldn't even provide her with a proper home or enough money to keep her adequately clothed, much less maintain her position in Athens's society.

In his utter misery because the problem was so unsolvable, he'd given serious thought to leaving Athens and starting over in some other town. But he'd come to love Athens, and to love even more his patients. Galen's patients liked him, trusted him, depended on him; to leave them would amount to desertion.

So he stayed on, miserable, spending sleepless nights tossing and turning on his hard bed at the back of Harding's house. He could have afforded to rent himself a room elsewhere, except that he was forever moved to spend what little hard cash came his way in buying nourishing food or adequate clothing for the children whose parents couldn't afford those things for them.

The children accepted the gifts shyly, their faces shining, taking a turn for the better because of the wonder of having them. Their parents were apt to be inarticulate with gratitude, but they loved him and they knew that his gifts were bestowed out of love, or else they would have been too proud to accept them even for their children.

What would they do if he were to leave? When one of their children became ill in the night, they didn't dare call Dr. Harding or one of the other doctors in Athens because they couldn't afford the fee. Galen would always wait. He never asked for money for his services if the family was experiencing hard times but only accepted it when it was offered, sometimes weeks after he'd been called and more often than not only a part of what was owed simply because they had no more to give.

His practice would build, with time. His reputation as a good physician was growing. But there would always be the poor, and he knew that even after Harding retired, he would still be compelled by his conscience to care for them.

He dressed in his best for the wedding, which was to take place at First Methodist, even though it was only a small affair, with only close friends of both families invited to attend. As a widow, Addie could not have an elaborate wedding—it would be beyond the dictates of good taste even for someone as uncaring about the mores of society as Bobo.

Galen knew how hard it had been to arrange for Addie and Bobo to be married in the church. If Herndon Livingston had had anything to do with it, there wouldn't have been a wedding at all. Galen, of course, had not been present at the confrontation between Herndon and his errant daughter, but Bobo had, and Bobo had given Galen a blow by blow account of it.

Herndon's fury when he'd learned that Addie was going to marry Bobo had been without bounds. For her to have the effrontery to marry at all, after her recent professional occupation, was enough to set his rage off, but the idea of her being married in Athens, and in church, was too much to be borne. To make a spectacle of herself, and worse, to make an item of low gossip and a laughingstock of him, had all but sent him into apoplexy.

Immediately he'd heard, he'd ordered Roxie to cross the street and instruct his daughter to present herself to him at once. Roxie's first impulse had been to refuse to run the errand, but on second thought she couldn't resist seeing the sparks that were sure to fly.

Addie's response had been for Roxie to tell her father that she had no intention of setting foot in his house, that if he wanted to see her he'd have to come to her. Roxie had had all she could do to suppress her grin when she'd relayed the message. For a moment, she'd thought that her father-in-law was actually going to have a stroke at the idea of entering Addie's house of infamy. But half an hour later, dressed as formally as though he were attending a funeral, he crossed the street and brought the knocker down once, very sharply.

If he'd expected that the door would be answered by some young lady of ill repute whom Addie was still harboring, his bracing for the encounter was unnecessary. It was Bobo who opened the door.

"Good afternoon, Mr. Livingston. Addie is expecting you. If you'll come into the parlor?"

His back stiff and his face registering his outrage, Herndon declined the chair that was offered, and turned first not to his daughter but to Bobo.

"Cyril, I am forced to believe that you have taken leave of your senses. If what Mrs. Livingston and my daughter-in-law have told me is true, that you intend to marry Mrs. Maynard, then you must indeed have gone mad. I can only hope that the condition is temporary, and that you will return to sanity as soon as you have had time to give the matter proper thought."

"If I'm loony, then I hope to stay that way forever!" Bobo told him cheerfully. He stood behind Addie's chair with his hands on her shoulders. "Because Addie and I are going to be married, and I've never been happier in my life."

"Young man, have you no conception of what such an alliance will do to your family's name?" Herndon demanded.

"It won't do anything but bring it additional honor," Bobo told him. "My family, and that includes not only my father and Geneva but my mother, are tickled to death about the whole thing. They only wish I'd been able to talk Addie into it sooner!"

For the first time, Herndon steeled himself to look at his

daughter, even though he still would not make the concession of calling her by her first name.

"Mrs. Maynard, you must be cognizant of what this alliance will do to Cyril, as well as to the Livingstons! It's beyond decency. I can't imagine that even you can be so depraved that you are willing to trample two fine families into the dirt!"

"Father,"—Addie's voice was as sweet and pleasant as if she were passing the time of day—"you forfeited any right to dictate to me when you sold me to that fat lecher Henry Maynard. I am going to marry Bobo, and there's nothing you can do to stop me."

Herndon's face became even more grim, although neither Addie nor Bobo would have thought it possible. "In that case, I trust that you are at least going to be married in some other town, and take up your residence well away from Athens."

"In a pig's eye," Bobo said. There was a smile on his face, but his eyes were steady and unflinching. "We're going to live right here in Athens where we belong, where our families have lived for generations and where our children will live, hopefully until they die. The wedding will take place at First Methodist, and you may come or not just as you please. But whether you come or not, it *is* going to take place, and Addie and I *are* going to be happy. You might as well resign yourself to that fact."

Addie rose and reached for Bobo's hand. He took hers and squeezed it, giving her the full support of his love.

"I think we've both said everything that needs to be said," Addie told her father. "If you will excuse me, I will bid you good day." And then her composure broke. "Father, if you'd once, even once, told me you were sorry for what you did to me! If you'd come to me and admitted that you were wrong, if you'd lifted one hand to help me when I needed you, while Henry was alive, I might have been willing to let bygones be bygones. I got even, and that could have been the end of it. But even now, you *dare* to come to my house and tell me that I have no right to marry Bobo. For that I will never forgive you! No, not ever! And . . . and you needn't expect me to name any of my children after you, either! I'd rather name them after the devil!"

Bobo's arms went around her and he held her shaking body close. His eyes were like steel as he looked at Herndon.

"I think you'd better leave. As Addie said, everything has been said that needs to be said."

Herndon left, but he hadn't finished with them yet. He used all of his influence to persuade Jebbidiah to refuse them a church wedding. Only the prospect of losing both the Burtons and Earl Fielding as his parishioners, as well as Wyatt and Roxanne, had persuaded the minister that a reformed madam should be granted readmittance to First Methodist. There were the Corinthians to be considered as well, all of whom would soon head their own substantial families. As Bobo's friends, their support would be lacking if Jebbidiah did not see fit to exercise Christian forgiveness.

And so the wedding was taking place in spite of Herndon Livingston's efforts to stop it, or at least force it to take place in some other locality. As nervous as Galen was, he couldn't help but notice that it was Wyatt, and not Herndon (who was conspicuous by his absence), who gave Addie away. But there was no doubt at all that neither Addie nor Bobo gave the absence of the father of the bride a thought. Bobo looked as if someone had just handed him a piece of heaven on a silver plate, and Addie's face glowed with a happiness that made Galen ache.

Everybody was getting married, Galen thought, swallowing past the tightness in his throat. First Philo O'Brian and Minnie Atkins. Two weddings for them, as a matter of fact, because Philo would never have believed it was a genuine marriage unless it was performed by a priest, and Minnie would never have believed it was legal unless that was followed by a ceremony by Jebbidiah Tucker, even though the later ceremony was a completely private one in the parsonage, with only her friends Marian and Walter Applegate as witnesses.

Galen remembered the weddings well, and even in his present state of misery he couldn't keep a grin from spreading across his face. After the Catholic ceremony, a few of Philo's friends had taken him and Minnie to the Cayuga for a celebration, and Philo had proceeded, in his euphoric happiness, to get roaring drunk. And, Philo having made myriads of friends in Athens, word of the celebration had spread like wildfire and more and more people had come to join in the celebration, until it had turned into a riotous shindig that those who participated in would remember fondly all the rest of their lives.

At the second ceremony, performed the following morning, the Irishman had hardly been able to stand on his feet and Minnie had been mortified. But not, by any means, as mortified as Philo had been when Minnie's friends had a special celebration of their own for the bride and groom, consisting of tea and cakes, prayer and the singing of hymns. To Philo, no other woman in the world would have been worth the misery of that hymn-singing day, with every booming amen reverberating against his hung-over head like a hammer on an anvil.

And come autumn, shortly before the canal closed down for the winter, Mary MacDonald and Jim Yarnell were going to be married. Jim had already bought the cottage around the corner from Minnie Atkins's house for them, and Mary was sewing curtains and fixing it up during what spare time she had from helping Roxanne and Lillian cater the mill mechanics' meals. The mill was already showing a small profit, nowhere near enough to satisfy Herndon, but enough so that Wyatt and his backers knew that it was possible to get it back on its feet.

There was no way that Galen could keep his eyes off Geneva, who served as one of Addie's two attendants, the other being Roxie. Geneva had chosen a dress of silvery gray, not wanting to detract one iota from Addie's splendor. Roxie was dazzling in her vivid green. And Addie herself was as lovely as an angel in blue that exactly matched her eyes. She looked too young and innocent to be a bride, much less an ex-madam.

But if Geneva thought that the gray she'd chosen would make her fade into the background, she was very much mistaken. The color brought out the luminous gray of her eyes; the creamy richness of her skin, so that just looking at her made Galen tremble. His patients were forever becoming ill or being injured at the most inconvenient times; why couldn't one of them have chosen to have his crisis today rather than tomorrow, so that he would have had an excuse to stay away?

His mouth tightened as he glared at Bob Maxwell, who acted as Bobo's best man. Young Maxwell was dressed in all his Corinthian splendor. His pearl gray trousers were skintight, and his ruffled shirt was dazzling. His moonstruck eyes were fastened on Geneva as though he wanted to eat her up. If it was miserable to see Geneva now, what would it be like after she'd married the young nincompoop? And it was distinctly possible that she would marry him. The Maxwells were one of Athens's leading families; Bob had money and breeding behind him, and a good education. Of all the infatuated young men who'd been hanging around Geneva like flies around a honeypot ever since she'd broken up with Wyatt, Bob was the most eligible. All the same, the idea made Galen sick to his stomach. The boy was nowhere near good enough for her. As far as that went, what man was? Geneva was one in a million, and seeing her mated to any of the young swains who were competing for her would be as bad as seeing pearls cast before swine.

His mouth tightened still more as he thought that the same thing held true in his own case. He wasn't good enough for Geneva either, and not only that, he was the biggest damned fool who'd ever walked the face of the earth. The way he'd treated her was enough to make her hate him, even if he'd been as well established as Stephen Harding and had family and social prestige behind him.

The knot in his stomach tightened painfully as he saw Geneva smile at Bob, and give a slight nod in response to some unheard question that must have formed on the young man's lips. Get a grip on yourself, damn it, Galen told himself. You're either going to have to get used to it, or leave town. And if he left town, left all the people who depended on him, because of a woman, he'd be as bad as David Harshey and not fit to call himself a doctor.

He was jolted out of his brooding as the final words were said and Addie lifted her face to accept Bobo's kiss. For a moment, Galen found himself grinning again, because the parson was beginning to look scandalized. Somewhere toward the back of the church a woman tittered as the kiss went on and on.

It was Roxie who broke it up, hissing "Bobo, you're in church, not in your bedroom!" Unfortunately, although the remark was intended to be a whisper, Roxanne's voice carried to all the nearest pews. Galen's grin widened. Another juicy tidbit for Athens to crow over.

Addie's face was scarlet but her eyes were shining with a

happiness that was enough to make the most disapproving matron feel tears sting her eyes. Bobo finally let her go, and as the bride and groom walked down the aisle, the guests rose from their pews to repair to the Burton house for the reception and wedding supper.

When he had gained the outside of the church and made to turn in the opposite direction, having no intention of attending the festivities where he'd have to eat his heart out over Geneva again, Galen found Jim Yarnell on one side of him and Mary MacDonald on the other.

"None of that!" Jim said. "Come along, you have no excuse to duck out and it would be an insult to the Burtons. Mary and I will stick close to you and you can leave early, but you're going!"

"Doctor Forbes, why don't you go after Miss Geneva, instead of letting Bob Maxwell court her?" Mary clapped her hand over her mouth, nearly dying of mortification. But all the same, why didn't he? She'd come so close to making a mistake that would have ruined her own life that she couldn't bear to see Galen being as great a fool as she'd almost been.

"I'm hardly in a position to court anybody, let alone Miss Burton. Besides, she hates me." Galen's voice was stiff.

"And I don't blame her," Mary said. "All the same, you could apologize, and tell her how you feel about her. It wouldn't hurt to try."

Galen shook his head. "I lost my chance a long time ago, and now I'll just have to make the best of it. But I'm happy for you and Jim. It's good to know that your friends get what they deserve, when what they deserve is the best."

Why was it, Mary wondered rebelliously, that the good Lord had seen fit to give men all the strength and women all the brains.

The Burton house was filled with freshly cut flowers, and every piece of furniture gleamed with beeswax and elbow grease. It was the perfect setting for a girl like Geneva, and it served to bring home to Galen even more forcibly that he had nothing to offer her that could in any way compare with what she would be giving up. Seeing her here, in the midst of her family and friends, in the position in life to which she'd been born, made him want to turn tail and run. But Jim's hand was clamped on his arm and Mary was still pressed close to his other side as they moved him on to the reception line

Somehow, he managed to compliment Cora Burton on the perfection of the wedding; he managed to congratulate Bobo and kiss Addie, a kiss that was heartfelt because she was one of his favorite people in the world. And then he was face-to-face with Geneva. She'd gained back most of the weight she'd lost while she'd been working at the hospital, and she had never been more beautiful, more desirable, more unobtainable.

"It was a beautiful wedding. I'm happy for Addie and Bobo." As inane as it was, it was all he could think of to say, and he felt like a fool.

"Yes, it was. I'm happy for them too."

Bob Maxwell was still sticking to her side as if he'd grown to her, and Galen felt a sudden murderous rage well up in him. Maxwell's air of proprietorship made Galen ache to knock that smug look of ownership off his face.

"I wouldn't if I were you," Jim warned him as Galen turned away before he could make an even bigger fool of himself. "You may not know it, but young Maxwell was the champion of his boxing club at Harvard. He'd floor you so fast you wouldn't know what hit you, and you might as well leave town afterward because men don't go around walloping their rivals at wedding parties, it isn't done."

The red tide of fury receded and Galen regained control of his sanity. He let Jim and Mary herd him to the refreshment table and accepted a glass of punch, well laced with brandy. Galen wasn't a drinking man. He held a strong conviction that doctors who drank were as bad as doctors who cared more about making money from their wealthy patients than about caring for the more unfortunate. But the punch hit the spot this time, and he helped himself to a second cup.

"Drowning your sorrows?" It was Roxanne, her voice cool and filled with amusement. "Galen, you're more of an idiot than I thought you were. Come along, I want to talk to you." She linked her hand under his arm, and he had no choice but to follow her. She led him to a small room tucked away at the end of the entrance hall, a room that he hadn't known existed.

"Marvin's sanctuary. He keeps his more valuable books and papers in here, and transcripts of cases that shouldn't come to anyone else's eyes. I'll bet he has enough secrets stashed away in here to turn this whole county on its ear, even if the place is hardly bigger than a closet."

Galen couldn't have been less interested in secrets that could turn the whole county on its ear. "You said you wanted to talk to me."

"And I do. Sit down." When Galen didn't move to obey her quickly enough to suit her, she gave him a push that plunked him into a leather chair, its seat and back indented from years of contact with Marvin Burton's body.

Her hands on her hips, Roxanne loomed over him, regarding him as though she wasn't sure whether he were a complete moron or merely someone who wasn't worth her attention.

"Are you just going to go on dragging your feet and let Geneva throw herself away on Bob Maxwell? What kind of a man are you, anyway? I would have thought you had more gumption!"

"If it's any of your business, which it isn't, Geneva wouldn't have me even if I asked her. And I'm not about to ask her. You ought to know as well as anyone that I'm in no position to ask her. And besides, she wouldn't have me even if I were a millionaire who could give her the moon."

"You're repeating yourself. How can you be drunk on just two cups of punch? I'd like to see what would happen if Earl ever got ahold of you with one of his bottles of rum! I'll lay odds I could drink you under the table, if I took a mind to."

"We'll never find out, because I have no intention of engaging in a drinking contest with a lady." Galen kept as much dignity in his voice as the situation would allow.

"Are you going to go after Geneva or aren't you?"

"I am not."

"Then you're a bigger fool than I thought you were. Would you mind telling me why you aren't? A valid reason, just one."

"Two valid reasons. Geneva hates me, and I can't afford her."

"Geneva doesn't hate you. Geneva isn't the kind who hates people. If they're horrid to her, she's sorry, more for their sakes than her own. As for not being able to afford her, do you know what Marvin Burton told me less than a week ago? He said it was a tragic shame that your pride is robbing him of bright, healthy grandchildren to comfort him in his old age, children who have a right to be born, the kind of children the world needs."

"Bobo and Addie will have children, and they'll be bright and healthy."

"But they won't be Geneva's children. Geneva's and yours. If you let Bob Maxwell get her, Marvin will love their children, but it won't be the same. They'll probably have Geneva's beauty and Bob's handsomeness and vitality and Geneva's brains, but Marvin would rather they were yours."

"He's never intimated any such thing to me." Even to himself, Galen sounded stuffy.

"A father can hardly ask a man to marry his daughter. Geneva would never forgive him, and with good reason. She may not hate people who are mean to her, but she has her pride."

"That doesn't change the fact that even if she'd have me, I couldn't afford her."

"Rot! Do you think Geneva cares all that much about money? And there's plenty of money. Bobo's going to make his own fortune on top of his share of the Burton estate, and half of *that* will go to Geneva, and if you're one of those utter male idiots who can't stand the thought of their wife having money, then you don't deserve her. What does money have to do with love and companionship and making a good life, anyway? If it's there, enjoy it. If it isn't there, do without it and be happy anyway."

A handclap from the doorway—the door had been opened a few inches without either Roxanne or Galen noticing—jerked Galen's head around. Marvin Burton was standing there, nodding at Roxanne with complete approval.

"I couldn't have said it better myself, Roxie. The question is, is this young man as intelligent as I thought he was, or is he so stiff-necked that he'll deprive me of the man of my choice for a son-in-law and the father of my grandchildren just because he still has a few years of struggle ahead of him?" Marvin's keen eyes fixed themselves on Galen's. "Well, Galen? If you were one of your own patients, what would your diagnosis be?"

There was an edge of desperation in Galen's voice. "Geneva wouldn't have me. You have no idea how I've treated her! If she doesn't hate me, then she ought to have her head examined!"

"There's only one way to find out, isn't there? Ask her!" Roxie glared at him. "I'll be darned if I'm going to stand by and let you ruin one of my best friends' life just because you're pigheaded and proud! Two of my best friends' lives, if I count you, which I won't anymore if you go on being such an all-fired fool!''

"How can I ask her? Bob Maxwell's sticking to her like he's sewn to her, and apparently that's the way she wants it.''

"You leave it to me. I'll set things in motion for you, but after that it's up to you, and if you don't come back and tell us it's settled, I'll never speak to you again!'' Roxie gave Galen one more disgusted glare, and swept from the room.

Marvin's glance after her was filled with admiration. "I wonder what she has up her sleeve? Whatever it is, you'd better cooperate. I'm getting a little tired of waiting for you and Geneva to get together. Now that Bobo finally talked sense into Addie, I'd like to have my other child's life settled so I can begin to enjoy my retirement.''

Galen stood up and began to pace, so agitated that he couldn't stand still. "All right. What if I do ask her, and what if, by some miracle so farfetched it doesn't even bear thinking about, she says yes? Do you want your daughter living in one room, going without everything she's taken for granted all her life?''

"If Geneva had to live in one room, with the man she loves, she'd live in that one room as happily as other women live in mansions. But it won't come to that.'' Marvin's tone was man-to-man. "Addie and Bobo are going to live here, and that leaves the Maynard house empty. People aren't buying houses right now, at least at anywhere near their worth, and somebody has to live in it to keep it from falling apart. Your practice is going to grow, there's no way it isn't. You'll be able to buy it as we pull out of this depression and things pick up. Stephen Harding isn't getting any younger. You'll have his paying patients soon, as well as others. I admire modesty in a man, but even you must realize that you're the best medical man in Athens, and a lot of other people realize it as well. Don't you have any faith in your own ability?''

"Of course I do.'' Galen banged his fist against the stone of the small fireplace. It hurt. "But she won't have me.''

Marvin put his hand under Galen's arm and propelled him out of the room. "As Roxie said, the only way to find out is to ask her. Let's go and see what that young woman is cooking up.''

438

Back in the parlor, where most of the guests had congregated to wait for the wedding supper to be served, Galen let Marvin give him another drink. This made three, which was two more than his usual limit, but this was a wedding celebration and it wouldn't be polite to refuse it. Besides, whatever Marvin's recipe was for punch, it was something special.

Jim Yarnell and Mary MacDonald were in the center of a small knot of people, obviously being congratulated about their own upcoming marriage. Mary's face was rosy, and Jim was beaming. Minnie Atkins—Galen corrected himself—Minnie O'Brian, was one of the group, but Galen didn't see Philo. He hoped that the little Irishman wasn't holed up with some of the men, away from the women's censuring eyes, sampling the punch cup after cup to make sure that each one was as good as the last had been. He had an idea that it was harder for Philo to find opportunities to enjoy his potations than it used to be, although Philo didn't seem to be suffering because of the deprivation. To Philo, Minnie was still worth any sacrifice, even his whiskey.

And there was Geneva, with Bob Maxwell still hovering at her side, his adoring eyes never leaving her face. And Geneva didn't seem to mind. There were four or five other men giving her all of their attention, but it was clear that Bob had the inside track. Boxing champion, was he? Once again, against all reason, Galen felt the urge to test it out, and this time the urge was stronger than it had been before. He didn't know what Roxie had up her sleeve and he didn't care. He didn't need a woman to help him speak up for the girl he loved, did he?

What was he, a man or a mouse? Why was he just standing here, when Geneva was being snatched away from him? Galen knew about weddings. One wedding brings on a rash of others. He'd bet that there were more proposals of marriage, and more acceptances, after a wedding than during any other time. Romance was contagious: come in proximity with it and it sticks to you. He was certain that Bob had proposed to Geneva already today, and although he didn't quite look elated enough for her to have accepted, the odds were too great for comfort that she might say yes before the evening was over.

He very carefully set his cup back on the table that held

the punch bowl, and with his face set in lines of determination, strode over to Geneva and the group of young dandies who surrounded her. Bob Maxwell saw him approaching, and his eyes turned wary, like a dog getting ready to defend its bone.

"Miss Burton? I'd like to speak to you, if I may." Galen was polite, custom dictated it, as this was a social affair. He couldn't very well lay Maxwell out with one well-aimed blow and throw Geneva over his shoulder and carry her off. It was a pity that some customs had changed.

"I say, Miss Burton is engaged at the moment. We're having a conversation." From his tone and the look on his face, Bob thought it was just as much of a pity that customs had changed as Galen did.

"I'll only keep her for a few moments." It wouldn't take longer than that to ask her and receive a definite yes or no.

"I'm sure that whatever you wish to speak to her about can wait." Bob pulled himself up to his full six-feet and flexed his muscles, all too evident, even under his ruffles.

"And I'm afraid that it can't. Miss Burton?" Galen pushed Bob aside and offered Geneva his arm. The garden would be the place to propose.

Bob thrust himself between Geneva and his rival, glowering. "May I point out that you're being demmed impolite?"

Galen smothered his impulse to laugh at Bob's British mannerism. Basically, young Maxwell was probably solid and decent, but why these young Corinthians insisted in imitating their British counterparts was something that Galen couldn't understand.

"And may I point out that you're blocking our way?"

The room had fallen silent. Galen realized, without much caring, that breaths were bated, that Cora Burton was looking at her husband imploringly, that Geneva was mortified. He'd no sooner realized it than Bob Maxwell burst out, "Sir, if you don't desist I'll be forced to challenge you!"

Galen's eyebrows rose. "You will? Well, if you must, but as the challenged party, I get to choose the weapons. Isn't that the rule? I expect you'd prefer pistols, but being a common man of medicine, I'm afraid it will have to be scalpels."

Bob's face turned the brightest shade of red that Galen had ever seen on a human being, even on those suffering from sunburn or scarlet fever. "Why, you . . . you . . ." he spluttered. His arm raised, his fist was already flashing toward Galen when Geneva commanded him to stop, and simultaneously, Philo O'Brian burst into the room, shouting something as he ran toward Galen.

"Doc, you're needed! There's been an accident—young Donald Emerson, out to the Emerson farm, got himself gored and trampled by their bull. Luke Emerson is wantin' to know where to find you!"

Galen had a little trouble taking in the sense of Philo's excited statement, as he was at the moment flat on his back on the floor, Geneva not having been able to divert Bob's angry blow. Now he struggled to sit up, succeeded with Wyatt's help, and shook his head to clear it.

"You'll be goin' right along, of course," Philo continued. "And they asked particularly if Miss Burton would come with you, rememberin' her so kindly an' how good she was to help when it was me that was hurt. And from what young Luke told me, they'll be needin' her to help because the boy's in a bad way, and I think you'd better be hurryin'. Doc, what in Gawd's . . . beg pardon, ladies . . . what in thunder happened to your eye?"

"It got in the way of a fist," Galen muttered.

Geneva was already in motion, hurrying toward the stairs. "I'll change, and be right with you."

"You can take my buggy and Red Boy," Wyatt said. "I'll go and hitch up."

"I'll be helpin' you, Mr. Livingston. I hope you can save the lad, Doc, it's a fine boy he is, as you'll remember. It's a good thing Miss Burton'll be goin' along with you, you'll be needin' her an' you with only one good eye. Now whose fist was it you ran into, if I might be askin'?"

"Come along, Philo, let's get Red Boy hitched up and over here." Wyatt propelled the Irishman toward the door, Philo reluctant to leave until he'd found out who'd had the lack of consideration to punch Galen in the eye. But he'd find out later. Whoever it was, the present of the black eye would be returned in kind and with interest before this evening was over, or his name wasn't Philo O'Brian. He might be small, but he was Irish, and an Irishman doesn't stand by and see a friend punched without doing something about it, even if only to keep the peace in the future.

By the time Red Boy and the buggy were brought around to the house, Geneva was ready, dressed in a practical cotton dress and carrying a small valise with another dress and night clothing, and two of the enveloping aprons she'd worn when she'd nursed the diphtheria victims at the hospital. The scene where Bob Maxwell and Galen had come to blows, or would have come to blows if Bob hadn't lost his head and struck without warning, was driven from her mind by her concern for Donald Emerson. If it was as bad as Philo said it was, she knew that it would take every ounce of Galen's skill to save him. She was prepared to stay at the Emerson farm for as long as was necessary, to nurse Donald and keep constant watch over him.

"We'll send word how things are," she told her mother. "Don't expect me back tonight. Doctor Forbes will let you know if I'll need to stay any length of time. You can send Father with some more clothes for me, and anything else we might need." She didn't even notice that Bob Maxwell, glowering because Geneva was being taken away from him in a way that he couldn't protest, was already being comforted by Dorothy Armstrong and Evelyn Moore, young, unmarried ladies determined to make the most of this opportunity.

"Let me know if there's anything I can do to help." Roxanne was beside Cora Burton. "I can come out and spell you, if the boy needs constant care. Lillian and Mary can hold down the catering kitchen. I'll find someone to come in and help them. You'd better hurry along, Galen's waiting."

As Geneva ran out of the door and down the porch steps to the buggy, Philo was already finding out, using his Irish charm, who it was who had punched Galen Forbes. Likely Minnie would be mightily put out with him tonight, but a man has his duty to perform.

"Do you want me to drive?" Geneva asked. "Your eye is swollen practically shut."

"I can manage. Red Boy has two good eyes." Galen picked up the lines and flicked them over Red Boy's shining back. The horse, fully as magnificent as Cato, stepped out as though he were in a trotting race. There was no need to push him, he'd maintain that pace the entire distance.

"I'm sorry that Bob hit you, but you provoked the attack." Geneva looked straight ahead.

"I'd had a little too much to drink. I'm not used to it."

"That's perfectly obvious. If I had as weak a head for spirits as you, I'd never touch it."

"I was working up my courage for something. It wasn't a success."

"Why were you working up your courage, or shouldn't I ask?"

"You should, but not now. I'll tell you after I've seen how bad Donald Emerson's hurt." Galen pulled Red Boy to a stop in front of Stephen Harding's house and handed Geneva the lines. "Hold him while I get my bag."

Geneva sat quietly during the long drive to the Emerson farm, her hands folded in her lap. She was curious, but she could wait. Galen's silence, as he evaluated as best he could without having seen his patient just what would have to be done to save him, gave her a chance to think about her own immediate problems.

It was ironic that this emergency should have thrown her into intimate contact with Galen again. She'd never been able to understand his hostility toward her. Hostility toward anyone was so foreign to her that she had no way of even imagining what could have caused it. It wasn't that Galen was one of those men who were natural woman-haters, because he liked Roxie and he'd come within a hair of marrying Mary MacDonald. No, it was she herself Galen disliked, disliked to the point of hatred.

And against all common sense, she had to love him! The one man in all the world she'd ever felt that she could love with all her heart and all her soul and all her body! And now she had to make a decision, the most important decision of her life.

Was she to go on loving Galen, resigning herself to a life of spinsterhood, because she couldn't have the man she loved? Or would she do what so many other women have had to do—marry a second choice and direct all of her energy toward making it work? Companionship, tenderness, being loved, and having a family of her own weighed heavily on the side of accepting the second choice and making the best of it.

Only she knew that second choice would never satisfy her. She should accept Bob. He'd be a good husband to her, and a good father to her children. Now that Wyatt had been snapped up, there was hardly an unattached girl in Athens who wouldn't welcome the chance to step into her shoes and take Bob Maxwell.

Damn Galen Forbes anyway! If it wasn't for Donald Emerson, she'd jump out of the buggy and walk back home, even if she wore her shoe soles out and had to finish the journey in her bare feet! She'd walk back, and find Bob and tell him that she'd marry him, and be done with it; she'd begin her search for inner peace and contentment without this man who sat beside her with a face like stone, his eyes on the road.

"Here we are." Galen turned Red Boy into the lane that led to the Emerson farmhouse. There was no one in sight. The farm lay peaceful under the late afternoon sunlight, with the scents of hay and clover so sweet and heavy in the air that it was like a dream of peace. Geneva jumped out of the buggy before Galen could walk around to help her down. If she had to do without him all the rest of her life, she didn't need his help now.

She was right behind him when he strode to the kitchen door and banged on it. Then, thinking that Samuel and Luke, who'd doubtless arrived back by now, were tending Donald, he pushed the door open and went in, again with Geneva right behind him.

Samuel Emerson was in the kitchen, poking up the fire in the black iron range. He looked up, startled, as Galen and Geneva burst in on him.

"Where is he? Did you manage to carry him upstairs?" Galen demanded. "You shouldn't have tried to move him."

"How's that again?" Samuel's startled look changed to one of bewilderment.

"Donald! Where have you put him?"

"Donald's helping Luke get in the hay. What's this all about, Doctor? Miss Burton, it's good to see you again."

It was Galen's turn to look bewildered. "Donald isn't hurt? He wasn't trampled and gored by your bull?"

"We don't have a bull. The critters are too dangerous. We have our cows serviced." Samuel looked at Geneva and his face flushed. "We borrow Zeke Hawkins's bull. I'm sorry if you've come all the way out here on a wild-goose chase. You can at least set a spell and have some coffee before you start back. The boys will be mighty glad to see you again, both of you."

Wild-goose chase! Galen's anger began as a small hot place in his chest and grew to the size of a pumpkin. That Philo! He must have been as drunk as a skunk to get the message garbled and send him to the wrong farm! Only, as much as Galen had seen Philo drink, he'd never seen him that drunk. It just wasn't reasonable.

"Nobody in this vicinity has been hurt, that you've heard of?"

"Not that we've heard."

The pumpkin in Galen's chest quivered and burst. As though some warp in time had propelled him back into Marvin Burton's private study. He heard Roxie's voice as clearly as if she were speaking the words now. "I'll set things in motion for you, but after that it'll be up to you, and if you don't come back and tell us it's settled, I'll never speak to you again!"

Geneva didn't fail to see the light of comprehension in his eyes. "Doctor Forbes, do you know what this is all about?"

"I think I do. Let's get started back. I'm glad that Donald isn't hurt, Samuel. Say hello to both boys for us."

Geneva controlled herself for several minutes after he'd handed her back into the buggy. Galen was driving slowly, holding Red Boy down. It wouldn't do to push him hard after the fast trip out.

"Well, are you going to tell me or not? If this was a practical joke, it was a cruel and thoughtless one, and I intend to find out whose idea it was!"

There was a pleasant place just ahead, where Galen could pull Red Boy off the road. The animal could use some rest anyway. He got out and took his time about seeing that Red Boy was standing in a lush growth of grass so that he could crop. Then he reached up and put his hands around Geneva's waist and lifted her down before she had an inkling of what he'd been going to do.

"Doctor Forbes, will you please answer me!" Geneva demanded, her face pale with anger.

His answer was to catch her in his arms and kiss her. There was no use in her struggling or trying to get away. He held her captive, and only tightened the grip of his arms around her as she twisted and squirmed and tried to beat at him with her doubled fists. He held her and went right on kissing her.

"I love you. I want you to marry me," he said when even he had to come up to catch his breath. But he still held her close, with no intention of letting her go.

"Well, I never! What do you mean, you love me? How do you dare tell me that you love me? You've made it plain ever since the first day we met that you can't stand the sight of me, that you detest me, and now you dare to tell me that you love me!" Geneva, with a supreme effort, extricated her right arm from his grasp and struck him in the face. She was livid with fury, she trembled and throbbed with it, she wanted nothing more than to have the strength, just for the time it would take, to beat him to a pulp.

"Stop that, damn it! I already have a black eye, do you want to give me another one?"

"Yes, I do!" Geneva's furious cry was smothered as Galen kissed her again. This time, with one arm free, she managed to break loose a great deal more quickly.

"Galen Forbes, don't you ever do that again! Have you taken leave of your senses? What's got into you?"

"The first lick of common sense I've had for years," Galen told her. "And some down-to-earth advice from two of the people I admire the most, your father and Roxanne."

"Roxanne! I might have known! This whole thing smacks of one of her wild ideas."

"And without her, I might not have got up the courage to admit I've been the biggest fool on earth, and try to undo all the harm I've done to both of us. Someday I'll tell you what motivated me, but not right now. Right now I only want one thing, and that's to hear that you'll forgive me, and that you'll marry me unless I've made you hate me so much that you can't bear the sight of me."

"I can't bear the sight of you! Let me go!"

"Do you mean that? Are you certain?"

"Yes, I'm cer . . . ."

He kissed her again. She fought him, her anger surging to even greater heights. How dared he treat her like this, how dared he lay hands on her and demand that she forgive him, after the way he'd treated her!

And how dared her knees go weak, so that she had to cling to him to keep from falling? How dared her blood race through her body, turning it to fire? Was she such a weak and pitiful creature that she had no pride, that she'd accept him just because he asked her, after all he'd done, after all the misery he'd caused her?

"Oh, God!" Galen moaned into her hair. Her hair smelled as sweet and fresh as the clover. Her skin was like satin, warm and silky, with a scent of its own that was hers alone. He loved her, he had to have her, or he'd never be more than half a man. "Geneva, Geneva!"

Her mouth was soft and moist and warm against his, as sweet as honey, filled with fire. "Geneva!" he said again, his voice like a prayer. "Will you take me, on faith, even before I explain why I've behaved toward you as I have? Because it's important to me, for some damned fool reason!"

No! The word screamed itself in Geneva's mind. But her heart had better sense. It knew better than to throw away the only thing in the world she wanted or would ever want.

There'd be another hurry-up wedding in Athens. Tongues would wag again, and the matrons would be counting on their fingers. It made her want to laugh. She wouldn't wait more than three months, there was no way that she was going to wait longer than that. She'd insist on being married tomorrow except that her mother would die of the shock. Now that she had Galen at last, she was going to make it legal as fast as she could, before the exasperating idiot could wriggle away from her for whatever even more idiotic reason he had for treating her so badly. A reason, she'd be bound, that was a man's reason entirely, something that wouldn't make any sense to a woman.

"Yes," she said.

"Thank God." Galen's face was a picture of deep and abiding joy. "Now I'll explain."

"Not now," Geneva said, and this time she was the one who cut off his words by kissing him, a kiss that threatened to disintegrate both of them where they stood. "Later. We have better things to do right now."

30

In spite of Jim's restraining hand on her arm, Mary was so excited that she kept breaking into little dancing steps in her eagerness to see everything. Her eyes glowed brighter than the torches and lanterns that beckoned people from miles around as they passed through the outskirts of the revival meeting at Chestnut Grove on this June evening in 1838.

"Easy, Mary! Remember that you're supposed to be careful!" Jim warned his young wife. His wife! Even now, it was hard for him to believe that Mary was actually his, that he'd never lose her, that they'd be together all the rest of their lives.

"But I want to see everything! I want to see who's here. And I want some of that gingerbread that smells so delicious, right now!"

Smiling, Jim shouldered a way for them through the milling crowds until they gained the booth from which the aroma of gingerbread emanated. If Mary wanted gingerbread, she should have gingerbread. If Mary wanted a chunk of green cheese from the moon, Jim would have found a way to get it for her.

"Don't eat too much. We can't have you getting sick."

"Pooh! Who's going to get sick? I'm as healthy as a horse!" Mary dimpled at him, her cheeks flushed with pleasure as her small white teeth bit into the gingerbread man. Snap, snap, and one arm was gone. Snap, snap, and one leg was gone. Jim watched her, his face filled with contentment, his eyes crinkling with amusement at her hearty appetite. After all, she was eating for two, even though the other one wouldn't show for a long time yet.

"Just think, we're going to hear Carlton Booth!" Mary said. "We'll get to hear all the preaching! I hope you haven't been sinning, Jim. I'd be mortified if you had to go forward to be saved."

"You heard him last year," Jim reminded her. "I doubt that he'll sound much different this year. No new sins have been invented, as far as I know."

"Yes, but I haven't got to hear him as often as you have! You must have heard him a dozen times at least."

"Not that many." Jim's smile deepened. "And I didn't really get to hear him back in '35. As you'll recall, I was sidetracked on my way in by a little mechanic who had no business here in the first place, getting herself into a pile of trouble and getting herself hurt in the bargain."

Mary sighed, but the sigh was a sound of pure happiness. "I know. Wasn't it wonderful? To think that I was scared half to death of you! I kept looking for horns under your captain's hat, because Mrs. Simms always warned us that all of you canallers were devils."

"And you kept right on thinking that for a long time afterwards!" Jim teased her. "I thought I never would be able to convince you that there was only hair under that hat, and not horns."

"I can't help it if I was stupid. Besides, nearly everybody in Athens, maybe in the whole world, is stupid that way—about canallers, I mean. Only really intelligent people like the Burtons and Roxanne and Mr. Fielding and Galen Forbes and Roxie and Wyatt Livingston seem to know that just because a man is a canaller doesn't mean that they'll be contaminated if they get within twenty feet of him!"

Snap, snap. The gingerbread man's head was gone. "It just makes me so angry! That people should think that way, when all the time it's us canallers who make this country prosperous and line their pockets!"

Us canallers! Jim chuckled deep in his throat. But then, Mary had some justification for lumping herself with the canallers now, because she'd made several trips with him on the *Undine*, and she'd taken to the life as if she'd been born to it. In a few months, that would have to stop because he couldn't risk having the baby born on the boat or in some strange town. Mary's baby had to be born right here in Athens, where Galen would look after her and all of their friends would be near. Babies and their new mothers needed womenfolk like Cora Burton and Lillian Livingston to do things right.

His musing was interrupted by a sharp pain in his foot. Mary had trod on it as she jumped up and down. "Oh, look! There's Miss Geneva and Doctor Galen!"

"Ouch!" For all that she was as little as a kitten and hardly weighed any more, it hurt. "Where? Oh, I see them. Hello, Geneva, Galen. It's good to see you." Even through his subsiding pain, Jim found himself amused by his satisfaction at being able to name Geneva and Galen among his friends; he could even call them by their first names. For a canaller, that was progress!

Galen's grip was as firm as his own as the two men shook hands, both of them inordinately pleased at running into each other.

"It's good to see you too. You're looking hale and hearty. If everybody was like you, doctors would be out of business. And you, Mary! You're looking wonderful, as pretty as a picture, but how do you feel?"

"I feel just fine. Jim's the one who gets sick, fretting about me. Right now I feel so good that I want another piece of gingerbread."

Geneva laughed. "Men are all alike. They insist on calling us the weaker sex, but I'd like to see one of them carry a baby for nine months and then have it, without whimpering and whining and raising the very devil about it! If it was up to the men to do the reproducing, the world would come to an end. I want some gingerbread, too, it's just the ticket for what ails us."

Mary's mouth dropped open, and then she smiled with delight. "You too?" she asked.

"Me, too. And for all he's a doctor, Galen's fretting almost as much as your Jim. I'll lay odds that after our babies are born, we'll be the ones to get up and dance and celebrate, while they'll have to take to their beds to recover!"

Mary put her lips close to Geneva's ear, her voice a whisper. "Is it true about Miss Addie? Her too?"

"She isn't sure yet. If it is true, there'll be three new babies, all about the same age. Mine will be the oldest, and yours the next, and then Addie's. We're giving the population of Athens a boost all by ourselves, aren't we?''

"Jim says that that's what this country needs, that there have to be more people, so the country can grow and get settled even way out to the west, and then there'll be more work and more money and everything. Only I'm glad we don't have to do it all by ourselves! Young'uns are a passel of work, no matter how sweet they are. Do you want a boy or a girl?''

"Galen wants a girl, or so he says.''

Mary giggled. "That's what Jim says, too. He wants a girl who looks just like me. Only do you know what I think? I think they want girls first so the girls can wait on and cater to the boys when they come along!''

"Well, if that's how they think, then Wyatt was disappointed. And speak of the devil! There they are now, just arriving. Roxie, Wyatt, over here! And Lillian! How did you manage to tear yourself away from David Philo? Who's baby-sitting him while you sneak out?''

"Cora's taking care of him. She and Marvin walked over and got him just before we left.'' Lillian Livingston's eyes were as bright and shining with excitement as Mary's. "I wouldn't have missed this for half a dozen grandsons! Herndon never would bring me, he always said that there was too much riffraff here and that this kind of meeting isn't dignified. All the time I was just dying to come and I never got to! What's that you're eating? Gingerbread? Wyatt, get me two! I have a lot of catching up to do!''

"Are you sure you don't want some kill-divvie or belly-whip vengeance to wash it down with?'' Wyatt asked her, his face perfectly straight but his eyes filled with laughter.

If he'd thought that his teasing would ruffle his mother, he was mistaken. "Yes, I do. Which is the best?''

"Either of them would eat the stomach lining right out of a lady like you,'' Galen told her. "But maybe we can locate some wine decent enough so that you won't be taking your life in your hands by drinking it.''

"No, not wine.'' Lillian paused, considering. "I want beer. I've never tasted beer, and I've always wanted to, and that can't be so very strong because it comes in such large mugs.''

"You aren't going to like it,'' Roxanne warned her. "But it would be a shame not to try it, at least once in your life. I've had more than a little of it myself, in my scandalous days on the canal before my father decided that I had to become a lady. He didn't know I had it, of course, but he couldn't keep an eye on me every blessed minute, could he? Wyatt, get your mother a mug of beer. And get one for me while you're at it, I'm feeling nostalgic."

Wyatt looked at his two womenfolk with an expression of dismay. "Beer! Do the two of you want all Athens buzzing? The two Mrs. Livingstons, drinking beer at the revival meeting!"

"Let Athens buzz. It won't be the first time, and we've always survived." Roxanne's eyes sparked.

"Me, too! I want some beer too!" Mary piped up, her feet dancing although she remained standing in one place because of the press of the crowd.

"Not for you," Galen told her. His voice was firm. "We don't want the coming member of your family to be born with bad habits. And none for Geneva, either. But there's no reason that Roxanne and Mrs. Livingston can't indulge, as long as they don't overdo it."

"Overdo it! Galen Forbes, someday I'm going to get you into a drinking contest, and we'll see which one of us ends up under the table first! I inherited my father's talent for handling the stuff. But Lillian had better take it easy, she isn't used to it."

"There'll be no drinking contests. You'll have to find some other way to outrage Athens. The young Mrs. Livingston has to set some sort of example for our mechanics."

"Mr. Wyatt . . ." Even now, Mary couldn't be comfortable calling Wyatt by only his first name. "I hope you didn't leave any of the girls on cleanup so they didn't get to come!"

"I didn't, Mary. I closed the mill an hour early, to make sure."

"And Herndon had a conniption!" Roxanne laughed. "To hear him rave, you'd have thought we'd go bankrupt because of that one hour!"

"And on top of that, the shock of Mother insisting that she was coming with us was almost too much for him," Wyatt finished for her.

"I wouldn't want anything to happen to him. I expect he can't help being the way he is," Lillian said. She looked at the mug of beer in her hand doubtfully, and then screwed up her eyes and took her first taste. "Ugh! But I don't care, I'm going to drink it anyway! I expect one has to develop a taste for it, like olives. As I was saying, I wouldn't want anything to happen to Herndon, but I've never had any fun in my life and it's time I started." With that statement, she upended the mug and drained it. Even Roxanne looked at her with awe.

"Would you care for another, Mother?" Wyatt's expression was correctly polite but his eyes were dancing with mirth.

"No, thank you, dear. I believe I have had enough for the moment. Perhaps later, after we've heard the preaching. But I will have some of that molasses candy." To take the taste of the beer away, she thought, although she wouldn't give them the satisfaction of hearing her say it.

"Look, look!" Mary's excitement threatened to make her seams, already a little tight even though the baby didn't show yet, burst. "There's a juggler, I want to see him!"

Indulgently, because they were all so fond of her, the entire group worked their way to the small platform where a juggler was keeping a number of bottles in the air without a one of them falling to the boards. A drunken canaller brazened his way up onto the platform and demanded to try it himself, and immediately bets were laid by other canallers as to how many he could keep up—one or two or three—before there was a crash.

"Why, that's gambling!" Lillian said, her eyes wide.

"You're darned tootin' it is! I make it three!" Roxanne called. "Three! Come on, Bert Callahan, you can do it!"

The canaller, so far blown even this early in the evening that he lost his balance as he attempted to bow in Roxanne's direction, scrambled back to his feet with a confident grin on his face.

"For you, Miss Roxie, I'll make it four!" he boasted.

"Four, then. But you'd better not let me down or Earl will hear about it!" Roxanne flung back.

One, then a second bottle, went up into the air and were caught by Bert Callahan; then a third, which he barely managed to catch. But the fourth proved to be his undoing, bringing on boos and catcalls. Callahan, his face bright red with embarrassment, looked at Roxanne with mute apology.

"Pay off, Wyatt," Roxie said. "And never mind, Bert.

We won't snitch on you. My father isn't here tonight anyway.''

"Who says he isn't?" Earl Fielding loomed up behind Roxie and spun her around, lifting her feet off the ground to give her a bear hug. "I took the Six Day Line to get here, even if it is the competition! How's that grandson of mine? David Philo—what a name! They're still talking about it all the way from New York to Buffalo. I still can't see why you didn't name him after me!"

"I wanted him to have a name all his own. Besides, you already have a child, me, and a grandson all your own even if he isn't named after you, but poor Philo doesn't have anyone to carry on his name and I wanted to do him the honor because of all he's done for Athens and the mill. Without him and other men like him, reforms might never have been made!"

"He did a magnificent job, for a fact," Roxanne's father agreed. "This country needs more men just like him, and I admit that I'm proud that you had the gumption to name my grandson after him, even if I do have to take a lot of joshing about it. It'd serve you right if I did what you so brazenly suggested back when the Canal Commission advanced the money to get the mill back on its feet, and had myself a boy of my own!"

"Nothing's stopping you, as far as I can see," Roxanne told him. "Miss Southern is still available, isn't she? It's about time you put a ring on her finger."

Earl frowned at her. Even for Roxanne, bringing up the subject of his mistress in a public place, among friends, was going a little too far. "That'll be enough of that. Miss Southern and I have decided that we're both happier single. You'll just have to produce another boy to name after me, and the next time, you'd better not find some other hero to name him after!"

As fond as Earl was of Jewel, he couldn't bring himself to marry another woman after having been married to Roxanne's mother. And Jewel didn't seem to mind. She was a woman who liked her independence as much as Earl liked his Things were better just as they were.

He had his first grandchild now, and a boy at that. And if he knew Roxanne, she'd provide him with a few more. As of this moment, Earl was a contented man, and he thanked whatever powers that be that in spite of his wealth and importance, he'd never gone sour the way Herndon Livingston had. Life was too filled with things to enjoy to let your self-importance cut you off from them.

The ladies' craving for food and other excitements satisfied for the time being, they made their way to the meeting ground proper, and found places near the middle of the rows of planks that served as benches. As always, the benches were well filled. The famous evangelist himself was speaking, and Geneva thought that it was just as well that they couldn't find places nearer the front, because Carlton Booth's voice was so powerful that it would have been painful to sit too close.

Booth was in fine form. Even as they made themselves as comfortable as possible on the hard benches, a man toward the front rose to his feet, shaking and crying, and stumbled toward the platform where Booth waited for him with his arms outstretched.

"Here's a sinner who's seen the error of his ways! God bless you, brother! Repent, and you will this very night gain your right to enter through the gates of heaven!"

"Good lord, it's Verne Baldwin!" Wyatt whispered to Roxie. She and Wyatt, and Jim as well, had to suppress their laughter as the town drunk threw himself into Booth's arms. The evangelist recoiled as the full force of the whiskey fumes hit him in the face. But Booth was equal to the occasion.

"From this moment forward, never again will the demon rum have a hold on you! Eschew it, brother! Promise the Lord that you will never touch another drop!"

Verne opened his mouth and tried to force the words out. "I pro—I prom—"

And then he broke from Carlton Booth's grasp, although Booth made a valiant effort to hang onto him.

"I'll be danged if I do! It's too much to ask of any man! Maybe next year, but not tonight!" Having gained his freedom from the evangelist's restraint, Verne turned and staggered down the aisle between the rows of benches, mopping at his forehead as he made his way to the perimeter of the meeting grounds to drown his terror at his narrow escape.

"Pray for that sinner, brethren and sistern! Pray with all your might!" Booth bellowed. "Pray for him, lest his soul be lost before he sees the light!"

Geneva and Roxanne tried to pray for Verne, and under the circumstances they made a pretty good job of it, although it was hard to suppress their giggles. Only Mary did her very best job of praying. Getting to pray for a lost soul right here at the revival meeting was too wonderful an opportunity not to make the most of it!

There was another small stir as Addie and Bobo, who had arrived late, made their way along the bench to sit by them, entailing a good deal of crowding. Addie hadn't been sure that she wanted to come, but at the last moment she'd decided that her bitter memories of Matthew Ramsey weren't bitter anymore, and that it wouldn't bother her in the slightest even if Matthew happened to be among the speakers. All the same, Bobo was just as glad that he wasn't. It wasn't because he was afraid of the effect on Addie, but because he wasn't sure that he cared to sit through any of Matthew's preaching. Booth at least held out the promise of redemption to even the worst of sinners if only they would repent, but Matthew's sermons seemed to convey the impression that if anyone had sinned up to the present time in his life, it very well might be too late.

Half a dozen prayers and three convulsive fits later, along with two repentant sinners who threw themselves at the seat of mercy, even Mary and Lillian were ready to admit that they'd had enough.

"Come on over to our house," Roxie said. "Lillian baked a cake this morning, and it's delicious."

"I can bake a good cake, if I do say so myself," Lillian said without the least trace of modesty. "I wanted to cook and bake all my life, but I never did get to until Roxanne married Wyatt and moved in. I just knew I'd be good at it, and I am!"

Herndon was in his study when they arrived. When Wyatt went to pick up David Philo and bring Marvin and Cora Burton back with him, he came out and greeted his guests civilly, as became a gentleman. But he declined to join them, explaining the pressure of business that kept him at his desk. His pressing business was a grandiose plan for expanding the mill and doubling its profits when Wyatt finally admitted that he'd failed at running it and would have to ask his father to step in and take over again.

The men huddled with their heads together over drinks while the women tiptoed upstairs to tuck David Philo into his cradle. He hadn't even wakened while he was being moved. At a little over six months, the baby's face, even in sleep, held a remarkable resemblance to Wyatt's, and his dark hair grew in the same peak over his forehead.

"Philo comes to see him almost every day," Roxanne told them, her eyes filled with laughter. "You never saw a man so proud to have a namesake! You'd think that cocky Irishman had fathered him himself, the way he carries on! It's a wonder that Minnie isn't jealous, but she isn't. She comes with him, and if I'm not careful the two of them will have Davie so spoiled there won't be any living with him!"

Downstairs, Earl held the floor. "We've come through the worst of it. That depression all but did this country in, but we weathered it, and I'm convinced that we'll weather anything else that's thrown at us. Things are moving, you're going to see progress such as no one has ever dreamed of! I'm buying more shares in railroads, and I've convinced Marvin here to do the same."

"If that means that traffic on the canals will be cut into, I'm not sure I'm for it," Jim said.

"It'll cut canal traffic all right, but that's a long way in the future. You don't have anything to worry about, Jim. The canal traffic will last as long as you need it. All the same, I'd advise you to save up some money and get your finger in the railroad pie, even on a small scale."

"For a while there, I thought that Van Buren was going to be the ruination of the country," Wyatt confessed.

"So did a lot of other men, but I'll tell you something, all of you. There isn't any one man going to ruin this country, even if he's the president. This country is crawling with men of vision, with men of ability, with men who aren't afraid to take a chance. The United States is going to expand, it's going to be settled from coast to coast, and I'm glad I'm still young enough to see a lot of it happen."

"There are other changes, too," Jim said. "It seems to me that just a few years ago, I wouldn't have had the chance of an icicle in July of sitting in a house like this, talking to men like you. Me, a canaller! It looks like democracy is really going to work. There's a long way to go yet, but when men like me and Philo O'Brian can call men like the Livingstons and the Burtons and the Fieldings friends, that's real progress."

Earl snorted. "A few years ago, I wouldn't have been

457

sitting in this house either! But here I am, and here you are, and there's going to be more and more of the same. Any man with guts and ability is going to be able to go as far as that ability will take him. I'm just glad that the new generation is coming along, to take over where we leave off.''

Coming back downstairs with the other women, Lillian felt only a moment's sadness that Addie and Bobo had refused to stop in with the others. It seemed that neither her daughter nor her husband would bend an inch. But then she brightened. Addie was only just around the corner, and with Wyatt and Roxie's backing, Herndon couldn't forbid her to see all of her she wanted. It seemed that for the first time in her life, she was really happy.

''I'll drink to that!'' Galen said just as the ladies entered the room. ''And with this new crop of babies coming along, it looks as if doctors aren't going to be out of work, either! From where I'm sitting, things are looking good.''

Their glasses were raised as they joined in their own private toast to Athens and to the country as a whole. The worst was over, and now no matter what surprises the future held in store for them, they knew that the Burtons and the Livingstons and the Fieldings and the Forbeses were going to make it, that they were all going to play their part in building the greatest and most prosperous country on the face of the earth.

BEST OF BESTSELLERS
FROM WARNER BOOKS

SCRUPLES
by Judith Krantz (A96-743, $3.50)
The ultimate romance! The spellbinding story of the rise of a fascinating
woman from fat, unhappy "poor relative" of an aristocratic Boston family
to a unique position among the super-beautiful and super-rich, a woman
who got everything she wanted—fame, wealth, power and love.

LOVERS & GAMBLERS
by Jackie Collins (A83-973, $2.95)
LOVERS & GAMBLERS is the bestseller whose foray into the world of the
beautiful people has left its scorch marks on night tables across two con-
tinents. In Al King, Jackie Collins has created a rock-and-roll superstud
who is everything any sex-crazed groupie ever imagined her hero to be. In
Dallas, she designed "Miss Coast-to-Coast" whose sky-high ambitions
stem from a secret sordid past—the type that tabloids tingle to tell.
Jackie Collins "writes bestsellers like a female Harold Robbins."
— *Penthouse*

THE WORLD IS FULL OF DIVORCED WOMEN
by Jackie Collins (A83-183, $2.95)
The world is their bedroom...Cleo James, British journalist who joined
the thrill seekers when she found her husband coupling with her best
friend. Muffin, a centerfold with a little girl charm and a big girl body.
Mike James, the record promoter who adores Cleo but whose addiction to
women is insatiable. Jon Clapton who took a little English girl from
Wimbledon and made her into Britain's top model. Daniel Ornel, an actor
grown older, wiser and hungrier for Cleo. And Butch Kaufman, all-
American, all-man who loves to live and lives to love.

THE LOVE KILLERS
by Jackie Collins (A92-842, $2.25)
Margaret Lawrence Brown has the voice of the liberated woman who
called to the prostitutes to give up selling their bodies. She offered them
hope for a new future, and they began to listen, but was silenced with a
bullet. It was a killing that would not go unavenged. In Los Angeles, New
York, and London, three women schemed to use their beauty and their sex
to destroy the man who ordered the hit, Enzio Bassolino, and he has three
sons who were all he valued in life. They were to be the victims of sexual
destruction.

RAGE OF ANGELS
by Sidney Sheldon (A36-007, $3.50)
A breath-taking novel that takes you behind the doors of the law and
inside the heart and mind of Jennifer Parker. She rises from the ashes of
her own courtroom disaster to become one of America's most brilliant
attorneys. Her story is interwoven with that of two very different men of
enormous power. As Jennifer inspires both men to passion, each is determined to destroy the other—and Jennifer, caught in the crossfire,
becomes the ultimate victim.

THE BEST OF BESTSELLERS FROM WARNER BOOKS

CALIFORNIA GENERATION
by Jacqueline Briskin   *(A95-146, $2.75)*
They're the CALIFORNIA GENERATION: the kids who go to L.A.'s California High, where the stars come out at night to see and be seen, where life imitates art, where everyone's planning to ride off into the sunset and make every dream come true.

PALOVERDE
by Jacqueline Briskin   *(A83-845, $2.95)*
The love story of Amelie—the sensitive, ardent, young girl whose uncompromising code of honor leads her to choices that will reverberate for generations, plus the chronicle of a unique city, Los Angeles, wrestling with the power of railroads, discovery of oil, and growing into the fabulous capital of filmdom, makes this one of the most talked about novels of the year.

DAZZLE
by Elinor Klein & Dora Landey   *(A93-476, $2.95)*
Only one man can make every fantasy come true—entertainers, industrialists, politicians, and society leaders all need Costigan. Costigan, the man with the power of PR, whose past is a mystery, whose present is hidden in hype, and whose future may be out of his own hands. In a few hours, a marriage will end, a love affair begin, a new star will be created, and an old score settled. And Costigan will know whether or not he has won or lost in the gamble of his life.

INTRODUCING
THE RAKEHELL DYNASTY

BOOK ONE: THE BOOK OF JONATHAN RAKEHELL
by Michael William Scott   (D36-233, $3.50)

BOOK TWO: CHINA BRIDE
by Michael William Scott   (D95-237, $2.75)

The bold, sweeping, passionate story of a great New England shipping family caught up in the winds of change — and of the one man who would dare to sail his dream ship to the frightening, beautiful land of China. He was Jonathan Rakehell, and his destiny would change the course of history.

THE RAKEHELL DYNASTY —
THE GRAND SAGA OF THE GREAT CLIPPER SHIPS
AND OF THE MEN WHO BUILT THEM
TO CONQUER THE SEAS AND
CHALLENGE THE WORLD!

Jonathan Rakehell—who staked his reputation and his place in the family on the clipper's amazing speed.

Lai-Tse Lu—the beautiful, independent daughter of a Chinese merchant. She could not know that Jonathan's proud clipper ship carried a cargo of love and pain, joy and tragedy for her.

Louise Graves—Jonathan's wife-to-be, who waits at home in New London keeping a secret of her own.

Bradford Walker—Jonathan's scheming brother-in-law, who scoffs at the clipper and plots to replace Jonathan as heir to the Rakehell shipping line.